KATHLEEN TAYLOR

A TORY BAUER MYSTERY

FOREIGN BODY

AVON BOOKS
An Imprint of HarperCollins*Publishers*

This is a work of fiction. Names, characters, places, and incidents are products of the author's imagination or are used fictitiously and are not to be construed as real. Any resemblance to actual events, locales, organizations, or persons, living or dead, is entirely coincidental.

AVON BOOKS
An Imprint of HarperCollins*Publishers*
10 East 53rd Street
New York, New York 10022-5299

ISBN: 0-380-81205-3
www.avonbooks.com

First Avon Books paperback printing: August 2001

Printed in the U.S.A.

10 9 8 7 6 5 4 3 2 1

"Aren't they awfully calm considering that their friend might just die in this dump?"

Del's voice carried further than she expected. At least one of the girls shot her an unreadable look before speaking softly to a friend behind a cupped hand.

"Shhh," I whispered sharply. "We don't know what's going on here. We don't know what's the matter with this girl, and we certainly don't know that *anyone* is going to die," I said fiercely but softly. "And it'd be better for everyone if you didn't speculate out loud."

Though I hated to admit it, she was right. It was odd that the young men and women were so grave and silent. Maybe the British aren't the only Stiff Upper Lippers in the world. Maybe Americans are the only ones whose emotions rise to the surface so easily.

And maybe the kids were only suffering from a delayed reaction compounded by a non-comprehension of both language and local custom.

The girl who'd been whispering earlier shot a questioning glance at Del, who ignored her completely.

She then looked at me searchingly.

Then she looked at Annelise. I mean *really* looked at her. Maybe for the first time.

The girl's eyes widened in horror. Color drained from her face. She opened her mouth and screamed.

After which, all hell broke loose . . .

Other Tory Bauer Mysteries by
Kathleen Taylor
from Avon Books

SEX AND SALMONELLA
THE HOTEL SOUTH DAKOTA
FUNERAL FOOD
MOURNING SHIFT
COLD FRONT

This book is for Shirley McDermott, Melanie Reuter and Ann Hilgeman, whose combined Evil Quotient leaves mine in the dust.

....

FOREIGN BODY

Prologue

I blame *Fargo.*

Not the town, which, like every other fair-size burg plopped down on the great flat plains, is wider than it is tall, with more inner city problems than real inner city types would expect, a couple of locally respected colleges bordered by stripper bars and the odd Chinese fast food place, and surrounded by fields for as far as the eye can see.

Fargo, which used to be famous only for *Fargo North, Decoder,* is nice enough.

I'm talking about *Fargo* the movie.

The one cinema buffs everywhere else hailed as a masterpiece. The one that focused attention not only on us (believe me, most coasties don't differentiate between the Dakotas, not to mention Minnesota, where most of the story took place), but on how we live.

And how we talk.

Or rather, how a couple of brothers who should have known better think we talk.

It's burden enough sharing the state with Mount Rushmore. The Slab Four have been South Dakota's default recognition point ever since Gutzon Borglum detonated his first stick of dynamite. Few non-natives know or care about the literal and philosophical distances within our borders, but they all recognize that great stone monument to one man's ego.

These days, people who've never seen a live prairie dog, or slogged their way through a fresh snow drift, much less lived in a town with fewer than fifty thousand people or farther away from a shoreline than forty miles, think that we Midwesterners all salt our speech with *yahs* and *you betchas* and *by gollys* and name our children Ole and Lena.

So now we're the butt of jokes, the estimation of our collective IQ lowered with each and every *fer shure*. Southerners have survived that sort of snap judgment and I suppose we can live with it too.

But the superficial observers are also certain that they know how we think and live, as though a cinematic peek at a pregnant cop's visit to a mythic Minneapolis that in no way resembles the real thing could impart actual wisdom about the reality of living where it gets damn cold in the winter.

And maybe they did pick up a pointer or two. I'll admit there's a sort of nasal twang to our speech patterns (not that I'd go so far as to call it an *accent*). And maybe most small town murders *can* be solved by the equivalent of a lucky drive around a frozen lake with a pregnant woman.

But the home truth, the underlying message, the thing most outsiders carried away from *Fargo* was dead wrong.

Isolation isn't insulation.

Regardless of how we comfort ourselves with statistics, evil visits small towns the same as it does Big Bad Cities.

And you're no safer in a place like Delphi, South Dakota, than you are anywhere else in the world.

1

Sprechen Sie?

FEBRUARY
NOON RUSH

Romantic city folk pining for an idyllic existence far from the madding crowd tend to visualize a simple life in the country—good friends, picturesque small town, a few adorably domesticated animals, and a little business quiet enough to soothe the soul with sufficient remuneration to fund a 401(k) and the occasional trek back into civilization.

A bed-and-breakfast, they think as they gaze out their fifty-seventh-story window at traffic snarls and big city squalor down below. *That would be just the ticket. Even better, a restaurant.*

A tiny cafe, nestled in the bosom of the heartland. The kind of place where everyone gathers for homemade food and homegrown fellowship. Where people sit in the same booths every day, where the company and conversation are comfortably predictable.

A little slice of heaven, a place where everybody knows your name.

Well, as the reluctant co-owner of just such an establishment, in just such a bosomy heartland, lemme tell ya—heaven ain't all it's cracked up to be.

In fact, if I had known what was coming, I'd have sold my share in the Delphi Cafe to the first idiot who made an offer and walked away without a backward glance.

Twenty-twenty hindsight being 100 percent accurate, I can see now that I shoulda stood in bed.

But I didn't.

I got up just like usual, slogged wearily through new drifts to the cafe, and spent a wonderfully rewarding, idyllic country morning dealing with frozen pipes, a faulty furnace, and booths that overflowed with energetic foreign teenagers all talking at once full blast in their own assorted languages.

"How long are we going to be stuck with the Trapp Family Singers?" Del whispered in my ear as she surveyed the chilly room, juggling plates of apple pie balanced precariously on top of glasses of Coke.

"Only a couple of days, I think," I said, suppressing a sigh and wrapping my arms around myself for warmth. It was barely 60 degrees in the cafe. "They sing day after tomorrow at the church and then they move on to Mobridge."

Where the furnaces probably functioned properly, I thought bitterly.

"Are they taking *her* with them when they go?" Del asked, maliciously eyeing a very pregnant Junior who tried to temper the noisy enthusiasm of her charges.

The fifteen or so kids ranged from apple-cheeked and hearty to sallow, bored smokers. They ignored the chill and pointed out the dusty sights of Delphi's main drag avidly to one another, the apple cheekers smiling, the sallow smokers wincing. Most of them laughed (probably *at* rather than *with* us) and wandered constantly from booth to booth, making it very difficult for beleaguered waitresses to remember which one was allergic to pickles and which one had insisted, in universal sign language, on fat-free margarine.

They babbled incomprehensibly to one another with their mouths full, or conversed with emphatic gestures that were both wild and dangerous to passing waitresses carrying trays filled with exotic American fare like hot beef combos and chicken fried steak.

My cousin Junior, who usually annoyed the hell out of me with her smug perfection and her Superwoman competence, looked tired and flustered. Her eyes were runny and her nose was red, which matched her mittens, which she did not remove. She seemed to be completely overwhelmed by the boundless energy of the European Traveling Lutheran Youth Choir, whose care and feeding had been dumped on her without warning after their concert in Cresbard, forty miles away, had been canceled.

Junior lumbered from booth to booth, flashing a wan imitation of her patented Minister's Wife Smile at each kid, shushing them politely and vainly trying to discourage underage smoking. In one hand she held a tissue that she used as a screen against secondhand smoke; her other hand seemed permanently attached to her lower back, kneading obviously aching muscles.

I surprised myself by saying to Del, "She's doing the best she can with them."

As we watched from a fairly safe distance, Junior tried to sidetrack one of the few nonverbal, nongesturing teens in the bunch from recording the whole scene for posterity with a handheld video camera. Even more energetic than the rest, he zoomed in gleefully on each of our faces with abandon and then swung the camera around to capture the next fascinating small-town detail.

Junior might as well have been trying to get the attention of the man in the moon. Except for a three-second close-up of her face, the young filmmaker ignored her completely, as enchanted by the texture of the gravy on the plate that Alanna Luna had just pushed through the opening from the kitchen, as he was by the scope and breadth of her chest.

Del raised an eyebrow. "Since when do you sympathize with Junior? I thought she was your mortal enemy."

Actually, she was closer to being Del's mortal enemy, though Junior's top spot on Del's hit list had been usurped by the unfortunately permanent addition of Alanna Luna to the Delphi social whirl.

"Getting mellow in my old age, I guess," I said, shrugging.

Too much had happened, too much had changed drastically in the last few months for me to dwell on old grudges against Junior.

Besides which, after the intimate family supper my mother had planned for that evening, during which she intended to reveal a few nasty secrets of her own, Junior would probably slink away from Delphi in shame, never to darken our lives again.

As little as I was looking forward to Mother's revelations or their inevitable public aftermath, it would almost be worth it to watch Junior and Aunt Juanita's faces when she finally confessed.

But such pleasures were hours away, and in the meantime I had to deal with chilly booths filled with not only foreign strangers, but disgruntled locals unused to waiting for their cheeseburgers and gossip.

"A tad nippy in here this morning, dontcha think?" Eldon McKee asked me, winking his good eye. A stroke a couple years back had permanently loosened the muscles along one side of his face, but had done nothing to hamper his need to monitor, and report, all the latest local news.

"Alanna called the furnace guy," I said, dreading the thought of another bill. Dreading even more another session of poring over the books without central heat during a South Dakota winter. "Maybe it's just a plugged filter."

Eldon shrugged at my unwarranted optimism.

"Don't all this foreign jabbering make you nervous?" Eldon asked, changing the subject. He squinted at the crowd with distrust from an unaccustomed perch at the counter. His usual window booth had been taken, and he was displeased. "They could be plotting to take over the U.S. government right now and we'd never know it."

"Seems unlikely," I said, refilling his cup, remembering at the last second that he'd recently switched to decaf, which probably accounted for his testiness. "But if they can get anyone in Washington to listen, more power to 'em."

"Well, you'd better keep an eye on 'em anyway," he said

darkly. "Don't trust no foreigners. Especially ones who can sleep through this noise."

He gestured toward the one silent and stationary person in the crowd—a pretty brown-haired girl in a back corner booth had given up on the letter she'd been writing, cradled her head in her arms, and slept soundly through the animated conversation around her.

"I thought it was the guilty who slept badly," I said. "It's the innocent who sleep like babies."

"Don't you believe it," he said, swiveling back around on his stool to frown at the counter.

"Tory," Alanna called sharply from the kitchen, "burger."

It was Alanna's day to cook and she was just about as pleased with being stuck away from the action as Eldon. She far preferred to be out in the crowd, wowing the masses with her Oklahoma accent and her enormous breasts, both of which I was certain were artificially enhanced.

If I wasn't so terrible in the kitchen, I'd have switched places with her. Dealing with the public, English-speaking or otherwise, was not exactly my strong suit.

Our last attempt at advertising for a cook had been disastrous and we were still seriously short-handed. Alanna's son Brian, who often filled in for us in the kitchen, was off gallivanting with Rhonda, our backup waitress who should have been in school but who had been cutting university classes a lot lately. Del absolutely refused to go near the grill.

So Alanna and I took turns.

Today was her turn, and as little as I enjoyed practicing phrases I barely remembered from high school Spanish, I was not about to let an ex-stripper loose on impressionable foreign youth.

Especially impressionable foreign male youth.

"Here's your order," Alanna said to me sweetly, tucking a tendril of blond hair behind an ear. She stood up to her full height, which was considerable, and threw back her shoulders and inhaled as deeply as possible, which was also considerable.

Her performance was obviously not meant for me.

I peeked over my shoulder and bumped my nose on the lens of a video cam.

Our intrepid recorder was directly behind me. I had yet to see him pull his eye away from the viewfinder, so intent was he on capturing our every movement.

Or rather, Alanna's every movement.

She breathed deeply again and slid my burger over. "Make sure you get that to our customer before it gets cold," she said slowly, drawing the syllables out. "The last thing we want are unhappy patrons. Our only job is to serve the public."

"Yeah, yeah," I said, grabbing the plate and dodging the kid. "Whatever." There was no point in arguing with Alanna when she was in full performance mode. I just hoped that she didn't intend to wow the room with an impromptu display of her ecdysiastical skills.

Which were also considerable.

Del, who had not yet reconciled herself to being the second most desirable middle-aged broad in Delphi, accidentally on purpose sashayed in front of the camera, flexing her own considerable chest and tossing her tousled red hair.

"You have my order ready yet, Alanna?" she asked sweetly. "I have a very important customer waiting."

"*Et tu?*" I muttered under my breath.

Del ignored me.

"What order?" Alanna asked, equally sweetly, managing to divest herself of a pesky cardigan and accidentally loosen the top two buttons on her blouse at the same time. Theatrically, she turned to face the camera, spatula in hand.

How she managed to make taking off a sweater look like a striptease, not to mention turning an ordinary spatula into a marital aid, I'll never know, but she did, and both Del and the kid noticed.

I shook my head. Never having been the object of mass male longing, I'll never understand the need to prove that the attraction still holds. Neither Del nor Alanna was going gently into middle age, and it was best to be at a safe distance when they decided to compete over turf.

Unfortunately Del, who was not above an artfully unbuttoned shirt herself, happened to be wearing a USD sweatshirt with no blouse underneath, which ended the competition right then and there.

The kid kept his lens focused on Alanna, who shot an artfully sweet but triumphant look at both Del and me.

Del turned away and looked out the window in disgust.

Her expression instantly became pained and contorted. She moaned.

"God, no," she said weakly. "Not today. Please."

I thought she was taking Alanna's temporary triumph a little too seriously.

There was no way, after all, that even Alanna would continue to undress right over the grill. And neither of them would be allowed to *keep* a foreign teenage boy however much they may want to.

And then I saw what Del saw out the window.

Alanna and the video boy, indeed the whole cafe and the rest of my awful, chilly morning, were instantly and completely forgotten.

I may have moaned myself.

2

Leave it to Weasel

Let's get back to our transplanted city slickers for a minute.

Having prepared in advance by poring over back issues of *Country Living*, stocking up on L. L. Bean essentials, and watching a couple seasons' worth of *Green Acres* reruns, they'll be more than ready to absorb a few home truths about small-town living.

They will not be surprised that the library doesn't carry a subscription to the *Wall Street Journal*. They'll know better than to look for shiitake mushrooms at the neighborhood mom-and-pop.

If they ever cherished a hope that movies would make it to the local theater before being available on video, they'll be disabused of that notion in a real hurry.

And, of course, they'll understand the universal truth about small towns: *Your news is my news.*

They won't understand the full ramifications of that particular maxim until they discover firsthand that their checkbook balance and hair coloring preference is common knowledge, but they'll still be marginally prepared for everyone to know everything.

What they won't expect, and what catches us off guard on

occasion too, is that sometimes even out on the plains, where there is no place to run and no place to hide, things, and people, can still sneak up on you.

The unpleasant and unexpected can show up and smack you right alongside the head.

"Oh my Lord," Del said, still looking out the window bleakly, her shoulders drooping. "Why didn't anyone warn us?"

It was a rhetorical question. She knew that if *anyone* had known, we *all* would have known.

Then we could have done the logical thing and barricaded the town, declaring a quarantine.

"I don't need this right now," I said sternly to the ceiling, expecting the cosmic glitch to be rectified immediately. "Things are complicated enough around here already."

"What're y'all moanin' about out there?" Alanna asked from the kitchen, leaning out over the counter that divided it from the rest of the cafe. "Did someone die or somethin'?"

"I wish *I* was dead," Del said.

Alanna looked at me for an explanation, but I figured there was no point. She'd understand soon enough.

I just shook my head and closed my eyes.

That was more mystery than Alanna could take. She threw the spatula down on the grill and pushed through the swinging half-door into the cafe and craned her neck over Del's head.

"That's it? *That's* what y'all are fussin' about?" she asked, incredulous. "That little bitty man out there? The one getting out of that furnace van? I woulda thought you'd be ecstatic that I got a repair man here so soon. We're all freezin' in here."

"That is not a man," Del said flatly. "That is an animal."

"Don't be ridiculous," Alanna said, surveying the interloper with a critical eye. "What can possibly be so awful about him that has y'all shakin' in your boots?"

"You'll find out in a minute," I said, sighing softly. "Just as soon as he gets inside." I turned to Del and said, "You'd better warn Junior that Weasel Cleaver's back. She'll need to get out of here and spread the word."

Del nodded. She didn't even question the order to talk civilly to Junior.

"Weasel? His name is *Weasel Cleaver*?" Alanna asked, disbelieving, as she watched the man wrestle a valise full of tools out of the side door of the van. "Y'all gotta be kiddin' me."

"Does he look like a *Beaver* to you?" Del asked over her shoulder.

I watched Weasel through the window and marveled at the justice of small-town nicknames.

Short and wiry, with small pointy teeth, sharp features, and dark beady little eyes, Weasel looked exactly like one, only less attractive. He stood up to his full height and slicked his shiny hair straight back and then wiped his palms on his striped overalls leaving greasy streaks down his thighs.

He smiled slowly at the cafe and picked up his valise.

"He's going to be in here in just a second," I said quickly to Alanna. "Whatever you do, do *not* give him any money. Don't *buy* anything from him. Don't write him a check. Don't leave him alone for more than two seconds with anything valuable. Do *not* believe a word he says. And especially," I emphasized the word, *"do not agree to go on a date, no matter how much he begs."*

"But why . . ." Her words trailed off as the cafe door swung open, allowing in a frigid blast of air.

"Ladies," Weasel stepped in grandly and addressed the whole cafe in the high-pitched voice that I had not missed for even one day of the three years he'd just spent in the state pen.

Cups slammed to a halt betwixt the table and the lip, slopping hot coffee down the fronts of many who were momentarily unaware of being scalded. Silverware clattered to the floor. Matches burned to the nub unnoticed.

Conversation died instantly.

Even the foreign teenagers stopped gaping out the window and jabbering to one another. They swiveled en masse toward the interloper.

Junior cast an accusatory glance at me, then reached

blindly for the nearest available chair and sat down without even checking first to see if it was dirty.

For a moment, the only sound in the cafe was Eldon McKee's ornery cackle and the soft whir of the video cam as our intrepid filmmaker recorded the scene for posterity.

Enjoying his entrance thoroughly, Weasel surveyed the cold, silent, surprised room and flashed a small and entirely evil grin at the assembly.

"Ladies, you surely are a sight for sore eyes." He paused, inspecting Del and me in turn, undressing us both with his eyes. Prison had evidently not changed him—he was still an equal opportunity letch. "The Weasel has returned. And *damn* . . ." He paused and slid a hand into his overall pocket and jostled himself enthusiastically as he caught sight of Alanna. His eyes glittered with delight.

Several foreign teenage jaws dropped open in surprise. The locals just averted their gaze and sighed. Alanna stared in total disbelief.

"I don't believe you've had the pleasure," Weasel said to Alanna. He withdrew his hand from his pocket, held it out to her, and said with a grin, "Do me a favor and pull my finger."

3

Merchant Semen

They say that which does not kill us only makes us stronger.

Jane Pauley goes out of her way to prove that point several times each and every week in TV news magazine installments overflowing with prime-time tales of heart-warming, resilient souls who have faced the vagaries of an uncaring world with a song in their hearts and an eye focused on triumph. They persevere in eleven-minute increments, buoyed by the certainty that Right Will Prevail and the possibility of living to see an HBO special detailing their heroic struggle starring Melanie Griffith and Judd Hirsch and a host of other actors on hiatus from their regular series.

But for the rest of us mortals, that which does not kill usually leaves us weary and weakened, with few reserves left to battle the next nasty surprise.

My entire last year was a pisser—I was still not recovered fully from the death of my husband, though Lord knows I should have been. Nick had been gone plenty long enough for me to gain some distance and perspective and I'd certainly had more than enough proof that I was better off without him, though that didn't stop me from making the mistake of getting involved with a married man.

Which, needless to say, led to all kinds of complications in the theoretically quiet life of a cranky, overweight, middle-aged waitress in a very small town. Some of those complications led me into even more complicated maneuvering with and around dead bodies, and a few especially nasty, long-held secrets, which in the end gave me the oomph to end the affair just in time for my life to be turned upside down by the death of my employer.

That landed me in the unenviable position of being co-owner of Delphi, South Dakota's only cafe, yoked in tandem with an ex-stripper, and suddenly the reluctant employer of my roommate (who didn't take to the transition very well), cautiously considering a romantic entanglement with my best friend, and facing very soon the public confession of the perpetrator of the crime that set my whole year into motion.

I would have liked nothing more than a few months of peace and quiet in which to weave those major life changes into a new normal.

I could have accepted, with pioneer stoicism, a furnace that wasn't working properly and the blizzards that had been hitting us with fierce regularity all winter. I could even have dealt with a cafe temporarily full of foreign teenagers with something approaching grace under pressure.

But I could not deal gracefully with the steadily mounting trials and tribulations of my life *and* the unexpected reappearance of Weasel Cleaver at the same time.

Something had to go.

And I knew what that *something* was.

He was still gaping at Alanna when I pulled him aside and whispered in his ear, "Weasel, I don't know why you're here or where you came from, but go back right now."

I was usually not that blunt. In fact I was usually a ray of sunshine, but this was an emergency. Tact would not get the point across.

"Tory," he said slowly, grinning with mock patience, like a professor explaining the obvious to a particularly obtuse student. He patted me on the shoulder gently, his hand slowly snaking down my back. I twisted away, which only made him grin more. "Now, now, is that any way to talk to someone you haven't seen for three whole years?"

"Weasel, last time I saw you, you were on your way out of town in a stolen car packed with fifteen thousand dollars that didn't belong to you, and a fourteen-year-old girl. Three years wasn't nearly long enough."

"Hey, she looked twenty-one, and told me she was eighteen, and screwed like she was thirty-five and twice divorced. What was I supposed to do? Check her ID?"

"Considering that her only ID was a school lunch ticket, that might not have been a bad idea," I said wearily, amazed that I had already been drawn into a useless debate.

Alanna had retreated to the kitchen to continue committing hamburger abuse, though she kept an eagle eye on Weasel and me. Her former life as a stripper had inured her to drunken male admiration. She may not have been fully prepared for sober, daylight obnoxiousness.

Weasel did not need the excuse of intoxication. He could be perfectly disgusting while completely sober. When he was drunk, you didn't even want to be in the same state.

Del had busied herself cleaning tables as far away from us as she could and still stay in the building. I think she'd even have offered to help Junior gather the choir and depart.

And Junior, who struggled mightily with her own near-term pregnancy and kids who were not so much recalcitrant as extremely slow, would probably have welcomed the assistance.

Amazing how a common adversary can bring together former enemies.

Their perfidy of course, left me to deal with Weasel alone.

I broadcast a glare in the general direction of the cowards, and then faced Weasel again and inhaled deeply. "That is neither here nor there. The simple fact is that I don't want you on the premises. I'm sorry if that hurts your feelings, but you have to leave. Now."

I might as well have been speaking to the air. He didn't even miss a beat.

"I couldn't possibly leave this fine establishment without fulfilling my assignment, Tory my dear. I came to fix the furnace, and I will stay to fix the furnace because that will not only please me, but will make my probation officer boundlessly happy. Anyway," he said, peering around the cafe, using that as an excuse to stand even closer to look over my shoulder at Alanna in the kitchen, "who died and put you in charge?"

"What did I do to deserve this?" I asked the ceiling out loud. *I've been good,* I thought. *I stopped having sex with a married man. I don't cheat on my taxes any more than anyone else. I haven't actually killed anyone. Yet. What more do you want?*

Weasel ignored me completely and asked the cafe in general, "Where's my sweet Aphrodite? *She'll* be happy to see me."

That was definitely an arguable statement, considering that some of the fifteen grand he'd absconded with in a phony stock scam had belonged to the cafe. Though given Aphrodite's current condition, that was a moot point.

Del caught my eye from the back of the cafe where she was still cleaning tables around immobile patrons. She pointed imperceptibly toward the back room.

I knew what she was suggesting—we'd never get rid of Weasel quickly or quietly. He'd come to fix the furnace—a skill he must have picked up at the expense of the state of South Dakota during the last three years—and said ailing furnace was in the back room, away from the general public.

Even Junior caught Del's meaning. They looked at each other, one enormously pregnant, tired, dark-haired woman and one faintly shopworn, red-haired, middle-aged sexpot, and then both nodded at me in uncharacteristic agreement.

It was time to put some physical distance between Weasel and a roomful of impressionable foreign teenagers (a church choir at that). It would be nice if their primary memory of South Dakota was not a disgusting little man with *Roman* eyes and *Russian* fingers.

Unfortunately, the videotaper had already discovered Weasel and was chattering to him happily. A couple of the girls had also shot curious, albeit knowing glances in his direction and he was sidling toward them, drawn like iron filings to a magnet until another girl gave him a cryptic, sidewise stare that stopped him momentarily in his tracks.

I used that pause to make my move. I grabbed his arm and tugged. "Come on, let's take a peek at the furnace."

My second-to-last desire in the world was to be closeted alone with Weasel Cleaver for even one minute, but my last desire was a toss-up between leaving him in the cafe proper where he was apt to molest those poor girls while simultaneously trying to sell them something, or sending him alone to the back room to wreak untold damage on an already fragile heating system and steal everything he could get away with.

"I knew she wanted to get me alone," Weasel said to the room loudly, pointing at my hand, which was still firmly latched to his arm. "The woman can't keep her hands off me. Never could." He turned back toward Del, who was picking up dishes by the still sleeping choir girl. "Sorry Del, gotta do Tory first and then I can take care of you. I got plenty for everyone."

Eldon McKee, who was still sitting at the counter watching everything, snickered.

"Sorry Weasel," Del said without missing a beat, without even looking up. "But I'll just have to pass. I'm celibate these days."

Eldon snickered even more loudly.

Actually everyone in the cafe who knew Del, and even a few who didn't know her, snickered.

Though she had not announced her intention, nor had she marked the passing days on a calendar, I realized, a tad belatedly, that she had not *seen* any man, in public or otherwise, since the death of Ian O'Hara.

I raised an eyebrow at Del myself, but she wasn't paying attention to me.

She was frowning down at the sleeping girl. The one who'd decided to nap instead of jabber or finish writing her letter.

Weasel burst into genuine, oily, amused laughter. "So Del's not screwing anyone, huh? It's the end of the world as we know it, that's for sure."

But Del ignored Weasel's laughter and commentary. She motioned Junior over to the girl.

"Kaboom." Weasel chuckled, miming an explosion with his hands. "All of Western civilization collapses because one of the fundamental laws of the universe has just been broken. Delphine Bauer is celibate. Fat fuckin' chance, eh Tory?"

He looked to me for confirmation.

"Shut up," I said, hoping suddenly that the appearance of Weasel Cleaver was going to be the absolute low point of my day. Afraid that I was just beginning to discover how low it could go. "Just shut up for a minute please."

Junior bent over the girl and slid the letter she'd been writing out from under her arm and scanned it quickly.

The page slipped from Junior's hand and drifted back down on the table as she turned toward me. Even from across the room I could see the color drain from her face.

4

Queen O' Denial

When it comes time to ring up my Celestial Ticket at the Till of Eternity, I think that I'll be able to stand proud and say that I rolled with the punches pretty well. With very little fudging, I can swear on my eternal soul that I cleaned up after myself, I played well with others, I was kind to animals and polite to the elderly.

I'll be able to say, truthfully, that I did my best, that I championed the underdog and, for the most part, that I *took it like a man.*

Given that fairly consistent performance, I hope I'll be forgiven for one teeny lapse in situational ethics—the one time when I knew I was needed and did not rise to the challenge. The single instance when I purposely put my own sanity ahead of the Group Welfare, when I opted out of Designated Grown-up status, perfectly willing to let someone else, anyone else, take charge for a change.

Not that it did me a damn bit of good.

"Come on," I said to Weasel, and pulled him in the direction of the swinging half-door that divided the cafe from the kitchen. "Let's go look at that furnace and see what you can do."

He stood stock still, unmoving.

Anxious to disappear into the depths of the back room before whatever was about to happen happened, I tugged again,

It was like trying to pull a boulder.

"It's cold in here," I said, trying one more time. "And I can't afford to pay you to stand around."

He didn't even look at me.

"Something's going on over there," he said, staring intently past the mostly oblivious crowd of teenagers at Junior and Del and the sleeping girl. Or maybe he was staring at the young, dark-eyed beauty who was staring back at him. Or maybe even at the video guy, who was still merrily recording the whole scene for posterity.

"This is an exciting place. Something's *always going on over there,*" I said, forcing a light tone. "Del can handle it."

"I don't think so," Weasel said quietly. "And you know it. There's something wrong with that girl. You'd better go and see."

"Who died and put me in charge?" I asked the ceiling under my breath, whining the eternal whine, *Why me? Why now? Why?*

I stood for a second, looking at Del and Junior who were quietly, but insistently, shaking the unresponsive, sleeping girl.

I watched the milling crowd, knowing soon that one of them would notice what was happening in the back booth and then all hell would break loose.

I stared intently at Weasel himself. He was awfully anxious to get rid of me, which was not a good sign. I mentally totaled all of the loose and portable valuables in the cafe. Fortunately there weren't that many.

Unfortunately, Weasel wasn't picky.

He grinned and shrugged and burped without covering his mouth. He'd eaten onions sometime in the recent past. "I'm amazed at you Tory. You're being mighty blasé about something that doesn't happen around here every day," he said with mock reproach.

"They didn't let you watch the news much in prison, did they?" I asked him wearily.

Knowing I had no choice, I turned toward Alanna and leaned over the stainless-steel counter and said, "We got a problem out here. You might as well shut the grill down and come and ring out the rest of these kids. I expect we'll be needing an ambulance soon, so keep the phone line free."

I turned away, ignoring her demand for an explanation, but turned back almost immediately and said, before she could get a word in edgewise, "Most important, keep an eye on Weasel. Don't let him go *anywhere* alone." I thought about adding *please,* but decided there was no point in pretending that it was a request.

I squarely faced Weasel, who was grinning widely, his beady little eyes sparkling at the possibility for committing mayhem while I was otherwise occupied.

"You," I said poking an insistent finger right into the middle of his chest, "you stay put. Don't touch anything. Don't go anywhere, unless it's back where you came from. And if anything turns up missing, I'll personally call your probation officer. Got it?"

"Moi?" he asked, laughing, pointing at himself in mock innocence. "You suspect little me of nefarious deeds? Tory, I am cut to the quick." He pouted and placed his hands over his heart and gave me a wounded puppy dog look.

"Just remember," I said darkly.

Alanna reentered the cafe from the kitchen with an annoyed expression on her face. She didn't like me bossing her around any more than I liked dealing with Weasel.

And she liked mysteries, especially mysteries that interfered with the cash flow, even less.

Which made for two unhappy cafe owners.

And an apparently unconscious girl in a back booth.

Please, I pleaded silently with the ceiling, *let her only be unconscious.*

5

Foreign Body

I've always wondered how fictional sleuths manage to view the continual mayhem with equanimity.

I mean, you never saw Hercule Poirot or Miss Marple turning primly away from those who unexpectedly ingested cyanide. Kinsey Millhone didn't run for the can with a hand clamped over her mouth every time she came across a gunshot wound. Even Cecil Younger, a sort of ordinary small-town guy, seemed able to view bodily remains with a calm resignation that was more sad than anything else.

They were able to see the unspeakable and process the unimaginable and unravel the Gordian Knot every ten months or so (depending on publishing schedules), and most of them seemed no worse for the wear (well, Cecil got battered about a bit, but he persevered too).

I suppose the operative word here is *fictional.*

Writers can make up whatever they want, and their poor creations have no choice but to deal with the overflow.

That's how it works in fiction.

Characters discover bodies, they investigate deaths, and they solve mysteries and then enjoy a bit of downtime between each installment.

In real life, you'd never expect to find an overweight, widowed, cafe owner in a small plains town, unfortunate enough to have tripped over (in one way or another) six bodies (several at her place of business) in less than seven months.

I doubt you'd expect her to have been able to solve the underlying mystery of each of those deaths in short order, while simultaneously trying to sort out her decidedly messy personal life and support herself in the trailer-house manner to which she'd become accustomed.

And you'd certainly not expect her to have to face the whole process again barely a month after the last grisly discovery.

If I was reading the story of my life, I'd have a hard time believing it myself.

Welcome to my world.

"Tell me she's not dead," I whispered to Del over her shoulder.

Most of the choir members were putting their coats on and talking to one another, but one or two had eyed Junior and Del with curiosity.

We didn't have much time to establish and maintain control, especially if the girl really had died right there in the booth.

In the middle of the day.

In my cafe.

"She's not dead," Del whispered back without looking at me.

The relief was instant and enormous.

Whatever was wrong with the poor girl, it wasn't going to get worse here and now. And best of all, I wasn't going to have to deal with it personally.

Maybe she was only sick. People got sick all the time and it was no one's fault and no one got blamed and no one had to investigate anything.

Unless they got sick because they ate something bad, the renegade voice in my mind said, just before it reminded me that this was the second meal the choir had eaten in the cafe. *Plenty of time for food poisoning to set in.*

I shot a surreptitious glance around the cafe, searching faces for traces of illness.

Eldon McKee, who ate two meals a day here as well as spending most of his breaks firmly seated in a window booth, looked hale and hearty. Or at least as hale and hearty as an elderly man who'd mostly recovered from a stroke a year or so ago. One eye drooped permanently at half-mast, and his smile was lopsided. But his mind was still sharp and there was nothing wrong with the eyesight in his good eye. He looked perfectly normal sitting at the counter sipping the coffee he personally spiked from a hip flask, keeping track of the proceedings.

Alanna was doing her best to ring the kids out. Though some of them could speak English, they had evidently been trained in the useless grammar of "What color is your pencil?" and "Can you direct me to the bathroom, please?" Wherever they'd been previously on their youth choir tour, it was obvious that they'd never practiced speaking Oklahoman.

Alanna was monolingual. Unfortunately, none of them seemed up to speed on the current value of a hamburger in deutsche marks. They tried to make each other understand, mostly to no avail, and they were all beginning to look flustered, but none looked ill.

Out of the corner of my eye, I spotted the dark-haired girl, the one who'd been watching us earlier, talking to, or at least gesturing at, Weasel. He had an unusual expression on his face, a mix of lust and what looked to be a trace of fear.

Weasel had not yet eaten anything from the cafe, so any illnesses he might have were his own problem. The girl looked healthy enough. Since she seemed to be holding her own with him, I decided not to interfere.

It was hard to assess the video recorder's health since I had yet to see his face. But he pranced around the cafe, still recording.

"Maybe she's just sick," I said out loud, helpfully.

"She's not sick," Junior said quietly. She'd taken the girl's pulse.

If anyone in the cafe looked ill, it was Junior. She was

pale and had begun to sweat. She let the girl's wrist go and brushed the hair off her forehead and closed her eyes, swaying a little.

"Maybe she's drunk," I said brightly.

The kid was young, she was in a strange country, surrounded by strange people speaking a strange language. Who could blame her for tippling a few before lunch?

I was tempted to do it myself, and I spoke the language just fine, thank you.

"She's not drunk either," Junior said, even more quietly.

I had been avoiding this moment ever since I'd spotted their charming little tableau from across the room.

I didn't want to do it, but I knew I was going to have to ask.

I took a deep breath, not wanting to hear whatever Junior was going to say.

"What's wrong with her then?"

Junior didn't say anything.

She just handed me a piece of paper.

The one the girl had been writing on.

6

Suicide Is Painless

Of course I should have known better than to think that I could get out of this unscathed.

Everything that happens in the Delphi Cafe affects me directly. From the arguments between formerly loving couples on their way to bitter custody settlements, to the bad checks written by sad souls sucked into the dark and smoky world of video gambling, to the underage drinkers who drop in to gobble scrambled eggs early in the morning after partying all night, only to throw up their unpaid breakfasts all over our unisex bathroom.

Everything that happens here affects me, because that's how it works in small towns. And everything that happens in the cafe affects me doubly because not only do I live and work in this godforsaken town, but I happen to have inherited a half-interest in the damn cafe.

The only one in town.

Which means it's the only local eatery in which young foreign choir members can attempt to commit public suicide.

"Jesus," I said, after having read what the girl had written.

Even Del was uncomfortable, though this may have been the very comeuppance she'd always wished on Junior. I don't think it was nearly as satisfying as she'd envisioned because she made a quick and awkward excuse and then hurried to the phone to call an ambulance.

There wasn't much we could do for the girl. She was unconscious but breathing, which meant that CPR was not necessary. Her lips had a bluish cast, but I suppose that was to be expected. I didn't think they'd want us to try to induce vomiting, which would have been difficult in her state anyway. If there were still pills in her shoulder bag, the paramedics could worry about them.

There was nothing we could do but wait and stand around and hope to hell that it wasn't too late.

And that people would have the sense not to believe the note the girl had written.

And, the inner voice I was too shamed to acknowledge added, *to hope that there was absolutely no truth to the note that the girl had written.*

I looked at Junior, not knowing what to say to her.

I belatedly realized that she had been the only adult in the cafe with the kids, that she'd been wrestling with them without the help of chaperones. "Where is their group leader? We'd better get her over here right away."

Junior nodded numbly. "Glenda Harrison. She's the American Lutheran liaison in charge of the tour. She was in here earlier, but she left for a meeting with Clay." She looked suddenly out the window, at the church across the street, blinking several times rapidly before continuing. "Over at the church. Now. To plan the concert with Jennifer Swanhorst, who's been taking over some of my duties." Her voice trailed off uncertainly. "He's been so"—she shrugged and looked down—"preoccupied lately. What with this coming." She put a hand on her swollen belly. "And this choir thing being dumped on us with no warning. He's a minister, it's in his job description to take on all of these responsibilities and deal with passports and things. No matter what's going on in our lives."

She tried a weak smile, but it fizzled.

It suddenly struck me that the unconscious girl wasn't an

American citizen and that this could turn into an international incident.

A well-publicized international incident.

I felt myself losing a little color.

"We don't even know this girl's name," I said, trying to think the situation through, though it was too late for damage control. "The dispatcher is going to want some information from Del about her age and nationality."

"Annelise," Junior said. "Her name is Annelise. She's Swedish, but I can't remember her last name. She's particular friends with the girl from Canada. The dark-haired one. Meg."

"Meg?" I asked. "The one who's talking over there with . . ." I turned around to point at Weasel, but he was nowhere in sight. Neither was the dark-haired girl, the Canadian Meg, who had seemed to be as intrigued with Weasel as he had been with her.

They weren't mixing with the other choir members, who were now gathered around Annelise's booth, watching gravely.

I had feared a rash of teenage panic when the group realized that one of their members was gravely ill. I had expected screams, and wailing, and tears. Maybe even a shouted accusation or two. But they stood there, watching us, almost eerily calm. They whispered quietly and waited for us to do something.

All of them except Meg, who had evidently disappeared.

For just a moment, I considered letting Junior stand watch over the unconscious girl alone in order to prevent an even worse international incident involving a teenage Canadian girl and a recently released American felon, but Junior touched my shoulder softly.

She inhaled and looked down at the girl, her expression unreadable and whispered, "She did stay with us last night, you know."

"I figured as much," I said quietly.

The choir members had been farmed out to assorted parishioners in town for the duration. It was common knowledge that Junior and Clay had taken in a couple themselves, as well as the tour liaison.

"No one's going to believe it," I said. "I can't imagine what made her write such a thing, but everyone will know it's not true."

I wanted to reach over and comfort Junior somehow but it was impossible.

Nothing I could say would make a bit of difference right now.

And Junior knew it.

This was going to be messy, and it was going to be very, very public.

Del spoke earnestly into the phone, relaying what little information we had, or at least what little information we were prepared to give, to the dispatcher.

There was no need to mention that Annelise had written in painfully correct English with a rounded girlish hand, her desire to kill herself by taking an overdose of aspirin because the Lutheran minister in Delphi, South Dakota, had snuck into her room the previous night and molested her.

7

In-a-Gadda-Da-Vida-Loca

Outsiders assume that the Great Plains is a huge, boring expanse in the middle of the country where nothing whatsoever happens. People who've never seen a tumbleweed up close and personal are absolutely certain that we spend one quiet day of desperation after another, with nothing more than the Weather Channel for entertainment and our own prejudices for company.

And under most circumstances they'd be right.

Our days do tend to blur, season blending into season seamlessly. Our journey from morning to night is rarely interesting enough to note, much less mark on a calendar. We've been known to pass from one millennium to another without cluttering the occasion with balloons and streamers.

But once in a while things go haywire in a big way.

And Delphi, for better or worse, seems to be Haywire Central.

We not only do *ordinary* different from everyone else, we manage to gussy up *out of the ordinary* in our own way too. It's one of our special skills.

"There's something wrong with these kids," Del whispered to me as we stood, gathered loosely around Annelise's booth. "Don't you think they're acting strange?"

I knew what Del meant. One of their own was obviously in trouble—a girl they'd been traveling with across the United States for over a month was draped unconscious over a table in a small cafe booth in the middle of nowhere.

She could be dying, for all they knew.

She could be dying, for all *we* knew.

Lord knows, we were on the verge of panic ourselves.

Junior was outwardly calm, but it was plain that she'd been flummoxed by the choir invasion. Her trademark I'm the Boss and Don't You Forget It persona had been replaced by a third trimester exhaustion that overruled her inborn need to be in charge. She'd been flustered even before the discovery of Annelise's condition. Absorbing the handwritten accusation in the suicide note had unfocused her even more.

Not that I was surprised—few are able to survive an accusation of sexual molestation unscathed.

The Reverend Clay Deibert was just about as blameless as they came. He was universally admired, genuinely respected, handsome, hearty, and, most amazing of all, sincerely spiritual without being obnoxious about it.

I forgave him a long time ago for marrying a pain in the rear whose list of obnoxious traits outstripped almost everyone's I knew.

Clay was a good man, and even he was going to have a hard time looking innocent when the inevitable cameras began to point his way.

Junior herself was so shaken by this unexpected wrench in the smoothly oiled machine of their lives that she hadn't attempted to get the rest of the choir out of the cafe.

She just sat in a booth, staring bleakly through the streaked window at the church across the street where her husband, all unaware, was still meeting with the choir liaison.

Though she was not in the least incapacitated by the morning's excitement, Del wasn't much help either. She'd been watching the kids with a keen and disapproving eye.

"Shouldn't they be more upset? Aren't they awfully calm considering that their friend might just die in this shit hole?"

Del's voice carried further than she expected. At least one of the girls shot her an unreadable look before whispering to a friend behind a cupped hand.

"Shhh," I whispered sharply. I had no idea how much English the choir members actually understood, but there was no point throwing a calm, if not fully cognizant, crowd of observers into a panic with the possibility that Annelise might die right here and now in Delphi.

Come to think of it, there was no point in panicking me with that notion either.

"We don't know what's going on here. We don't know what's the matter with this girl, and we certainly don't know that *anyone* is going to die," I said fiercely but softly. "And it'd be better for everyone if you didn't speculate out loud."

"Well, all I know," Del said darkly, picking up a few empty glasses and crumpled napkins from a neighboring table, "is that these guys remind me of that creepy old movie *The Village of the Damned*. Remember it?" She eyed the unnaturally quiet choir members, most of whom stood in a loose circle around us, staring wide-eyed but unemotionally at the unconscious girl. "Or even worse yet, they're like Stepford Children. They just aren't acting normally. They should be upset. They should be running around screaming and crying and being hysterical. All this quiet is just too weird."

Del shivered theatrically.

Though I hated to admit it, she was right. It was odd that the young men and women were so grave and silent, though I didn't suspect them of being aliens, only foreign.

Maybe the British aren't the only Stiff Upper Lippers in the world. Maybe all other carbon-based life forms are able to view disaster with aplomb. Maybe Americans are the only ones whose emotions rise to the surface so easily.

And maybe the kids were only suffering from a delayed reaction compounded by a noncomprehension of both language and local custom.

The girl who'd been whispering earlier shot a questioning glance at Del, who ignored her completely.

She then looked at me searchingly.

I wasn't sure what she was asking, and could only shrug in reply.

Then she looked at Annelise. I mean *really* looked at her. Maybe for the first time.

The girl's eyes widened in horror. Color drained from her face.

She opened her mouth and screamed.

After which, all hell broke loose.

"Happy now?" I asked Del a frantic few minutes later.

We suddenly had mayhem galore—weeping and wailing teenagers, boys trying to throw themselves at Annelise's unconscious body, insisting via mime on performing CPR even though the girl was breathing and her heartbeat was slow but steady. There were despondent but very vocal demands that *something be done immediately* in several languages that did not have to be translated for the gist to be absorbed.

We even had a few English exhortations from the locals, not all of whom were entertained by the spectacle.

The melee did snap Junior out of her stupor. The first scream pulled her back from whatever mental terrain she'd been exploring. Her eyes widened, she inhaled deeply, shook her head, and jumped into action, finally realizing that getting the mobile choir members out of the cafe was the best possible option for everyone.

Of course, she was handicapped by an inability to speak most of the languages being babbled around us, but she did make it clear to those nearby that they should put on their coats and wade through the snow across the street and gather at the church for further instructions.

The uproar also flipped Alanna's panic switch.

"We got to get these kids outta here," she shouted at me over the bedlam. "We cain't have them running around and screaming like this. Lookit the mess they're making!"

Alanna was right. In the space of a couple of minutes, we'd gone from unnaturally quiet to total chaos. Chairs had been overturned, tables were moved out of place, tipped-over glasses dribbled pop and melting ice cubes onto the floor.

"They're not even payin' for their food," Alanna mourned.

"Junior will come back in later and pick up the tab," I said, trying to reassure Alanna, whose eyesight only strayed from the bottom line when men were involved. "Won't you, Junior?"

Junior, who had her hands full trying to persuade the video recorder, who was still merrily fulfilling his function, to leave the cafe, nodded. "I'll send someone over with a checkbook as soon as possible," she panted.

Alanna was not mollified. She surveyed the disorder and moaned, "This is *not* good for business."

"Dead bodies on the premises aren't good for business either," Del said under her breath as she gently pushed a weeping girl toward the door.

"Dead bodies?" Alanna said, her voice rising. "Who said anything about dead bodies?"

"No one said *anything* about dead bodies." I glared at Del, hoping to hell that the kids who were still in the cafe were not fluent in English, though I'd be hard-pressed to imagine how they could be more panicked than what they were already. "But the fact remains that we're still better off getting these kids out of here right now. Even if no one ever picks up the tickets."

Alanna reluctantly agreed. "Okay. But someone's gonna have to explain this to the accountant," she said darkly.

"I'm pretty sure that expenses incurred in the removal of suicide victims is a legitimate expense," Del said, clamping her lips into a straight line with sheer force.

Amazingly enough, she was enjoying herself. The kids had finally reacted in a way that felt normal to her. Junior's perfect husband had been accused of a crime worse than adultery. She was going to get an unexpected afternoon off.

I doubt Del thought that Annelise was actually going to die or that Clay had been dallying with the youngsters, so the afternoon's excitement would provide plenty to talk over at the bar later with no lasting aftereffects. It would give Del a perfect chance to be the center of attention, and there was nothing she liked more.

For that reason alone, I suspected she was goading Alanna, who would in turn make my shabby life even more miserable, though I certainly didn't need Del to perform that particular function.

"Where's Meg?" Junior asked.

I didn't think she was actually talking to me. Or to anyone else in the cafe.

No one looked at her, and she didn't seem to be focusing on anyone in particular.

I treated her question as rhetorical and began instead to push tables back into position, righting upset napkin holders and sopping up spilled Coke as I kept an ear open for the distant wail of the ambulance and a weary eye on Annelise, who was still sprawled unconscious in the back booth.

"Tory, where's Meg?" Junior said again, this time tapping me on the shoulder to get my attention.

"Oh, were you talking to me?" I asked innocently.

"Yes," she said distractedly. "Where's Meg?"

Most of the kids had bundled themselves up and left the cafe. Through the window I watched them straggle across the street valiantly through the snow. A few seemed to have gotten over their hysteria very quickly. Some laughed, and others threw chunks of snow at each other.

With the exception of Annelise, they were all interchangeable. I'd never have singled her out if she hadn't been so rude as to try to commit suicide in my cafe.

"Didn't she leave with the rest of the kids?" I pointed at the window at the church across the street. "I'm sure she's with them."

"I'm sure she isn't," Junior said firmly, regaining a little of her Queen of the World attitude, the one that hadn't been gone long enough for me to miss. "In fact I haven't seen her since she was talking to Weasel earlier."

"Oh," I said, remembering the pretty, dark-haired girl who'd been talking to Weasel when Annelise's condition was first discovered.

I looked around the cafe.

There was no Meg in sight.

"You sure she wasn't with the others?" I asked, with a sinking heart.

Oh please, I thought, *let her be with the others.*

Junior looked at me bleakly, a terrible realization dawning on her face.

We both looked around the cafe, which was now bereft of teenagers and customers of all nationalities. In fact it was completely empty of ambulatory adults except for Del, Alanna, Junior, and me.

"Where's Weasel?" we asked together.

8

When in Danger, or in Doubt

Somewhere there must be a listing of proper responses to chaos, turmoil, and uncertainty—published guidelines to help those facing on-the-job disaster meet their fate with aplomb, a book of practical suggestions gathered by some famous pundit's ghost writer that would apply to our present situation.

Lord knows, I was out of ideas.

My usual source of calm in the face of unexpected workplace travail was not exactly available at the moment. Aphrodite Ferguson's death a few months ago had upset the balance of my life in ways that I was still discovering. I missed her hoarse laugh and her bad cooking and even her cigarette smoke. I missed her monosyllabic acceptance of everything that fate threw at us.

But most of all, I missed having her as an employer. While she was alive and owner of the Delphi Cafe, everything that happened within its walls was her responsibility, and not mine.

Now that Aphrodite was gone, I was yoked in tandem with Alanna, who was more than useless in a crisis situation.

Del, as she often took pains to remind me, was now my employee. But even without that resentment, she was far more interested in her own journey than in any of my problems, however much they affected her steady employment.

These days, the brunt of every cafe disaster falls squarely on my shoulders.

I'm a big girl, but even I have my limits.

And we'd pretty much reached them.

We had on the premises an unconscious foreign suicide attempt whose farewell note spelled out a bombshell accusation that could blow the town, not to mention my own family, apart.

And we had, unfortunately not on the premises, a recently released felon with a history of enjoying the company of underaged females and a proven propensity to steal anything he could get his hands on.

We'd already taken the run-in-circles route, and that hadn't gotten us anywhere.

I was open for suggestions from anyone as to what to do next.

"Maybe we should call Clay to come over here. He's the one who's really responsible for these kids while they're in Delphi," Junior said softly. She was still looking out the window at the church across the street. "Or maybe I should go over there and talk to him.

"Oh no you don't," I said. "The ambulance will be here any minute now. You have to stay and talk to them about the girl. I don't even know her last name, much less anything else about her. They're going to need a lot more concrete information than I can give. You have to stay. Besides, I'm sure Clay has his hands full at the church with hysterical kids."

I didn't add that it was probably politic for Clay to stay as far away from the unconscious girl as possible, given his prominent mention in her suicide note.

Junior seemed to realize this without being told.

She nodded. "But I should at least call him, let him know what's going on. Tell him what we know so far. Maybe he can send the liaison over—she's the one who really knows these kids. She can tell the paramedics what they need to know. And she'll know who to contact from here."

That was the best idea I'd heard so far.

"Yeah," I said, patting her on the shoulder, actually relieved that Junior in Charge had returned. "That's a good idea. Clay really needs to be informed." *Especially since he's materially involved,* I added mentally as Junior made her way to the pay phone on the wall and deposited a quarter in the slot.

I did not for one minute think that Clay Deibert had been sexually involved with any teenager, American or foreign. But I had to assume that there'd been some connection between him and the girl. It seemed highly unlikely that out of all the towns the traveling choir had visited so far, she'd picked him at random as a target for her accusations.

It was a conundrum.

And luckily for me, it wasn't *my* conundrum.

Unfortunately, however I tried to duck responsibility for Weasel Cleaver's activities, his disappearance *was* my conundrum.

Even if he hadn't absconded with a young foreign national (albeit from Canada) on a goodwill tour of the American Midwest, he'd surely relieved me of some portable goods.

The cafe, under the stewardship of Alanna and me, was tottering on the brink of extinction. We could ill afford another monetary setback (though if Weasel thought he was going to steal from us the amounts he'd already stolen from Aphrodite, he was in for a real surprise).

"I *told* you to keep an eye on Weasel," I *said* wearily to Alanna. "I said that he couldn't be trusted out of our sight for more than a minute."

"What I wanna know is why is this my fault all of a sudden?" Alanna was in no mood to be reprimanded. "I'm not from this dipshit town. How in the hell can I tell which locals are colorful and which ones are dangerous?"

As always when she was upset, Alanna's Okie accent magnified. She inhaled deeply, a move she usually reserved for an appreciative male audience. This time, I don't think she was doing it for visual effect, she was simply storing up enough oxygen to continue her tirade.

"Well, you could always go back to where you came from," Del said, wickedly imitating Alanna's accent. "I don't recall anyone inviting you here in the first place, and I'm not sure anyone would miss you if you packed up your bags and left."

Instead of cleaning up the mess, she'd been listening to our exchange, as well as keeping an eye on the window for the ambulance, and probably taking notes on Junior's phone conversation as well.

Alanna, who needed no goading from Del to come unglued, inhaled again (something I would not have thought possible) and opened her mouth, probably to scream at us at full volume.

But Del cut her off at the pass. "Have either of you two managed to notice that Weasel's van is gone?" she asked before Alanna could even make a peep.

Del's sudden change of direction caught us off guard.

"What?" we both asked at the same time.

"Weasel's van is gone," Del said slowly, enunciating each word clearly. "Vanished. Disappeared into the thin prairie air." Del fluttered her hands in a flyaway motion. "Weasel Cleaver has not only left the building, I'll bet he's well on his way to the state line."

Of course I couldn't take Del's word for it, I had to look for myself.

Sure enough, the battered furnace company van was no longer in the diagonal parking spot in front of the cafe. During the uproar, Weasel had somehow gotten out of the building, entered his vehicle in full view of the three picture windows, and driven off with a cargo once again including an underage girl, and surely other items of varying value that did not belong to him.

"Fuck," I said, though what I really meant was *Dammit, Aphrodite, what in the hell am I supposed to do now?*

"No kidding," Del said, grinning. It was a small consolation that our burdens had livened her day up considerably. "But I think you got more pressing problems right now than Weasel."

She pointed out the window.

9

Dangerous Liaison

There is a certain truth to the adage that the way to get over a headache is to whack your thumb with a hammer. Not that distraction is a cure exactly, but it'll sure as hell take your mind off that pounding head.

By the same token, an intramural problem involving feuding fellow employees, compounded by a possible theft triggered by the twin disasters of a broken furnace and an attempted suicide in an already floundering business establishment, might seem completely and totally engrossing to those in the middle of the brouhaha. But at least the problem was still confined to the family so to speak.

By strict Delphi definitions, Alanna might still be an outsider, but for better or worse, she was a permanent part of the cafe. And as such, she'd put the priorities of the business ahead of any other considerations.

However much Del was enjoying the predicament for the predicament's sake, she was a Delphi native, and like the bully older brother, she might push us around, but she would not stand by while someone else tried to lord it over us.

Given the content of Annelise's suicide note, and Junior's

tendency to protect and preserve her own, it went without saying that she could be counted on to present a united front.

Which was a good thing because the Outside World was about to come crashing in on us.

"Who *is* that?" I asked, watching an impeccably dressed woman tiptoe her way across the snowy street toward us.

She wore a finely tailored charcoal wool pant suit with a matching overcoat and coordinating shoes. Around her neck was a loosely tied cashmere scarf. Her perfectly sculpted chestnut hair didn't move, even in the fairly stiff breeze. It was obvious that the woman had either money or lots of credit cards. She moved with the kind of professional elegance that makes personal beauty downright irrelevant. In the bright afternoon sunlight, and from our distance, it was impossible to tell if she was an eerily mature twenty-two or a well preserved forty-nine, but I'll bet that she turned heads regardless.

Only one thing was certain: The woman was upset.

"That's Glenda Harrison," Junior said bleakly. She'd hung up the pay phone and was now standing with the rest of us, looking out the window, marking the woman's steady progress across the street. "She's the American liaison for the traveling choir. It's her responsibility to get them from place to place. She's been staying with us for the last two nights."

Something in the way Junior said that made all three of us look directly at her.

"Don't get me wrong, she's a nice enough woman," Junior lied hastily. "But she's, well, forceful. Once upon a time, she was a Miss America third runner-up and I think she vowed never to let anything she wanted get away from her again."

The woman certainly looked capable of getting all she wanted and more.

And what she wanted right now, I think, was our heads on pikes at the town gates.

"She's gunnin' for bear, that's for sure," Alanna said. With that, she beat a hasty retreat to the kitchen. "I'd best see to getting things organized in here. Y'all let me know when the ambulance arrives."

"Like you won't hear it when it does," Del said darkly, as annoyed by Alanna's desertion as she usually was by her presence.

Actually, getting Alanna safely out of the way was a help, not a hindrance. She had a tendency to go all cute and fluttery around males, especially males in uniform. She was also not above lying outright to authority figures, and she felt no compunction whatsoever in fudging the minor details if she could come out looking better.

What she usually did was make things worse, and since things were about to get worse on their own, I was glad to have her in the kitchen when Glenda Harrison, age unknown, mood definitely dark, stormed into the cafe.

"Where is she?" Glenda shouted without a preamble or an introduction, not bothering to close the door behind her. "What have you done with that poor girl?"

"We haven't done anything with her," I said, pointing toward the back of the cafe. "She's still in the booth, exactly as we found her."

"Oh my God," Glenda wailed, running to Annelise's side. "Why did you just leave her like this? Why haven't you laid her down? What in the world is the matter with you people? Can't you see that this girl is in deep trouble?"

"Of course we can see that she's in trouble," Del said sharply. "What do you think we are, a bunch of dim-witted *beauty pageant contestants*?"

Behind me, Junior snorted and then coughed politely into her hand. It was probably the first time in Delphi history that she and Del were in agreement, and certainly the only time that Junior had actually shown audible support for anything Del had said.

Even Alanna, ostensibly too busy in the kitchen to pay attention to our piddling concerns, whooped delicately.

But Glenda Harrison, former Miss America finalist, was made of stern stuff. It took more than a single blow from a small-town floozie to phase her.

"No," she said with a frozen smile, "it's obvious that you're not quite ready for the pageant world. Which does nothing to explain why this poor girl is sitting here, unattended."

"She's not unattended," I said sharply.

Now that Glenda was nearby, I could see the fine tracings of wrinkles at the corners of her eyes and along her down-turned mouth. I was instantly pleased to realize that her tragic pageant loss had been a good decade and a half earlier. I decided to be kind. After all, the poor, pitiful woman was living in her own past, and like most ex–high school jocks, deserved our pity.

"We've been right here since her condition was discovered. The paramedics told us by phone not to move her as long as she was breathing steadily."

Glenda was not mollified. If anything, she seemed to be even more incensed. Her nostrils flared, she inhaled sharply, she turned and honed in on Junior with narrowed, glittering eyes.

"And is *this* how you discharge your responsibilities? You're left with that wonderful group of kids for no more than a half-hour, given the barest of duties, and look what happened! You can't even be trusted to feed them properly." A look of distaste clouded elegant Glenda's features. "Poor Annelise probably has food poisoning from this horrible place."

"Hey," Alanna said from the kitchen.

She furiously untied her apron in preparation for hand-to-hand combat with the interloper.

"The kid didn't get food poisoning," Del said, her voice dangerously flat. She was getting angry too, and maybe ready to take Glenda on herself.

The woman certainly knew how to push buttons. Maybe that was part of the Miss America training.

"She tried to kill herself," Junior said softly but firmly. "But her attempted suicide occurred while you were off doing *something else*." Junior took a step toward Glenda, who held her ground. "Luckily, *we* saw her in time and called the emergency crew."

Junior had made that *something else* sound decidedly sinister. Almost like an accusation. Del and I looked at each other in surprise.

Annelise had accused Clay of molesting her. In fact,

she'd given that as sufficient reason for shuffling off this mortal coil.

Did Junior want to divert attention from the explosive charges contained in the suicide note by implying that Glenda had neglected her duties while one of her charges overdosed?

It made sense. I couldn't imagine Junior wanting the accusations against her husband released to the public, and she'd do anything necessary to keep that from happening.

But Del was more than willing to sacrifice Clay for the cafe. She turned to me and said with a theatrical flourish, "Show her, Tory."

"Show her what?" I asked, wary.

"Show Glenda that Annelise didn't succumb to *food poisoning,*" Del said fiercely.

"How can I do that?" I asked. What did she want me to do? Call the County Health office and have the premises tested for E. coli and salmonella?

Del sighed mightily. "Show her the note," she said slowly and mimed writing on her own hand. "The suicide note."

I hated to hand Glenda such explosive ammunition, but the contents of that note would be public knowledge very soon anyway. There was really no point in keeping it a secret. Certainly the paramedics would want to take it with them when they transported Annelise to the hospital.

"Okay, go ahead and show her," I said to Junior, steeling myself for Glenda's reaction.

"Me?" Junior asked, surprised. "What makes you think I have the note? I thought you had it."

10

Taking Note

This kind of stuff doesn't happen in books, you know.

Agatha Christie never once let Hercule Poirot get caught flat footed.

Ed McBain would not allow Steve Carella to lose valuable evidence.

Even Jessica Fletcher would not have let so vital a piece of paper as a suicide note out of her sight, knowing instinctively that it would be important in the third act right before the last spate of commercials.

Of course, it helped enormously that Herc, Steve, and Jess were fictional characters, not exactly creatures of free will, doing their own bidding, making or breaking it on their own, like me.

But it still seems that I would by now know enough to realize that nothing in Delphi is what it appears to be.

And that everything that happens here has a larger meaning.

And a larger circle of consequences than we ever expected.

And finally, that no matter what, I was going to get the blame.

They say that God is in the details.

Well, around here the Devil is in the details, and most of the time he has the upper hand.

"What do you mean, you don't have the note?" I asked Junior, not really wanting to hear her answer because I had a sinking feeling that I knew what it was going to be.

"Why would I have the note?" she answered archly. "It wasn't up to me to keep track of it. This is *your* cafe."

The old annoying Junior was suddenly back in full force, reappearing as quickly and mysteriously as she'd disappeared earlier.

Personally, I would have waited until the paramedics arrived before mentioning the note at all. And then to spare her feelings and Clay's reputation, I probably would have slipped it to the emergency crew without fanfare.

I'd have done my best, Lord knows why, to protect her, or at least to delay the public dissemination of the note's contents. But now that the cat was out of the bag, she was being snotty about it.

"Well I sure as hell don't have it," I said, biting back a few expletives.

We weren't alone after all. We were being observed by an outsider, and a hostile one at that.

"What note?" Glenda asked suspiciously. She eyed each of us in turn, silently demanding an answer.

Junior stood her ground silently, crossed her arms over her huge belly, and arched an eyebrow at me.

I glanced at Del, hoping for some backup, but she just smirked.

Though Alanna had been leaning over the stainless-steel countertop that divided the cafe from the kitchen, listening to our every word, she now busied herself doing nonexistent chores in the kitchen and avoided eye contact completely. She wouldn't have been able to help anyway. I was pretty sure that she hadn't known that there even was a suicide note, much less that it had vanished.

I mentally deleted a few more expletives and inhaled. "The girl was writing a note when she lost consciousness. It was on the table under her arm when Del and Junior discovered her condition." I figured there was no sense in absorbing all of the blame. Next time maybe they wouldn't be so damn observant. "They left it on the table beside her and that's where it was the last time I saw it."

I double-checked my own story by striding to the table in question. It still held some of the jumble from the post-discovery chaos, but nowhere on it was a handwritten note.

"It must be on the floor," I said to the air. That was a logical conclusion, after all. The door had been opened and closed several times in the interim, the cold winter wind had swirled into the cafe each time. Any one of those gusts would have been enough to sweep a single sheet of paper off a table and hide it across the room, under something else.

The cafe door was still open, as a matter of fact, and the wind still blew through the room, cutting right to the bone. The already chilly interior air was cooling rapidly. If we didn't get the furnace working soon, the place would be dripping with icicles.

"Well, you'd better find it quick, the ambulance is coming," Del said from the open doorway where she stood, arms wrapped around herself for warmth, watching the flashing lights in the distance. "They'll want to take it with them for sure."

"Exactly what did this *alleged* note say?" Glenda asked.

The relief in knowing that the ambulance would arrive soon to take this mess off my hands disappeared in the instant it took to understand what Glenda had actually said.

What she'd accused us of doing.

"Alleged," Junior snarled. "What is that supposed to mean?"

"Exactly what you think it means," Glenda snarled right back. "I don't think there ever was a note. None of the others mentioned a note at all. If Annelise had actually written something, don't you think they would have noticed it?"

"It was there," Del said, still standing in the doorway. The ambulance was very close now, the wail of the siren echoed through the cafe. "I read it. Junior read it. Tory read it. We *all* read it." She ignored Alanna in the kitchen, but since Alanna had been the only one not to read the note, it didn't really matter.

"It exists," I said defiantly. "We all saw it."

"Oh, I see where you're going now," Glenda said, a slightly panicked understanding dawning on her finely sculpted features. "You're implying that this mythical note accuses *me* of something terrible, aren't you?" Her voice rose in agitation.

I could sense Glenda's panic, the fear that her glamorous Almost Miss America Career would disappear in a flash if the blame for Annelise's suicide (please, let it be an attempt only) fell on her.

She could kiss good-bye all those paid vacations touring the hot spots of the American Midwest as she shepherded motley crews of foreign teenagers hither and yon. She could forget being spotlighted on a zillion local evening news broadcasts. Her excuse to wear better clothes than anyone else in the room would vanish in an instant if Annelise were to die while in her care. There had to be hundreds of desperate Miss America runners-up chomping at the bit for such a high-profile job.

"You want to point the finger in my direction," she continued, eyes narrowed dangerously.

"We're not pointing anything," Junior said quietly. "But we did see a suicide note. And I doubt you'd want it to be flashed around either."

I shot a confused look at Del, who had moved out of the doorway to give access to the emergency crew. Junior was technically speaking the truth. It would do the choir no good to have the accusations be made public, but they'd be hurt far less than Junior herself by what it contained.

Del shot an equally confused look back my way and shrugged.

There was only one way that Junior would dare to imply that Glenda had been mentioned in the note. Only one circumstance in which she could make the statements she'd made without fear that the note would be discovered under another table, or behind the counter.

Only one way she would feel safe enough to torment Glenda.

Del and I looked at each other at the same instant, bathed in the light of simultaneous revelation.

11

Ursa Major

It's common knowledge in nature, not to mention artfully staged nature programming, that the mothers of all species are fierce when crossed. I have no doubt that Marty Stauffer and Marlin Perkins's staff knew firsthand that while Ben himself may have been gentle, Ben's mother was a real handful when riled.

I'll bet that even parameciums scuttle for cover when Mama Amoeba is on the warpath.

How much more awesome then, in the true sense of the word, is a carbon-based biped when the safety of her family is on the line?

I think we were about to find out just how far the Uber Mother would go in order to protect her nearest and dearest.

Though Del and I don't claim anything like a psychic link, our many years of sharing living quarters, not to mention jobs and the fact that my dead husband was her first cousin, have made it possible for us to understand each other without the bother of speaking out loud.

Sometimes, when I am trying to keep my private life private, for example, this is not an especially good thing. But right now, with the cafe suddenly hectic as paramedics calmly but quickly lifted the still unconscious Annelise from the booth to a gurney that had been positioned next to her booth, I was pleased that Del and I had come to an unspoken understanding.

We'd both realized in the same instant that Junior herself must have taken Annelise's suicide note. There was no other explanation for her having drawn attention to a document so damning unless she knew it would not come to light. She'd skillfully turned Glenda's own insecurities against her, hoping that would provide camouflage for her own actions.

On the surface, it wasn't such a surprising move. After all, Junior's own husband had been accused of the unspeakable. It didn't take a rocket scientist to know that the permanent repercussions from such a charge would end life as she knew it. Even a minister as liked and respected as Clay Deibert would not be able to shrug off the smear of child abuse, and innocent or not (and I would bet the cafe on the former), the muck would stick.

But even so, both Del and I were shocked.

Maybe you had to know Junior the way we do to understand the depth of the deception she was currently engaged in. My first cousin, younger than me by a few years, has spent her entire life being good. Not only has she been *good,* she's made it her life's work to see to it that everyone else lives up to her standards. She runs her children with an iron fist, and tries to do the same with her husband, and largely succeeds in imposing her will on all of Delphi.

But the thing about Junior is that, as annoying as she usually was, as forceful and humorless and relentless as her general nature, she wasn't a hypocrite. She tried to live the life she expected others to achieve.

She took on more responsibility than anyone I knew.

She volunteered for every committee in town.

You could eat out of her toilets if you had a mind to.

I didn't like her; she made that impossible. But I trusted her.

Del actively hated Junior.

But I'd bet that she trusted her too.

The fact that Junior would not only lie and steal, but that

she implicitly expected us to back her up in those deceptions, was nothing short of astonishing.

Mama Bear ain't got nothin' on Mrs. Bear.

And there was no mistaking the formidably pregnant Junior for anything stuffed and cuddly.

"Ma'am," one of the paramedics said to Junior as his two companions examined Annelise efficiently. The pair took her blood pressure, flashed lights into her pupils, listened to her heart, all the while talking back and forth to each other.

The young man who'd addressed Junior stood with a clipboard in hand, pencil poised. "Are you responsible for this young girl? We're going to need some information on her and what she took if you can help us."

Junior opened her mouth to reply, but Glenda shouldered her aside before she could speak.

"*I'm* in charge of Annelise, as well as fifteen other European teenagers who are visiting the United States on a goodwill choir tour," she said forcefully, glaring at each of us in turn, daring us to contradict her. "I can answer anything you might want to know about the girl herself."

You had to admire Junior's skill as a master manipulator.

Without uttering a word of direct accusation, she'd managed to put Glenda Harrison on the defensive. So defensive in fact, and so afraid of what we might say that could implicate her, that she wasn't going to allow us a word in edgewise.

"We've only been in this town for two days. I've been traveling with this girl for the past month and a half and I know her well. These people don't know her at all," Glenda said, indicating the rest of us. "Whatever you need to know, you can ask me."

"Okay," the paramedic said genially. "I'll ask you then. When was the girl's present condition discovered?"

In the kitchen, Alanna, whose duties weren't so onerous that she couldn't keep track of what was going on in the cafe proper, laughed out loud.

Del and I managed to keep straight faces. After all, this

was a serious situation, despite the fact that the young paramedic had asked one of the few questions that Glenda could not answer.

"We found her at about twelve-thirty," Del said quietly. "She'd been sitting in that booth by herself for at least a half-hour, writing a letter." She shot a look at Glenda, but Glenda didn't interrupt. "We assumed she'd just put her head down on her arms to sleep for a bit. It was noisy and busy in here, but I expect that people who've been on the road a long time get used to napping whenever and wherever they can."

Del was being uncharacteristically gentle. She could have blown the lid on the suicide note right then and there, but she was holding back for reasons I could not understand.

I decided to wait and see what her plan was before spilling the beans myself. The note had held no actual information about the suicide attempt, after all. It had not listed what drugs she'd taken or the amount, or even given a real reason for the attempt besides a vague accusation that Clay had molested her.

When Annelise woke up, she could reiterate her accusations, if she wanted to. People in authority, not to mention the media, would sit up and take notice then. Nothing would be gained by an early release of that information.

And if she didn't wake up at all, well there was time enough to think about that scenario later.

"Do any of you have any idea what she took?" the young paramedic asked us. The other paramedics were nearly done with their preliminary examination. They exchanged despairing looks that made my heart sink. "Do you have any idea which drugs she used, how much, or when she took them?"

I had not only not seen her take anything, I hadn't noticed her at all until Eldon McKee had pointed her out.

"She kept to herself mostly," Glenda said finally. "She didn't have any particular friends on the tour. The one she was closest to was a Canadian girl named Meg. If anyone would have a clue as to what drugs she might have had access to, it would be Meg. I know that she wasn't taking any prescriptions because those have to come through me, and I monitor their administration personally."

Glenda, who'd seen the looks the paramedics had exchanged too, lost a little of her belligerence. The severity of the situation seemed to dawn on her, the realization that more than her job and reputation was at stake finally clear.

She turned to us, "Call Meg out here and ask. She'll know."

12

Blame Canada

As a rule, the Great White North slumbers peacefully within her own borders, offending no one, polluting no rivers, adding no acid to southern air, accepting stoically the near global notion that North America consists only of the United States. She sends us the cream of her entertainers, accepting draft dodgers and dissatisfied film crews in return, a trade so lopsided that arctic cold fonts seem a mild response.

When we think about Canada at all, and I'm embarrassed to say that it isn't often, it's with a sort of patronizing goodwill one reserves for a somewhat less-than-bright nephew who's finally found a job that will keep him occupied and out from underfoot.

If Canada had done nothing but send down a few brands of really good beer, she'd have earned her keep, and our respect, admirably.

But once in a while, Canada does something so thoughtless, whose consequences are so fraught with the possibility of evil, that all the Molsons in the world can't make up for it.

And when that happens, like the rude and crude citizens of South Park, Colorado, I am fully prepared to declare war on the entire nation single-handedly.

"Meg?" I asked carefully, keeping my face neutral. "I don't know who you're talking about. There's no *Meg from Canada* here." Aware of my tendency to babble under pressure, I clamped my mouth shut. I was careful to meet no one's eye, I concentrated instead on Annelise, who could not see my hypocrisy.

Not two minutes after registering my disappointment in Junior's perfidy, I was committing some of my own. Though in my favor, I never set myself up as a role model for the rest of Delphi.

Still, I knew very well who Meg was.

And I knew that she wasn't currently on the premises.

And I had a fairly good idea who she was with, if not exactly where, though I doubted they were headed toward the Canadian border.

I wasn't even sure why I was playing stupid. The cafe, after all, could not be held responsible for Weasel's actions, and Meg had looked to be at least eighteen years old and therefore responsible for making her own bad decisions.

It's just that the day, which had started out badly, was deteriorating quickly. I was cold, I was tired, I was sad for the unconscious girl and for the trouble that surely lay ahead for Junior. I simply did not have the energy to face another Miss America Runner-up tantrum, especially in front of the emergency crew, who would gleefully reenact the scene from here to Redfield.

"Well Meg was here earlier," Glenda said sharply. "She certainly came across with the rest of the choir group." She shot a questioning glance at Junior, who nodded an assent. "Dark hair, pretty. You must have noticed her."

"Amazing as it may seem to you," Del said, dropping an almost imperceptible wink at me, "we don't memorize the faces of our customers. We had a cafe full of noisy, not particularly well-behaved kids who couldn't speak the language. It was all we could do just to take their orders and feed them without counting heads."

"Yeah," Alanna said from the kitchen.

"I lost track of her myself," Junior said, telling the absolute truth. "She was certainly here earlier. But I haven't seen her seen since the cafe cleared out after we discovered Annelise. I am pretty sure none of the rest have seen her either. Right?"

We all nodded. I had never truly appreciated Junior's amazing talent for twisting the truth before.

Of course, she'd never used it on my behalf, so we'd never been on the same side.

"She had to have gone back with the others," I said. "When they did. Across the street. To the church."

I was babbling again.

"Maybe she was in the bathroom when you took count," Del said, interrupting me, thank goodness.

"You know how kids are," Junior said. "They spend hours giggling in the bathroom."

"Yeah," Alanna echoed from the kitchen.

Glenda narrowed her eyes at us. She knew something was up, but we were able to meet her gaze full on because we were mostly telling the truth.

Maybe Meg *was* back at the church, sneaking a smoke in the girls' can.

And maybe pigs can fly.

"Ma'am," the young paramedic said, making me feel old in a single syllable, "we're going to have to transport now."

He turned to Glenda. "Since you seem to be in charge, and she is a foreign national, we'll have to ask you to come along with us. You'll need to sign for her at the hospital. And you can tell the doctors who to contact in her home country."

Glenda moved aside so the other paramedics could wheel the gurney past her. She watched them silently as they rolled her through the door and out into the bitter cold. A few locals had gathered, shivering in a loose circle around the ambulance, watching the proceedings carefully.

"Can you see to the others while I'm gone?" she asked Junior. There was real concern in her voice, and a measurable sadness. "Reverend Deibert has my cell phone number. If any of them has any information, please let me know right away. Try to keep them calm. Get them to their guest homes and keep them quiet for the night. I expect we'll need to cancel the performance, but we can wait a bit before making a formal announcement."

"Ma'am," the young man said from the doorway. "We really do need to get going now."

"Yes, yes," Glenda said distractedly, gathering her coat around her, searching for her purse, wrapping the soft cashmere scarf back around her neck. "I'd appreciate it if you'd call me when you locate Meg. I'll feel better when all the heads are counted properly."

"I'll give her a good talking-to," Junior said, with a straight face.

"Okay. Thank you." Glenda hurried to the door, paused, and turned. "I'm sorry I snapped before. This whole thing"—she swung her arm wide—"is just so distressing that I forgot my manners for a minute. I hope you'll forgive me."

Before any of us had a chance to answer, the driver beeped the ambulance horn. Glenda scrambled out the door. The wind caught it behind her and slammed it shut.

With the siren wailing, the ambulance reversed and sped off.

The four of us stood in the cold, empty cafe and just looked at one another, unspoken questions volleying back and forth like a fast and furious game of air tennis.

Junior broke the silence first. "Oops," she said suddenly, bending over, "I think they forgot something."

She reached down on the floor behind the back booth, grabbed a shapeless cloth bag, and held it up.

"This must belong to Annelise," she said far too casually. "I wonder how it got back there."

13

Maintaining Deniability

Never apologize. Never explain.

That would be my motto if I was ever faced with thronging hordes of reporters and cameramen. Luckily, my experience with reporters has been pretty mild; a simple "no comment" did the trick for me. But if I ever was faced with real paparazzi, that's the credo I'd live by.

I learned it from watching Junior, who ruled her world, and yours too if you didn't watch out, with an iron fist and no footnotes. I've seen her in action, and her resolve is unshakable, nothing short of awe-inspiring.

She stuck to that policy when she was being good. And I had no doubt that she'd stick to it even more closely when she was being bad.

Which was why I was pretty sure that we weren't going to get any explanations from her now.

More's the pity because I really *really* wanted to know exactly how she'd spirited that note away right from under all of our noses.

And how she'd managed to hide Annelise's bag behind the booth.

And, far more importantly, why.

But I knew better than to ask.

"So where the hell *is* that note, anyway?" Del, who should have known better, demanded the minute that the ambulance carried Glenda Harrison safely out of earshot.

"Huh?" Junior asked distractedly. She wasn't looking at Del at all. In fact, I think she barely heard her question.

Or maybe she heard the question and was just practicing selective deafness.

That was another of her mottoes: *Hear no evil.*

"Don't play coy," Del ordered. She'd cooperated for the outsiders, but now that we were alone again she'd reverted to true form. "What did you do with that note?"

I decided not to get into the middle. Del had a better chance of getting an answer out of Junior than I did, which wasn't saying much. Playing the percentages was our only option at the moment.

"What do you mean, *what did I do with the note*?" Junior asked, giving a marvelous imitation of confusion.

I'd seen this ploy before. They called it *maintaining deniability*. No matter the circumstance, no matter the evidence, or even eyewitness confirmation, never admit guilt. Even if you're caught red-handed. It was the fall-back position of politicians, philandering husbands, and unlucky felons. And, evidently, ministers' wives who'd recently ventured into Broken Ten Commandments Territory.

"The note. The note," Del said, shaking her finger at Junior. "The damn suicide note! What did you do with it?"

"Me?" Junior snorted. "Don't be ridiculous. I didn't do anything with the note. In fact, I thought Tory had taken it."

"Me?" I said, voice rising. I shook my head. "Oh no. Uh-uh."

I'd seen this ploy too. It was called misdirection. Guilty parties used it to rebound accusations onto an innocent party. My late husband Nick was especially good at this sort of obfuscation.

"I didn't do *anything* with the note, I can tell you that."

I'd have continued, but it would have done no good. Junior had played her card and, come hell or high water, she was going to stand.

I could deny that I'd taken the note, that no one in their right mind would actually believe that I had done it. I could announce that she had stashed it somewhere about her ample person until my voice was hoarse and the cows came home. But she'd simply widen her eyes, and cluck at me, while assuring everyone else in the room that I certainly was the guilty party.

So convincing was she, and so well-practiced in this art, that by the time she was done, even I would believe her. Nothing short of an on-the-spot full-body cousin search would prove me right, and I wasn't about to try a move like that. Especially since she was fully capable of having hidden the note somewhere in the cafe for future retrieval when none of us was looking, not to mention beating the hell out of me before I gave up such a silly notion.

I sighed and surrendered without a fight.

Junior didn't even acknowledge her victory. She was too busy contemplating Annelise's bag. With a handle looped around one hand, she judged its heft, raising and lowering it experimentally. She twisted her wrist and set the bag into a slow, swinging rotation.

Del and I exchanged glances. She shrugged. I snuck a peek back at Alanna, who watched from the kitchen, fascinated.

Without taking her eyes off the slowly twisting bag, Junior said, "What do you say girls? Shall we see what's inside this thing?"

"Yes," Del and Alanna both said quickly.

"No," I said at the same time. "You can't just look inside there. It's not right." I thought about the unconscious girl on the gurney and this invasion of her privacy. "We should just call the paramedics and turn the bag in. They're the officials, let them do the searching." I was amazed to find myself doing an eerie imitation of Junior during all those childhood escapades where she'd played the Tattle-tale Goody-Goody and I was the Bold Explorer.

It suddenly felt as though my entire world had turned upside down.

"Come on, Tory," Junior said slowly, with a smile that was entirely evil. "Where's your sense of adventure? Besides, they said specifically that we should try to discover what she'd taken. This seems like a perfect opportunity to investigate."

"Do it," Alanna said from the kitchen.

"Do it," Del chorused softly from beside me.

"Don't do it," I said. I don't know why I was so worried about snooping through an unconscious girl's bag, but it just seemed wrong.

More wrong than lying about the suicide note.

More wrong than pretending we had no idea where the mysterious Canadian Meg was.

Wrong for no reason that I could name specifically, though watching Junior grin evilly at the bag, knowing that the girl's health was not her prime consideration, made me profoundly uncomfortable.

"Do it," Del said again.

And before I could protest or intervene, Junior upended the bag and dumped all its contents out on the table at the booth where Annelise had been just a few minutes earlier.

"You guys, we really shouldn't do this," I said, with an eye on the door. Though we'd intended to close the cafe for the rest of the afternoon, we hadn't locked up and the *Open* sign was still in the window.

"Jesus, Tory, will you get a backbone?" Del asked harshly. "This stuff could be very important. We could be saving that girl's life."

"Yeah," Junior said, not looking up.

It was safe to say that I'd just witnessed the end of my world as I knew it—Del and Junior had both used sarcasm on me at the same time for the same reason.

I hoped to enlist Alanna in my cause before we got caught by returning customers, but she'd already left the kitchen and pushed her way past me to look over Junior and Del's shoulders.

"Ah, this might explain something," Junior said, a hint of triumph in her voice. "You ought to come over here, Tory."

And of course, I chucked my principles and trotted right over.

Scattered on the table was the usual assortment of teenage

portables, the kind of things every girl in the world carried in her purse: lipstick, Chapstick, safety pins, a wallet, loose change, a few toothpicks, a comb, some colorful hair bands, a small mirror, a half-empty pack of gum, a couple of hard candies, bits and pieces of paper covered with girlish scribbles, a plastic aspirin bottle, a pair of sunglasses, and a fair accumulation of lint.

But there were also items not found in every teenage girl's purse: a Midwestern United States guidebook; a small and well-thumbed paperback of English/Swedish phrases; a stamped, sealed, and addressed letter to Switzerland; and three perfectly rolled marijuana joints.

14

Reefer Madness

I'm from the sixties, or at least I was a teenager during the latter portion of that turbulent decade, so there isn't much in the way of youthful excess that I didn't encounter, either in my own heyday or during the ensuing years.

I am, against every effort to disprove the notion, famous for being an all-knowing, worldly wise, Earth Mother type, and therefore it takes a whole lot to surprise me these days. I mean, I lived long enough to witness the revival of disco, for crying out loud.

I haven't seen it all, but I've seen enough to keep me from being blindsided by most of humankind's sillier mistakes.

But even I was surprised to find marijuana among Annelise's possessions. Cynical and worldly-wise I may be, I still couldn't picture the European Traveling Lutheran Youth Choir relaxing after a tough gig by passing doobies around.

"This stuff standard equipment for young Lutherans these days?" Del asked. Del was a lapsed Catholic, but that didn't keep her from finding Protestant failings amusing.

"And so nicely rolled," Alanna said with admiration in her voice. "Someone knew what they were doing with these."

She reached over Del's shoulder, intending to grab the joints, but Junior slapped her hand.

"Don't touch," Junior said sharply. "They may be evidence."

Del snorted. "What do you think happened? That the girl smoked up right here in the cafe? We're not *that* unobservant."

Annelise could very well have popped enough pills to render her unconscious while we'd scurried around trying to translate the choir's orders into some semblance of English, but the sweet, acrid scent of pot on the air would have caught our attention.

"She wasn't smoking, Junior," I said. "And neither was anyone else. Well, there were kids who smoked, even you saw that." Junior had tried in vain to get several of the choir members to put out their cigarettes. "But no one was smoking anything illegal. I can swear to that."

"Of course they weren't smoking up in front of anyone," Junior said, her old sharpness returning. "I was here too, remember? But the fact that she had *these* in her possession means something. We'd better let the police sort it out."

"You're not going to turn her in, are you?" I asked. I was flabbergasted. "You'll get her in a whole lot of trouble."

"Not just her," Del said, "but the rest of the kids too. And the Miss America Bitch too. They'll probably deport them all."

There was a certain satisfaction in Del's voice that was echoed in Junior's complacent expression. Del was always delighted when trouble visited attractive women. I was afraid that Junior's subtle pleasure had a deeper, darker meaning. A deported Annelise would not be able to press charges against Clay.

Deport all of the kids, especially under the shadow of illegal drug use, and the chance of the accusations ever being resurrected was suddenly eliminated.

If I didn't know her better, I would have suspected Junior of planting the marijuana on Annelise for just that purpose.

But I did know her better. A sudden proficiency for lies and theft notwithstanding, Junior had no more personal knowledge of marijuana dealers than I did, and I was pretty sure that she didn't keep a stash of her own at the parsonage. No matter how much she might want to sweep this incident under the rug (or how much she might bend the rules to make sure that happened), she would not frame an innocent girl.

"Whatever else they do, they can't deport the Miss America Bitch," I said, looking over the rest of Annelise's possessions. "She's an American citizen."

"Well, they can lock her up at least," Junior said firmly. "She's the one who's in charge of these kids. She's ultimately responsible for their behavior while on foreign soil. It was her lapse that allowed this happen in the first place."

The bitterness in Junior's voice was palpable. She knew more about Glenda than she was telling.

"You're not going to turn the kid in for drug possession, and you know it," I said firmly. As law and order as Junior was, she wasn't the Zero Tolerance, Throw Away the Key type. She firmly believed in rehabilitation according to the Principles of Junior Deibert. And she was more than willing to oversee the instruction personally.

"The kid has enough going against her as it is," I said sadly. "I mean, happy, healthy, well-adjusted traveling European Lutheran choir members don't attempt suicide in ratty American cafes in the first place. The minimum they're going to do is send her home, and who knows what'll happen to her there."

"And that's if she lives," Del said bluntly. "She could die you know."

Alanna reached for the joints again. "In which case, we'll be doing her a favor by getting rid of these, right?"

We all turned and looked at her.

"I was just going to keep them in a safe place," Alanna said weakly.

"*I'll* keep them in a safe place," Junior said firmly. "And when the time comes, we can decide if turning them over to the police is necessary."

I was sort of amazed that Junior was allowing for a committee decision.

"Why would it *ever* be necessary?" Alanna asked, pouting.

"Because," Junior said, her voice dripping with sarcasm.

"Annelise got these somewhere. Maybe that somewhere was Delphi. Do we want this sort of thing going on in our town?"

Alanna bit her lip. I think she wasn't sure of the correct answer.

"I'm more interested in this," I said, reaching past Junior, daring her to slap my hand too.

I picked up the white plastic aspirin bottle and shook it.

It was empty.

"You suppose that was what she took?" Del asked.

"Could be," I said, shrugging. "Aspirin overdoses can kill."

"That isn't a plain aspirin bottle," Junior said, taking it from me and inspecting it closely. The bottle's label had the numbers 222 printed boldly on it. "This is, or at least it was, aspirin with codeine."

"Codeine?" I asked. "How can you tell?"

Junior shrugged. "I've seen this stuff. They sell it over the counter in Canada. It's legal to buy it there without a prescription."

"But it's not legal to have it here, is it?" I asked. "At least not without a doctor's okay?"

"Nope," Junior said. "I know people who drive up through North Dakota and cross the border just to buy it though."

I thought about that for a minute. The obvious connection between the missing Meg and the Canadian codeine had occurred to me instantly. But as Junior had pointed out, you didn't have to be Canadian to buy or possess the stuff.

"Did the choir spend time in Canada on this trip?" I asked.

"Not that I know of," Junior said, "but I can find out. Clay has their itinerary."

Maybe Annelise had bought her own pain killers. Maybe aspirin with codeine was legal in Switzerland. Maybe she had a prescription for the pills. Glenda had mentioned that she monitored the choir members' medications.

But I doubted that she had a prescription for the marijuana, which was still lying on the table, in plain sight.

"Hey, you open or what?" Eldon McKee said loudly right behind me, startling the living shit out of all of us.

We'd been so intent on our discussion, so distracted by the very presence of the pot, that we hadn't heard him open the door, much less sneak up behind us.

Instantly, Junior scooped the bag's contents back from whence they came, making sure that the marijuana went in first. Notes, aspirin bottle, and the rest disappeared into the ratty green and yellow cloth bag before Eldon could peek over our shoulders to see what we were doing.

Dell, Alanna, and I turned in unison and faced Eldon, doing our best to look relaxed and cheerful and ready for business. We tried not to look like we'd been contemplating illegal drugs, which I suddenly realized were now in our possession, and any charges made concerning them would likely fall directly on us.

The three of us closed ranks, with Junior standing behind us, still facing the booth.

"Whatchu doin' ladies?" Eldon asked, peering at us closely. "You look like you got caught passin' notes in the classroom."

"We were discussing the tragic occurrence this morning," Junior said, primly stepping around us. She had Annelise's bag tucked firmly but casually under her arm. "We have been doing our level best to work out what happened to that poor girl in order to assist in her recovery."

Junior herself had recovered remarkably fast. Her face was composed, her voice was even, and her shoulders were thrown back. It would take someone far braver, not to mention brighter, than Eldon McKee to ruffle her self-confidence.

And it would probably take someone who knew her as well as I did to recognize the hint of panic in her eyes.

"Yes indeed." I took Eldon's arm and led him away from Junior. Over my shoulder I said to her, "Isn't it time for you to go back and check on the other choir members and pass our conclusions to the paramedics?"

"Don't forget to keep the *valuables* in a safe place," Del said sweetly.

I could have smacked her.

"I still think some of those valuables would be safer here at the cafe," Alanna said firmly.

Del did smack her.

Alanna rubbed her shoulder and then muttered a few nearly intelligible expletives on her way back into the kitchen.

"I'll see you all later," Junior said lightly from the door. "I'll keep in touch."

"You do that now, ya hear," Del said, equally lightly.

Eldon may have been old and recovering from a stroke, but he'd lost none of his observational powers or his ability to recognize bullshit when he stepped in it. He frowned at all of us.

"Let's get you seated," I chirped. "How would you like a nice big piece of pie a la mode on the house? That'll help make up for the disruption this morning."

Eldon never saw a freebie that he didn't like. His face brightened considerably as he sat in his usual booth by the window.

"Can you get me some of that caramel syrup for the ice cream too?" he asked. "You know the stuff I like so much?"

He was committing a minor species of extortion. He knew very well that something was up and he knew that we were trying to distract him. He also knew that we'd never tell him what it was, so he upped the stakes.

"And a big cup of coffee?" he wheedled.

"Coffee, pie, and ice cream, it is," Del said cheerily from behind the counter. She flexed her chest for Eldon's benefit before opening up the pie cooler and selecting the biggest piece of apple pie that we had left. "Tory, I think we're out of that syrup that Eldon likes. Would you mind going to the storeroom for another can?"

"It would be my pleasure," I said grimly, glad for an excuse to get away before I collapsed from an overdose of perkiness.

I marched through the kitchen, sending an exasperated look at Alanna on the way just out of general principle. I walked down the short hallway, pushed into the pitch-black storeroom, and reached blindly at the wall for the light switch, muttering crabbily about marijuana, caramel syrup, old men, and not remembering to lock the door.

Before I could turn the light on a hand reached suddenly out of the darkness and clamped itself roughly to my mouth.

15

The Quicker Picker Upper

Though the County Extension Office sponsors them occasionally, I've never taken one of those self-defense classes that purports to teach women how to disarm burly male attackers with just a flick of an elbow or a carefully aimed jab with a set of car keys.

Infomercials, magazine articles, and flyers make it look oh-so-easy to break a stranglehold, whirl around, poke the creep in the eyeballs, and send a swift kick to his nether regions while at the same time screaming your head off to attract attention and rescue.

Staged reenactments make it seem not only possible, but inevitable that a woman could, should, and would emerge triumphant—safe and sound, ready to take on a whole group of slimeballs if necessary.

She is woman, hear her roar.

Of course the little voice in the back of my head, the one that reminds me *after* I've bought the shirt that there is no such thing as One Size Fits All, always says that if it was that easy for women to deflect men bent on doing them harm, there would be a lot more bad guys writhing on the tarmac in the parking lots of America.

That said, I have always thought that a little common sense could, if you were swift and lucky, give you the upper hand if you found yourself in a *situation.* Unfortunately, I never quite formulated a workable definition of common sense under pressure. I'm pretty sure that *grace* doesn't enter into it.

Time to formulate a plan doesn't come into it either.

In fact I didn't have time to think at all.

I just reacted instinctively when the sweaty hand clamped suddenly over my mouth in the darkness.

The hand removed itself immediately.

"Oh, ow! Jesus! Goddamn!" wailed an aggrieved, whiny voice that I recognized instantly. "Son of a bitch! Tory what the hell did you bite me for?"

I reached out blindly and flipped the switch, and then turned to face my attacker, hands at the ready, more than willing to poke his damn eyes out if he looked like he was even considering lunging at me again.

But what I saw drove all thoughts of self-defense from my head.

What I saw drove coherent thought from my head completely, leaving only the urge to flip the light switch back off.

"Oh my God, Weasel," I said, clamping my eyes shut, trying to erase what had just been imprinted on my retinas. "What the fuck are you doing in here? And where the hell are your clothes?" I spun around on one heel, facing away from him so I could open my eyes again. "And why did you grab me like that? You scared the shit out of me!"

The sudden adrenaline rush that had left my heart pounding had also left me thoroughly pissed. Now that I knew who my assailant was, I was no longer afraid. Weasel Cleaver was a liar, a felon, and a miscreant, with a penchant for coveting other people's portable goods and pathological inability to say no to any breathing female who agreed to dally with him.

He had no history of violence.

But even if his recent stint as a guest of the state of South Dakota had taught him the finer points of literal back-stabbing, I was willing to take that chance rather than risk another peek in his direction.

"You're going to pay for those paper towels, you know," I said, "and any other damage you've done in here."

"And I'm going to sue you for assault," he said, not in the least embarrassed to have been found in my storage room, naked except for what looked to be an entire roll of paper towels wrapped round and round his middle, up and over his shoulder, and then tucked back in, toga style. "You had no call to bite me like that."

"Oh for chrissakes, Weasel, I walk into a dark room and a hand pops out of nowhere and tries to smother me. What did you expect me to do?"

"I figured you'd scream, that's why I tried to calm you down first," he said, still whining. "I didn't expect you to hurt me."

Poor Weasel, always the victim.

"Well, you got a weird way of calming someone down. Why didn't you just say something, or better yet turn on the light so I'd know you were there?"

"Yeah right, Tory. I turn on the light and you find me standing here like this and you just go about your business like nothing is happening? You'd have screamed your fool head off and brought the whole damn cafe there back to see what the ruckus was."

"The *whole damn cafe* consists of about three people right now," I said, not factoring in the unexpected store-room population explosion. "It wouldn't have been much of a ruckus."

"Wouldn't have to be a big ruckus," he said mournfully. "You live in this piss-ant town. You know it'd take just one of them shit kickers to see me like this and the story'd be spread from here to Minneapolis."

"What makes you think that I won't spread the story?" I asked wickedly, mentally taking inventory of the depleted shelves in front of me since there was no place else I could safely look. "Finding you here dressed, or shall we say undressed, like this, would be worth its weight in free beer at the bar for a very long time."

"You won't tell anyone about this, Tory," he said, with a superior air, "because it's in your best interest not to."

I turned around, furious. Eyeballs be damned.

And was instantly sorry.

God, he had a lot of hair. Everywhere.

"What do you mean, *it's in my best interest*?" I demanded, squinting a little, doing my best not to notice how inadequate paper toweling was for covering intimate body parts.

Weasel indicated himself, with a crafty grin. "You think it would do your thriving restaurant business any good for *people* to know that I'd spent time in your storeroom? Like this? What if I'd sat on the bags of rice. What if I blew snot all over the napkins? What if I'd fingered the hamburger buns?"

"We don't keep the hamburger buns in here," I said stubbornly, not about to be held hostage by Weasel Cleaver. "And besides, I'd tell them that you were back here stealing the petty cash. They wouldn't care about anything else."

"And I'd say that I peed in the flour," he countered triumphantly. "I think you'd find out how much the citizens of this fine town care about your slush fund when it comes down to having blueberry and urine waffles for Sunday brunch."

I crossed my arms and glared at him, knowing that he would do exactly what he'd threatened.

"So," I said finally, unable to think of a way to up the ante. I could feel my blood pressure rising dangerously, veins pounding painfully at my temples. I tapped my foot.

"So," he said right back at me, defiant, hairy, naked, and cold, wrapped in a roll of paper towels that didn't exactly cover the subject adequately, if you get my drift.

We were at in impasse. I could tell his parole officer that Weasel had been committing atrocities here, but he'd do an equal amount of reciprocal damage on his way back to jail.

"So get your clothes on, and then get yourself, *and her*," I said, enunciating each word carefully, "the hell out of here."

I hadn't had time to do a thorough inspection, but it was a

sure bet that Weasel had ducked into the storeroom with the obviously evil Canadian Meg for some sort of truly sick encounter on top of the paper plates.

The very thought made me shudder.

It made Weasel shudder too, though whether he shivered in delight or because he was barefoot and the storeroom was no warmer than the rest of the cafe was a moot point.

"*You* get her the hell out of here," he said petulantly. "It's your damn cafe. Besides, I heard the ambulance sirens while I was back here. I know something went on out there. I hope to hell someone killed that little bitch."

"What do you mean, *me get her out of here*?" I asked, completely bewildered. "You're the one who brought a foreign girl, probably underaged, back to *my* storeroom, endangering your parole."

"Me?" he asked, putting on a good show of amazement for a man with an established record of committing exactly such crimes. "I didn't bring no foreign girl back here."

"I hope to hell you didn't come back here and get naked in my storeroom all by yourself," I said, thinking that would be too weird, even for Weasel.

"Oh she came back here, all right," Weasel declared. "But it was her idea. *All* her idea. She gave me the eye, and then the wink, and then the come-hither walk, and while you all was lookin' over that other girl, she walked right through the kitchen pretty as you please and did the finger thing to me."

"The *finger thing*?" I asked, almost too disgusted to be curious. "In the *kitchen*?"

"Oh for Jesus Christ, Tory, *not that*," he said, annoyed at my stupidity. "I mean this." In demonstration, he waggled his index finger in the international signal to *come and get it, big boy*.

"And so of course you just followed her right into the storeroom, expecting all kinds of exotic Canadian delights," I said, still disgusted, thinking of health code violations and bodily fluids. And heavy applications of bleach.

"Well, of course I followed her right into the storeroom," he said, imitating my inflection. "I been inside for three years, you think offers like that come along every day there?"

"So you followed her into the storeroom and had kinky Canadian sex all over the freeze-dried potatoes," I said, not conceding anything to the possibility that prison seducers probably weren't quite as pretty as Meg.

"No I did not have sex all over anything," Weasel said. "We got in here and she shut the light off and said we should take off all our clothes, that it would be cheap and dirty if we were dressed."

"Like being naked would magically transform banging your eyeballs out against gallon jugs of ketchup into a classy encounter," I said sarcastically. "You didn't even question her amazing and sudden interest in you? You didn't worry about being caught? You didn't think her offer was bogus?"

"I been inside for three years," he repeated stubbornly. "I wasn't about to miss this chance. You don't know what it's like in there, Tory."

I closed my eyes and rubbed my forehead.

"Anyway," he continued. "I was already undressed and fully ready to rumble, if you get my drift and she said, '*Oh just a minute, I need to get some sheiks. I'll be right back.*' "

"*Sheiks?* What the hell are sheiks?" This whole scenario was a new one on me. I had never realized the untamed, and evidently not-too-picky depravity that slumbered just beyond the North Dakota border. "Some kind of drug?"

"I guess they're some kind of fancy Canuck rubber," Weasel said and shrugged. "She said it'd be worth my wait and she'd be right back. And I wasn't about to argue with her."

"And then she picked up your clothes and left the room with them and hasn't come back," I finished for him. Sounded like a shakedown, though I doubted that Weasel had anything a young and pretty girl would want badly enough to risk the chance of seeing him naked. Especially after a fifteen-minute acquaintance.

And of course Weasel, being Weasel, didn't doubt her sincerity or desire for a second.

Something occurred to me. "How did you know that I wasn't her when I came in just now? Would you have grabbed Meg and scared the shit out of her too?"

"No offense, Tory, but you don't exactly walk like a naked

eighteen-year-old Canadian goddess with a pocketful of condoms. I could tell it was you," he said wryly. "Besides, it'd been a good hour since she left, I been freezin' my balls off in here ever since with nothin' to wear except these stupid paper towels. I was too pissed to give her Mr. Happy even if she begged. I just want my clothes back. And I wanna get outta here and outta this town. So why don't you trot right back out there and find that girl and make her bring me my clothes and I'll be gone before you even notice."

"As much as I'd love to do just that, Weasel, I'm sorry to say that your clothes aren't out there. Neither is Meg. Both seem to be missing at the moment."

"Well, you just run your butt out to my van then," Weasel said snottily. "Way in the back is an extra set of coveralls. I can at least put them on until we find the little bitch and wring her neck."

16

Pop Goes the Weasel

I've seen and done some pretty strange things in my forty-some years. The last few months have served up an especially interesting mix of odd and unusual life experiences for me to savor and later regale to someone else's grandchildren (there being none of my own on the horizon) in my dotage.

But nothing, not living on wide open prairie, not growing up and working in the same small town for my entire life, had prepared me for the task of giving an ex-felon dressed only in hair, paper toweling, and goose bumps some very bad news indeed.

"What do you mean the van's gone?" Weasel shouted, his voice echoing in the small room.

"Shhh," I cautioned. "Do you want everyone else to hear you?"

I certainly didn't want anyone else to hear him.

"What do you mean the fucking van's gone?" he repeated in a forceful whisper. "It can't be gone. I parked it right in front of this shit hole not two hours ago."

"Well it's not there now," I said simply, waiting for him to put two and two together.

His eyes widened as realization sank in. His jaw dropped

and he stood there stunned, frozen for half a heartbeat before uttering a stream of oaths that left me gaping in admiration. If nothing else, his years as a guest of the state of South Dakota had taught him some really imaginative bad words.

He swore at the ceiling. He swore at the floor. He swore at the shelves. He consigned Canada and all her progeny to the fires of hell while jumping up and down in fury, which was not a good idea considering the ease with which his clothing could perforate.

He spun around and faced me.

"You!" he shouted. "It's all your fault!"

"Me?" I repeated, incredulous. "How the hell can this be my fault? You're the one who let some Lutheran chickie steal your clothes and car keys. You're the one who snuck into the storeroom intent on depravity."

He ignored me completely and continued raving. "You shoulda been watching them. You shoulda been watching the cars. You shoulda kept track of what was going on. You shoulda known that girl was sneaky."

"Listen you," I said, taking a step toward Weasel, locking his eyes with mine. "The only person in this whole damn cafe who needed watching was you. *You're* the felon. *You're* the one who stole from the cafe last time you were in town. *You're* the one who snuck back where you shouldn't have been and lost your clothes and vehicle. You got no one to blame but yourself and I am not about to take any shit from you. Got it?"

I was pissed.

And I was perfectly willing to continue my diatribe but at that moment the storeroom door swung open and Del stormed in.

"Tory, for chrissakes, we coulda made that caramel sauce by now. Jesus, Eldon is gonna start asking questions if we don't fill his mouth with . . . *eeeek.*"

The unexpected sight of Weasel in his swaddled glory sent Del stumbling backward. Startled, she held a hand to her heart, looking from Weasel to me and back to Weasel with an openmouthed stare, though I noticed that she kept her eyes firmly above his shoulder level.

"You gotta be kidding me," she said finally.

"I wish," I said.

"So *she* stole the van," Del said, quicker on the draw than either Weasel or I had been. "And left him back here with nothing but Brawny to keep him company."

"Little bitch," Weasel agreed bitterly.

Del had good ears and an even better memory and a capacity to hold grudges for a long time. She'd heard Weasel's comments in the cafe and she wasn't in a forgiving mood. "Well, call the police then, report the van and the girl missing, and get this creep out of our storeroom before he shits in the corner."

"No," Weasel said. "Don't. Please."

"You know, as much as it hurts me to disappoint men who wrap their wieners with paper towels," Del said, reaching for a jar of caramel sauce on the shelf just above my head, "I think calling the police is our best bet. It'd get rid of you and let us tend to our day. I don't know about anyone else, but *I* have work to do."

"Me too," I said, nodding. "We can have the Highway Patrol here in fifteen minutes and they'll take this little problem right off our hands."

The potential for peripheral Weasel-related damage paled in comparison to the relief of getting him out of the place. The cafe had recovered from dead bodies on the premises; it would surely survive a live naked one.

"There's no need to call police," Weasel said quickly. Instead of being cocky and angry, not to mention demanding and threatening, he was suddenly anxious. "We can work this out without calling them." His face took on an expression that was pitiful to behold. "Come on, we can talk this out, can't we?"

In fact if I didn't know better, I would have sworn that he was begging.

"I'm begging you," he said. "You can't call the police. I already lost three jobs and if I lose this one, they're gonna throw me back in jail."

Del just shook her head and turned to go.

"Jesus, Del, have a heart. Do you really want the incarceration of an innocent man on your conscience?"

She paused by the open door, jar of caramel sauce in hand. "You better shut up right now, Weasel, you're talking me into it."

"No, you don't understand, I didn't come here to steal anything or cause you problems," he said. "And I didn't come here to boff no jailbait either."

"You coulda fooled me," I said, curious against my will as to why he was so adamant about not calling the authorities. As little as I wanted to give him the benefit of any doubt, he was actually blameless for the theft of the furnace van. His employer couldn't hold being scammed against him.

And even if his employer could hold it against him, it wasn't against the law to be cheated.

Not that I'd expect him to go back to jail willingly, but it seemed to me that Weasel was exactly the kind of guy who would thrive in prison—he was sneaky enough to cheat the system and milk it for all it was worth, while at the same time he wasn't pretty or young or smart enough to be a target.

Weasel sat down on a pallet of pork and beans cans and put his head in his hands.

Del and I exchanged glances. There was no sympathy in hers.

I don't know what was in mine except an indication that I was willing to hear him out before turning him in.

Del sighed.

From the kitchen, Alanna hollered theatrically, her voice echoing down the short hallway with faux cheer, "Delphine, I declare, what are you and Tory doin' back there? It can't be *that* difficult to locate some ice cream sauce for Mr. McKee who is right *anxious* for his pie."

"I'd better get moving or we'll have The Tits back here too." She raised an eyebrow in my direction. "Unless you want her as a witness. Gather a few more people and we'd have a quorum, you know."

"No," Weasel and I both said simultaneously.

"I'll take care of it," I said hastily. Torturing Weasel was fun in its own twisted way, but the fewer people who knew that he'd been in the storeroom in this particular state of undress, the better it would be in the long run.

Especially if one of the people who didn't know was Alanna Luna. She had a tendency to make my life miserable as it was.

"Well, whatever you do, you probably should think about sneaking him out the back," Del said as she left. "Soon."

". . . Delphine . . ." Alanna's voice sounded closer than before. And more annoyed.

"Coming, Mom," Del chirped. With a parting glare for Weasel, and a deep and clearly decipherable look at me, one that said that this situation was my responsibility, she exited the room and closed the door firmly behind her.

"So," I said, sitting down on a crate of canned peaches, knowing that Del was right. No matter what chain of events had set this particular complication in motion, no matter who was involved, no matter what strange cosmic coincidences had put these particular players in this particular position, this mess was my responsibility.

It was always my responsibility.

I looked Weasel right in the eye because the way he was sitting left me no alternative, and sighed.

17

Mighty Aphrodite

As a culture, we've lost the ability to listen to storytellers. We live in a land where the longest we ever have to sit still is the eight minutes between commercials. Sound bites are the lead story on the evening news, and even advertisers manage to fit their hard sell into thirty seconds or less.

We've become far too impatient for a leisurely approach to the climax.

At a time when fame lasts no more than fifteen minutes, we've decided that we want it all and we want it now. So when the occasion arises where sitting and listening is required, with neither channel changer nor mute buttons by our side, what we want most is to cut to the chase.

Especially when you're pretty sure that you don't want to hear what's coming next.

"Well, you see, it's like this," Weasel said after the silence finally lengthened beyond his endurance. He leaned forward and placed his hands on his knees. He was perched on a pallet of canned goods, which could not have been comfortable no matter how many layers of quilted paper toweling were sandwiched between him and cold, ridged metal. "It's really sort of funny if you stop to think about it."

"I'll bet," I said, not meaning it.

He chuckled weakly. "Actually, it'd be better if you got Aphrodite down here for this since it mostly concerns her. The fewer times I have to repeat myself the better it'll be for all of us." He shifted his knees together so that they were touching. "And the quicker I can get outta this refrigerator and into some clothes."

A needle of pain lodged itself behind my eyes as I rubbed my forehead, wondering where to begin. I opted for the cowardly route.

"Aphrodite can't come right now," I said, and for the briefest of moments, I was sure I'd caught a faint whiff of cigarette smoke. I shook my head and it disappeared. "Take my word for it, whatever you have to say, you can say to me."

"No," he said firmly, "I need to talk to Aphrodite herself. It's a part of my program. I gotta apologize to everyone I hurt, tell 'em right to their faces that I'm sorry for what I done, even when I didn't mean to hurt 'em. And I didn't mean to hurt Aphrodite. She was always good to me."

Actually, he was right about that—at least about Aphrodite having been good to him. For some reason unknown to anyone but herself, she'd actually liked Weasel. She'd given him odd jobs over the years, and when he tried his hand at owning his own investment firm, she'd trusted him to broker some deals for her.

Which is how he happened to be able to leave town with a fair amount of her cash theoretically slated for some hot new stock.

The fact that Weasel and the money and a certain well-developed fourteen-year-old all disappeared together left the town buzzing with public sympathy and private glee.

Aphrodite herself swore that it must be a mistake, and refused to believe the worst about Weasel until it was proven in court. And even then she did what she could to keep charges from being pressed on her behalf. But the parents of the girl, not to mention several other scammed clients, banded together, and between them they managed to put Weasel away for three incredibly short years.

During which much had happened in Delphi that had evidently escaped his notice.

"I'm just not going to be able to get Aphrodite here," I said sadly, refusing to inhale through my nose. Ignoring the almost definite whiff of smoke.

"Oh but you gotta, Tory. I know she's mad at me and I wouldn't blame her if she never wanted to speak to me again. But she doesn't have to talk, she just has to listen for a minute. And afterward, if she never wants to see me again, I'll go away and stay away."

Periodically out-of-town regulars, truckers and salesmen on long routes who only come to Delphi every few months or so, stop in the cafe. They always ask for Aphrodite.

And it always falls to me to tell them what happened.

It never got easier.

"Weasel, Aphrodite can't come down and listen to your apology because she's dead."

I'd discovered with practice that short and to the point worked best. Get the awful truth out in the open, let it sink in, fill in a few details, pat a shoulder, dab a tear or two (usually my own), and then get on with life.

"Dead?" Weasel's voice rose in agitation. "No. She can't be dead. She's gotta be here. I been planning this for three whole years." He stood up and began to pace back and forth. "It's why I took the van today and snuck down to Delphi."

He stopped pacing and pointed a finger at me. "Do you know what I risked to come here today?" He addressed the ceiling, "You couldn't have let me know sooner? So I coulda taken care of this while it still woulda done some good?"

I didn't have a clue as to what he was talking about, but it seemed clear that his anxiety about not calling the police over the stolen van had more to do with not getting permission to leave a certain jurisdiction than the fact that the vehicle was now missing, along with a comely Canadian lass.

"For real?" he turned and asked me finally.

"Sorry, Weasel."

I gave him an abbreviated version of the story.

He sat back down on the pallet, and for a second I could swear that there were tears in his eyes, though the second passed quickly and the lighting in the storeroom was bad.

After all the man was nearly naked and freezing, he had any number of reasons to tear up beyond sorrow over a friend's unexpected demise.

"So who owns the cafe?" he asked quietly. "Who's running it?"

Something in his demeanor had changed. He'd always been cocky, as a child and as an adult. Even when he was on the defensive. As though his very presence was enough to make up for all the aggravation he caused.

In fact, cockiness, even in the face of judicial disapproval, was Weasel Cleaver's defining characteristic.

Now he just seemed deflated—a sad, sorry, pitiful, hairy little man bound in rapidly deteriorating paper towels.

"Me," I said, equally deflated. "And Alanna out there. We own it together. Though who knows for how long. The way things are going, we'll be closing the doors in a couple of months."

"You and The Tits, huh?" he asked, chewing his lip, contemplating something in the far distance.

I nodded and then looked down at my feet, the weight of the trust that Aphrodite had placed in me to carry on after her death felt like a stone mantle.

Weasel wasn't the only one who'd let her down.

"Well, maybe things will work out after all," he said quietly, reaching out to pat me on the shoulder.

The storeroom door swung open suddenly and Del, looking furtively back over her shoulder, stepped in carrying a paper grocery sack.

"Well, isn't this a sweet tableau," she said, surveying us as she closed the door. "Did I interrupt something?" She grinned wickedly at me and then tossed the sack to Weasel. "They won't be perfect, but they're the best I could do on such short notice."

He'd already opened the sack and dumped out a pair of worn jeans, a plaid flannel shirt, some old white underwear, and a pair of socks rolled in a ball. He squealed in delight and began dressing immediately, not waiting for us to turn our backs. "Damn, Del, I'm going to take back all those bad things I said about you."

"Don't bother," she said, facing the door. "I didn't do it for you, I did it to get you the hell outta here."

"Mighty kind of you, Del. Mighty kind," he said. He sighed in obvious relief as he zipped the pants. "They're a mite snug, but they'll do. No shoes?"

"Jesus, Weasel, do I look like a cobbler?" Del asked sharply, turning around. "Just be glad I got you that stuff. Besides, I think there's a pair of Aphrodite's old mop shoes around in here somewhere."

Del was right, I'd forgotten about the old rubber boots we wore while cleaning up our periodic toilet overflows. I dug them out from a far corner and handed them to Weasel. The boots were big enough to fit over Aphrodite's shoes, which meant that Weasel could squeeze his feet into them.

"So what do we do now, honeys?"

"Yeah, *honey*, what *are* you going to do now?" Del repeated, with a raised eyebrow. "I take it we're not calling the police."

Both of them looked at me.

It was evidently my call.

I made a split-second decision, one that I'd probably live to regret.

"Maybe later," I said. "But first we need to talk to someone."

18

Goin' to the Chapel

I suppose there are those who would dispute me on this point, but I really am not that easy.

Sure, I married the first guy who even took an interest in me. During my marriage, I did my level best to transform Nicky Bauer from a good-natured philanderer into a good-natured husband with firmly-zipped pants. And when it became clear early on that no force on earth could keep Nick from jumping into bed with any woman who'd have him, I made do by looking the other way, figuring that when we were good we were very, very good, and when he was bad I played ostrich.

When he died in a one-car rollover with a college cheerleader, I firmly squashed that small voice that said at least I wouldn't come home and find someone else's diaphragm case sitting on my bedside table again.

That doesn't make me easy.

And a couple of years later, when I sort of fell into a sort of secret affair with a firmly married feed and seed dealer, mostly because he was the first guy after Nick's death to take an interest in me (that I knew of anyway), I did my best to reconcile the afternoon delights with the fact that Stuart

McKee never once, in bed or out, mentioned a desire to get unmarried.

By the time his on-again-off-again estranged wife's pregnancy became obvious, I finally got the courage to walk away almost without looking back.

That surely proves that I am not easy.

And now that Neil Pascoe, my best friend in the whole world, a man who could always make me laugh, who has been there for me through bereavement and adultery with the patience of a saint most of the time, and whose warm brown eyes have been haunting my dreams of late (oh and let us not forget the twelve million dollars he won in the Iowa State Lottery some years back) seems to have made a romantic move in my direction, I still moved slowly, afraid to look directly at my first chance for real happiness. Afraid it'd vanish before I even get to know what it looks like.

Easy? Hah!

So why was I giving Weasel Cleaver, a guy who made my skin crawl, a felon with a habit for prevarication and pilfering, an all-purpose creep who should have been thrown to the wolves at birth, another chance? Why hadn't I called the police instantly and cheered as his sorry ass was hauled back to jail?

Because I thought I'd seen a glint of a tear in his eye when he learned of Aphrodite's death. And that glint seemed to prove, outside appearances notwithstanding, that there was an actual human being under all that hair.

I figured that an actual human being deserved a second opinion before being turned in.

Maybe I am easy.

"Tell me again why we're going to church," Weasel groused as we slogged over the deeply rutted snow pack after having snuck out the cafe back door without being spotted by Alanna or the few patrons inside. Del had somehow found clothes that mostly fit him, but she hadn't come up with a coat or gloves. He shivered and tucked his uncovered hands into his armpits as we worked our way across the street. "God ain't going to get me my van back. And the last person I want to see is that uptight bitch Junior Deibert. And it's too fucking cold for a hike."

"We're not going to see Junior," I said, stepping over the deep clumps of snow and ice piled on the curb by the last pass of the snowplow. I didn't want to talk to Junior either, not because she was an uptight bitch, as Weasel had so aptly put it, but because she'd become the exact opposite.

I had learned through long years of practice how to deal with Goody Two Shoes Junior—ignore her as much as possible, spit in her face when it wasn't, and deny everything when she tattled.

I had no idea now to react to the New Junior, a woman who was willing to bend the rules and steal a suicide note in order to redirect a possible investigation away from her husband. There was no doubt that she would have to be told about Meg taking Weasel's van, and soon, but I was hoping not to be the one to break the news to her.

"*I'm* going to talk to Clay," I said, moving up the sidewalk as quickly as possible. Even with a coat, hat, and gloves, the wind, with a chill factor of minus 20 degrees easily, cut like a knife. I was too old to saunter, and poor Weasel courted frostbite with each second outside.

"And why do *I* have to come along?" Weasel panted behind me.

"Because I'm not letting you out of my sight until we figure out what to do with you," I said, pulling the door to the St. John's Lutheran Church Annex open.

The annex was a long low brick building, built in the sixties when farming was still a viable enterprise, when tithes had been plentiful and the coffers full. It was a modern abomination, designed by a committee and built by volunteers with mostly donated materials, tacked to the side of a truly lovely, hundred-year-old clapboard church.

Weasel hesitated, squinting at the church itself. He'd evidently not undergone a jailhouse conversion, and was probably uncomfortable trespassing in a place where goodness had the theoretical upper hand. But it was too cold to waffle on theological technicalities, and too late for him to manage a miraculous transformation. I took his arm and pulled him inside.

Faint strains of music drifted to us from the church proper, which was up the stairs and through the double doors to our left. From the right, along the long annex hallway, came the assorted sounds of ordinary church business—keyboards clacking, small voices laughing, dishes clinking in the kitchen/reception room. Warmth settled on us like a blanket and we stood still for a moment, absorbing the wonderful heat.

You had to hand it to the Lutherans, they might be a dour and generally humorless bunch, but they liked their pews warm.

They also liked their floors clean. We stomped the excess snow from our boots so as not to track on the worn rust and avocado indoor/outdoor carpeting, and headed down the hall in search of Clay.

"I don't know why we gotta talk to the preacher," Weasel whined as he rubbed his hands together to warm them up.

"Well, *we* don't gotta talk to the preacher," I said, realizing that there were things I needed to discuss with Clay out of Weasel's earshot—like the contents of Annelise's suicide note. I had been willing to delay telling the police and medical authorities what the note had said, but I thought Clay needed some warning for the firestorm that was about to hit.

As a rule, I would have left being the bearer of bad news to Clay's ever-vigilant wife, but she seemed to have been replaced by an alien.

Besides which, though I had no use for churches or churchmen in general, Clay was a good and intelligent man, possessing an inner core of steel he'd used not only to lead his congregation, but to defy Junior's concentrated effort to remake him in her own image.

He was good without being boring. He was a nonpreachy preacher. He often saw through to the heart of things, and I trusted his judgment in most matters except his choice of wife (which was sort of out of my purview anyway).

I wanted to talk to Clay because I thought he might have a clue as to what we should do next. And because he was as deeply embroiled in this problem as me, or Weasel, or his pregnant and suddenly unpredictable wife.

Given that this was a weekday afternoon, and that he was as tidy and punctual and dependable as Junior used to be, I knew exactly where to find him.

I hadn't been in either the annex or the church since Aphrodite's funeral, but nothing had changed. The same cheery, homemade felt-appliquéd wall hangings adorned the brick in all their doweled and tasseled glory. The same classrooms had the same laminated Bible story cut-outs tacked to the same bulletin boards. The building even had the same smell, a combination of moldy books, chalk dust, and coffee cake.

"You sit here," I commanded, pointing to a row of plastic kiddie chairs lined up in the hallway against the wall that was opposite Clay's office. "And don't you move."

"Jesus, you're bossy all of a sudden," Weasel complained. "Where the hell am I going to go anyway? I got no vehicle. I got no coat. And I got no way to get back to Aberdeen before my boss realizes I left town again, not to mention that the whole reason I came here in the first place died and nobody bothered to tell me. I might as well sit here and wait for the cops to come and haul me off."

"Oh, quit your bitching," I said. "It's nice and warm here and at least you have pants again."

Weasel sat down on the low chair reluctantly, knowing that he really had no choice.

"Just stay put, okay? I won't be long. I promise."

I looked him straight in the eye and by sheer force of will, forced him to respond in kind.

"Yeah, yeah, yeah," he said finally, arms crossed, feet planted firmly on the floor, patience sorely tried.

And since he said it without a waffle or a blink, looking me straight in the eye, I believed him.

19

Son of a Preacher Man

It's human nature to want what you can't have.

One of the very first concepts that a baby completely and fully comprehends, even before the true meaning of *hot* sinks in, is that the all powerful *they* would not say *no* if they weren't selfishly keeping all the fun to themselves.

Even after we come to understand that the cat doesn't taste good, or that there's a perfectly sound reason not to spit in electrical outlets or that smoking pot really is bad for you, especially if your mother catches you half-naked and giggling wildly in your bedroom with your boyfriend when you thought she was safely stuck at a city council meeting for hours, there's still a small and insistent voice in the backs of our heads telling us to go ahead, it can't be that bad.

The forbidden is always enticing, always enchanting, always sending out a siren call to the unconscious.

Another chocolate chip cookie won't hurt.

I've already let him put his hand *there*, why stop now?

Just one more drink for the road.

So what if I'm over my credit limit?

His wife doesn't understand him. Really.

Even those of us who understand our universal human failings and are prepared to defy temptation are susceptible.

How less able, then, are those who are simply not equipped to realize or resist?

Especially when the target is so very forbidden.

I actually thought I had Annelise's suicide note figured out. In fact there was no other explanation for her bizarre claim: *She* had been attracted to Clay, not the other way around. And he'd spurned her advances, which explained the suicide attempt and an effort to shift blame.

It's happened before (propositions, not suicide attempts), and to women who are a whole lot better judges of the susceptibility of males to sexual dalliance than a teenage girl in a strange land.

Clay is a handsome man. He's hearty and cheery and relentlessly upbeat without being perky. He's kind and intelligent and he genuinely cares about people, whether they are his congregants or not. The fact that he's a minister, and therefore completely out of reach, is just the icing on the cake for some.

Even Del tried to seduce him, to no avail (a rarity in her universe), and if he could resist Del's overblown charms, then he'd have no trouble gently refusing foreign jailbait.

Besides which, though I would not say this out loud about many citizens of our fair city, including myself, I sincerely thought that Clay Deibert was above temptation.

Not that he didn't feel it (he was human after all, and with Junior he'd created four plus children, so the plumbing obviously worked), but I'd bet the farm that he just wouldn't give in.

Which was why I opened the door to his outer office and stepped in, knowing that I'd find him back in his inner sanctum, working diligently on church business or some other charitable project. Or maybe counseling a troubled teen. Or overseeing any of the zillion details that crop up daily in the care and feeding of modern Christianity.

The outer office reception area, decorated in Lutheran Modern with abstract mosaic crucifixes on the wall and donated shag carpeting on the floor, was quiet and dark. Clay's office, a windowless cubicle just off the outer office was also quiet and dark.

And empty.

I stood for a moment, nonplussed. Then I remembered the music wafting down from the church as Weasel and I warmed ourselves in the doorway.

I decided that Clay was in the church, overseeing choir practice.

Or maybe he was in the kitchen, checking out the supplies for the potluck supper that had been scheduled to raise the funds necessary to underwrite the traveling choir's visit to Delphi.

I turned to go, satisfied with my own conclusions, certain I'd find him somewhere in the building, and ran smack into Junior as she came in the door.

"Jesus, Tory, what are you doing sneaking around in here?" she asked, hastily stuffing a piece of paper she held deep into the pocket of her maternity top. "This is not a public area, you know."

"I'm not sneaking around," I said crabbily. Evidently whatever bond we'd formed at the cafe had evaporated. Junior was back to being her old charming self again. "I was looking for Clay."

"Well get in line," she said cryptically.

Or maybe she was speaking rhetorically.

Or even metaphorically.

In any case she wasn't making any sense so I decided to ignore her.

"I figured he'd be in here, working, being this is a weekday afternoon and all."

"Yeah, you would figure that, wouldn't you," she said flatly, not looking at me.

"Well, I suppose I *would* figure that, considering he's been in his office every weekday afternoon for as long as I can remember," I said a tad acerbically, though I was beginning to realize that there was more wrong with Junior than her usual testiness.

After her surprise at finding me in her husband's office, she hadn't looked straight at me even once. It wasn't unusual for Junior to multitask—she was good at doing a dozen things at once—so holding a conversation while rifling through papers on the secretary's desk didn't seem unusual.

What seemed unusual is that she'd waddled from there to the long table next to the copier, and from there to the computer, all without looking over her shoulder at me, even to emphasize her own snappy retorts.

And she'd done it all in the dark. The weak late-winter afternoon sun had lost almost all of its power and the outer office was deeply shadowed. It was too dark to read any of the papers Junior had carefully inspected while keeping her back to me.

I reached out and flipped the light switch on. Junior flinched as though she'd been hit.

"Are you okay?" I asked, keeping my voice neutral. Offering sympathy to Junior was a dicey business. She was just as apt to bite a hand extended in friendship as any other.

She shrugged. "Not really," she said wearily. "It's been a hectic afternoon, you know."

"Yeah," I agreed. And Junior didn't even know about Weasel and the paper towels yet. Or Meg and the van. "That's partly why I wanted to talk to Clay. There've been some developments that he should know about." I had hoped to talk to Clay alone, but since Junior was here, and she'd have to know about Meg eventually, there was no point in excluding her from the conversation.

"*Developments,*" Junior parroted. Her voice sounded odd. She still hadn't turned around.

"You know, more stuff happening," I said, too confused to be snotty. I think it'd be a good idea to tell Clay everything that happened today, including the contents of the girl's note, before things get completely out of hand."

If it isn't too late already, I added silently.

"Well good luck," Junior said, with a harsh chuckle that ended in a choked sob.

"What do you mean?" I asked, taking a tentative step toward her, but she flinched as though I'd hit her.

I realized that Junior was crying, and that was why she hadn't faced me yet.

Tears were not her usual response to dire circumstances. In fact, I've only seen her cry a couple times in my whole life. I had no idea what to do or how to react.

I couldn't very well ignore the fact that she was sniffling. On the other hand, she was obviously reluctant to acknowledge the truth. If she'd been anyone else, I would have put a protective arm around her shoulders and murmured a few reassuring words, but hugging Junior was every bit as dicey a proposition as offering sympathy.

And with our checkered past, I couldn't exactly blame her for refusing my pity.

"Should I go get Clay?" I asked gently.

That seemed like an excellent strategy. If nothing else, having him here would relieve me of the responsibility of cheering Junior up.

"You can't get Clay," she said emphatically, breaking down completely. "He's not here."

She ran into the inner office and plopped herself down in Clay's desk chair and began to cry in earnest.

I followed her, pulling a wad of Kleenex from the box on the outer office desk, and awkwardly handed them to her. She took them wordlessly and held them to her streaming eyes.

"Well, tell me where he is, and I'll go find him. You shouldn't be alone," I said.

"I don't know where he is," she said through the tissue.

"Huh?"

Junior always knew where Clay was. And all four of her children. And most of the other citizens of Delphi.

She dug into her pocket and handed me a wrinkled piece of paper.

I flipped the light switch on and smoothed it out. Typewritten on the sheet were the words: *Went ice fishing. Will be back later. Don't wait supper for me.*

Now I *was* confused.

Clay didn't do much fishing. Clay didn't do much hunting. Clay didn't play much golf. Clay didn't do most of the things that most of the Delphi men considered essential to their sanity and recreational well-being.

And when he indulged in any of the above, he certainly

didn't do them on weekdays when he was needed at work. Or without letting his wife know exactly where he was going. Or when he was coming back.

"Clay doesn't ice fish," I said finally.

"No shit, Sherlock," Junior said bitterly. "I guess that means he's not ice fishing then, doesn't it?"

"Well, if he's not here, and he's not ice fishing, where is he?"

"Well, let's see if you can figure it out," Junior said nastily. Sadness didn't preclude her general snappish nature. "For the last month he's been late home to supper a good three nights a week. At least once a week he's out for evening calls and doesn't get home until very late. He's been away from his desk almost every afternoon this week. And there have been calls at the house. Hang-up calls. The kind where when I answer the phone, the person on the other end puts down the receiver without saying anything. He's been moody, distracted, not himself at all. He's been avoiding me and all of his responsibilities." She looked at me directly for the first time, tears streaking down her face unchecked, pain plainly visible in her eyes. "You've lived through this. Hell, you've caused this. Don't tell me that you don't know what all these things add up to."

I sat there stunned.

Sure, when Nick was late home from work (when he worked, that is), it meant just one thing. And when he was out for unexplained evenings, it meant just one thing. And when there were mysterious hang-up calls to our house, it meant exactly the same thing.

And I imagine that it meant much the same thing at Stu McKee's house, though I had not called him there, and we'd never spent so much as an evening together while his wife was living in residence.

For nearly every married man in modern America, such behaviors would add up to the same obvious conclusion.

But we were talking about Clay Deibert.

Reverend Clay Deibert.

"Oh, Junior," I said, reaching across the desk to touch her shoulder. "There's gotta be some other explanation. Clay wouldn't . . ." I fumbled for words, not wanting to say it out loud, not wanting the pictures in my head. Not wanting my illusions shattered.

"Yes he would," she said with the force of certainty backed by a broken heart. "He's having an affair. And I have proof."

20

Immaculate Perceptions

Okay, so I don't believe in Santa Claus anymore. Or election year tax cuts. Or Oprah's permanent weight loss. My innocence in such matters is long gone, and good riddance to it.

I'd rather face the world with an eye unclouded by juvenile expectations of happily ever afters. Gimme a double shot of reality straight up, barkeep.

But somewhere, deep inside this cynical shell, there is a giddy girl who still thinks that out there a few faithful married men exist. Men who feel the tug but who resist. Men who dream of warm bodies other than their wives but who don't turn the dream into reality. Men who look but who don't touch. Men who just say no.

This idiot living inside me not only thinks that there *are* fairy-tale husbands, she thought she'd actually discovered one in his native habitat.

And she wasn't about to give up her illusions without a fight.

"You gotta be kidding, Junior," I said. I was sitting in the chair opposite Clay's desk in his office. The bright fluorescent light turned Junior's red and now tear-swollen face yellow. "Clay is one of the few honorable men I know. He'd never fool around on you."

"Yeah, well, that's what I used to think too," she said, blowing her nose. "Back before I knew better."

"You have proof?" I asked. "*Real* proof, not just . . ." I hesitated. I couldn't very well say *pregnancy delusion*, which I figured was the wellspring of Junior's present dementia.

"You mean, am I making it all up because I'm due soon and miserable and not able to think clearly?" she asked sharply. "Because if you think that, then how do you explain the fact that I saw him coming out of her room in the middle of the night last night?"

I slumped back on the couch and rubbed my forehead. "Her?"

"Yes, *her*," Junior said sharply. "Annelise. The one who took an overdose of pills just before naming Clay as the reason. Her."

"You couldn't have been mistaken? You weren't dreaming? You didn't misinterpret whatever it was that *really* happened?"I was grasping at straws.

"Tory, I got up to go to the bathroom like I do six times every night these days. When I get up I usually check on the kids too. I saw him backing out of her bedroom at two A.M. After that he tiptoed down into the living room and sat there by himself in the dark until after five, at which time he put on his coat and left the house. I haven't seen or talked to him alone since."

She'd stopped crying, but a deep and very familiar pain was etched on her face and in her voice and I did not doubt her account.

I still hoped it was a matter of misinterpretation.

"But there could be any number of good reasons for him to have been in her room. And certainly a good reason for him to have left the house without saying good-bye," I insisted. *Yeah, like he'd been boinking the foreign choir member and couldn't face his pregnant wife*, the rebel voice in my head said. "You can't know that he did in there."

"Oh yes I can," she said bitterly.

Junior reached into her overflowing purse and pulled out a little black box that looked sort of like one of those old transistor radios, the kind we used to have in the early sixties to listen to the Beatles while wearing earphones. It had some knobs and dials and a bright green LCD screen. She handed it to me.

"What the heck is this?" There was no manufacturer name, no indication of purpose on the outside.

"A body fluid detector," Junior said miserably.

I just looked at her, disbelieving. Maybe even a little horrified.

"There was a segment on *20/20* last year about how dirty motel rooms really are, and how you could use one of these things to check to see if there was blood or urine in the room, whether it was properly cleaned or not. You would have been disgusted."

I *was* disgusted.

"I suppose blood and urine aren't the only things it indicates."

Actually, that went without saying. I was pretty sure that Junior didn't suspect Clay of sneaking into Annelise's room in the middle of the night and peeing in the corner.

"It'll pick up fecal matter too," she said.

"Ick," I said, turning it over, but the device was just as mysterious on the back as on the front. "You know there are some things you really don't need to know."

"Yeah," she said. "I figured that out just a little too late."

"So it also picks up semen stains too, huh?"

"Unfortunately," Junior said.

If the subject hadn't been so deadly serious, and if Junior hadn't been heartbroken, the vision of her prowling around motel rooms looking for old wet spots on the bedspreads would have been funny.

And under any other circumstance, I would have thought that finding traces in her own home would have been a just reward for being such a doofus.

But this was deadly serious. She truly thought that her husband, the Lutheran minister, had molested a young foreign girl who'd been so despondent over the incident that she'd tried to kill herself. There was precious little humor in the scenario.

I squinted at the thing. "How does it work? Does it beep or something?"

"You turn off all the lights and an ultraviolet light highlights bodily fluids and other contaminants. They show up bright purple in the dark."

"It doesn't differentiate between fluids?"

"Except for blood, which is a different color or something like that. I haven't seen a bloodstain yet. Otherwise they all look the same."

"Well, there you go," I said, delighted to have found a loophole. "Obviously you found *something* on Annelise's sheets or you wouldn't be so upset. But there's no reason to think that it was semen."

"Tory, do you think he spit in the middle of her bed? There's nothing else a stain in that location could be."

"Well, there's no real reason to think that Clay left it there," I said adamantly. "Does it indicate age? I mean how old the stain is? How long ago it was left?"

"No," Junior said slowly.

"See? Then it could have been left by someone a couple of days ago. Maybe Annelise has a boyfriend in the choir. Someone she's fooling around with. Are there any boys staying at your house this week?"

"Just Jurgen," Junior said, the light in her eye dying. "He's the one who videotapes everything. But Annelise doesn't like him. They try to pretend otherwise because they're supposed to present a picture of global friendship, but they avoid each other completely. It couldn't have been him."

"Pretending to hate someone is a good way to cover up an affair," I reminded her gently.

"So is sneaking out of the house so you don't have to face your wife," Junior said.

I had a brainstorm. "Wait a minute, didn't you say that Clay's been acting strange for at least a month? These kids have only been in Delphi for a couple of days. Unless you're accusing him of fooling around with someone else *and* Annelise at the same time, and that I won't believe without pictures, his weird behavior couldn't be caused by *this* particular girl."

Junior sighed. It was a ragged sound, one that said she'd thought through that argument already. And dismissed it.

"Unfortunately, the timeline *is* right," Junior said. "He's been working with some of the other preachers on bringing the group to Delphi for a couple of months already. He's met with all of them at least a dozen times, he's driven to the cities where they were appearing. He met all the kids a long time ago." She dabbed at her eyes again. "Plenty of time. More than enough. In fact he made a special point of having Annelise stay with us and not with any of the other host families."

"Oh," I said, deflated.

I didn't want to believe that Clay would have sex with anyone except his wife, and I surely didn't want to contemplate him fooling with girls almost young enough to be his daughter.

In his own guest bedroom.

While his very pregnant wife prowled the halls at night.

"I take it you haven't confronted him with any of this yet," I said, handing the magic black box back to Junior.

"What would be the point?" she asked the ceiling. "Did you ever confront Nick?"

"No," I said. "I never really wanted to know the whole truth. What I knew for sure was bad enough."

Terrible memories flashed in my head, images of Nick with other women. Some I'd encountered in person. Some I'd conjured up in my imagination. They all hurt. Even years after his death.

"You know, I'd always thought you were such a chump for allowing your husband to cat around like that. I thought you were every bit as much to blame as he was since you didn't stop him."

"Yeah, well, you can lead a horse to the altar but you can't make him keep his pants on," I said softly. "I suppose I could have forced the issue. But I figured he'd leave me. And somehow that seemed worse than living through the awful times."

And in a way I'd been right. There had been good times interspersed with the bad ones. And I know that Nick loved me in the best way he could. And then he left me anyway, just not the way I'd expected.

"You still don't know for sure," I said gently.

I had known for sure. I'd caught Nick in the act. There had been no doubt.

There was still room for explanation in Clay's case.

Explanation and exoneration.

"I know," Junior said, sounding like a very old and very tired woman. "Take my word for it, I know."

There wasn't much to say to that.

We sat for a moment, both of us wrapped in our own misery—Junior's fresh and painful, mine old and still surprisingly painful.

"We're going to have to say something to the authorities," I said finally.

"You're right," she said sadly. "But can we wait a little while? Until after tonight? I'd like a chance to talk to Clay before it all becomes public."

I was about to agree that another few hours of silence wouldn't hurt, when the office door opened and an attractive and extremely disgruntled woman stormed in. She had Weasel's forearm clenched in an iron grip as she dragged him into the office behind her.

Junior instantly jumped up and began to ruffle papers on Clay's desk. She stood with her back to the door.

"He says he belongs to you, Tory," the woman said angrily, shooting a swift glare at Weasel, who grinned in return while miming innocence.

She shot an equally nasty look at me. I'd known Jennifer Swanhorst for years but we weren't friends. In fact she'd been one of the disapproving dozens who'd spent time whispering behind cupped hands at the cafe when it came out that I'd seen Stu before his wife left Delphi. Though she carried out her myriad church and civil duties with a cheery smile and a platitude, sort of a Junior Jr., she'd been little more than civil to me ever since. "I caught him up in the church, bothering the choir. They're trying to rehearse and they don't need any distractions."

Though I had no intention of claiming Weasel as *mine*, her snotty tone set my teeth on edge. And as angry as I was with Weasel for not staying put, I was even more annoyed with the church police.

"Sit him there," I said, pointing to a chair against the far wall. I shot a pretty lethal glare at him myself. Amazingly enough he didn't spontaneously burst into flames. "I doubt he did any real damage."

"Well, you never know with *some* people," Jennifer said, obviously including me in the group. For someone who was a good ten years younger than Junior, she'd picked up her mannerisms very well. She wiped her hand, the one that had held on to Weasel, delicately on her sweatshirt and then composed her face into a bright smile. "I had to come down here in any case. I need to see Clay. Where is he?"

She glanced at Junior's back, waiting for an answer. Junior shrugged imperceptibly without turning around.

Jennifer stood her ground, prepared, evidently, to wait in the office with us for Clay to return. She probably wanted to tattle on Weasel *and* me.

Unwilling to spend any more time with her, and surprised by how protective I suddenly felt toward Junior, I said firmly, "Clay's ice fishing." I ushered Jennifer out the door before she had a chance to protest. "We'll tell him that you stopped by. I'm sure he'll get back to you later."

21

Preaching to the Choir

It's a topsy-turvy world. In the space of one afternoon, a fair number of my deeply held convictions had sailed right out the window.

Delphine Bauer embarked on a mission of celibacy. Junior Deibert took to lying and stealing. Clay Deibert, the Reverend Clay Deibert, I should add, may or may not have dallied with a foreign teenager under his pregnant wife's nose, but he was certainly in her room late at night. And he wasn't in his office in the middle of the afternoon, which was almost as disconcerting. I was treating Junior not only as a fellow human being, but as a sister under the skin—a person worthy of my trust and sympathy.

It was enough to make me stop and scratch my head and wonder how things got so strange so quickly.

So, in the middle of all this turmoil, it was almost comforting to find that some things hadn't changed.

"You couldn't stay put for even a half-hour?" I asked Weasel sharply. "You have to wander off and embarrass me, huh?"

It was one thing to have Jennifer Swanhorst and her ilk condemning me for my own bad, albeit freely chosen, actions. It was another to be saddled with, and held responsible for, Weasel Cleaver.

Adultery I could live down.

"Embarrass *you*?" he replied, voice rising in indignation. "You aren't wearing some dickhead's hand-me-downs and a dead woman's rubber boots. You didn't freeze *your* balls off in a storage room with only paper towels for company . . ."

Out of the corner of my eye I saw Junior frown in confusion.

Weasel continued. "You weren't dragged out of a church, for chrissakes, by Miss Snootnose and trotted down to the principal's office like a kid who got caught shooting spit wads in class. I was just sitting there minding my own business watching the kids sing. I wasn't hurting nothing."

That last stopped me short. I forgot the rest of my rant.

"Kids? What kids?" I asked. "I thought the choir was practicing."

"It *is* the choir," he said slowly and emphatically. "Or at least it's that bunch of yahoos who were in the cafe this morning. They're a choir, aren't they?"

I turned to Junior, who'd stopped pretending to go through piles of papers on Clay's desk and instead was rearranging supplies in the green double-door cupboard against the far wall. "I thought the choir kids were going to their guest homes and wait for word on Annelise. That's what Glenda said for them to do anyway."

Junior shrugged. If her eyes hadn't been red and puffy, and if I hadn't seen it myself, I'd never have known she'd been crying and confessing grave doubts about her marriage less than five minutes ago. "They didn't want to go home." Her voice was calm and even again. "Once they came back here, they got together and took a vote and decided to stay and rehearse. I think they felt better being together. They may still decide to perform so rehearsing makes sense."

That seemed pretty coldhearted to me.

"Do you *really* think that they'll go on with the concert while Annelise's in the hospital?" I asked, surprised.

"I don't know why not," Junior said. "These kids are pros. They've been on the road for months already, and they're used to being onstage without members all the time. They all take turns going ahead to the next couple of towns in order to connect with the local liaison and do some publicity stuff. They move in with a host family and help to organize temporary homes for the whole choir and get their schedule settled. I expect they're just pretending that Annelise has gone ahead to the next town."

"Maybe they just don't care," Weasel said suddenly.

I'd almost forgotten that he was in the office with us.

"What do you mean?" Junior and I asked together.

"Well, this girl, this Annelise you're talking about. She's the one they took off in the ambulance, right?"

We nodded.

"I don't know for sure what happened since I was stuck elsewhere at the time." He shot a sideways glance at me, waiting to see if I was going to add anything. "But something happened to that girl and it wasn't good, and she's in the hospital now, right?"

We nodded again.

"And the prognosis isn't good either, right?"

We got tired of nodding. "And your point is?" I asked.

"Well, for a group of kids that's been traveling together for the last few months, bonding and all that in a strange country where hardly anyone speaks their language, where they don't get much chance to get to know people from the outside world, where they're supposed to be pretty good friends—you know, one for all and all for one, that kind of thing—"

"What the hell are you trying to say?" Junior demanded, interrupting his narrative.

"Well, for a group of kids who should be all shook up because one of their good friends is hurt or sick and maybe dying, they're a pretty fucking jolly group."

"What, they're not weeping and wailing and carrying on enough to suit you, is that it?" I asked.

"Why the hell would it suit me?" he asked, a little wounded by my tone. "I could give a shit if all of them died, especially that bitch who stole my van."

"What?" Junior asked. "Stole your van?"

"In a minute," I said to Junior. To Weasel I said, "Well then, what *do* you mean? They're singing and practicing, right? What's suspicious about that?"

"That's just what I was trying to tell you, Tory, but you ain't been listening to me. They're down there in the church all right, singing and practicing. But they're not just *carrying on in the face of adversity*." He intoned those words with mock sadness. "They're laughing and dancing. They're whooping it up like they're having a gay old time. Like they're celebrating something wonderful. Like they're all of 'em real damn happy that this other girl, the one who is supposed to be their friend, is in the hospital."

"How would you know?" I asked. "They teach you psychology in jail?"

"Tory, it don't take an expert to see that those kids aren't in the least bit sad about that girl. Oh, when someone pays attention, they all put on their hang-dog faces and they work up a few crocodile tears. But when they're alone, and they thought they *were* alone back before Miss Tightass yanked me outta there, it's a whole different story."

"Are you sure?" I asked, looking him right in the eye, daring him to play me for a fool. Lord knows, I could do that easily enough on my own.

"Cross my heart," he said, crisscrossing his chest on the wrong side and holding up two left fingers in sort of backward Boy Scout salute.

It was not a declaration destined to inspire confidence. On the other hand, there didn't seem to be any reason in the world for him to be making it up.

Junior and I looked at each other, plainly skeptical.

"You don't believe me, why don't you two trot your asses down there and take a peek. There is something weird going on with those kids."

22

Youth Hostile

I wasn't all that good at understanding the adolescent psyche even when I was one. My own teen years were mostly packed with unfulfilled longings and huge stretches curled up alone with stacks of books. I spent most of that decade standing on the outside with my nose pressed against the window, wanting desperately to join the others in the fun they seemed to be having without me.

At least I'd stood on the outside until Nick Bauer came into my life, by which time it was too late to be careful what I wished for.

But however badly I might judge proper behavior in today's teens, I figured I had a better shot at sussing them out than Weasel Cleaver, whose entire experience consisted of spending time with the few sorry specimens who could be talked into going to bed with him.

Hardly a representative sample.

"What do you mean by weird?" I asked Weasel as the three of us left Clay's office and headed down the long hall toward the church. "Weird, odd? Or weird, ha ha?"

He shook his head at my sad lack of intelligence. "Now what do you think, Tory? You think I was vastly amused by these dipshit kids? That their antics were endearing and engaging?" He was making fun of me. "No. They were acting weird—they were laughing and smiling and no one in their right mind, and I am most definitely in my right mind, would think that they were worried about anything." He shook an admonitory finger at me. "I'll bet everything I own that they don't care about that girl at all."

"Well, that'd be a whole lot, now wouldn't it?" Junior mumbled from beside me.

She'd yet to ask what I was doing with Delphi's creepiest former citizen in tow, but I knew that her inquiring mind wanted to know. She'd positioned herself as far away from Weasel as she possibly could, so as to avoid contamination.

It was too late for me to worry about contagion—I'd seen the man naked. Or at least I'd seen enough of him that he might as well have been naked, paper toweling not being quite as opaque, not to mention pliable, as many might think. Something about that intimacy, however unintended and unwanted, had put me on Weasel's side.

Maybe it was easier to spot his vulnerability when he was undressed.

And maybe the tear I thought I'd seen when he learned that Aphrodite was dead had addled my brain.

In either case, I was surprised to feel a little protective toward Weasel, though that didn't preclude keeping one hand on my wallet at all times.

"I suppose he knows *happy* and *sad* when he sees them," I said in a reasonable tone, as we mounted the stairs up into the church.

Junior just looked at me and shook her head. "Yup, they look plenty jolly to me."

There were several entrances to the church from the annex. We'd entered at the rear through the door by the very back pews. Though the choir hadn't spotted us yet, we could see them clearly in front.

The group of about fifteen or so, the same kids who'd been in the cafe earlier, was up on the stage. One was playing the piano, one was leading, and the boy with the video cam was taping the rehearsal. The rest were singing.

But no one in their right mind would have called them happy.

Many of the girls had red and swollen eyes. Some clenched tissues that they used to dab tears away as they sang. A few of the boys had been crying too, and the rest were somber.

They sang, except for the boy who still recorded everything, following the young director's baton like clockwork. They were carrying on bravely in the grand show biz tradition.

But they weren't carefree. Their voices held a distinct note of sadness despite the upbeat tune. They smiled mechanically where the lyrics and choreography demanded it, but they weren't happy. Anyone could see that this was one sad bunch of teenagers dancin' and singin' a happy tune.

Junior and I looked at Weasel.

"No, no, no," he said emphatically. "*No*. They *weren't* like this. They weren't crying. They were laughing."

"Yeah, it looks like they're having a wonderful time," Junior said nastily. "Like they don't have a care in the world."

I wasn't quite ready to kick Weasel when he was down, but I had to agree with Junior. The choir *was* behaving exactly as you'd expect a group of young people to behave when a dear companion's life hung in the balance.

"Dammit," Weasel said, his voice rising. "They *were* laughing before. I sat back here for a good ten minutes watching them. Not a one of them saw me, and they laughed and joked around. A couple of them were even kissing each other."

"Sure," Junior said, lapsing wearily into *Fargo*-speak. "Yah. You betcha."

The choir finished their song. While they stood, talking quietly and somberly to one another, the accompanist and leader rifled through more sheet music and the boy lowered his camera and ejected a cassette, which he put in a large black cloth bag set on the first pew. He pulled another out of the bag and inserted it into the camera.

"I know it looks bad," Weasel said, eyeing the group maliciously. "But take my word for it, these kids ain't what they seem. We already know they're thieves. And I say they're putting on an act now."

I squinted at the stage, watching and listening intently. If they were acting a part, they were doing it not only convincingly, but in unison.

"Acting for whom?" I whispered, not wanting to draw their attention. They were between numbers and the big old church was quiet except for their hushed, multilanguage conversations. So far as I could tell, they hadn't spotted us yet.

"For everyone. They're on their guard," Weasel said darkly. "They really didn't know I was in here until whatsername squealed and drug me out by my ear. That's why they were acting that way now. I could tell that they were surprised."

It was certainly possible that the singers hadn't noticed Weasel's entrance. But Weasel's presence rarely went unnoticed for long anywhere. I had to assume that someone in the choir would have spotted him leering at the girls fairly early on.

"So they're just putting on an act?" Junior asked. She slid into a pew and sat down. Her exhaustion was obvious. Also her lack of patience. "And why would they do that?"

"I don't know," he said, leaning against a post. He crossed his arms and narrowed his eyes at the singing troupe. "But they're up to something. You better stay on guard."

That was one bit of advice that I didn't think Junior needed. I was pretty sure her guard was so far up that no one would be able to breach the perimeter ever again. She already thought she had plenty of reason to distrust and dislike this particular band of kids, though the main offender was not on the premises at the moment.

I would have expected her to jump on Weasel's bandwagon with both feet. I had a feeling that nothing would have pleased her more than to hustle the whole European Traveling Lutheran Youth Choir out of Delphi on a rail, never to darken our city limits again.

But aligning herself with Weasel Cleaver, a move I seem to have made without even thinking about it, was beyond her ken.

"They look fine to me," she said wearily. "At least they look like a bunch of kids who are worried sick about a friend."

I had to agree. Their sadness seemed real, their eyes truly red, their tissues damp.

"Listen, I *know* what you two think of me and I can't really blame you. But I saw what I saw," Weasel declared firmly. "And I know a scam when I see one. You'll wish you'd believed me when they pull whatever it is they're planning."

A wide and entirely evil smile spread across his pointy little features. He pointed toward the doorway closest to the stage. "And I think it may be starting right about now."

23

Eh?

Outsiders, especially big-city outsiders, often make mistake South Dakota's vast and empty plains for a good hidey-hole. They assume that it would be easy to get lost, to disappear, in a place with a population density of less than .5 person per square mile, when in truth, it's almost impossible to get lost here.

You can get *physically* lost on the our vast grid of unmarked, unpaved and mostly unmaintained country roads, but any fool with a full gas tank who can figure out which way is north can find his way to a city big enough to get situated without too much trouble.

But for an outsider, an obvious *other,* to blend in with the native population, to disappear into our crowds, is almost impossible. We all know ourselves and one another too well to be fooled by imitators, however clever.

Whether we sound like Frances McDormand's notion of what we sound like or not (a matter hotly debated in Midwest cafes), we certainly don't sound like anyone else.

And no one else sounds like us.

Especially Canadians.

It was for that reason, if no other, that I didn't worry much about Meg getting too far with Weasel's furnace repair van. Once we called the theft in to the police, something I was going to insist be done as soon as we informed Junior of the disappearance, it was just an *oot* and *aboot the hoose* before someone spotted her.

After all, there wasn't anyplace a pretty, obviously Canadian teenager driving a repair van by herself could blend in unless she headed directly back to Canada, at which time she'd be stopped by the border guards if the North Dakota HiPos didn't spot her first.

And if she tried to go east, west, or south, the same thing applied. Iowa and Minnesota might be more heavily populated, but she'd still stand out like a sore Canadian thumb, as she would in Nebraska or Montana.

So I was confident that Meg would be found and the van returned, and Weasel's life, for better or worse, would get back on the road where it belonged. I figured her heist and flight might even be video worthy on a slow news day, which is most days in Delphi.

I would not have been surprised to see her next on the evening news.

I was therefore astonished to look up and find Meg, the missing Canadian van thief, standing in front of St. John's Lutheran Church with a fistful of tissues and a tearstained face.

I wasn't the only one.

"Why you little bitch!" Weasel shouted at full furious volume. He pushed me aside and sprinted down the outside aisle toward Meg. "What the hell did you do with my van?"

The church was old and well-built, with sturdy beams and very tall ceilings. It had been constructed with a special eye toward acoustics, which was why it was ideal for choir rehearsal.

That unfortunately also made it an ideal microphone for Weasel's outrage.

"Where are my clothes?" His booming voice echoed from the walls and ceilings. The startled choir turned in unison to stare at Weasel. Meg herself squealed and hid behind Jurgen, who continued to tape merrily. "My wallet! My keys! When I get hold of you I'm going to make you wish you'd stayed in fucking Canada!"

Not certain what mayhem Weasel intended to wreak on Meg, I hurried up the aisle behind him as quickly as possible. Not that I blamed Weasel for being upset—I was pretty annoyed myself at the complications she'd caused in an already complicated day, and *I* hadn't been forced to sit naked on a pallet of canned beans.

But I also didn't want to watch Weasel wring her neck right in front of everyone. He was short, but he was stocky and powerful. I didn't think I could actually keep him from attacking Meg if that was his intent, but I could try to slow him down a little while one of the other kids ran for help.

Junior lumbered behind me, shouting at Weasel to watch his language, that this was a church for chrissakes.

Under other circumstances, I would have savored the humor of Junior taking the Lord's name in vain in her own church, especially in order to express disapproval over someone else's swearing, but there wasn't time to chuckle.

I had a murder to prevent.

"Weasel," I shouted, trying to get his attention. "Weasel, calm down. We can talk about this like adults. At least she's here. That means you can have your van back without calling the police at all."

That last seemed worthy of pause and consideration, but Weasel would have none of it.

"I'm gonna kill her," he shouted over his shoulder at me. "So help me God, I'm gonna kill her."

The rest of the kids milled around, wide-eyed and confused, like a herd of startled gazelles. They got in my way and Junior's, but somehow left a wide-open path directly to Meg, who danced around the others as Weasel chased her.

There was no doubting the apprehension in her eyes, or the real fury in Weasel's voice.

"Damn!" he shouted, making a sudden lunge to the left and grabbing Meg's shoulder bag. "I got you now!"

Instead of just dropping her bag, Meg held tight and

screamed, a sound that could have pierced eardrums for miles around.

"All right!" Junior boomed from behind me. Her voice echoed from the rafters and enveloped the melee like God Herself speaking from above. "This is a church, and such behavior and language *will not be tolerated*!"

She enunciated each word and syllable clearly and at more decibels than I would have thought she was capable of.

They all froze exactly as they stood, like an old-fashioned tableau or a Three Stooges movie. Everyone stared wide-eyed at Junior. Even Weasel.

"This is a house of God," Junior continued. Now that she had everyone's attention, she'd lowered the volume without losing any vehemence.

No one within hearing distance doubted for one second that the red-eyed, pregnant lady meant exactly what she said. I had known that she could command the masses, and though I had built up an immunity from long exposure, even I was in awe. The poor unprepared choir kids were caught completely in her spell.

"Good, I have your attention," she continued, lowering her voice even more and moderating the tone, though there was no question who was in charge at the moment. "Now we will all sit down quietly. You, you, and you"—she included most of the choir with an accusatory finger—"move into the second and third pews and sit quietly."

The boys and girls obeyed, sliding into the pews wordlessly, casting guilty looks at one another and looking sheepish.

"You"—Junior pointed at Meg—"sit here." She indicated the first pew.

Meg, still clutching her shoulder bag, sat meekly.

"And *you*," Junior said, reserving an extra special disgust for Weasel, who, it went without saying, should have known better, "sit here."

She pointed to a spot at the edge of the pew, a safe few feet from Meg.

Without even a murmur of protest, Weasel sat down.

With Junior in charge and a large camera bag between

them as a buffer, Meg relaxed just a little. Her eyes lost their hunted look and she loosened the death grip on her bag.

Weasel narrowed his eyes and glared at her silently.

"Now," Junior said, so quietly that the kids in the other pews probably had to strain to hear her, "I'd appreciate it if you would tell me just what the hell is going on here."

24

Pants on Fire

There are times when small towns are the greatest show on earth.

The rest of the country dismisses rural America as a bucolic backwater, where watching paint dry is the official sport and bitching about the price of gas the main topic of conversation.

And sometimes they're right—a paint crew can attract a sizable crowd of sidewalk supervisors, especially on a soft spring day when the breeze has dwindled to a mere twenty miles per hour.

But that isn't all that happens here, nosiree.

We have all the excitement, drama, and suspense of bigger cities, and we get it without waiting in line.

Sometimes, if we're patient and observe carefully, we're rewarded for the weeks when the best a day has to offer is recording moisture accumulations in hundredth-inch increments. Occasionally, if we stand very still, our bossy, pregnant first cousins forget we're right beside them, and we get to listen in on what promises to be a *really* interesting conversation.

"Who wants to go first?" Junior asked sweetly.

Of course she didn't mean it sweetly, and neither Meg nor Weasel interpreted what amounted to a command to *talk and talk fast* as a gentle request.

So they both began talking at the same time.

"She stole my"—Weasel said in an emphatic voice, and then paused, as if remembering where he was, and then decided to ignore it—"goddamn van!" He pointed at Meg just so that Junior would know exactly who was the accused. "And she took my clothes. Just check that bag of hers, I'll bet you'll find all of my stuff in there."

"He's a crazy man," Meg said at exactly the same time. "I've never even seen him before in my life and he attacks me in a church. I can't believe you haven't called the police yet. I want to file an assault charge."

They both paused, processing what the other had just said.

"Took your van?" Meg said, voice rising in righteous indignation. "Have your clothes? You really *are* crazy!" She turned to Junior for emphasis and repeated, "He really is crazy."

"Never seen me before?" Weasel asked, his own indignation matching Meg's. "What the hell do you mean never seen me before?" To me he said, "Tory, you know she saw me before. You saw us together at the cafe, right? And not only that, but I met her and the rest in Cresbard last week. Don't let that Little Miss Innocent act fool you. We know each other. Hoo boy, we *know* each other. You damn betcha."

"Liar!" Meg shouted.

"Bitch!" Weasel shouted.

"Quiet!" Junior shouted.

They were.

"You first." Junior pointed at Meg. "And you"—she pointed at Weasel—"sit there and keep your mouth shut. You'll get your turn. Understood?"

Weasel nodded meekly, though he did send a beseeching look in my direction.

I could only shrug in reply. I would back him up on Meg having met him earlier in the cafe, but I knew nothing about prior meetings in Cresbard or anywhere else.

"I honestly don't know what he's talking about," Meg said firmly in her Canadian accent. "I never met that man before, and I don't know anything about any stolen vans. And I certainly don't have his clothes in my bag."

"My ass," Weasel muttered.

Junior flashed a withering glare that shut him up. He scrunched down in the pew and ducked his head into his shoulders. I sort of felt sorry for him. Junior's glares can be nearly lethal.

"Go on," Junior said.

"That's all," Meg said. "We realized that poor Annelise was really ill, and we decided together that continuing our rehearsal was a way to honor her. We thought we'd be too sad and scared if we didn't stay together, so we did."

"Wait a minute," I interrupted, ignoring Junior's eagle eye and addressing Meg directly. "You're trying to say that you've been here, in *this* church, ever since the ambulance left?"

Meg, wide-eyed and as innocent a Canadian as ever was born, nodded at me. "Yes, that's exactly what I am saying. I left the diner with the rest of the group and I've been here singing ever since. Well, I was singing until a few minutes ago when I visited the ladies' room. I stopped there for a small cry, and then when that was over, I came back in to rejoin the rest."

Though his jaw had dropped open in shock, and his eyes fairly popped out of his head, Weasel stayed silent during Meg's testimony.

He was a better man than me.

"Give me a break," I said harshly. "You have not been here ever since. You disappeared even before the ambulance arrived. Disappeared with this man's vehicle. And it's not just Mr. Cleaver who says this. I saw that the van was gone, and Mrs. Deibert can confirm it."

I pointed to Weasel, who nodded in emphatic agreement.

I looked to Junior for backup. She'd been at the cafe during all of the excitement before Weasel's discovery in the storage room. She'd known that the van was gone. She'd even helped cover up Meg's absence with Glenda.

I waited for her to nod in agreement.

But Junior just looked at me, confused.

She even dropped her Major General persona enough to say, "Huh?"

"What do you mean *huh?*" I asked her. Mindful of our avid audience, I stepped over and pulled her aside a little and said quietly, "You were there. You saw that Weasel's van was gone. You know that we thought he'd run off with Meg."

She just looked at me.

"Tory, did you smoke those joints? I don't know what you're talking about."

"Junior," I said emphatically, "you *know* that Weasel's van was gone. You *know* that we thought that he left with her. It was only later that we realized that she'd taken the van by herself. That's what I wanted to talk to Clay about. *That's* what I needed to tell you. That Meg had stolen Weasel's van and we needed to call the police."

Junior looked at me like I had lost my mind entirely.

"What the hell are you talking about?" she asked me. There was no doubt that she was genuinely confused.

I thought back to the cafe. Del had first noticed that the van was gone after the kids left the cafe. She'd pointed that fact out to me. And to Alanna.

But had she pointed it out to Junior?

I retraced the conversation in my memory.

No, Junior had been on the phone.

But I'd assumed, we'd all assumed, that ol' Eagle Ears had heard our entire conversation and that she was up to speed on the latest complication in our lives. But she'd been talking to Clay, or to someone who'd told her that Clay was unavailable, and given the recent complications in her own life, complications I'd known nothing about at the time, Junior could be forgiven for just this once not eavesdropping.

But she sure picked a helluva time to keep to herself.

"You really didn't notice that the van was gone? You *really* didn't know that we thought Meg and Weasel had run off together?"

"Meg and Weasel? Together?" Junior asked, horrified. "Ick."

"Yeah, yeah, yeah," I said. We'd all felt the same way. "But it turned out that they *didn't* leave together. Meg lured Weasel into the cafe storage room, talked him out of his clothes, and then disappeared with the clothes *and* the van to God knows where. I found Weasel naked in the storeroom—"

"Ick," said Junior again. It was her new favorite word.

"—and Del found him some clothes and we high-tailed it over here to tell Clay that one of the choir members had a bent for grand theft auto."

"But she's here," Junior pointed out reasonably.

"Well, she must have come back then," I said, just as reasonably. "So there's no real harm done. Weasel can take his van, and Meg can return his clothes, and he can get the hell out of Delphi without anyone having to call the police."

"Except that she says that she didn't take the van, that she was here all along," Junior said. She was being stubborn on purpose, fixating on an irrelevant notion and obsessing.

"It doesn't matter if she *says* she was here," I said. "We all know she wasn't. Del and Alanna know that the van was gone. I know that the van was gone. Weasel sure as hell knows that his van was gone. And I saw the man naked for crying out loud. Do you think he undressed in a cold storeroom for shits and giggles? She was gone."

Junior still wasn't ready to concede.

"Weasel Cleaver is not exactly an unimpeachable source," she said.

And of course that was as true a statement as any ever made. But given what I'd seen, and what I hoped never to see again, I believed him.

"Meg wasn't in here singing just now. We know that for sure. And she wasn't here earlier when Weasel sat listening to them by himself."

Junior chewed her lip, mulling for a moment.

"Did *you* see her here this afternoon? I mean after lunch? In the church? With the rest of the kids?"

Junior looked at the floor and replied very quietly, "I did what I could to avoid seeing anyone this afternoon. The President of the United States could have been here and I wouldn't have noticed. I guess I figured that she *was* in the bathroom. I really didn't think about it."

"Oh," I said softly. Junior was in the middle of a pretty major personal crisis, and taking a headcount of the possible authors of her discontent would have been pretty low on her list of priorities.

She turned to the group, who had been watching our conversation silently but closely. "Meg, were you here all afternoon, singing with the others?"

"Yes ma'am," Meg said solemnly.

If I hadn't known better, I'd have sworn she was telling the truth.

"And you say that she disappeared with both your clothes *and* your van?" Junior asked Weasel."

"Damn right," he said.

If I hadn't know better, I'd have sworn that he'd never told a lie in his whole life.

"And you all," Junior addressed the rest of the choir, "was Meg here with you, singing all afternoon?"

"Yes," they chorused in unison.

25

Van Go

Even if you live where each day is the same and life rolls on through the weeks and years without so much as a hairstyle change or a new paint job, it's still never a good idea to make assumptions. Especially in public because the minute you declare something (anything at all) to be the absolute truth, Jolly Old Fate will come along and prove you wrong.

The bigger the audience the better.

Given my last year, I should have known better than to jump to any conclusions no matter how logical, without hard proof and eyewitness backup. And surely I should know that a publicly declared assumption would be just too great a temptation for the powers-that-be to make an ass outta me, forget *u* altogether.

"What do you mean, she's been here *all* afternoon?" I demanded of the choir.

Everyone answered at once, including Meg and Weasel.

Weasel I ignored because I knew what he was going to say.

Meg was pretty easy to ignore too, considering that she'd already said her piece and wasn't likely to change her story now.

It was the others' commentary that I wanted to hear because frankly, I didn't know what the fuck was going on.

Unfortunately the choir was excited, or at least agitated too, so not only did everyone talk at once, loudly, they didn't all remember to speak in English.

The best I could come up with was that they were indeed all insisting, some using wild affirmative head nods and hand gestures, that Meg had been on the premises all afternoon, singing her sad little heart out with the rest of them.

I shot a confused and questioning look at Weasel.

At first he shook his head vigorously, denying the group response, which he'd understood as well as I had. Then a puzzled look crossed his face as he worked through the permutations of this new wrinkle. He slumped back in the pew, squinting, all of the anger seemingly drained from his body.

I expect we'd come up with the same burning question.

If Meg had not taken Weasel's van, then who had? And, more importantly, if Meg had not intended to steal Weasel's van, then why abscond with his clothes?

I peered at Weasel through narrowed eyes, though he seemed to be contemplating the old oak of the pew, and the items on it closely.

Or maybe he was just avoiding eye contact.

Had Meg taken Weasel's clothes at all? Had she even been in the cafe storeroom with him?

Weasel had declared that to be the case. And he'd been so convincing that I'd not doubted his story for a second. Even Del had believed him.

But was he telling the truth?

I peered at him some more, remembering his outrage. Remembering, against my will, his nudity. He still didn't look up, but it wouldn't have mattered.

Nothing that had happened on this long afternoon added up.

Meg, looking sweet and innocent, had declared herself to be on-premise the whole time, and she had the backup of a theoretically unimpeachable majority of those present, all of whom, it should be remembered, were good churchgoing Lutheran youth.

She looked innocent. They looked innocent. There was no one to prove them otherwise.

On the other hand, Weasel Cleaver, a known felon, an ex-con, a thief, and a creep, absolutely and convincingly declared that a not-so-innocent Meg had lured him into the cafe storeroom with the express intent of relieving him of his clothes and motor vehicle in that order.

Which declaration I'd believed without hesitation myself. He'd been naked, paper toweling notwithstanding. And the van *had* been gone, after all.

"Wait a minute," I said. "What about Weasel's van?"

"What about it?" Junior asked wearily, one hand kneading the small of her back. She was near exhaustion and losing interest in the proceedings.

Weasel caught my drift, however.

"Yeah, what *about* my van?" he asked Meg slyly.

If Meg had not stolen Weasel's van, then who had?

There was absolutely no disputing the fact that it was missing. Not only had Del noticed, but she'd pointed out the empty parking slot to all of us. Even if Junior had been too distracted to notice, Del knew. I knew. Alanna knew.

And Weasel knew.

Three sort of unimpeachable sources and an ex-con who happened to concur about an undeniably missing van.

"Is this van *actually* gone?" Meg asked. "I mean, did it truly disappear at all?"

"What? You think I lost it or something? This ain't that big a town, sweetie," Weasel sneered. "It was gone and I still think you took it."

She shook her head, pitying the mistaken man across from her on the pew.

"I'm afraid you're wrong," she said reasonably and sadly. "I've been here all afternoon. I don't even know which vehicle you're talking about."

"*Is* the damn van gone?" Junior asked wearily.

"Of course it is," I said sharply. "It was gone before you left the cafe."

Without preamble, I stalked back down the outside aisle,

out through the lobby. The choir kids scrambled after me, and Junior followed behind them, much more slowly.

"See?" I said as I pushed open the big double exterior doors, shivering in the sudden blast of arctic air. I faced my audience and triumphantly pointed across the street toward the cafe. "See?"

"Uh, Tory," Junior said, as the kids in the choir began to giggle and whisper. "I got news for you."

26

Ass Outta Me

I really ought to start listening to myself. Not five minutes ago I made it very clear that assumptions were the wrong way to go. That drawing conclusions based only on alleged and unsubstantiated facts was a bad idea, a *really bad* idea. That public declarations were an irresistible invitation to the gods to prove you wrong.

And while I didn't say it out loud, I certainly understood the corollary to the above—that once you've jumped and declared, someone surely will point out the error of your ways in the most embarrassing manner possible.

"But . . . but . . ." I said, sputtering.

Junior, who allowed herself the ghost of a smile, said, "Looks like a van to me. In fact, it looks exactly like the ratty van Weasel Cleaver drove into Delphi, parked exactly where Weasel Cleaver parked it, just waiting for Weasel Cleaver to drive it away again. The sooner the better."

The kids, all of whom had gathered in a tight knot behind Junior, tittered and shivered discreetly.

"But it wasn't there before," I said weakly, shoulders sagging.

Wherever it had been, the van was back in all its beige

glory, right in front of the cafe where it'd been earlier, looking for all the world like it had never been moved.

Junior shrugged and the kids laughed a little louder, a little more impolitely.

"Dammit," I said firmly. "The van was gone. Someone took it *and* Weasel's clothes. And someone brought it back and parked it in the exact same spot."

"And what exactly do you expect me to do about it?" Junior asked wearily. "You come to me with a wild story that one of the choir kids stole a vehicle. You name the perpetrator specifically, and accuse her of other disgusting acts. Only problem is, the girl in question is not only here, she has multiple witnesses to back her up."

"But Weasel said . . ." I said and then paused, listening to myself.

Whether Junior had noticed its absence was irrelevant. The van *had* been gone. I did not doubt my own eyes, and I sure as hell didn't doubt Del's.

But who had taken it?

At first we'd assumed that Weasel and Meg had disappeared together. It was a logical conclusion, given his history and the smoldering look I'd witnessed in the cafe.

When Weasel proved to be on the premises sans clothing, we'd all jumped to the same conclusion—that Meg (who seemed to be missing herself) had taken the van for reasons of her own.

But did we have any proof to back up that assumption?

It suddenly occurred to me that Weasel could very well have moved the van himself during the ambulance chaos, snuck back into the cafe through the unlocked back door, and undressed in the storeroom in plenty of time for me to discover him there, wrapping his weenie with Bounty and blaming it all on some innocent Canadian girl.

I closed my eyes tightly against the realization that I'd probably been had. I suddenly wondered if Weasel Cleaver, for reasons unknown to anyone but himself, had taken to indecent exposure in cafe storerooms and had come up with the stolen van story to cover his hairy butt once I'd proven less than interested in the rest of him. I'd not only believed him, I'd become his champion. Maybe even his friend in the process.

I was going to have to have a long talk with Weasel.

Junior, who was adept at reading expressions, especially when it afforded her a chance to lord it over others, was on my wavelength. "You'd best talk to him, right?" Her eyes locked on mine in a steady and unwavering gaze that plainly said she didn't care one way or another. If there was a problem, it certainly wasn't hers, and she'd appreciate it if I'd gather my petty concerns and get them out of her sight.

Super Junior had returned.

And I had no choice but to tuck my tail between my legs and run for home. Or somewhere away from her condescending pity. "Yeah," I said, inhaling deeply, hating what I was going to have to say next with all my heart. "You're right."

Junior had the grace to drop her eyes, to allow my defeat without crowing.

I stepped back into the church lobby and let the door close. In the brief time we'd stood in the open doorway, the temperature in the lobby had dropped a good 20 degrees, our breath puffed in great white clouds.

The kids, who'd been watching avidly, parted like the Red Sea and let Moses Bauer walk through the empty middle. They'd stopped laughing. They'd stopped whispering. They'd stopped doing everything and watched me solemnly the way they'd watched us in the cafe before the ambulance had come for Annelise.

Their gaze had spooked Del, but it didn't spook me. They had just witnessed a middle-aged American widow making a fool of herself. I imagine they were memorizing the moment in order to amuse the folks back home around the fire.

I silently vowed to make Weasel Cleaver's life a living hell. I vowed to report him to his parole officer for being out of town without permission. I vowed to tattle to his employer, to tell them that they'd hired a liar and a pervert who'd never quite gotten around to fixing our damn furnace, what with taking his clothes off in the storeroom and all.

Out loud, I vowed to wring the bastard's hairy little neck.

Warmed by my own righteous anger, I reentered the church and actually got halfway up the aisle before I realized that the front pew was empty.

27

Swan Song

Nothing like a big honkin' dose of stupidity to dull your senses.

Weasel hadn't been standing at the church doorway with the rest of us, gaping at the miraculous reappearance of his own van. I'd sensed his absence in the way you know without being told that there aren't any agitated skunks in the vicinity. But I'd been too wrapped up, first in my certainty and then in embarrassment, to think through what a missing Weasel might signify in the larger scope of things.

It appeared that I was going to have plenty of time to rectify that oversight.

I stopped short in the aisle and muttered, "Fuck," under my breath.

"Oof," Junior said as she ran into me from behind. "Tory, for crying out loud, would you be careful please?"

I muttered something slightly more impolite.

"And remember where you are," she said, frowning. "There's no need to take it out on me."

"Yeah, I know," I said, sighing.

We stood in the aisle for a moment together as the kids arranged themselves in formation, getting ready to practice another number. Jurgen, the ever jolly camcorder operator, rummaged in his black bag while speaking to one of the other girls.

They didn't seem to notice that Weasel was gone, which was not surprising given that there was no reason for them to have registered his existence in the first place. The tenuous connection between him and the group had vanished into the cold prairie air.

"Does it actually matter?" Junior asked finally, apropos, evidently, of nothing.

"Does *anything* actually matter?" I replied existentially.

She frowned, not in the mood for semantic tomfoolery. "I *mean*," she said sharply, "does it matter that Weasel is gone? Whether his van disappeared or not seems to be a moot point. And given that Meg is here, and that all he does is upset and disturb the populace, it strikes me as a good thing that he took the opportunity to sneak out without causing any further damage."

"Yeah, well, if we could count on that," I said, not willing to give Weasel the benefit of even that doubt.

But Junior had a point. What difference did it actually make that he said his van had been stolen when it might not have been? What did it matter that he'd blamed a Canadian choir girl for duping him out of his keys and clothes, even if that was not exactly the way events had unfolded?

Why did it bug the living shit out of me that nothing that had happened since the discovery of the unconscious Annelise added up properly?

Because it didn't, that's why.

Not a damn thing made sense and that made me crabby.

"Even if you can't count on it," Junior said wearily, "there's no need for you to hang around here any longer. I'm sure you have plenty to do before tonight."

"Tonight?" I asked, confused.

"Supper tonight? The whole family? Your mother, my mother, everyone? My house?" she said. "Remember?"

I almost muttered another impoliteness. "Oh yeah," I said instead.

I had forgotten that tonight was the night that Mother had

planned on making a few revelations and confessions *en famille*, and that my presence was required.

I had not been looking forward to the commotion that was sure to ensue after she dropped her bomb. After learning of the disarray in Junior's life, I was even less enthusiastic.

Junior was a royal pain in the ass, and she deserved any number of comeuppances, but to whack her in the family pride when she was already reeling from the certainty that her perfect husband was not quite so perfect, was more than even I could enjoy.

Maybe I could talk Mother into postponing the revelatory portion of the evening. Especially if we weren't going to be alone.

"Will some of *them* be eating with us too?" I asked, almost enthusiastic about the prospect.

"Of course," Junior said, annoyed. "A couple of the kids and Glenda Harrison too. They're staying at my house, I can't very well tell them to go elsewhere for supper can I?"

I realized with relief that Mother would not be able to execute her plan after all. One of the weights disappeared from my shoulders. "Good."

"Good?" Junior asked.

"Never mind," I said. She'd find out soon enough. "I'd better get going."

"Must be an echo in here," Junior muttered just loudly enough for me to hear.

I realized that I was also too tired to engage in semantic tomfoolery and decided to declare a unilateral truce with Junior by leaving the gauntlet on the floor where she'd dropped it. "I'll see you later," I said wearily. "Sorry for disturbing your afternoon."

That last I meant sincerely. I was sorry that everyone's afternoon had been disturbed.

She nodded, and then lumbered up the aisle toward the kids, who were solemnly tuning up.

I followed her, grimly determined go home and play Scarlett O'Hara and think about it tomorrow at the very earliest. By the time I got to the front row of pews, I'd almost convinced myself that not thinking about it was possible.

And as always, fate proved me wrong immediately.

I looked up to see Jennifer Swanhorst, pale and obviously near tears, standing in the doorway, frozen.

"Yes?" Junior asked. She shot me a look that I returned with a shrug. "Something we can do for you, Jennifer?"

"Um," Jennifer said, her voice faltering. She swallowed and then opened her mouth again to speak.

By now, the choir had noticed Jennifer in the doorway. They all watched her with their patented spooky intensity. All but Jurgen, who was still rooting around in his black bag. And even he noticed the sudden silence in the church and looked first at the others, and then toward the door.

"Uh, I called Clay just now," Jennifer said, her voice wavering. "Reverend Deibert, that is. At the hospital. That's where he's been."

I risked a peek at Junior to see how she took the news that Clay was not ice fishing after all, that he'd instead rushed to the bedside of the girl who'd accused him of molesting her.

"Yes," Junior said again, only this time her voice wavered a little. "Go on."

"Well, um," Jennifer began again. She inhaled deeply and continued, "Clay wanted me to tell you"—she paused, looking directly at Junior with an odd expression on her face—"and all the rest that Annelise . . ."

She stopped for a moment, looking down at the floor, then raised her eyes and announced in a nearly steady voice, "They did what they could for her, but it was too late. I am so sorry to have to tell you all that Annelise died about fifteen minutes ago."

28

Shrimp on the Aga

Same Day
Early Evening

Death always catches you off guard. It doesn't matter if the recently deceased had been terminally ill for years, gasping for breath as doctors declared it could be any minute now for days on end. It doesn't matter that we've been presented with repeated, concrete, physical evidence that the death rate on this here planet is 100 percent.

It doesn't even matter if you and the corpse were complete and utter strangers, with an acquaintance consisting entirely of a polite request for ice water but nothing else thank you.

No matter how well you think you've prepared yourself, you never actually expect anyone to die. Friend or foe, family or stranger, innocent victim or coldblooded murderer, you simply don't think that anyone ever stops breathing or settles into the final mystery, or boldly goes where no man has come back from.

Death is always a shock to the system, an unwelcome reminder of your own and everyone else's mortality.

And in this case, the old cliché rang true—some people were just too damn young to die.

"So what happened then?" Neil Pascoe asked without looking up from the counter where he was slicing pink, thawed shrimp, getting ready to sauté his supper. Neil may have been able to buy, thanks to the Iowa State Lottery Commission, exactly what he wanted when he wanted it without ceremony or notice, but like the rest of us, he lived in Delphi, where fresh shrimp were not to be found for any amount of money.

"All hell broke loose," I said, reaching quickly from my perch on a bar stool across the counter from Neil and grabbing a hunk of shrimp, which I popped into my mouth. "Actually, it's too bad that Weasel decamped before Jennifer showed up with the awful news. He'd have seen some real weeping and wailing from the choir as they scattered."

"I take it that the kids were genuinely upset this time, not faking it?" Neil asked. He scooped the shrimp up by hand and dumped them into a hot frying pan in which he'd already melted butter and tossed in a couple cloves of crushed garlic.

"Yeah," I said. "If they were faking shock and horror at Annelise's death, I'll eat my shoe. And what's more, I'll bet that they were just as sad earlier. I think Weasel probably wouldn't know a real emotion if it bit him right on his hairy ass."

Said ass had already been described in detail, to Neil's great delight.

"Maybe," Neil said cryptically. The shrimp sizzled and popped as he stirred. The concoction smelled absolutely wonderful.

"God, I wish I could eat here," I said, annoyed that Junior still insisted on hosting a family meal after the unexpected outcome of today's events. There seemed no reason now to invoke a command audience. Mother would not be able to drop her bombshell in the midst of chaos and strangers, and I'd expect that Junior, of all people, would really prefer to be alone. "This is so much better than anything I'll get out at the farm."

"Junior still on a health food kick?" Neil asked, smiling.

He'd recently switched from tortoiseshell to gold wire-rim glasses, which made him look even younger, though his dark hair was prematurely shot with gray.

Considering that he was already ten years younger than me, I thought that gave him a decidedly unfair advantage.

"Sprouts and fat-free cheese," I said glumly. "Yogurt instead of sour cream. No egg yolks. Skim milk. Fake margarine."

"Margarine is already fake." He laughed, pushing his glasses back up on his nose. I don't know if the new frames slid down the way his old ones had, or if he was just reverting to an old habit.

"Well, the shit she serves is even fakier," I said. "It's like yellow grease."

"You could just call Junior and tell her that you're stuck in town without transportation," he said as he stirred. "Or that I gave you a note excusing you from healthy food tonight. You could say that you've been grounded and can't leave the city limits."

"I wish," I said, looking around Neil's state-of-the-art kitchen, taking in the gleaming chrome and the subtle lighting.

The first two floors of his house were strictly restored Victorian—quarter-sawn oak, dowel and ball-lattice trim, narrow plank flooring, soft muted colors, and antimacassar overabundance. So beautiful, and so painstakingly perfect, was the library that he ran from the first floor that it had been featured in both the *South Dakota Magazine* and *Old Home Journal* as cover stories.

But upstairs was his home. And it reflected the complex tastes of a complex man. There was an eclectic mix of old and new, all finely crafted, some by his own hand, that didn't speak to any period.

It just said Neil Pascoe.

And Neil Pascoe's kitchen spoke to efficiency and no spared expense when it came to tools and equipment. It looked just like him.

"I wish I didn't have to leave at all," I said aloud without thinking.

"You don't have to, you know," he said without looking up. "You *can* stay."

A silence hung between us as the shrimp sizzled and Sarah MacLachlan wailed plaintively from speakers hidden above the cabinets.

It was an awkward silence, but not too awkward.

Neil is my best friend. He stood beside me after Nick's death. He waited for me to get over a foolish and unfortunate entanglement with the very married Stuart McKee. He'd been patient, oh so very patient, while I worked through my own jumbled feelings, and more importantly, my terror of trading in a most wonderful friendship for something deeper.

On New Year's Eve, he'd made it clear that it was time to think about us as an *us.* And I'd blown it by making a decision that resulted in Neil's withdrawal for a while.

We were just barely coming to terms again, both with the old life and with new possibilities.

And we'd been moving incredibly slowly, pretending that nothing had changed while knowing (and knowing full well that the other was equally aware) that nothing would ever be the same again.

This was the first time in a month that either of us had dared to refer out loud to the possibility of a deeper relationship.

I knew very well what Neil had just offered. And I knew what I wanted to do.

Unfortunately, it wasn't possible.

"I *have* to go," I said softly. "This thing with Annelise is just the tip of the iceberg. Her death means that all of the accusations about Clay will come out."

I'd already filled Neil in on the note and its contents, as well as the rest of the afternoon's amazing revelations. He knew as well as I did the effect that Clay's defrocking could have on Delphi. And he understood the effect it would have on Junior herself.

He'd always championed Junior in his own understated way.

"You're right," he said as he pulled a plateful of cooked penne pasta from the warming oven. "There's a lot more going on here than shows on the surface." He expertly dumped the shrimp on top of the noodles and sprinkled the mound with fresh Parmesan cheese and then sat down on the stool across from me. "She needs you."

I nodded.

He was right. As little as I liked Junior, as much as I would have rooted for a comeuppance just a day or so ago, I would never have wished for public humiliation or the destruction of her marriage.

"And she needs you to prove that none of it is true," Neil said simply.

"You think it isn't?" I asked, stealing another piece of shrimp from his plate. "You think Clay was *counseling* Annelise in her room at two-thirty in the morning?"

"I don't know *what* he was doing in there," Neil said, slapping my hand as I reached for more. "But whatever it was, he wasn't boinking jailbait. On that I'd bet the farm. Hell, I'd bet the library."

"I would have bet the same thing too," I said sadly. "In fact I would never have believed it if anyone else had told me. But you didn't see Junior's face. And you didn't see that awful little device she had, that body fluid detector thing."

"It might have detected semen," Neil said with his mouth full, "but it couldn't say whose it was. Maybe Clay just happened to be up and caught the girl with someone else doing the horizontal polka. That Jurgen kid, the one you said tapes everything. He's staying there, right?"

"He's staying there, but Junior insists that he and Annelise avoided each other."

"Well, maybe Junior is wrong."

I poured myself a small glass of Riesling from the chilled bottle Neil had set between us, and thought about that for a moment. "But she was so certain."

"She was also certain that Satanists were invading the carnival last summer, remember?"

"Yeah, but this time . . ." I paused, trying to put my feeling into words. "This time she made it seem so real. She *made* me believe that Clay was fooling around with the kid."

"That's because *she* believes it with all her heart. It's up to you to prove her wrong before things really fall apart."

"Oh, gee, thanks," I said, swallowing the wine in a single gulp, not relishing the notion of being Junior's All-Purpose Savior. "Exactly how am I supposed to do that?"

"Well, for starters, you can find out who it was that Annelise was really fooling around with," Neil said, grinning.

I looked at him and raised an eyebrow and waited for instructions as to how to go about unobtrusively investigating a teenage suicide's sex life.

"Ask around tonight at supper. Annelise is bound to be the main topic of conversation anyway. Listen and watch. If the kids are as sad as you said they are, they won't be on their guard, and they may let something slip. You'll know what you're looking for when you see it."

"Yeah, sure," I said. "Tofu and skullduggery among the bereaved. Sounds like a blast."

He cuffed me lightly on the shoulder. "You can do it, kiddo. Talk to them all, but check out that Jurgen kid especially. I'll bet he knows something."

"What, you have a psychic link with him?"

"Nope, I just know that he's a teenage boy, and teenage boys are all hormones and radar. If he wasn't getting any from her himself, he knows who was. Take my word for it."

"They can just tell, huh?"

"It's a *guy* thing," Neil said laughing.

"Well why don't you just come along with me and hone your *guy radar* in on him and save me the trouble?" I asked, only half-joking. "You could wrap up the Weasel conundrum and Clay's little adultery mess in one fell swoop."

"Can't," he said, indicating his plate. "Besides, Junior didn't invite me specifically and you know how she is about drop-ins."

I sighed. I knew how Junior was about everything.

Neil tilted his head and thought for a moment and then said, "Just talk to him. Your radar's as good as anyone's. Try getting him to show you some highlights from his videotape collection. He's bound to have caught something interesting."

29

My Dinner With Junior

I don't know how it always ends up like this—I start out wanting nothing more than to get through my days, one at a time, in one piece, with enough energy to face the dawn. I don't want to make unwelcome discoveries. I certainly don't want to trip over dead bodies. And I never ever want to investigate anything, especially on behalf of a cousin who, on her good days, can accurately be described as a pain in the ass.

And yet, as always, I find myself investigating, keeping an eye peeled and an ear to the door and a snoopy question on my lips as I root through the sordid underbelly of small-town life.

Well, okay, so it's not quite as bad as all that, but I still end up going to my drippy cousin's house for supper in order to find out for myself if her minister husband really was fooling around with a young girl who may or may not have killed herself as a result of the alleged involvement.

Which was sordid enough for my tastes.

Especially when I would much rather have stayed at Neil's house, exploring other far more pleasant things instead.

"What are *you* doing here?" Junior asked me testily, blocking the doorway.

She didn't move aside, which I took as a signal that my boots weren't clean enough for her immaculate home. "What do you mean, *what am I doing here?*" I replied as I went back on the step and stomped more snow off the boots so as not to have it melt all over the parquet flooring. "You insisted that I come to supper. That's what I'm doing here."

It was incredibly cold on the porch, and I was already crabby about having to come out at all, so I sidled past her into the entry without stopping to play Twenty Questions.

Junior shot a furtive glance over her shoulder and then turned back to me. "Didn't Del tell you?"

"I haven't seen Del since this afternoon," I said, taking off my coat and hanging it on a hook. I pulled soft house slippers from a pocket and took my boots off on the rug.

"Del was *supposed* to tell you that supper was postponed. I called a while ago to tell you that you didn't need to come tonight," she said, whispering frantically. "Del said that she'd get the message to you."

I was still divesting myself of the usual complement of South Dakota winter outerwear when Junior's statement finally sank in. I froze in mid-muffler-unwind.

"What do you mean, I didn't have to come out here tonight?" I asked dangerously. "You've been insisting all week that it was not only polite, but necessary for me to attend your little soiree. Do you think I drove all the way out here on a night like this just for my own amusement?"

Do you think I left Neil's in order to sift through your husband's possibly illegal activities because I wanted to? I added mentally.

"Well Del said she'd tell you," Junior said, pulling my coat back off the hook and handing it to me. "You'll have to take it up with her. Sorry for the inconvenience. Drive safely back into town."

"Whoa," I said, trying to sort out what was actually happening. If I read the signals right, Junior not only did not want me to eat supper with her, she wanted me out of her house immediately. If not sooner. "Slow down. Didn't it occur to either of you to try Neil's house? I left straight from there to come here. In fact, I'm driving his truck because he didn't think that Del's car would make it through the drifts."

"No," Junior said stubbornly. "Del said she'd let you know. You have to go."

All of my alarm bells were ringing. Why the hell was Junior so anxious to get me out of her house?

I'd come with the express purpose of sniffing out Annelise's dark secrets, which would, theoretically, exonerate Clay. Which would, in turn, ease my cousin's troubled mind. Which was a favor, an evidently unwanted favor.

The only explanation I could supply for Junior's sudden, rude anxiety was that Clay's innocence truly was long gone and she was bent on preserving the image for as long as possible.

Back at Neil's house, I had been convinced that he was right, that Junior's hyperventilating certainty of her husband's guilt in dallying with Annelise was an illusion, supplied by Junior's own pregnancy-addled brain.

Now that I was in her presence again, my certainty was fading.

I had no clue what it was that Junior didn't want me to see. But whatever it was, she *really* didn't want me to see it.

Which only intensified my desire to get in and take a gander for myself.

Neil would be proud.

"Well, it's too late for Del to tell me not to drive this far," I said simply, hanging my coat back on the hook. "I'm here now, and I haven't had any supper yet, and it's been a long and tiring day," I said as I put the house slippers on. "And I am not about to turn around and go home without at least warming up and saying hello to everyone first."

Without looking at her directly, I pushed past Junior and into the entry proper.

"Wait Tory," she said from behind me. "You don't understand . . ."

I stopped short, at the end of the hallway, just before entering the brightly lit dining room, from which floated assorted voices, and delicious smells that could not possibly have emanated from anything made with tofu or fat-free cheese. I turned around and faced her. "Don't understand what?" I asked sweetly, with an eyebrow raised.

I silently dared her to thwart my mission. To come up with a reason good enough to leave without scoping out the territory, or sampling whatever was cooking in the kitchen.

"Why in the world should I turn around and go back home now?" I asked.

Junior merely closed her eyes, and let her shoulders slump. "I tried," she said weakly. "I really tried."

And given that I will evidently never learn how dangerous it is to tempt the gods, Junior unfortunately gave me a perfectly good reason to turn tail and run back out into the snow.

In fact she'd supplied the only reason in the world that I would have considered good enough.

If only I'd heeded her warning.

Instead, I turned on one heel, and ran smack into Stuart McKee.

And his pregnant wife.

30

A Stranger in a Strange Land

Wouldn't it be nice if stupid mistakes had a half-life, if there was a statute of limitations on the consequences of your own bad decisions?

Maybe in bigger cities you can actually walk away from an old life and leave it behind, with none of your acquaintances any the wiser. But that's not how it works in Delphi, where the only thing longer than the dark winter nights are the memories of your friends and neighbors.

You can bet none of them would ever forget that your good-girl reputation died the minute someone let it slip that you'd been sleeping with your married boyfriend *before* his wife left him.

Not that I wasted time or emotion regretting the afternoons, and rare evenings, that I'd spent with Stuart McKee. Expending energy over something that could not be changed was a self-indulgence I tried not to allow myself. Besides which, we'd had some decidedly good times together, and in the end Stu and I had come to a sort of peace about the whole thing, a bittersweet acceptance of what was, and more importantly, what never could be.

But that peace didn't extend to being observed together in public, especially in the same room as his pregnant wife.

In the last month, Stu had stayed away from the cafe for the most part, ambling over from the Feed and Seed Store he ran with his father only when in the company of valued customers or when the cafe was too busy for people to spend time watching for stray sparks to fly between us.

And since there were no stray sparks to observe, we gradually became old, and boring, news. Not worth speculation or contemplation.

I hoped that eventually he'd be able to resume normal lunches and coffee breaks as long as someone else waited on his table. And I hoped that eventually we'd be able to resume at least a guarded friendship, the sort of casual friendship that occasionally grew between ex-spouses.

Of course, I was fooling myself there because Stu McKee, despite ignoring at least a few of his marriage vows, was never going to have an ex-wife. That last had become clear to me in the waning days of the affair, and that had prompted its end, which, to give Stu credit, had been mutual and amicable.

The breakup had left me with no bitterness and only marginal pangs of regret over the whole business despite it having been wrong from the start. But nowhere in the Handbook of Illicit Affairs was there instructions on how to deal with sudden and unexpected and absolutely unwanted meetings with ex-lovers in the company of their spouses and a fair portion of the rest of your hometown.

My first glance had revealed not only Stu and Renee McKee standing in Junior's kitchen, but easily fifteen more adults, the surviving members of the European Traveling Lutheran Youth Choir, and a passel of Junior's children, all crammed together in ranch-style comfort.

The children laughed and giggled, but the rest milled somberly around the food-laden countertop that divided the kitchen from the dining room, whose table was similarly loaded. They spilled over into the living room, each carrying a paper plate filled with the kind of plain and hearty food that South Dakotans prepare when there is a death in the family.

I'd bet that there was not a speck of tofu or fat-free cheese anywhere among the casserole dishes and cake pans.

I realized immediately what was going on—Junior had jettisoned the family meal and convened the choir members and their host families, which had evidently included the McKees, for an early wake, as it were, for Annelise.

Her suspicions about the relationship between Clay and the dead girl would have been firmly suppressed in the obligation of being a minister's wife. And like the very good minister's wife that she was, she'd tucked away her own sorrow and done what was expected of her.

And though Junior had never been a member of the Tory Bauer fan club—in fact she'd been one of my biggest detractors—she had at least tried to spare me further public humiliation.

If only I'd listened to her. But it was too late to turn and run now.

The Delphi natives in the room froze in mid-syllable, mid-bite, or mid-sniffle and turned to stare at me en masse. The choir members and the couple of adults with them, including a frazzled Glenda Harrison, looked first at one another in confusion, and then at me.

Though no one raised an arm and hissed at me, it was obvious that I'd stumbled into an alien conclave, a Pod of Lutherans in their natural habitat. Even without my Honorary Harlot status, I would not have been more out of place if I'd had three eyes and tentacles.

"Uh . . ." I said stupidly, quickly considering and discarding a dozen escape plans.

I'd been seen, recognized, categorized, and memorized. Leaving now would serve no purpose beyond ending the humiliation early while at the same time signaling my defeat to one and all. My sudden appearance in Junior's kitchen would go down in the Delphi annals as a historic example of being in the wrong place at the wrong time.

Determined to salvage what little dignity I could from the

situation, I mumbled, "Stu," an acknowledgement necessary because I'd literally bumped into him, nodded an impartial greeting, and stepped around him into the throng, which suddenly sprung back to life from suspended animation.

Out of the corner of my eye, I caught a silent exchange between Renee and Junior—Junior mimed a helpless apology, Renee stoically accepted the situation.

I'd known they were casual acquaintances, both socially and through their church, but had not realized that Junior and Renee had become particularly close, though their advanced pregnancies probably explained the sudden friendship.

That Renee knew about Stu's and my relationship—and was not particularly upset about it before she left him—was known only to Renee and me. How they'd come to terms with it after her return wasn't something Stu and I had discussed, given that the affair had ended pretty much at the same time. But as far as the room was concerned, I was a Home Wrecker and Renee was the Wronged Wife, and I would rather have set my feet on fire than make chit-chat with any of them.

Luckily, I didn't have to.

"Tory," Clay said loudly enough to trigger guilty conversations all around us. "I'm so glad you're here. I wanted to thank you for all the help you gave Junior this afternoon. I don't think she'd have gotten through it without you."

His statement was arguable, but his vote of confidence was gratefully received. Junior *had* been on the verge of breakdown this afternoon, though Annelise's death was the least of her worries.

I focused on Clay's face, studying it carefully, looking for traces of shame and guilt in his clear blue eyes and concerned expression. At this stage of my life, I ought to be able to recognize the symptoms of adultery in the dark, but all I saw in Clay's face was Clay the way I'd always known him: hearty, healthy, handsome, and as happy as possible under the circumstances.

If he was struggling to cope with the loss of a lover to suicide, he covered it masterfully.

I had to conclude that either Clay had not been having an affair or he'd been having them all along and I simply could not tell the difference. He was the same Clay I'd always known, and I could not bring myself to believe that he'd acted so shabbily.

Of course, I have a history of pulling the wool over my own eyes.

"When Jennifer called me, she said that you were there to help Junior when the awful news came this afternoon," Clay said. "I'm so happy you were with her."

A red-eyed Jennifer Swanhorst had been conversing with Clay in a corner when I'd made my less than graceful entrance. At the sound of her own name, she acknowledged my presence with a frosty nod and then turned to find her husband, who was loading his plate at the table.

Clay seemed blissfully unaware of the undercurrents in the room. He was either the most unobservant man in the world or the best actor.

"I don't think I helped Junior much," I said quietly and truthfully.

Jennifer had tearfully announced Annelise's death, the reaction to which had been stunned silence from everyone in the church. She'd gone on to say that preliminary conclusions were that death had resulted from an overdose of aspirin compounded by Annelise's own allergy to codeine.

I'd remembered the empty 222 bottle from Annelise's cloth bag, the one that had held codeine aspirin from Canada, and realized grimly that she'd left nothing to chance in her suicide attempt. If the aspirin hadn't done the trick, her own allergic reaction had taken care of the rest.

I also remember locking eyes with Meg, and the wide-eyed horror that spread across her face as the news of her friend's death finally sunk in.

She'd begun to wail and the rest of the group had instantly joined in a cacophony of sobs in assorted languages that echoed and reverberated throughout the church. Even Weasel would have believed their grief to be real.

Junior herself had done what she could to hustle me out

after Jennifer's announcement, preferring to deal with the weeping teenagers on her own. Any misapplied credit for help during the crisis must have come, erroneously, from Junior herself.

I wondered why she'd purposely given Clay the wrong impression.

I shot a furtive glance at Junior, but she was still talking to Renee McKee by the doorway. I didn't want to make eye contact with either of them so I looked away and out of the corner of my eye caught Stu glancing in my direction.

Making eye contact with him seemed just as unwise, so I turned brightly to Clay and asked, "What's going to happen now? I mean will the choir continue on with their tour?"

With a firm hand at the small of my back, Clay steered me toward the dining room table, picked up a paper plate, and handed it to me. "That's up in the air still. This afternoon the entire group wanted to go home, their own real homes, immediately, but they may change their minds after a night of thought. Glenda is trying to get a real consensus from the kids, and then she can make a decision about continuing on or not."

Glenda Harrison, still wearing the perfectly tailored outfit she'd had on earlier, but looking rumpled and exhausted, was standing near the sliding glass doors on the far side of the dining room table, talking earnestly with Meg and Jurgen, who amazingly was not videotaping the gathering.

They'd all shot unreadable looks at me when I came in and continued to send periodic puzzled glances in my direction.

I suppose it was obvious to their Lutheran radar that I didn't belong, that my outsider status was somehow visible to the True Elect. Either that or they didn't remember who I was, and were trying to fix me in their memories—it's not like we'd had any real conversations. Glenda had been too harried, too immersed in her performance as a Harried Former Miss America Runner-up, for introductions as the ambulance arrived, and I had not spoken directly to the Mad Cameraman.

"But regardless of what the choir decides, we'll be holding a memorial service at the church tomorrow morning," Clay said, filling my plate methodically with scoops of tuna noodle casserole and a square of lime Jell-O studded with pineapple chunks and mini-marshmallows. "Though none of us knew her well, Annelise deserves a respectful good-bye from the citizens of Delphi."

I thought about a girl miserable enough to have swallowed a lethal dose of aspirin while sitting in cafe in strange country, surrounded by her close friends and traveling companions. I thought about her suicide note and the awful accusation it held. I thought about the disappearance of that note and looked again at Clay Deibert's open, handsome, honest face, his clear blue eyes clouded by a deep sadness and the vestiges of exhaustion.

I studied him carefully and tried to be objective, but try as I might, I could not see in him the eyes of a monster. I didn't think he was perfect, incapable of making mistakes or inflicting pain. Clay's most attractive trait was the effort he put into being good because it was the right thing to do, not because it was part of his job description.

He was as human as the rest of us. And like the rest of us, he was probably capable of making entirely stupid mistakes, the consequences of which were unclear until it was too late to remedy the situation.

But I realized that in my heart of hearts, I would never believe him capable of molesting a young girl regardless of what that girl herself had written in her own suicide note. Regardless of what his own wife believed.

And I realized, as Neil had said already, that it would to be up to me to prove Clay's innocence.

The only way to do that would be to discover the real reason for Annelise's suicide.

31

Bag Lady

So, against my better judgment, against my common sense, and almost against my will, I was once again investigating a death. This happens many more times and I'll get to join the union.

Of course, my track record is not unblemished—granted I've unraveled a couple of puzzles, but not without false starts and certainly not without grave errors and misjudgments. And never without a great deal of soul searching as to what should ultimately be done with the information uncovered.

Usually I dig deeply in order to know who committed the unthinkable. This time I chose to dig because someone I know and trust was about to be accused of an act of which I did not believe him capable.

Of course the specific accusation could not come out against Clay without Annelise's suicide note, which Junior was still keeping hidden somewhere. As far as I knew, Annelise had not regained consciousness after passing out in the cafe, and therefore she'd not been able to repeat her charge to other, less discreet, audiences.

There was, however, a possibility that she'd confided in

some of the choir members, and I meant to talk to as many as I could before leaving Junior's house.

Not that they would tell me, a complete stranger and a foreigner at that, anything of a deep and personal nature. But I could at least test the radar that Neil was certain I possessed. Maybe I could catch an undercurrent—a lead on what had really been happening in Annelise's life. A clue as to why she would accuse a good man of an evil deed.

Unfortunately there's no set way to go about conducting such an investigation—no handbook available listing specific instructions for grilling the bereaved for clues so nebulous that I could not even name them. All I could do was talk. And listen. And observe.

Happens I have experience in all three.

So I stood in the corner by the dining room table, munching idly on carrot sticks and home-canned dill pickle spears from the plate that Clay had overloaded for me, as I watched the throng.

The first thing I noticed was that I was also being watched surreptitiously.

I automatically discounted the Delphi natives' stares and glares. They were watching me all right, but not because of Annelise or the choir. They were keeping an eye out just in case something *interesting* happened vis-à-vis Stu and Renee, a complication I'd managed to forget entirely in the last few moments, but which had livened up a routinely somber evening for all of them.

Determined not to provide any peripheral entertainment for the masses, I avoided eye contact with locals, except for Clay, who smiled occasionally in my direction.

Junior was still deep in conversation with Renee McKee and studiously ignoring me altogether. Renee kept her back to me, which, thank goodness, eliminated the possibility of our having to converse accidentally.

Stu was huddled with a small group of farmers, all of whom talked in low and serious voices, Styrofoam cups of coffee in one hand, and empty paper plates in the other. The few times I dared to glance his way, he'd not been looking mine, which was just as well. Though I was over being attracted to him, and the rare pangs of regret I'd felt at ending the relationship were long gone, I could still see very well from whence the desire had sprung.

Stu was medium height, medium build, with soft brown hair that was beginning to recede at the temples and the kind of weathered face sported by midwestern men who spent most of their working hours outdoors. He was generally well-liked, smarter than I gave him credit for, and quick to laugh. He wasn't *GQ* handsome, but he was good-looking enough for a confused widow to get herself in way over her head.

Though I'd never expected or even wanted him to leave his trim and pretty Minnesota-born wife, I was still caught off guard by proof, in the form of a pending second child, that it was just never going to happen.

By then, of course, our affair was widely known, and it was far too late for me to keep the involvement under wraps. If we intended to continue living in the same town, then both Stu and I, as well as Renee, would just have to get used to being in the same room together occasionally. And we'd just have pretend not to notice how closely we were observed by our fellow citizens.

Delphi being what it is, unexpected public meetings were inevitable. It was just as well that I had other things on my mind at the moment.

Like trying to understand why the very sad choir members, who seemed mostly confused by this calorie-laden American tribute to the dead, also sent curious and puzzled glances in my direction. One or two, I could have ignored. But they all did it.

The kids milled, weaving in and out among the natives, at whom they nodded impartially. Occasionally they would engage in short somber exchanges with people I assumed were their host families, each of whom urged refilling barely touched paper plates. But mostly they formed small clumps from which they eyed the rest of us, me in particular, as though we were alien creatures.

They were the walking wounded, exhausted and bleary

eyed—blindsided by both the method and the madness of Annelise's departure. They didn't weep openly and there certainly was no wailing—in fact the whole room spoke only in hushed, funereal tones—but there was no doubt whatsoever that the remaining choir members were numb with a grief genuine enough to satisfy even discerning observers like Weasel Cleaver.

They weren't the only ones.

Glenda Harrison was still well put-together, an attractive not-quite-middle-aged woman whose her hair wasn't disheveled, whose makeup was faded but intact, whose clothes weren't dirty or wrinkled, but who was just as obviously struggling with a crisis far beyond anything she'd anticipated. I suppose being a Miss America third-runner-up did not prepare one for the suicide of a minor left in your care.

She smiled weakly at the assorted condolences as they were offered, but she was plainly cresting the leading edge of a breakdown.

I even felt sorry for her, though I rarely extend sympathy to pushy former beauty queens. I expect she'd taken what seemed to be a cushy job, shepherding a photogenic group of youngsters around the countryside, in the hopes of parlaying the gig into even grander PR/media-style adventures.

I also expect that her job prospects had plummeted the minute Annelise flat-lined.

Who would hire a chaperone who couldn't keep her charges alive, for crying out loud? An accident was one thing, a suicide another entirely. The rest of her career would now be filled with condescending clucks and second-guessing about which distress signals she'd chosen to ignore. Which symptoms she'd disregarded. What supervisory snafu had lead to the preventable death of one so young.

Since Glenda was standing nearby, still deep in conversation with Meg and Jurgen, I figured they were a good starting point for oblique questioning.

I sorted through conversational gambits, but rejected them all as over the top. I may not be socially correct on most occasions, but I do know that it is not the done thing to dissect the deceased's sex life at the wake, at least not directly. And even Neil would not expect me to grill Glenda on new career options.

Luckily, I was saved the trouble of working out an opening line.

Meg spotted me, tapped Glenda on the shoulder, and glanced in my direction. Glenda turned and with a small, artificial smile said, "Ah yes," in an *I'm In Charge Here* voice that was decidedly louder than the one she'd been using to whisper with Meg and Jurgen. "You're Ms. Bauer from the cafe, aren't you?"

I allowed as how that was the case while at the same time wondering why she was suddenly talking loud enough for half the room to hear.

"Oh good, I thought that was you," Glenda continued, smoothing back her hair. "I wanted to ask you something."

She still had the volume cranked up and everyone else made like they were auditioning for an E. F. Hutton commercial. Conversation didn't exactly grind to a halt, but all ears were trained in our direction.

"Okay," I said warily.

"I believe we left some of our dear Annelise's personal belongings in your cafe during the confusion this afternoon," Glenda declared.

I blinked. The only thing belonging to Annelise that might still be in the cafe was the suicide note that Junior had either spirited away or stashed in some corner.

"Uh . . . um . . ." I said, sounding like an idiot. And a guilty one at that. "Not that I know of. I mean, I don't think there was anything of hers left in the cafe, but I can check tomorrow morning for you if you like."

Judging by the puzzled expressions and whispered asides, no else one in the room knew what Glenda was driving at either, but they were surely entertained by the conversation. Even Junior had paused in her confab with Renee McKee to listen.

No one outside of Del, Junior, Neil, and I even knew that there had *been* a suicide note. And though that's fully three more people than can actually keep a secret in a small town, I was pretty sure that none of them had confided in Glenda Harrison in the interim.

I wasn't even that sure that keeping the note a secret was a good idea. It was probably not only wrong, it was illegal to boot.

Clearing Clay was one thing, obstructing the law was another altogether.

I opened my mouth to blather some more. I wasn't sure exactly what I would say but I wasn't about to mention the note. At least not while the whole town was listening. But I didn't get a chance to say anything.

"I can understand your confusion about the matter," Glenda said patronizingly, regaining even more of the attitude that had set my teeth on edge earlier. "In fact, with the hubbub going on around you, and the rarity of this sort of tragedy in your little town cafes . . ."

Someone snorted.

Whatever Glenda had been doing in the last six months, like Weasel, she hadn't exactly kept abreast of Delphi news.

A small frown crossed her elegant features, causing her brow to wrinkle momentarily, and then smooth out again. "At any rate, you rural people can't be accustomed to such unpleasant discoveries . . ."

This time someone actually chuckled.

Glenda flashed a puzzled look in the general direction of the crowd, leaned in, took my arm, and finally lowered her voice. "At any rate, I am certain that Annelise's cloth shoulder bag, the one she always carried, was left behind in your cafe this afternoon. I'd like it back as soon as possible as we're gathering her personal belongings to ship back to her parents."

I finally got her drift.

She wasn't talking about the suicide note at all.

The last time I'd seen Annelise's bag, Junior was carrying it out the door. It was now somewhere at the church, and not my responsibility.

The relief was enormous.

"Ah," I said, nodding. "Annelise's bag. Well, you see . . ."

"Yes, the bag . . ." Junior had materialized suddenly at my elbow and startled me with an interruption. "Yes. That bag is definitely still at the cafe. It was still there right on the table when I left this afternoon, isn't that right, Tory?"

Junior gazed at me with a wide-eyed innocence so genuine that a bystander might have thought that she was asking me a legitimate question.

But I knew better. Behind her eyes was the steely glint of a battlefield general issuing a direct order to lie on her behalf.

32

Inspector Gadget

An outside observer would very quickly get the impression that I enjoy lying, seeing as how I do it so often. They'd have a hard time believing that I prefer to go through life without weaving any tangled webs at all. It's not that I'm morally aghast at practicing to deceive, I just learned a long time ago that it's too damn hard to keep all of the stories straight.

But sometimes life forces you into corners and gives you no other choice. Or maybe it's pushy pregnant cousins who do the maneuvering.

In either case, sometimes ya just gotta lie.

"In fact," Junior said, placing a companionable arm around my shoulders, "it happens that I have to go by the cafe early tomorrow morning anyway, why don't I just pick the bag up for you and bring it back here? That'll save you a trip out into the cold when you have so many other details that need your attention during this terrible time."

I didn't dare look directly at Junior because I would not have been able to maintain the pretense that Junior ever, and I do mean *ever,* darkened the cafe door early in the morning, especially to save someone else the trouble of going out in the cold. So I just nodded enthusiastically at Glenda, signaling that it was fine with me if Junior wanted to drop in and pick up Annelise's bag, which Junior and I both well knew wasn't at the cafe anyway.

Junior beamed an entirely phony smile and gave me a vigorous shoulder jostle.

"I'll just drop in, say seven-ish and pick it up then, okay?" Junior continued genially.

"Well, actually, I need to do a few things in town early myself," Glenda said, smiling right back at Junior. "So I wouldn't dream of forcing you out of your lovely, warm home on my account. It won't be any trouble at all for me to pick up the bag in the morning."

If I hadn't been smack in the center of this little drama, I would have enjoyed (as the rest of the room surely did) the battle of wills between these two women. It's true that Junior had never been a former Miss America third runner-up, but it's equally true that surviving the loss of a major beauty pageant was no preparation for a tug-o'-war against Super Minister's Wife.

I have no idea why she didn't tell Glenda outright that the bag was at the church, but it was too late for the truth to set us free now. And it was too late for Junior to prevail.

"You just take care of yourself." Glenda patted Junior on the cheek, a move that would have netted her a bloody stub if she hadn't been performing in front of most of Clay's congregation. "And I'll get the bag in the morning. Thank you so very much. You small-town people are truly the best."

Before Junior could protest, Glenda turned away and gathered a pale Meg and an even paler Jurgen, and herded them toward the table, urging them to *eat, it would help to keep up their strength.*

Junior stood, stunned for a moment, watching Glenda's back, logging the curious glances Meg and Jurgen sent our way, ignoring the curious glances of the rest of the room. She then pasted on a public smile and grabbed my arm.

"Come on," she whispered fiercely through clenched teeth. "We need to talk."

She dragged me through the crowd and back down the

hallway, engaging in chit-chat and accepting small condolences and deflecting inquiring glances with ease while at the same time making a beeline for the laundry room that was near the back door.

"There," she said, closing the door firmly behind us.

"Indeed," I said, taking in the narrow room, which was as neat and tidy as the rest of Junior's house. An almond-color Maytag set stood next to a water heater along one wall, while a sink with a small vanity and medicine cabinet, a toilet, and several empty clothes baskets took up the other. A wooden shelf above the washer held a couple different kinds of detergent, an open box of dryer sheets, and a lint roller. The back of the door was filled with coat hooks, all presently occupied.

The space between the washer and the sink was barely big enough for a nonpregnant maneuvering, and there was certainly no room for me to stand, so I sat on the toilet lid and squinted up at Junior.

"You wanna tell me what the hell is going on?"

I hoped she would condense because I not only had questions to ask other people, but the dryer was running merrily so the room was hot and stuffy.

"Listen," she said briskly as though I hadn't spoken at all. "I need you to go to the church tonight. Now. I want you to get that damn bag and take it over to the cafe so that Glenda can pick it up there in the morning."

"Why?"

I didn't just mean *why me?* Or *why now?* Or *why did you lie?* I also wanted to know why she had taken the bag with her in the first place. And why, if she had taken the bag, was she suddenly willing to turn it over to Glenda?

"Because if you don't get the bag to the cafe tonight, it won't be there for her in the morning," Junior said, being obtuse on purpose.

"I understand that," I said sharply. "But why don't you just tell her where it is and let her pick it up there? Why do *I* have to go tromping out in the snow trying to undo your mistakes?"

And a mistake it had been—hiding the suicide note, taking the bag, and then pretending not to know the whereabouts of either made obverse sense since Junior thought that her husband was somehow involved with the dead girl. But it took very little rationality to know that both would have to come to light sooner or later.

"I *can't* tell Glenda that I took it," Junior said miserably. "When all of"—she hesitated— "it . . . comes out, it's going to be awful. Devastating. I hoped that I could keep all of that *other* stuff under wraps. But I realized later that wasn't possible. And I also realized that it'd look even worse for Clay if it seemed like I interfered. It won't help either of us if anyone thinks I covered up, or worse yet tampered with, evidence."

Which made perfect sense, except for one thing. "Why the hell didn't you figure that out in the first place?" I demanded.

"Because I didn't think she'd die," Junior said simply.

The power in her statement stopped me short.

None of us thought Annelise was going to die.

We all thought she'd be whisked off in the ambulance, magically relieved of the toxic substances, and made good as new, ready to continue with the tour.

If it was hard for adults to wrap their minds around the fact that Annelise's life was truly hanging in the balance, it was no wonder that the kids hadn't shown enough grief to satisfy Weasel.

We'd all thought that Annelise would live happily ever after, and we'd been wrong.

"I thought I could talk to her when she came out of it," Junior said softly. "I thought I could get to the bottom of her story. Find the truth. Salvage something from this mess without sacrificing my whole life. And Clay's.

"So I took her bag, intending to go through it, to learn what I could about her, and maybe even find out why she'd said the things she did. I hadn't had a chance to do that yet when Jennifer came in and told us the news. Then things got hectic and by the time I realized that the bag should be put back in the cafe, you were already gone and there were too many people around for me to make the transfer myself."

She looked at me, pleading. "So you have to do it for me. I tried to put Glenda off. I would have gotten up early, come into town and got the damn bag myself and trotted it over to the cafe. But you saw how she was. There's no way I can do it in the morning now. And there's no way I can leave and do it tonight. There are too many people here; they'd notice I was gone. And I'll never get away later."

The dryer buzzed and Junior bent over, opened the door, and pulled out a load of hot, white cotton sheets and wearily began to fold them.

"I can't leave yet," I said. "I have stuff to finish here first."

She stopped in mid-fold, sweat beading on her forehead. "What do you mean *stuff to finish here?* I'd think you'd be thrilled for the opportunity to get out quietly."

Under ordinary circumstances, she would have been right—leaving McKee Central would have been my highest priority. But these weren't ordinary circumstances.

"There are people I still want to talk to and this may be my only chance," I said. "I want to talk to Meg. I want to talk to Jurgen. And I really want to talk to Glenda some more. They'll be leaving town soon."

"Why in the world do you want to talk to them?" She smoothed and patted the sheets, satisfied with their precise folds and corners.

I thought about repeating Neil's instructions as well my own silent decision to help prove Clay's innocence, but decided that Junior would not appreciate my having told her secrets to Neil.

Besides, I was beginning to feel the need to know the truth, whatever the truth was. When I was with Clay, I believed with all my heart that he could not have done such terrible things. But Junior's belief in her husband's guilt was contagious. Five minutes with her in a hot and cramped laundry room and I was ready to believe him capable *and* culpable.

"There's more going on here than just Annelise's death, remember?" I finally said. "I want to know what really happened with Weasel this afternoon. He swore up and down that Meg stole his clothes and his van. I know she denies it, but he could have been telling the truth."

Junior grimaced as though the mere mention of Weasel's name was painful.

"And Jurgen may have a lead on Annelise's real life. He's the official recorder of the tour; I'll bet he knows more details than anyone. He may know who she was sleeping with."

"We already know who she was sleeping with," Junior said bitterly.

"No we don't," I said. "All we know is that someone had sex on those sheets. We don't even know for sure that it was Annelise, much less Clay. It could have been Jurgen. It could have been anyone who's been in and out of your house since you washed the sheets last. In fact, the bedding should be tested. That might be the only way to know for sure who was and was not involved."

"Too late," Junior said, patting the sheets again.

"Oh God, Junior, you didn't," I said, realizing what she'd just been doing.

"Of course I did. And no one would ever question my washing the sheets either. The girl is dead. The room had to be cleaned."

"But you might have destroyed evidence," I pointed out.

"Yes, I might have."

"But you might have destroyed the only thing that could exonerate Clay."

"I had no choice, Tory. In fact it would have looked odd if I hadn't stripped the bed immediately."

She had a point. Junior was a fanatic about propriety and cleanliness. Leaving the sheets on the bed would have raised eyebrows.

"What about the rest?"

"The rest of what?"

"The rest of the sheets," I said testily. "Have you washed them? Did you run your little beeper gadget over them to see if anyone else in the house has been engaging in extracurricular activities?"

Junior turned and looked at me. "No I haven't. That's a good idea. I'll do that in the morning as soon as everyone clears out."

"And . . ." I hesitated, not exactly sure how to proceed with my next indelicate suggestion. "How about Clay's . . .

um . . . underwear? Or have you washed them already too?"

Her face wrinkled in disgust. "He's still wearing the same clothes he put on when he left last night. Besides, I'd never do that, Tory."

"Why the hell not? You already believe that he's fooling around. Run your magic machine over them and find out for sure. Unless the two of you have . . ."

"Jesus Tory, I'm about ready to pop. I am not in the mood, and Clay hasn't come near me for two months . . ."

We both paused. The conversation had suddenly turned too personal, and the naked pain on Junior's face far too real to continue.

"Anyway," I said, looking away. "I wanted to talk to those three, and anyone else I could get hold of tonight, just to pick up impressions."

"Well, I can do that for you," Junior said. "I'll have plenty of opportunity to talk to Jurgen and Glenda. And I can talk to Renee about Meg."

"Renee?"

There was only one.

"Meg is staying with them. Maybe she noticed some unusual behavior. I can talk to Stu too. Unless you want to."

"God no," I said, shivering. "And will you please talk to Clay? The best thing would be for you to sit down with him and have an honest conversation tonight after everyone goes home. He can either clear this up, or you can face it together."

"I'll try. But I bet that he drums up another excuse to leave the room. Maybe even the house. He hasn't slept in the same bed with me for over a week. There's no reason to think that'll change now."

I would never have thought I'd feel empathy for Junior. But I remembered nights alone and empty beds and horrible suspicions and pain so acute that my vision clouded. And I remembered finally giving up my illusions, accepting what everyone else could see clearly but I'd continued to deny.

I didn't wish that on anyone. Even Junior.

"You know, it's *all* going to come out sooner or later," I said softly.

By *all*, I was including the suicide note, which Junior had yet to mention but which would have to be produced tomorrow at the latest.

"I know," Junior said. "But let us retain a little dignity. At least for tonight?"

This was as close to begging as Junior would allow herself. It would hurt nothing, in the forensic sense, for me to return the bag to the cafe for Glenda to pick up in the morning. No one need ever know that it had left the site. No one need ever know that I'd returned it.

And in doing so, I could let Junior pretend for just a little longer that everything was okay.

It was small comfort, but small comforts were all she had these days.

"Okay," I said finally. "Give me the keys."

33

I Sing the Body Selectric

It wasn't *exactly* like breaking and entering. I had a key after all, and express permission from the key holder to enter the premises. That the key holder wasn't technically able to extend formal invitations was a moot point.

At least until lately, Clay and Junior had been a team, and Junior's orders were always considered as carrying the weight of two. And since she'd pretty much ordered me to enter Clay's office in the dark of a cold winter night, I felt only the slightest twinge of conscience.

And that was exacerbated by the fact that I really didn't belong in a church building under any circumstances, given my basically irreverent view of organized religion. So even though the temporal authorities could not really quarrel with my being where I was, some not-so-temporal ones just might.

It was with that in mind that, even though I was obviously alone in the annex, I tiptoed along the industrial carpet that blanketed the hallway and was careful to make no noise beyond that of my own beating heart, which to my ears at least echoed madly.

I'd been able to sneak out of Junior's house unobserved except by Jennifer Swanhorst, who'd been about to tap on the laundry/bathroom door when Junior and I emerged. She'd given each of us a questioning glance, but since she'd never been one to make pleasantries with adulteresses, I was able to get by with just a nod as I began to reassemble my voluminous outerwear.

Junior herself slid past us with a generic mumble. Without even a parting glance, she'd rejoined the throng as though all was as right with her world as could be, given that she was in her third trimester and trying to deal with the oh-so-tragic suicide of such a lovely young girl.

I'd been slipping into my boots, after having already buttoned up a sweater, arranged earmuffs, wrapped a muffler around my head, and zipped up my coat, when Jennifer remerged.

"Do you think Junior is all right?" she'd asked me as I pulled on my gloves.

"Junior's a brick," I answered, meaning it. She drove me crazy most of the time, but I was beginning to admire her against my will. It was a grudging admiration, but it was admiration just the same.

Jennifer had chewed her lip and peered down the hallway. "I know that Clay is worried about her," she said more to herself than me. "And the baby and all. And he's been under such a strain lately."

"Haven't we all," I'd said, deliberately cutting short her sudden interest in chit-chat by opening the back door. The resultant blast of arctic air had driven Jennifer back into the warmth of the kitchen.

The blast of arctic air would have driven me back too, if I'd had any choice in the matter. Instead, I hoped to discharge this long day's last obligation as quickly as possible, and to crawl back into the warmth of Neil's house.

I'd already decided to take Annelise's bag home with me rather than tromping it across the street to the cafe. In fact that was one of the reasons I'd agreed to Junior's plan.

I didn't have the cafe keys with me anyway—Del and Alanna had closed this afternoon. Besides, that would give

Neil and me a chance to do what Junior had not—paw through Annelise's belongings to look for clues to her life.

Since Glenda wasn't coming by the cafe until seven-ish, and I had to open at five-thirty, taking the bag with me made perfect sense even without ulterior motives.

My motive at the moment, however, was to grab the damn bag and get out of the silent and disapproving Lutheran church annex.

The heat had been turned down for the night and the drive had not been long enough to warm the cab of Neil's truck and my hands were still cold. So without taking my gloves off, I fumbled a bit and unlocked Clay's office outer door and entered. Since the outer office windows faced several other buildings, including the Feed and Seed Store and post office, I didn't turn on the lights, preferring to avoid undue attention (Junior's permission or no).

I stumbled my way in the dark through the outer area where the computer and church secretary usually sat, and into the inner sanctum, which had a separate door that wasn't locked.

Clay's real office, his home away from home, was a small, airless interior room with no windows. It was pitch-black except for the red light on the little TV/VCR combo that sat on a rolling stand in front of the bookshelves. I could safely flick the light switch without fear of being seen from the outside. The fluorescent lights hummed to life, illuminating Clay's office, which was neat but not quite as compulsively arranged as his home.

The smallish desktop was cluttered with stacks of papers, church flyers, a telephone, a framed picture of all four Deibert children, a half-eaten Snickers bar, and smack in the middle, taking up most of the room, an old behemoth of an IBM typewriter.

Though Junior and the secretary were computer-savvy, I knew that Clay preferred to write his sermons first in longhand on yellow legal pads. He'd then type them up himself, clacking happily away on the noisiest electric typewriter this side of the new millennium.

Junior and Jennifer, who filled in occasionally when neither Junior nor Clay's secretary could make it, had both tried mightily to get him to upgrade, but he'd stubbornly clung to his old tools.

In fact, a piece of paper was rolled into the machine. Evidently Clay had returned to his office after his ice fishing/hospital visit, probably to begin work on tomorrow's memorial service, slated for mid-morning.

Which was neither here nor there.

I'd hear what Clay planned to say on Annelise's behalf soon enough and did not need a preview nearly as much as I needed to do my job and get the hell out of his office.

I'd never suffered from claustrophobia, never been afraid of the dark or being alone. But I was acutely aware of being the only human being in the large building complex. The vast silence beyond was oppressive and vaguely frightening.

Suddenly the office walls seemed to close in on me—the emptiness of the annex and the attached church raised the hairs on the back of my neck.

Shaking off my nerves, I quickly strode to the tall green metal storage cupboard where Junior said she'd stashed Annelise's bag on the upper shelf behind the big box of educational VCR tapes that they kept on hand for the little kids' Sunday school classes. She didn't figure anyone would spot it up there even if they were rooting around in the lower part of the cabinet.

I pulled the double doors open, and knew instantly that Junior would have been right.

She'd shoved the bag so far back into the dark recesses of the shelf that only a hint of green striped cloth showed at eye level. You'd have to have known what you were looking for even to have seen it.

But given the present circumstances and the current contents of the cupboard, it didn't seem likely that anyone would have noticed the bag, even if it had been right there on the front of the shelf.

Even if there'd been a label that announced in bright bold

lettering: *Here's the bag Junior took from the cafe.*

No one would ever have noticed that bag, no matter where it was, because the only thing anyone would see when they opened the cupboard doors was Weasel Cleaver's lifeless body stuffed into the large lower cavity.

34

Weasel, We Hardly Knew Ye

The notion that there are some people who need killing pretty much went by the wayside about the same time it stopped being okay to slap your wife up if she got a little mouthy. We as a society have basically decreed that everyone, no matter how often they prove otherwise, is worthy of respect. We tell ourselves that no one is inherently bad. We declare that bad behavior can be fixed with equal doses of national self-esteem coupled with a zero-tolerance policy as regards plastic cutlery in schoolrooms, and blanket prescriptions for Ritalin.

Everyone's a victim, no one is responsible, and we're all one big happy family until something goes drastically wrong, at which time we react the way we always do: with genuine confusion as to how it could happen to us instead of to the ones who really deserve ill fortune.

We all speak one philosophy while privately believing another. I believe they call that hypocrisy. And I'm no different.

Though I'd never have said it out loud, if someone had told me this morning that Weasel Cleaver had been killed in a jailhouse brawl, my first, and honest, reaction would have been: *Couldn't happen to a nicer guy.*

Don't get me wrong, I would have chided Del for saying that very thing, as she would have immediately. I would have frowned at Eldon McKee's rueful chuckle. I would have reminded everyone in the cafe that Weasel was a human being like the rest of us and he deserved to be mourned, all the while thinking, *Good riddance to bad rubbish.*

But somewhere during a long and confusing day, I had begun to see Weasel as more than just a supremely annoying carbon-based biped. I don't know where or how it happened, and I certainly would not have believed it if anyone had told me, but I'd not only started to see him as a fellow traveler, but, Lord help me, I even started to like the little creep so long as he kept his pants on.

It's not like I wanted to be friends with him or anything, I'd just thought I detected a spark of humanity in him, and I'd have liked that spark to have been kindled.

But even if I hadn't come to that conclusion, even if I'd wanted nothing more than to see Weasel Cleaver's back as he left town, I would, after today, at least have wanted him to stay alive awhile longer.

Which task he, unfortunately, didn't quite manage.

And even more than any wishes I would have spared for Weasel, I would have selfishly wished that someone, anyone, else had found him.

"Jeez Weasel," I said sadly out loud, though even as I spoke, I realized that I was talking to a dead man in a dark and deserted church. "Who the hell did you piss off this time?"

I belatedly realized that the church might not be all that deserted. I froze, standing perfectly still as I listened, trying to hear over the sound of my own beating heart.

As far as I could tell, there were no stealthy footfalls, no heavy breathing, no hockey-masked mass murderers waiting for me in the dark with an upraised axe.

I tiptoed carefully toward the doorway, noting that the outer office door was still open, a good sign. I flipped the light switch off and listened some more. St. John's Lutheran Church and annex, a place that had been specifically designed for acoustic reverberation, was silent.

Dead silent.

I decided to proceed on the assumption that I was alone in the building with Weasel, and that whoever'd stuffed him in the cupboard was long gone, waiting for morning and the news of the fateful discovery.

Which, given the usual course of things, would have been made by Clay Deibert.

I wondered, amazed at my own calm contemplation, if that had any significance.

Weasel had left the church sometime during the few moments that the rest of us had been gazing out the door at his van across the street. He was gone before we got the news of Annelise's death, which mostly seemed irrelevant to his situation and condition.

Or was it?

Did the death of a middle-aged ex-con have any connection at all to the suicide of a young foreign girl?

As nice as it would have been to tie the two events together neatly, there didn't seem to be any connection between the two occurrences beyond their happening on the same day. It was no more relevant than the fact that I'd had to deal with both.

Life was full of nasty coincidences. At least my life was. And unless I had a very good reason to think otherwise, I was going to assume that the two events were unrelated.

Annelise had purposely taken an overdose of aspirin laced with codeine, to which she was allergic.

Weasel had not stuffed himself onto the lower shelf of the supply cabinet in the office of the reverend of the Delphi Lutheran church.

One was self-inflicted, the other was not.

And it was the other that concerned me at the moment.

I ran through the sequence of this afternoon's events.

It was obvious that Weasel had either left the church and returned later only to be killed, or he'd been dispatched earlier, somewhere else on the premises, and brought to this spot and hidden after everyone else left for the night.

I tried to remember if Junior had mentioned exactly when she'd crammed Annelise's bag behind the videocassette box—had it been before Weasel disappeared, before we'd heard the news of Annelise's death?

Or had she returned to the office later, after the choir had dispersed, after the church was deserted and empty, to hide the bag?

Whenever she'd done it, she certainly would have noticed a body crammed onto the lower shelf of the cupboard. And if she'd seen a body, I would have expected her to have brought up the subject sometime during our little laundry room conversation.

Unless, of course, Junior had killed Weasel herself and then engineered my return to make this discovery.

Common sense told me that even if a pregnant Junior was capable of murder (and given her behavior lately, I wouldn't have taken any bets), she wouldn't have been able to drag the body and cram it into a small space.

I had to believe that Junior'd had no clue to what I'd find in her husband's office, if for no other reason than that I also believed that Junior wanted desperately to keep the present location of that damn bag a secret.

Which, given the situation, was hardly likely to continue.

Or was it?

The moonlight reflected off the snow outside, shining in through the outer office windows, making it bright enough to see even with the lights off.

I stood in the silent room and looked at my hands.

My gloved hands.

It was cold, and I'd not taken the gloves off, which meant that I'd not left any fresh fingerprints. No one but Junior would know that I'd been here, and she wouldn't tell. I could quietly sneak right back out of the office, lock all the doors, leave the church, and pretend I'd gone straight home from Junior's.

I'd taken the precaution of parking Neil's truck behind the bar, rather than in front of the church, so as to avoid undue notice. If anyone saw the truck, they'd think that Neil was having a drink, or that he'd lent his truck to someone else. Both were likely scenarios.

I'd entered the back annex door, also to avoid notice. No

one would ever know I'd been here and my leaving Weasel exactly where he was for the night would not hurt him.

With the exception of opening the cupboard door, I'd not disturbed the crime scene and therefore I'd not hurt any future police investigation. I could leave right now and concoct a story for Junior that she'd have no choice but to believe.

I truly could walk away with no one the wiser.

It was a plan, and a good one at that. I'd already been involved in more than my share of death during the last year. I'd already done more investigating than I ever wanted to do, and I certainly didn't want to take on another quest.

But I knew, even as I formulated my escape plan, that however much I was tempted to play ostrich, I wouldn't do it.

I knew that I'd call the police.

And with a sinking heart, I knew that I'd do whatever I could to restore a little dignity to Weasel Cleaver's death, if not his life, and help Junior in the process if at all possible.

But first, I needed to talk to someone.

I looked at my gloved hands one more time and picked up the phone.

35

All You Have To Do Is Call

We all know that there is nothing certain except death and taxes. Every lit student in the United States knows that home is the place where, when you go there, they have to take you in. Any James Taylor fan understands that winter, spring, summer, or fall, help is just a phone call away.

And I firmly hoped that while friends won't let friends drive drunk, *real* friends just might help you hide the bodies.

Metaphorically speaking anyway.

"I'm not sure this is such a good idea, Tory," Neil whispered from Clay's inner office doorway. He was more than nervous, he was downright spooked.

Of course, he didn't have quite as much experience in these situations as me. And he definitely wasn't thrilled about being there. But despite his misgivings, he'd come as I'd requested. Just like I knew he would.

"You don't have to whisper," I said softly. "There isn't anyone here except us."

I'd made sure of that while I waited for Neil to arrive, tiptoeing from room to room, listening at doorways, opening the few that were unlocked. My eyes had adjusted to the dark and I could see fairly well in the dim hallways. I could also hear fairly well—and unless we were about to be set on by intruders who could hold their breaths indefinitely, we truly were alone in the building.

Just Neil Pascoe, me, and a dead guy.

No wonder Neil was unsettled.

I wasn't all that calm myself, but for some reason I didn't want Neil to know just how upset I was. Not that I wanted to give him the impression that I *liked* spending time with dead people, but I also didn't want to go all girlie and weak in the knees.

"Jesus," he said, still whispering. "How can you be so calm?"

"I'm faking it," I said. "And the quicker we get finished here, the quicker we can leave so I can have a breakdown."

"You really think we should do this?" he asked, shivering. He'd walked the four blocks from his house to the church along the back alley, as per my directions, and even dressed for a South Dakota winter outing, he'd gotten chilled to the bone.

"Not really," I said, being honest. "That's why I wanted you here."

"Yeah, you just wanted an accomplice," he said with a weak chuckle. "Someone to go to jail with you when we get caught destroying evidence at the scene of a crime."

"They won't send us to the same place anyway," I said, "so we'd best not get caught." Even in the dark, I could see the skepticism in Neil's eyes. "Well, we're not actually tampering with anything. We're not going to move or alter or change anything, so we're not technically destroying evidence. We won't leave any fingerprints, the snow by the back entrance was trampled before I got here tonight, and any tracks we make on the carpet will dry and disappear by morning. No one will ever know that we were here. Besides, all we're doing is very carefully looking at it all before we go home and make what I hope will be an untraceable anonymous call to the police."

"What do you mean, *we're not removing anything?* What about the bag?"

"Well, that," I said.

"Yeah, that," he said, closing the inner office door and flicking the switch back on. I think he wanted to remind me exactly what we were doing.

And who was in the office with us.

I had to fight the urge to duck even though I knew that no one would be able to see us in the windowless inner office. But after I'd wandered in the dark for the last half-hour, the harsh light was so bright that it hurt my eyes. I could not bear to look at what it illuminated clearly.

Obviously feeling the same way, Neil had leaned back against the inner office door jamb and crossed his arms. When he first arrived, he'd stepped into Clay's office, taken a quick squint at Weasel in the dark, mostly to assure himself that I wasn't losing my mind, and then he'd retreated to the doorway and held his position.

Not that I blamed him.

I'd hovered in the general area behind Clay's desk. Close enough to Weasel to acknowledge his presence without actually having to look anywhere near him. It seemed like a Big Brave Girl sort of compromise.

"Well, the bag wasn't *supposed* to be here to begin with," I reasoned. "And since it's still exactly where Junior said it'd be, we can assume that whoever put Weasel here didn't see it. Besides which, we already agreed that Junior had nothing to do with Weasel's death, so the bag should be irrelevant. Right?"

This was why I'd wanted him with me—to serve as a sounding board and to point out obvious inconsistencies or errors in my logic.

"Unless whoever killed Weasel planted something in the bag as well," Neil said softly.

I turned and looked at him. "But they wouldn't know that the bag was there, would they?"

"Depends," Neil said, shrugging. "Junior didn't tell anyone that she had the bag, but that doesn't mean that no one saw her with it. And that doesn't mean that the killer didn't spot it, and recognize it. And tamper with it."

"But there'd be no point in tying the two deaths together.

Weasel had nothing to do with Annelise, and she was gone before he died. I just don't see where there's a connection."

"I didn't necessarily mean that Weasel knew Annelise," Neil said. "Maybe the killer knew both of *them.*"

"But only one person knew them both—" I said, then stopped.

"Meg," we said together.

"You think *she* really could have done it?" I asked, a little breathless.

"I have yet to make the young lady's acquaintance," Neil said. "And we don't even know how Weasel died." From our vantage point, there was no visible trauma, no strategically inserted knives, no blood, nothing but a body in a very unusual place. Neither of us was willing to shift him in order to do an inspection, which was just as well. The police would surely frown if we did. "But we can't afford to rule it out. He did say that she'd stolen his van and clothing."

"And the rest of the choir swears that she was rehearsing all afternoon," I reminded Neil.

"Well someone was obviously lying, or deeply mistaken. And since Weasel is dead, I'm disposed to take his version of the events a bit more seriously than I would have otherwise."

I thought about that for a moment. I'd never completely discounted Weasel's version of how the afternoon had unraveled, even in the face of seemingly incontrovertible eyewitness testimony.

He'd been so adamant. And so angry.

Weasel Cleaver was many things, but a thespian he wasn't. I would swear that he'd been genuinely angry at Meg. But I would have also sworn that she was completely surprised and confused by his anger.

"Damn," I said out loud.

"No shit," Neil agreed.

"So what do we do then?"

He crossed his arms and looked at me seriously. He was a true and loyal friend who'd swallowed his entirely reasonable doubts and objections and tromped in the subzero cold to help me do something he plainly wished I would not attempt. It would be very easy to love Neil Pascoe.

"My first choice," he said, "would be to call the police right here and now. But since you've vetoed that option, I say we take that bag back to my house right now with the proviso that if we find anything, anything at all, that ties these two deaths together, we turn it over to the authorities with a full explanation and take our lumps."

I wasn't thrilled with the notion of giving myself up. Or with tattling Junior's secrets. One of the reasons I had resisted calling the police to begin with centered around trying to help Junior, whose marital problems had no connection to Weasel.

"Okay," I said, slowly sinking into Clay's swivel chair, hoping mightily that we could pull this off without the need for formal confessions. "Howzabout we grab the bag, and then—"

I was about to suggest that we commence step two of my basically illegal and probably foolish plan, but in order to avoid looking at Weasel at near eye level less than five feet away, I instead glanced at the typewriter on Clay's desk.

And read what was typed on the paper rolled into it.

36

QWERTYUIOP

The only D I ever got was in typing.

Mostly school was easy for me, I cranked out A's and B's without even thinking about it, and the worst I ever got was a C in physics and that's mostly because I don't like math and I didn't work very hard. So it was a complete and total shock to my system to do so badly in typing, especially since I was really trying.

I concentrated. I strained. Mother even bought me a portable typewriter for Christmas that year so I could practice at home. But nothing helped because the whole grade rested on timed typing tests, one taken per class, with the top three test grades comprising the whole quarter mark. Sounds like a piece of cake, right?

And certainly everyone else seemed to catch on quickly. Even the football players and the greasers tippy-tapped their way to an A in the first two weeks of the quarter. Me, I'd start sweating the minute I entered the classroom.

It didn't matter that I could type just fine when writing letters or term papers, I could not pass those damn timed writings. Any more than five errors in a given amount of time resulted in a failure. I was lucky not to have six or seven typos, and the few times I had fewer, I always missed one or two during the self-correct. Failure to properly proof a timed writing dropped the grade even more. I only pulled a D in the course because the teacher took pity and didn't flunk me outright.

That experience, my first exposure to true failure, left me with a lasting and permanent distaste for keyboards of any kind. Even two decades beyond my shame, the fear of not being able to measure up makes me freeze anytime I'm even near a typewriter.

To compensate, I pretend they don't exist; they simply fall into my own personal blind spot. Unfortunately, as much as I dislike typing machines or reminders of my failings, I liked looking directly at a dead man even less, so I really had no choice but to stare directly at the typewriter on the desk in front of me.

And even so, I might have missed what had been sitting right there the whole time if I had not been feeling slightly guilty for dragging Neil out on a such a miserable night on such a miserable errand, and was therefore reluctant to meet his eye since I'd also neglected to mention part two of my little plan over the phone.

"Jesus, Neil, come and look at this," I said, barely breathing.

He tiptoed over, making a special point not to look at the open supply cupboard.

"Holy shit," he said, reading over my shoulder. "Was this here when you were here earlier with Junior?"

"I don't think so," I said, not taking my eyes off the page. "I wasn't in here for all that long, but I'm pretty certain that the typewriter was empty."

"Which means that it could have been written later."

"But how much later?" I asked. That was the sixty-four-thousand-dollar question. "And why is it still here?" A one-hundred-twenty-thousand-dollar question if ever there was one.

" 'My darling,' " Neil read out loud softly, " 'I can't bear the thought of losing you. My heart is breaking . . . ' "

". . . 'though our short time together is all we'll ever have, the memory of our love will keep me and sustain me for the rest of my life . . . ' " I finished.

"Damn," Neil said.

"But who could he have been writing it to?" I asked, still staring at the words.

"She was already dead when he got back from the hospital, right?" Neil asked.

Without saying the names out loud, we both knew that we were talking about Annelise and Clay. This piece of paper seemed to confirm Junior's worst suspicions.

"But as far as I know, Annelise died *while* he was at the hospital. Right there, with her," I said. "I don't even know if he came back here before going home."

I was grasping at straws, wanting to hold on to my illusions awhile longer. I wanted to believe that Clay would not have cheated on Junior at all, much less with a young girl. I desperately wanted to believe that even if he had, he'd never have put such damning sentiments in writing.

Nor would he have left them to be found by others.

"Maybe Clay didn't write this," I said weakly.

"This is his office, Tory," Neil said simply. "And this is his typewriter. The one he uses exclusively, right?"

"No one else will even touch the thing," I said sadly. "They all switched to computers years ago. In fact Clay is the only one I know who still types anything."

"Ergo," Neil said softly.

"But it doesn't make sense," I insisted. "If he *was* having an affair with her, why would he write a letter to her *after* she died? And why would he leave it here, right out in plain sight?"

I had been married to a serial philanderer who didn't much care if he got caught. And even he hadn't left love letters lying around.

Clay, on the other hand, had every reason in the world to keep an affair secret. Besides hurting his reputation in the community and endangering his livelihood, he'd have every reason to believe that his wife would not accept straying as meekly as I had done.

"There's gotta be another explanation."

Neil put a gloved hand gently on my shoulder. "People do odd things, stupid things, when they're in love. And even odder things when they're in shock."

"But I talked to Clay this evening. I watched him in a roomful of people. If he was in shock, he kept it under wraps pretty well. There's no doubt that he was sad, but I'd swear that he wasn't mourning a lost love. Other people have access to this office. I spent time in here this afternoon myself." I pointed to the supply cupboard. "Weasel found his way in here somehow. And so did whoever put him there. There's no reason at all to think that Clay wrote this. The timing is way off and the content makes no sense."

"Tory," Neil said softly. "Typewritten sentences aren't like computer files. There's no way to know by looking at a piece of paper when something was written on it. Just because this is in the typewriter now doesn't mean it was written this evening. Maybe Clay started this letter earlier, maybe it's a rough draft of something he already delivered." He paused and swallowed. "Maybe Clay had already ended the relationship."

I looked up at Neil, knowing what he was going to say next.

"And maybe that's why she took an overdose."

It made terrible sense but I was still not convinced.

"So why is it here now? If the affair was over, if the poor girl was already dead, why leave something like this where it's sure to be found?" I asked.

"Maybe he wanted to get caught," Neil said.

"Or maybe," I said slowly, "*someone else* wanted him to be caught. Maybe someone else knew about the affair and wanted it brought to light."

"And maybe," Neil said, looking at the supply cupboard, "these two deaths aren't such a coincidence after all."

37

*69

It comes as something of a shock when your devious ways tempt a good and righteous soul down the path to perfidy. It is one thing to suggest a means to an end, knowing that arrival at the latter means you'll be taking your companion on a side trip through the dark side.

It is another entirely when the partner you expected to demur not only seconds the notion but comes up with a few wrinkles of his own.

"Say what?" I asked Neil, not quite believing what he'd just said.

"I said, I don't think we should call the police," he repeated slowly. He wasn't quite grinning—it was too serious a situation for that—but I could swear that I spotted a twinkle in his eye.

"We *have* to call the police," I said. "There's a dead body where a dead body absolutely does not belong. This is the sort of thing that officials like to know about. I can't help but think that this particular body was put here specifically so that someone *would* do exactly that."

"You're right," Neil agreed. "Whoever left Weasel here wanted a big, public fuss made over the discovery. But unless it was Junior who put him in the cupboard, whoever did it didn't expect him to be found until tomorrow morning. And they most assuredly didn't think that *you* would make the discovery."

He'd retreated to the doorway, leaned back, and crossed his arms, waiting for me to argue with his logic.

I swiveled in Clay's desk chair to face him. "But leaving poor Weasel here like this until morning seems wrong. Cruel," I said, searching for a way to explain a feeling that mostly couldn't be explained. "I mean we sort of made a connection today. I feel like I owe him some help. And he deserves not to be left overnight like this."

"He's already as dead as he's going to be," Neil said simply. "We haven't touched him, so whatever evidence is in or on his body will remain intact for investigators to gather. I know it's hard to leave him like that. It feels weird to me too. But I just honestly think it'll do Weasel more good in the long run to leave things as they are, for a couple of reasons."

"Such as?"

"Well, first of all, whoever killed him certainly doesn't know that anyone else knows he's dead. That means they'll probably be waiting anxiously, and watching very carefully in the morning for all hell to break loose. I imagine that someone is going to be mighty jumpy come breakfast time, and maybe we can spot 'em in the act."

He had a point. The cafe was almost directly across the street from the church, with our big front windows providing a panoramic view of both the church and the annex entrances. Not only could I keep a surreptitious eye on the comings and goings there, but I could watch whoever might also be watching from inside the cafe.

I risked a quick peek at Weasel and reconfirmed that the damage, such as it was, had already been done. The church itself was cold, an unfortunate consideration when contemplating the overnight storage of dead bodies.

We had truly not disturbed anything, and since we were both wearing gloves, we'd left no trace of our presence on the few surfaces we had touched—like the cupboard door handle.

"What's the other reason?" I asked finally.

"What other reason?"

"You said that there were a couple of good reasons for us not to call the police. I concede the first, but I want to know the other one before we decide."

"Well," Neil said, "you want to keep Junior and Clay's marital problems out of this, right?"

I nodded.

"And you're not completely convinced that Annelise's suicide had anything to do with either Clay or Weasel's death?"

"Right again."

"And you'd rather not betray Junior's confidences before it's absolutely necessary?"

"Yeah, yeah, yeah," I said testily.

"Well, then we can't call the police because they'll know it was us and you'll have one hell of a time explaining to them what you were doing inside Clay Deibert's office by yourself at this time of night. If you want to keep Junior's suspicions a secret, then you'll have to keep it *all*"— he indicated the whole room—"a secret. At least for the time being."

"How the hell will they know it's us? I thought we were going to make an anonymous phone call?" I demanded.

"Which century do you think we're living in, Tory? Even South Dakota has access to *69. The dispatchers probably have telephone-tracing capabilities anyway, but even if they don't, all they have to do is punch the code in and they'll instantly get the number that made the call. If we call from my house, they'll be able to trace it. If we call from a cell phone, they'll use the satellite to pinpoint the number and location."

"How about if we call from here and let them worry about tracing it?"

"The dispatcher records all incoming calls. Someone down there is sure to recognize your voice. There is simply no way that either of us can make that call without our identities being discovered."

"How about if we called from the bar?"

"And you think no one would notice us tromping in together, heading for the phone, making a quick call, and then leaving again? Especially once the police come in and question every single barfly?"

I sighed. Neil was absolutely right on all counts. Unless I wanted to take full credit for discovering Weasel's body—a situation that would involve a great many explanations I'd rather not make—there was no way I could call the police.

I was in Clay's office at night to do a deliberately bad thing for good reasons. And those good reasons would be negated by doing the obvious right thing in this situation.

"What about the bag?" I asked, giving up. This whole mess had come about because I'd been sent to retrieve Annelise's ill-gotten property. "Do we leave that for the morning too?"

"Nope," Neil declared. This time he was smiling. "We take the bag *and* the page in the typewriter."

"Come again?" I was flabbergasted by his offhand suggestion. "Taking the bag is one thing. Taking the note is another entirely. That's tampering with evidence."

"A little late to find your sticking point, isn't it?" Neil laughed. "If you won't call the police because that would highlight the reason for your being here, then it wouldn't do to leave behind road signs that lead right back to Junior and Clay, would it?"

"Noooo," I said slowly, searching for a hole in his logic and not finding one. It's not that I would not have considered taking both the bag and the note on my own, it's that I was completely shocked to hear Neil suggest it. I'd called him over mostly to curb my felonious tendencies. I didn't expect to have to squash his.

Neil shrugged. "Well, it's either that or we call the police and take our lumps and let Junior's and Clay's lumps fall where they may. That's probably the best course of action anyway—it'd certainly make the police happier. And someone would get to the bottom of all of the puzzles eventually."

"Or?"

"Or we take the bag and the note over to my house, pore over both all night if it takes that long, go back to the cafe in the morning where I can keep an eye on the church and you can keep an eye on the customers, and between us, we might just discover something important."

I'd created a monster. He was not only embracing this cockamamie plan, one sure to raise the ire of the police when it finally came to light, but he was doing it enthusiastically, with little regard for the final consequences.

And what would be the final consequences if our actions came to light?

We would look like interfering fools. But if we were lucky, we'd also look like we did it for the best of reasons.

If Clay was guilty of tampering with the heart and body of a minor, he would surely be caught with or without our help. But if he was innocent, this could be the only chance to keep a terrible story quiet.

I looked at Weasel one more time.

Nothing had changed—he was dead and he'd be every bit as dead in the morning, no better and no worse for having rested in cramped peace for another eight or so hours.

"Okay," I said, barely acknowledging that this was what I wanted to do in the first place, repressing a small thrill of excitement that Neil had not only not objected, but had become a full-fledged accomplice.

"I'll grab the bag," I said, not looking forward to that part of the plan. "You go around back and get the truck and I'll meet you out front."

He paused at the doorway. "Why not just come with me?"

"I have a feeling that there's something out front that we need to check."

38

Vandals

Actually, I wasn't proposing to do anything illegal. I wasn't even considering anything immoral. In fact, what I had in mind was barely, by Delphi standards, much beyond regular snoopiness.

That is if you forgot about that dead body tucked in a cupboard across the street.

And since I didn't officially know nothin' about no dead bodies nowhere, no one would have wondered why I was freezing my ass off out in the subzero cold, hovering around a vehicle parked right in front of my place of business, right where it had been, on and off, for going on eight hours now.

On the other hand, if I'd known that Neil was going to dive into the investigation business headfirst instead of fighting it tooth and nail, I'd have told him about this wrinkle to begin with.

Which, as I said, wasn't anything compared to what we'd just done across the street.

"How did you know it'd still be here?" Neil asked, getting out of his truck, shivering. The wind, which had picked up in the last hour or so, blew unimpeded down Delphi's main drag and lowered the temperature to at least 25 degrees below zero.

"I didn't," I said, standing on my tiptoes, trying to see into the darkened passenger side windows without breathing on them since my breath instantly crystallized on the frozen windows, making them even more opaque, if that was at all possible.

In fact everything was opaque. Clouds now obscured the moonlight, and since Delphi didn't have streetlights, the diagonal parking spaces in front of the cafe were bathed in shadow.

Though Neil had left his truck running, he'd turned off the headlights so as not to draw attention from the bar across the street, or from the few vehicles out on this windy and cold night.

The van's interior was as black as coal. Or at least as black as the interior of a ratty van with tinted windows sitting in the cold darkness of a South Dakota winter evening.

"Well, you've come this far," Neil said, wrapping his arms around himself for warmth. "Aren't you going to open the door and look inside?"

"Can't," I said, tromping around to the back and trying the handle there. "It's locked up tight."

"Interesting," Neil said, following me. "Who locks their vehicles in Delphi?"

"Only people who know that things get stolen sometimes. You know, thief-type people," I said, moving back to the passenger side again. I'd already tried that door, but I'm an optimist. I also wanted to stay out of the wind as much as possible. "The rest of us are trusting souls."

"Who wouldn't survive in the real world for five minutes," Neil said, stomping his feet for warmth.

"Look who's talking, Mr. I Can't Lock My Library, What If Someone Needs a Book After Hours?"

"Well"—he laughed—"we're probably the last people in the world who actually leave the keys in our vehicles."

"That's what I was hoping anyway," I said, giving up on the door handle. "Weasel's a native; I thought a little of the old trust might have been left in him."

"I'll bet some was—the part that knew that all the other doors in town would be open, just waiting for him to enter, which gave him an even better reason to lock his stuff up tight. Did you happen to notice if Weasel locked it when he got here this afternoon?"

"Del saw him drive up before I did, and by the time I realized that he was actually here and intending to come into the cafe, all rational thought had deserted me. I saw Weasel and that's all I saw."

"Completely understandable," Neil agreed. "We'll have to call Del and ask if she noticed."

"I doubt if she's any more observant than me," I said, annoyed for some reason, that he might even think it. "Besides, there are other people who lock vehicles too." I turned to face him, squinting at him in the darkness, trying to make out his features. "Outsiders, for example."

"You mean like Meg?"

"If she really did take his van, it would never occur to her *not* to lock it when she brought it back. No one from any population center, even in Canada, leaves an unattended vehicle unlocked. You know how coasties are—they scurry into the cafe and then sit in a window booth keeping an eagle eye on the Winnebago the whole time they eat, just in case someone tries to make off with it."

"So who has the keys then?" Neil asked. "And can we please talk about this back at my house? Unless you happen to know a lock picker, you're not going to get inside the van tonight. We're courting frostbite for no good reason."

"In a minute," I said distractedly, trying to think, a process becoming more and more difficult as I stood in the snow and slowly froze.

Or maybe the whole process of finding another body and taking on yet another round of inquiries had slowed down my synapses, making it harder to perform my usual leaps of logic. I needed to think something through to the end right then and there, and my difficulty had more to do with mental weariness than any physical slowdown.

If Meg had taken the van, I reasoned, then she'd still have the keys in her possession. Unless she killed Weasel and planted the van keys back on him to draw attention away from herself.

The only way to know for sure was to talk to Meg, though just talk would probably not net actual results. Searching her was, for better or worse, out of the question. Given that she was staying with the McKees, even talking to her seemed to be an impossible mission.

But if Meg hadn't taken the keys, then Weasel should still have them.

The thought of going through his pockets made me shudder.

I turned to face Neil and then looked at the darkened church across the street.

"I can't do it," I said out loud, making the decision as I said it. Maybe I was getting old and losing my nerve. I began to shiver. "Even if it means that we don't know about the keys."

"What the heck are you talking about?"

I'd forgotten that Neil wasn't psychic. "Even if Meg took the van," I explained, "she may have managed to give them back to Weasel, or at least plant them on him." That implication chilled me even more. "Which means that they may be with Weasel's body—in his pockets or somewhere nearby. But I don't have the heart to go back inside and look for them."

"Of course you aren't going back in there," Neil said adamantly. "I'm already feeling guilty about what we did. We are not about to compound the problem or court obstruction of justice charges by reentering a crime scene on purpose. It doesn't really matter who has the keys anyway. Weasel may well have made up the whole Meg saga. He could have moved the van for his own reasons while you were dealing with the ambulance. And he could have moved it back while you and Junior were confabbing in Clay's office the first time, when he disappeared from the hallway.

"In fact Jennifer may have come on him in the church just after he'd put the van back in its original parking place. His Meg Wasn't There spiel could have been a cover up for the fact that he was nowhere near the kids while they rehearsed."

"The whole choir backed up her story," I said quietly.

"It's one of those things that we just aren't going to be able to solve. Especially here on a frozen street. Come on." He looped an arm around my shoulder and pointed me toward his truck. "See that? I guarantee, it's warm in there."

"But I really wanted to get inside the van," I said, knowing that Neil was right. And knowing that I absolutely did not want to go back across the street and actually rifle through Weasel's pockets looking for keys that probably weren't there in the first place.

But still I didn't move. There were things that only the van could tell us.

"I'd hoped that his clothes, his original ones, the ones he wore *to* Delphi, would be in there," I said finally, looking down at the snow-packed ground.

"What difference would that make?" Neil asked, confused. "His clothes are like the keys—a riddle inside a mystery. Weasel could have gotten naked in your storeroom for some perverted reason of his own and stashed the clothes in the van himself. Or Meg may have stolen them all just like he said, and she may have left the clothes and the keys locked inside. Either or both of them may have stashed either or both anywhere in the countryside. For all we know, the Overall Fairy might have whisked them over the rainbow. Just finding them wouldn't tell you anything."

"Yes it would," I said stubbornly. "I'd be able to check the pockets for a work order or some other documentation. And if the info wasn't in his pockets, it'd be inside the van somewhere."

"Documentation for what?"

"A work order. Some invoices. Something on paper that will tell us who Weasel's employer was, and how we can contact him. We'll get a better handle on him *and* his movements if we know that much at least."

"Tory," Neil said softly, "you're tired and worn down. This has been far too long and awful a day for you and you're too cold to think straight."

"That's not very nice," I said peevishly, even though I knew it was true. More than true.

"Well, if you were warm and rested and firing on all cylinders, I wouldn't have to do this," he said, leading me to the driver's side of the van and pointing at the foot-tall letters painted there.

39

In the Bag

Okay, so I was too cold and tired, and hungry come to think of it, not to mention frazzled by a long and awful day, to process things very quickly or clearly. But it's not my fault that Weasel's chintzy employer only sprang for lettering on the driver's side of the furnace repair van.

Around here there's nothing much to block anyone's view of anything, and even so, businessmen plaster their names all over their vehicles—on the sides, on the back, on the cab, even backward on the grill if there's room.

Since I'd seen no writing on either the passenger side of the van (which incidentally had been the view I had from inside the cafe) or on the back (which I'd observed fairly closely as I'd tried to rattle open the locked doors out in the cold), I assumed that there wasn't any writing anywhere else on the van either.

It was only luck that Neil had noticed the lettering himself, or I'd have trudged back without that vital information.

"So what do you intend to do with this?" Neil tapped the back of the deposit slip where I'd hastily scribbled the furnace repair company's name, address, and phone number.

"I'm going to call them," I said, with my mouth full. Neil had reheated a plateful of shrimp and pasta for me. Junior'd hustled me out of her house so quickly that I hadn't had a chance to eat anything off the Styrofoam plate that Clay had so kindly overfilled. I was starving.

If I'd had even an inkling of how the rest of the evening was going to go, I'd have blown Junior off and stayed in Neil's warm kitchen in the first place. As it was, I was more than happy to be right back where we started, with me on the bar stool and Neil standing on the other side of the counter and a full plate sitting between us. Even reheated, the soggy noodles and limp garlic shrimp tasted wonderful. Especially with Jose Feliciano floating softly from the speakers.

My toes and fingers were regaining sensation, probably aided by the two glasses of Riesling I'd inhaled while waiting for Neil to dish out the leftovers. I was beginning to warm up from the inside out, and my brain was starting to thaw.

And it was beginning to function again.

"Waldlach Furnace Repair of Aberdeen, South Dakota, Faithfully Serving the Area for Twenty-five Years," I said, reading from the slip of paper, "sent a repairman to my place of business this noon in order to fix a faulty furnace. However, it has been"—I glanced up at the wall clock over the sink and did a quick calculation—"nine hours since then and my furnace is still not running. The repairman they sent not only did not fix my furnace, he seems to have abandoned his work vehicle in front of my cafe, where it is blocking some of the limited parking area we reserve for our valued patrons."

I grinned and took another bite.

Neil grinned back. "You have every right to be disgruntled with Waldlach Furnace Repair of Aberdeen, South Dakota. And every right to demand some sort of accounting for the behavior of their employee. Exactly what kind of accounting were you looking for? I mean you're not about to announce to them that their former star worker is no longer among the living, are you?"

"God no," I said, spearing another shrimp. "But if I push a little I might be able to get them to name some of Weasel's satisfied customers just to prove that today was a glitch in his otherwise smooth employment record."

"And you will do what with that information?"

Neil reached over and grabbed one of the last shrimps from the plate before I could stop him, though he almost got a fork in his hand for his trouble.

"Hey, you had yours already," I said, sliding the plate closer to me and looping a protective arm around it. "Whatever else may or may not have happened between Meg and Weasel today, I got the impression this noon at the cafe that they knew each other already."

"Smoldering glances across the hamburger specials, eh?" Neil emptied the wine bottle into his glass. "Want more wine, or should we have an after-dinner drink?"

"A black Russian would do nicely, thank you very much," I said. I never worried about overtaxing Neil's liquor cabinet. It was always overstocked. "And yes, there *were* smoldering glances, or something very like that. I thought at the time that they at least recognized each other. It's possible that they ran into each other on one of the choir's earlier appearances."

"You got someone checking out the tour schedule for you?" He eyeballed shots of vodka, followed by Kahlua, into a pair of glasses and then filled them with crushed ice.

"Junior," I said, sopping up the last bit of sauce with a piece of sourdough bread. "She's going to get me their whole itinerary. She's also going to talk to Jurgen and try to pump him gently about Annelise."

"You realize that you corrupt everyone you come in contact with, don't you?" Neil handed me a drink. "People who would have no inclination on their own to dabble in death and destruction are drawn to it after being in your presence."

"What can I say? It's a gift."

"Well, life is never dull around you, that's for sure." He clinked rims with me, and then got serious. "So what do we do next? You're not going to call Mr. Waldlach now, are you?"

"Nah. I could probably get them to send an emergency crew to the cafe tonight, but the old furnace was at least keeping the interior temp above freezing, so there won't be any real damage if we wait. As you pointed out, I'm not exactly at my sharpest right now, and I don't want to give away more to him than I have to. It's perfectly reasonable for me, as a business owner, to call them in the morning and do some heavy duty complaining. I just want to do it before the shit hits the fan."

"What do we do in the meantime then?" Neil asked. "Besides get sloshed on black Russians?"

"That sounds fine to me actually," I said. "But I suppose we'd better take a peek at that bag. We went through an awful lot to get it here, and this is our only opportunity to see what's inside. I have to take it back to the cafe in the morning and hand it over to Glenda."

Neil sighed. "I was afraid you were going to say that. You know, all of our ideas sounded perfectly reasonable while we were cold and shivering, with a dead body for company in Clay's office. But here and now, the whole thing seems a little silly. And more than a little dangerous."

"I know what you mean," I said, taking a sip, letting the alcohol warm me all the way down. "A part of me wants to turn the bag in and be done with it. Let the authorities find whatever they find, and let everyone else cover their own asses. But it's already too late to do that, unless we want to tell the police *everything*. Unless we want to tell them that Junior already took Annelise's suicide note, that she's obstructing justice in order to protect her husband. Unless we want to mention that we're helping her to do just that."

"When you put it that way, it doesn't seem like we have any choice, does it?" Neil said quietly.

"Nope," I said, "so let's get busy."

40

De-Liver De-Letter

For some reason, it hadn't felt quite so weird pawing through Annelise's belongings while she was alive. This afternoon we thought she was going to recover, and while it seemed impolite to rifle through her bag, it didn't feel *wrong,* the way it felt *wrong* sitting in Neil Pascoe's kitchen as we stared at the jumble of half-scribbled pages, used tissues and empty gum wrappers spread out on the countertop.

Of course, this afternoon it had been Junior's decision to inspect Annelise's bag, and she'd been the one to dump it out right in front of us. It wasn't really our fault that we'd let our eyes stray over the legal and illegal contents. It was a little different to upend the shabby green and yellow striped canvas bag myself.

"Someone knew what they were doing with those," Neil said, eyeing the three neatly rolled marijuana joints that had already caught Alanna's fancy.

"And how would you know?" I asked, laughing.

"I was in high school in the seventies too, you know. I'm not that much younger than you," he said archly.

I snorted. "Yeah, if you count 1981 as the seventies."

"The seventies are in the mind of the beholder," he declared. "I wore my share of powder-blue leisure suits and big bow ties. I'll have you know that I can do the Hustle." He performed a little Travolta arm fling to prove his point. "Besides, I don't exactly remember seeing you in platform shoes under a glitter ball at Studio 54 either."

"Okay, okay, so the seventies in Delphi were mostly like the fifties in polyester," I conceded. "But that still doesn't explain how *you* know a quality joint from any other kind."

"I have a checkered and sordid past which I have paid dearly to keep under wraps. And someday, if you are very lucky, I'll tell you the whole story. But in the meantime"—he cleared his throat and assumed a serious expression and pushed his glasses up on his nose—"we have a whole lot more to consider here than a dead girl's pitiful little stash."

I made a face. "You're no fun at all. I'd much rather hear about your indiscretions."

"All in good time, my dear," he said without looking at me. He pulled a pencil from the canister under the phone and prodded the empty pill bottle. "This is the one that held the codeine aspirin, right?" The 222 label rolled into view and I nodded and reached for it, but he grabbed my hand gently. "Fingerprints, remember?"

"Too late," I said, not pulling my hand away. "I already touched this stuff with my bare hands in the cafe. So did Junior. And Del. If they end up dusting it, our fingerprints are going to show up on everything anyway. We implicated ourselves before we knew there was anything to be implicated for."

I generally try to limit my dangling prepositions, but I'd just realized that Neil was still holding my hand and for some reason that garbled my syntax.

"It's not just your fingerprints I'm worried about. We still don't know what we're dealing with here. There may be other sets of fingerprints that you don't want to smudge. At least not any more than they are already."

"You think someone else tampered with the bag? Annelise had it with her in the cafe, and we, or at least Junior, had it after that. There wasn't much chance for anyone else to snoop around in it."

"Well, there was enough time for someone to stuff Weasel Cleaver's body into the same cupboard where we found this. Obviously there was opportunity enough."

"To do what?" I asked, reluctant to look Neil in the eye. He'd let go of my hand, but I had not pulled it away. He hadn't pulled his hand away either. They both just sort of sat there, next to each other, warm and touching.

"I don't know," he said softly. "That's the problem. Anyone trying implicate Clay by rolling that note into his typewriter would have to have suspected the *alleged* affair before any of today's events occurred. If they're serious about exposing him, they also might have been able to plant something in the bag—either before or after she overdosed." He paused and then continued, his hand still touching mine. "We can continue on, we just have to be very careful."

"You're right," I said, suddenly aware that the subtext of our conversation had changed. We were no longer talking about Annelise or Clay or the assorted contents of a stupid canvas bag.

Afraid to meet his eye, afraid not of what I would see, but of what I might not see, I looked down at our hands, which were still resting on the counter side by side. Neil's strength, his loyalty, his warmth—all felt so right. And so frightening at the same time.

"We can do it," Neil said simply. "We're both smart. And we're both grown-ups. And we both know what we're doing."

"Are you sure?" I asked, looking up finally and seeing more than I ever expected in his eyes.

"I've never been more sure in my life," he said with a soft smile.

He picked up his glass and clinked the rim of mine without saying anything. He didn't have to.

"Okay then," I said, nodding my head, knowing that as much as I'd like to continue on, there were other issues more pressing at the moment. Knowing that there was plenty of time for the rest. Knowing that Neil knew it too.

We rooted around the pile on the counter in companionable silence, using pencils to flip objects or move them around.

"What about the letter?" I asked. Back in the cafe we'd noticed that the bag also held a stamped and addressed envelope to someone in Sweden. Even a cursory glance had shown the handwriting on the envelope to be the same as that on the suicide note. I wondered if we dared to open it.

He was on my wavelength. "Well, we wouldn't exactly be tampering with the U.S. mail since it hasn't officially been mailed yet."

"Good point. But will it do us any good to take a peek? I mean, my Swedish is pretty rusty."

"Mine too," Neil said, laughing. "But I have a Swedish friend who'll tackle this for us if I ask."

"Where, in Minnesota?"

Minnesota was pretty much the Nordic capital of the U.S. That and Wisconsin.

Us Dakotans were mostly sturdy German stock. Yah, you betcha.

"Nope," Neil said, grinning. "A little farther away than that." He pulled open a drawer and rooted around and came up with a pair of tongs, which he used to grab the envelope by a corner, and motioned for me to follow him. "Come on, I'll introduce you."

41

Mamma Mia

I'll be the first to admit that Neil Pascoe was a pretty amazing guy. How many small-town lottery winners, especially young small-town lottery winners, take their money and stay put?

Neil's twelve-point-something-million-dollar take from the Iowa Lottery Commission, back when there were no other state lotteries and a twelve-thousand-dollar jackpot on *Jeopardy!* was a big win, before Regis Philbin was even a blip on anyone's annoyance meter, was more than enough to enable him to put Delphi in his rearview mirror.

Young, very smart, and with enough money to live exactly where and how he pleased, Neil chose to stay in Delphi and open a library, which he runs happily from the lower floor of his restored three-story Victorian home. A Delphi native, he lives quietly enough that most of the time, people forget how much money he has. Without ever chairing a committee or drawing attention specifically to himself, he helps the community in ways that most people will never realize because his donations are sizable and anonymous.

He is truly an asset to the community.

Don't get me wrong, Neil is no sackcloth-wearing saint.

He's a regular guy, with a wicked and occasionally raunchy sense of humor. He travels when he feels like it. He doesn't buy his clothes at Target. His refrigerator and wine cellar are fully stocked and he's not afraid of real butter or Bud Light.

He likes his toys too—he indulges himself in ratty old pickup trucks and then restores them and sells them for a goodly profit. He keeps a state-of-the-art kitchen. His stereo and music collection is to die for, it goes without saying that he has the least obsolete computer system in town, and we haven't even gotten into the books that line shelves throughout the lower floor of his house and lay stacked haphazardly everywhere upstairs.

But even Neil Pascoe, millionaire librarian and all-around great fella, did not keep a Swedish translator in his bedroom. At least, I hoped not.

"Where you got him stashed?" I asked, carrying our drinks as I followed Neil into a dark room whose only illumination was the digital clock on the bed stand, the red pinpoint of light on the VCR across from the bed, and the glowing computer monitor in the corner. "Gillian Anderson?" I asked, looking at the picture on the screen.

"What can I say, I like the *X-Files*." Neil laughed. "And you gotta admit that she's hot."

"If you like dour, red-haired pouters, I guess," I said, knowing full well that I harbored an embarrassing little crush on Fox Mulder myself, and therefore had no room to talk.

"They're nice to look at anyway," Neil said, sitting in the office chair in at the computer. "Here." He patted the chair next to him. "Behold the wonders of the Internet."

As I sat and sipped, he clicked on something, typed in something, and listened to an array of beeps, boops, and squawks, all of which must have been normal because he ignored them completely. A few more things happened on the screen, boxes whizzed into view and then back into oblivion before I had a chance to read them. But at each juncture, Neil typed or clicked, or possibly hit random keys as though the whole rigmarole was routine.

Which I suppose it is for a vast majority of Americans these days.

"There," Neil said, staring at the screen, his face bathed in a blue light. "We're online, let's see if Jorg is on."

I'd finally realized that Neil knew someone in Sweden who might be able to translate Annelise's letter for us, though how he was going to get him a copy of the letter was beyond me. I didn't think Neil's keyboard had any umlauts or those O's with slashes through them, so typing it seemed out of the question.

"You going to e-mail him?" I said, proud of knowing at least that much lingo.

"Nah, e-mail is too slow. I'm going to ICQ Jorg."

"IC what?"

"ICQ," Neil said, laughing. "It's a program that tells you when certain people are online. You click here," he positioned the arrow over a green flower on the lower edge of his screen. A box appeared with a list of names and more flowers, "and instantly know if the person you want to talk to is online. And luckily for us, Jorg is online."

"So you just happen to know this guy in Sweden who has no life and spends his evenings at the computer, waiting and hoping that someone will contact him so that he has something to do?" I was skeptical of the whole process.

"I know this guy in Sweden who has a job that keeps him online during the daytime, and yes he's perfectly happy to be distracted," Neil said, his eyes still not leaving the screen as he typed a message into another box that had popped up.

"What kind of job does this Swedish guy have that he gets to be online all night?" I asked, watching Neil's fingers fly across the keys. I'd had no idea he was such a good typist. No D's for him.

"It's morning in Sweden, Tory," Neil said gently. "He's at work—just like you'll be in about eight hours. Ah, there we go." He clicked something again and the box disappeared. Neil sat back in the chair and stretched his arms over his head. "Now we just wait and hope he has time to look at this letter for us."

"Are you going to retype it for him?"

"Nope," he said, carefully holding the envelope up with the tongs and using a small X-acto knife to loosen the flap.

One sheet of paper, in a schoolgirl handwriting in what I assume was Swedish, slid out on the desk in front of him.

We both looked at it for a minute.

"You sure this is a good idea?" I asked.

"The law is against tampering with the mail, not translating it," he said, not touching the page either. "We've already tampered and interfered, finding out what we're risking incarceration for won't make it any harder on us."

"So you say," I said doubtfully.

He stood up and used the tongs again to move the letter over to a long, flat, rectangular box next to his computer.

"I'm going to scan it," Neil explained, lifting the lid of the contraption and laying the sheet facedown on a glass screen. "Then I'll save it as a .jpg and send it as an attachment to Jorg and he can read it and ICQ the translation back to us."

"Hokay," I said, not understanding a word he'd said, but trusting his judgment and skill. If Neil said it could be done that way, then it could be done that way.

Back in his office chair, Neil clicked a few more things. Suddenly the scanner emitted a whole series of high-pitched, vaguely musical noises that would surely have carried a deeper meaning in *Close Encounters of the Third Kind.*

"Is it in pain?" I asked, worried. "It sounds like it's trying to contact the mother ship."

"Scanning is not something you can do in secret." Neil laughed. "Watch."

He pointed to the computer monitor. As a very bright light traveled the length of the scanner under the lid, an exact copy of Annelise's letter showed up, in increments, on the screen.

"Wow," I said, impressed. "It's like a copier, right?"

"Sorta," he said, as the scanner emitted a couple more beeps and the light swiftly moved back to from whence it came. "You can use a scanner as a copier to make individual color or black and white copies, but what it really does is take a picture of an object and translate it into a computer graphics file. This picture"—he tapped the screen—"is what we'll send to Jorg. He'll be able to see it well enough to read what's written on it. And hopefully he'll be able to tell us what it says."

He clicked some more and typed something and hit a few more keys, then looked at me. "There, the letter is all scanned and saved and ready to send to Jorg. If she'd written on both sides of the paper, I would have scanned the back the same way and saved it in another file. I think, though, I'd best scan the envelope so that he can tell us if it says anything interesting. I mean I've sort of assumed the letter was to her parents, but we don't know that for sure."

As Neil repeated the scanner procedure, I watched an exact copy of the envelope show up on his monitor, fascinated, until I noticed something.

"Your flower is blinking," I said. The green flower in the corner of Neil's screen had started to flash on and off.

"Oh good, that's Jorg."

He sat down again and opened up a small screen and read what had been written halfway across the world just a few moments before.

"Jorg will be delighted to translate the letter for us," Neil said. "Things aren't too busy for him right now, so he should be able to get to it right away and if we wait around, he'll have a rough translation in a half-hour or so. He says 'Hi.' "

"To me?" I asked, surprised and suddenly worried that this Jorg guy could see me sitting next to Neil in his bedroom. "How does he know I'm here?"

"I told him, silly," Neil said. "I also told him the basic details about Annelise, that she'd committed suicide and in doing so had implicated someone we trust in something we don't believe him capable, so we want to know if her last letter can help us to understand both her death and the accusation she made."

"He's not worried about mail-tampering laws?"

"He's in Sweden; what's the U.S. Post Office going to do to him there?"

In the midst of these instant communications, I had forgotten that this Jorg guy was out of the reach of most of our laws.

"A handy system for miscreants," I commented.

"And Webmasters," Neil added as he typed furiously.

"What the heck is a Webmaster? Sounds kinky."

He clicked one or two more things. "There, the .jpgs are

on their way." He swiveled to face me. "Depending on the individual Web sites, kinky may well be the order of the day. But Jorg isn't a kinky Webmaster. He manages the technical aspects of several large Web pages. That's how I met him."

"And what kind of Web sites does he manage?"

I pictured cyber gatherings of lottery winners, confabbing over the mutual problems of having so damn much money. Or maybe librarians moaning about book availability together. Or even convocations of old truck restorers looking for '60 Ford radios.

"You don't want to know," Neil said sheepishly.

"I thought you said it wasn't kinky," I laughed.

"It's worse than kinky. Jorg runs, among other things, an ABBA fan site."

"Oh my Lord, Neil, you met this guy because you cherish a secret love for 'Dancing Queen'?" I didn't know whether to be amused or horrified.

That Neil Pascoe was a man of many facets. Not all of them savory.

"More like 'Chiquitita,'" he said, ducking. "And 'Fernando.'"

"Well, I'm glad you admitted this shameful addiction before I became too involved with you," I said, cuffing him on the shoulder. "I don't know if I can be seen in public with an acknowledged ABBA fan."

"Hey, you like the Monkees, Ms. Glass Trailer."

"Yeah, but I don't go online looking for other Monkee lovers," I said, laughing.

"That's only because you don't have a computer. You hang out with me long enough, honey, and you'll be doing all sorts of shameful things."

I would have challenged Neil to prove it right then and there, but his flower was blinking again.

42

Babelfish

I could see why technophobes and autocrats feared the kind of technology where without ever meeting in person, a Neil Pascoe in Delphi, South Dakota, could become good enough friends with a Jorg Whateverthehellhislastnameis in Sweden to trouble him during busy daytime office hours for a translation of a letter that neither should have been reading in the first place.

Prohibiting access to information is the mainstay of dictators and conservative parents around the world.

I mean not only is it all, and I do mean *all*, right there at your fingertips—or at least keyboard and monitor—but it's all there instantly.

"Good grief, did he finish the translation already? It hasn't even been five minutes," I said, thinking I might need to get one of these amazing machines myself. And then realizing that it'd cost a decade worth of accumulated tips, by which time we'll probably be communicating via chips implanted in our heads and won't need computers anyway.

"Jorg is fast, Tory, but he's not the Swedish Superman," Neil said, after clicking on the flashing flower. "He's just letting me know that he got the files and will have something for us soon."

"Oh," I said, vaguely disappointed. A half-hour ago, I had not even considered the possibility of knowing someone halfway around the world, and now I was sad that he wasn't performing miracles fast enough.

On the other hand, why were humans needed at all?

"Aren't there computer translators?" I asked. It seemed reasonable—there were machines that translated pictures into digital files, there ought to be files that translate English words into Swedish. "I mean do you have to rely on chance every time you need something Swedish translated? What if our next emergency case is from Belgium and you don't know any English-speaking Europeans who are fluent in Belgian. Or Flemish, or whatever."

"There are translation engines on the Net, Tory, but you don't want to rely on them for anything important," Neil said, grinning. "Here, let me show you." He did a little more clicking and typing and a new picture came up. "Meet Babelfish."

"Like from Douglas Adams?"

"Yup," Neil said, typing as he talked. "This jobbie will change whatever you write in English into French, German, Italian, Spanish, or Portuguese, and back again. It's not especially sophisticated but it'll give you a notion of why it's better to ask a living human to translate for you."

He read out loud what he'd just typed: " 'Dear Tory Bauer, My name is Neil. I run a library in Delphi, South Dakota, and I know that you own a small-town cafe. Would you like to have supper with me some day? I am a good cook. Perhaps we share some common interests. Sincerely, Neil Pascoe.' "

"Oh come on," I said. "That's too easy. A kid could translate that paragraph without messing it up."

"Au contraire," he said, clicking on the English to German option. Within thirty seconds a new message appeared in a window above where he'd typed originally. "Wanna try to read this out loud?"

It said: "Lieber Tory Bauer, Mein Name ist Neil. Ich laufen lasse eine Bibliothek in Delphi, South Dakota, und ich weiß, daß Sie einen kleinen Stadtkaffee besitzen. Wurden Sie mögen das Abendessen mit mir eines Tages haben? Ich bin ein guter Koch. Möglicherweise teilen wir etwas öffentliche Interessen. Aufrichtig Neil Pascoe."

I looked at it and shook my head. "Nope."

"Me neither," he said. "So let's change it back to English. I'll just copy and paste the translation back into the engine and switch it to German to English, and voilà."

He did a little Vanna White motion at the screen, which now read: *"Dear Tory Farmer, My name is Neil. I to run leave a library in Delphi, South Dakota and I know that you possess a small city coffee. Did you become to like the dinner with me a daily to have? I am a good cook. Possibly we divide somewhat public interests. Sincerely Neil Pascoe."*

I nearly choked on my drink.

"Well at least you're a good cook and sincere in English and German both," I said finally.

"You got some public interests you wanna divide with me?" he asked, waggling his eyebrows.

"Maybe somewhat later," I said, still laughing. "But it looks like Jorg is done. Or at least he wants to talk to you."

That damn green flower was flashing again, right when things were getting interesting.

"Oh, right," Neil said, turning to the screen again, all business. He closed down the translator and clicked on the flower again. Another message window popped up. As he read the contents, his face became inexpressibly sad.

I wanted to reach out, to stroke his cheek, to comfort him in the darkness.

"Listen to this, Tory," he said softly, " 'Dearest Mother and Father, I know you will be frightened when you hear the news about me from America. I want you both to know how much I value your love and guidance and how badly I long to come home. Please try not to worry about me or the decision I have made here in this foreign land. My love has forsaken me and my heart is broken. This is my only option, my only way to return. I will be seeing Grandmother very soon and I am very happy for that because I have missed her a great deal since she went away. Until we meet again, dearest parents, know that I have loved you. Your daughter, Annelise.' "

43

Feet of Clay

That old seek and ye shall find routine doesn't quite cover the investigation scenario anymore. In this day and age, you can find out just about anything you want about anything, or anyone, in the world with a click of a finger, right from the comfort of your own bedroom with very little seeking involved.

Neil had proven the irrelevance of our inability to speak Swedish. The fact that we were not likely to hop on the next plane to do our research in person made no difference at all. Even the realization that he was depending on the kindness of foreign strangers for the delivery of vital information in a timely manner was not considered miraculous in our increasingly connected society.

But in the excitement of the hunt, in our search for answers, we forgot that what we discovered might not be what we expected, or wanted to know.

Unfortunately, once we had an answer, it was too late to take the question back.

"Damn," Neil said, not taking his eyes off the computer monitor. He sat in the dark, his shoulders slumped, his face grave.

I reached over and gave his hand a small squeeze.

"I know how you feel," I said, sadly. "I was still hoping it was some kind of mistake. Even with the suicide note, I thought there might be a rational explanation—that she'd taken an accidental overdose. Or that she was playing some kind of nasty prank that just got out of hand."

"I know what you mean," Neil said, placing a warm hand over mine. "I didn't want to believe it about Clay."

"I suppose there's no doubt now. Between Annelise's direct accusation and Junior catching him sneaking out of her room at two A.M., not to mention the wet spot on the sheets, and this"—I pointed at the screen—"there aren't many other conclusions you can draw."

"She could have been lying," Neil said.

"For what purpose?" I asked. "What good does it do to accuse an innocent man of an atrocity if you aren't going to stick around to watch the fallout? If Annelise had lived, I might have wondered if the whole thing was concocted to cover up something else. But she wasn't fooling around when she took those aspirins. And she's too dead to take any of it back now."

I was near tears. It's not that I thought Clay was a saint. I knew he was as human as the rest of us.

And I have every reason to understand fully that even the best of people make stupid choices, and the best of marriages have hard times, and the best of intentions can sometimes hurt the greatest number of people.

I'd have been no happier about it, but I could have believed that Clay was fooling around with a parishioner, or at least with another grown-up, without having to give up many of my cherished notions. I would have thought less of Clay of course, but I would not have thought less of the world in general.

But forcing myself to believe that Clay Deibert was capable of having sex with a young girl in his care made me despair of my entire species.

"So what do we do now?" Neil asked finally.

"I suppose we put the letter back in the envelope and glue it shut. Then we put it in the bag, and in the morning I'll take the bag back to the cafe. Then we sit back and wait for the shit to hit the fan. If Glenda Harrison doesn't go through Annelise's belongs herself, then someone surely will. It's all going to come to light now. And I guess there's nothing we should do to try to stop it."

"What about the suicide note? The real one, the one Annelise wrote in the cafe?"

"Junior probably destroyed it. That's what I would have done if life as I knew it revolved around a single piece of paper," I said, shrugging. "I doubt we'll ever see it again."

Neil swiveled his chair around to face me. "Then how is any of this going to come to light? If the suicide note is gone, there's nothing else that ties Clay specifically to Annelise. She didn't mention him by name in her farewell letter home. Junior certainly isn't going to mention a connection. And if Clay is the man that Annelise says he is, he's not going to step forward and confess either."

"Well, first of all, she may have had a confidant in the choir. I think Junior said that Annelise was good friends with Meg. One of the other kids may have noticed something odd about their behavior together. Glenda may have seen something and not processed it. We can ask around tomorrow at the cafe, and later at the memorial service."

"But all of that is hearsay stuff," Neil said adamantly. He turned back to the screen and typed a swift thank you to Jorg, then shut down all of the programs and logged off. Without looking at me he said, "None of it will stand up in court, you know, including our interpretation of what may or may not have happened. None of it will really hurt Clay in the long run because no one will believe the accusation without an actual videotape of them together. But none of it will help him either; once the seed is planted, it won't go away. You know what kind of memories people have around here. We have to be very, very careful because no matter what we think right now, this could still all be smoke and mirrors. I'm ashamed that we're sitting here, honestly believing something awful about one of the best people we know, and we're believing it on circumstantial evidence alone. We're tired and overloaded. You've dealt with two dead bodies today, which is twice as many as me, and more than I ever want to see again. I think we're both overreacting, letting ourselves be carried along on an emotional tide with not one shred of physical evidence to back up this awful theory."

"I wish you were right," I said softly. "But for better or worse, we *do* have physical evidence, and more than just a shred. We have a whole typewriter page. We just have to decide what to do with it."

44

Junior Mints

Knowing that we had a vital piece of information, a clue that no one else knew existed, was not quite the same as figuring out exactly what to do with it. And it wasn't the same as wanting to figure out what to do with it.

Which neither of us did.

So we pretended that the piece of typewriter paper was not still in my coat pocket as we returned to the kitchen and carefully spread glue on the flap of Annelise's last letter.

Neil had opened it very carefully and there were no wrinkles or tears to show that it had been unsealed. By the meticulous way he was resealing it, there would be no outward evidence that it had been resealed either.

But I had watched enough *X-Files* episodes to know that forensic types armed with tweezers and microscopes would know not only that the envelope had been opened, but that it had been resealed with an ordinary, non–postal regulation, glue stick. For all I knew, they'd be able to tell that we beamed a picture off to Sweden for a translation.

"It looks good, but won't they be know that it's been opened and glued back together?" I asked as Neil carefully smoothed the flap back into place with the back of a bread knife.

So far, neither of us had touched the paper with our bare fingers.

Neil shrugged. "They'd be able to tell if they really looked. But I doubt anyone will ever look. Annelise wasn't murdered, she committed suicide. No one is even going to suggest a full-blown investigation. At least not the kind you're worrying about."

"I thought that suicides were always treated like murders until proven otherwise," I said, drawing on my vast experience in reading mysteries and watching TV.

"They might be, in bigger cities," Neil said, using the tongs to pick up the resealed envelope and wave it around a little to hurry the glue drying. "But this is Delphi. We don't exactly have a crack forensic team ready to jump into action when a girl commits very public suicide. We've been careful with this"—he waved the envelope some more—"just on general principle, but I'll bet no one else will hesitate to touch it. Watch Glenda in the morning, I'll bet she paws through the whole bag the second you hand it over to her. And she won't be wearing gloves either."

He held up Annelise's bag by the strap and dropped the envelope in. He began to transfer the rest of the jumble on the counter back from whence it came, using the tongs to pick up each item, piece by piece.

When he got to the marijuana joints, he shot me a wicked grin and then shrugged and dropped them into the bag.

"Got a line in front of you for them anyway," I said, laughing. "I believe Alanna has first dibs. Just to keep them safe."

He was almost finished. He'd picked up a crumpled sheet of paper, torn evidently from a small pad that had already been added to the rest.

"Wait a second," I said, putting a hand on his arm. "There's writing on that page."

He'd already transferred a couple other pieces of paper which had been obviously torn from the same pad, but they'd held nothing but an indecipherable scribble or two, or a dried wad of gum.

He dropped the page, and with a knife and the tongs spread it open carefully.

The small sheet was filled with cramped and sloppy handwriting. Words were crossed out and insertions had been made. Though the penmanship was obviously hurried, it resembled Annelise's.

"Looks like she wrote a rough draft of something," I said finally.

It was in Swedish of course, so we had no idea what it said. The envelope was already resealed and replaced and unavailable for comparison, though we'd probably not be able to work out meanings anyway since Jorg's translation had not been the kind of literal word-for-word insertion in which the automated online Babelfish seemed to specialize.

"I'd better see if Jorg can take a look at this," Neil said, picking up the sheet with the tongs. He headed for his bedroom.

"My thoughts exactly," I said, getting ready to follow him, looking forward to another demonstration of scanning and e-mailing and instant communication with people on the other side of the globe, but the phone rang.

"Get that, will you, Tory?" Neil asked over his shoulder.

"Sure," I said, reaching over to the avocado retro wall phone. We had one just like it at the trailer, only it wasn't retro. It was just old. "Neil Pascoe's residence," I said, feeling like a receptionist.

"Oh good, it's you," Junior said without a preamble. "Don't you ever go home?"

"And good evening to you too," I said sarcastically. I could worry about Junior. I could even break a few laws to try to help her, but being nice to her was almost impossible. She was just so damn bossy and irritating.

"I tried your house, but Del said that she she'd told everyone who called that she hadn't seen you since early afternoon," she continued testily. "So I've been calling Neil's number for the last hour and the damn line has been busy the whole time."

"We were online," I said simply, deciding that an explanation of exactly *what* we were doing online wasn't necessary.

"Well, how's a person supposed to be able to get hold of you if you're never home or you're always online?" she asked, I'm assuming rhetorically. I opted out of answering her question and volleyed one of my own back at her. "Well you have me now. What did you want?"

Junior lowered her voice. "Is Neil there in the room with you? Be careful how you answer if he is."

"No, he's in his bedroom scanning something," I said in a normal voice.

Junior understood computer stuff; I figured she wouldn't need further explanation of the processes involved.

"Good," she continued, her voice normal again. "I had to make sure that you got *it* out of the church."

Under ordinary circumstances, I'd have toyed with her awhile, making her spell out exactly what she was asking. But these weren't ordinary circumstances, and for some reason, annoyance factor notwithstanding, I'd been more on Junior's side than otherwise lately.

"Yeah, I got it," I said, remembering to leave Neil out of the conversation since she didn't know I'd included him in the festivities. "And obviously I'm out of the church since you found me here."

"Well, there was no guarantee of either now, was there?" she asked. "Del didn't know where you were. Neil's phone is busy a lot—I think he leaves that damn computer on even when he's not home, so there was no telling if you were there or not. I already tried the bar—"

"You called the bar looking for me, Junior?" I interrupted. "Jeez."

"I had to find out where you were, and I couldn't very well call the church, could I?"

"You could have, but I wouldn't have answered even if I had been there."

Neil had reappeared in the kitchen doorway. He raised an eyebrow in a silent question.

Junior, I mouthed.

"I *know* that," she said sharply. "I couldn't call the church no matter what because Clay was going there himself."

"What?"

She finally had my full attention.

"Clay is going back to his office *tonight*?" I said out loud, mostly for Neil's benefit.

Holy shit, he mouthed at me.

"Yes," Junior said emphatically. "You see why I was anxious to find out if you'd left yet."

I saw why she was so anxious. Problem is, she had no way of knowing why I shared her anxiety.

"Jesus, Junior, why didn't you tell me that right away?" I demanded, envisioning Clay's nighttime discovery of Weasel Cleaver's lifeless body, not waiting until daylight so that those of us in the cafe across the street could keep an eye on the action.

"I tried to tell you that right away," Junior said, with a small hint of triumph in her voice, which got louder with every word. "But the goddamn phone line was busy!"

"Oh," I said, chastened. "Well, I've been here for a couple of hours already. Has Clay been gone that long?"

Maybe he'd already made the awful discovery. Maybe there were police cars and ambulances circled around the Lutheran church annex already.

"No, he's been gone for less than an hour. Everyone else was gone before that. Glenda decided to have a private meeting with all of the kids, so she left with Jurgen. We got our kids put to bed and I thought I could try to talk to Clay after. I tried a couple of times to get hold of you just to make sure you'd gotten the bag, but the last time I dialed, Clay tapped me on the shoulder and said that he was going back to his office to work on the memorial service for tomorrow and he was out the door before I could say a word. You can see why I needed to make sure you weren't still inside the church, since he was headed directly there."

I had another thought.

If Clay had indeed been the one to roll that piece of paper into his own typewriter, he might already have realized that it had disappeared. Which would mean that he already knew that someone had been in his office since he'd left it this afternoon.

Mornings were busy at the church, with people in and out

of Clay's office. I had counted on that jumble to distract Clay, to keep him from noticing the missing paper at least until after he'd made the gruesome discovery in his supply cupboard.

It would be all too easy to narrow down who had been in his office if he realized the note was gone tonight.

The scenario played in full Technicolor in my head: *A frantic Clay calls Junior telling her that he's just found Weasel Cleaver's dead body in his supply cupboard (he of course does not mention the missing page from his typewriter, something he noticed as soon as he turned on the light). A horrified Junior replies without thinking, I wonder if Tory noticed the body when she took the bag from the closet?*

So much for gloves. So much for tongs. So much for trying to keep our interference a secret. I was definitely feeling weak in the knees.

Neil, who didn't have to hear the entire conversation, or see the scenes in my head, to know exactly what I was thinking, had already dug into the pocket of my coat and pulled the typewritten sheet out, forgetting all about tongs and fingerprints.

I know he was regretting the decision to take it. I know he was feverishly thinking of ways to put it back without getting caught. I know he was every bit as frightened as me.

But I didn't know everything.

I didn't know that he was going to turn the sheet over.

And I sure as hell hadn't known that there was something written on the back.

45

Playing the Numbers

Some kind of hotshot investigator I am. If Miss Marple was a tad more corporeal, she'd be laughing her ass off right about now.

Well, maybe Miss Marple would be too ladylike to indulge in anything more than a slightly superior smile over the scones. But Nero Wolfe would be *pfui*-ing all over the place. And Kinsey Millhone would not be able to respectfully submit anything presented by a person who went to the trouble to steal a seemingly vital piece of paper, who didn't have the sense to turn it over and check out the back.

Maintaining an outwardly calm phone voice, I reassured Junior that Clay was not about to stumble into me as I snooped around in his office. With a completely false statement that I had already taken Annelise's bag to the cafe where it would wait safely for Glenda to reclaim it in the morning, I hung up as quickly as I could.

Neil had already placed the sheet, typewritten side down on the counter, and was silently studying what had been written on the reverse.

"What do you make of these, Tory?" he asked without looking up.

I leaned over his shoulder and saw that there were three sets of numbers penciled on the page, a set scribbled across the top and another pair written a couple of inches below the first. The pencil had been dull and the marks were very light, which made the fact that I hadn't noticed them earlier a little easier to swallow.

"1593–1679," I read out loud. "800–1247. 4011–5729." I stopped to think for a minute. "Phone numbers, do you think? Maybe they're all 1–800 places."

"But where are the prefixes?" Neil asked. "Who writes partial phone numbers down?"

"You're probably right," I said, scratching my head. "There aren't any dollar signs, so I don't think it's money. The numbers are too big to be dates. Do you suppose it's a credit card number or some other kind of ID? Maybe PIN?"

"Could be," Neil said, tracing a finger over the writing. It was too late to worry about fingerprints anyway. "Whoever wrote on this wrote very lightly. There's no impression on the paper at all."

"Good. That makes it a little less embarrassing that I didn't notice it before."

"That also means that they didn't write on top of a stack of paper, or anything soft. If they had, you'd be able to feel the numbers on the other side. This was written on a hard surface."

"Like a desk?" I asked, thinking of Clay's, which had few bare surfaces.

"Or the typewriter itself. Almost anywhere, actually," Neil said wearily.

"So what does it mean?" I asked.

"Damned if I know. But it means something or whoever it was wouldn't have taken the time to write it down. We'll probably make more progress if we can figure out why it was in Clay's office. And why it was in the typewriter."

"Which came first, the pencil or the typewriter?" I mused. "And did the same person write both? Clay uses an old Selectric, can you feel the letters on the back of the sheet?" My frugal typing teacher used to make us use both sides of every sheet of paper, and I remembered that sometimes the pages felt more like Braille than regular homework.

Neil swept his fingers lightly across the whole sheet. "Hard to tell. I think that I can feel some letter impressions under the numbers. If I had to make an educated guess, I'd say that the numbers were written first and the page rolled into the typewriter after."

"In that case, maybe they don't mean anything at all. Maybe Clay . . . or whoever," I amended, "was merely recycling old checkbook scribbles. Or catalog order numbers. Or Bible verse notations."

"Or hymn selections," Neil said, sagging a little. "This came from a minister's office, after all. A minister who is known to write his sermons and schedules by hand before typing them out on a dinosaur."

I sagged a little myself.

"We're never going to figure it out with just this much to go on," I said.

"Not likely," Neil agreed. "But we aren't limited to just what we have here, you know."

"Uhuh. I'm not going back to that office," I said adamantly. "Even if there wasn't a body in the cupboard. Besides, Clay is there now. What would we do, knock and ask if we can come in and snoop for a bit as he works?"

"We don't have to go back there, we can keep an eye on things from here," Neil said, grabbing his glass and beckoning. "Follow me."

He headed down the hallway for a door at the far end.

I grabbed my glass and trotted down the hall, through the door, up the stairs after him, at a much slower pace of course.

"Why didn't *I* think of this?" I asked, settling myself sideways on a padded window seat. I leaned over the back cushion, put my glass on the windowsill, and gazed at the silent, snow-covered town below.

Neil had recently completed the interior work on his tower, which was a lovely little hexagonal cupola with a 360-degree view of the surrounding prairie, perched on the top of his already tall house. Except for the church steeple, the grain elevator and the WEB water tower, we were sitting in the highest point in Delphi.

Before he sat on the window seat beside me, Neil put a CD in the small boom box in the corner and by the time he sat next to me, Jose Feliciano was strumming "California Dreamin' " softly in the dark.

"We can't see much even from up here," I said quietly.

We had a perfect view of the length of Delphi's main drag, the snow-packed two-lane gravel road that ran the length of the town, but there were no streetlights. The moon was shrouded in clouds so even the solid blanket of snow was gray and full of shadows. The most we could make out were a few house lights and occasional headlights backing in and out from the bar.

"The annex is on the other side of the church, we wouldn't be able to see it even in the daylight," Neil said. "Besides which, Clay's office is an interior room. We'll notice if a whole bunch of red lights come barreling into town, though. As long as the street stays dark and quiet, we'll know that Clay hasn't opened that cupboard door yet."

"And what do we do when he does?" I asked, settling back against Neil, who wrapped his arms around me and propped his chin on top of my head.

"We bundle up and go outside into the street and watch the excitement, with the rest of Delphi's good little citizens."

The thought of watching Weasel's body as it was wheeled out of the annex made me shudder.

"Are you cold?" Neil reached back and grabbed a cotton comforter from a rocking chair and wrapped it around my shoulders and tucked it under my chin. "I insulated as best I could up here, but we're exposed on all sides and it's never going to be warm in the winter up this high."

"Thanks," I said, drawing the comforter in tightly. It was cool in the tower, though not nearly as chilly as either the annex or the cafe had been earlier today. Which reminded me of the broken furnace.

"Why do you suppose he came here in the first place?"

Neil knew who I was talking about. "Probably just to scope the joint, casing it for further felonies."

"Call me silly," I said, "but I think he had some higher purpose."

"Weasel Cleaver only had lower purposes," Neil assured me.

"Usually, I'd agree with you," I said. "But he seemed genuinely sad that he couldn't talk to Aphrodite. Maybe he wanted to apologize to her."

"Well, he's probably getting his chance right now," Neil said simply.

I chuckled. "You think he's not destined for the fiery pits? Or do you think Aphrodite is down there too?"

"Lord no. Aphrodite was a good human being, she's not only not *there*," he emphasized the word, "sometimes, I think she's still *here*."

Though I'd never told him about the odd occurrences after Aphrodite died, I agreed with Neil completely.

"But Weasel wasn't a good human being," Neil pointed out.

"He wasn't so terribly bad either. Most of his crimes were misdemeanors. They were more pitiful than anything else. He tried hard, but he never quite managed being a badass. He was just a pain, and a clumsy one at that. Even the escapade with the underage girl was pathetic. I think he really thought she was eighteen years old."

The girl had been troubled long before Weasel came into her life. And she'd testified sincerely under oath that she'd convinced him of her legal ability to give consent.

"But once he knew that Aphrodite was dead, why didn't he just leave town?" I asked. "Why was he still in the church?"

And of course, there was the big unspoken question: *Why did someone kill him?*

"We don't know that he *was* still in the church. He could have been moved back there after he was killed. Or he could have been forced back before being killed."

I'd had no real fondness for Weasel, but I found both of

those scenarios chilling. I didn't like picturing him frightened or hurt or begging for his life in vain. I shivered under the comforter.

Neil tightened his arms around me.

"That whole period of time between when he disappeared and you found him is completely unaccounted for," Neil continued. "We're not all that sure about what happened before that either."

"None of it makes sense," I said, shaking my head.

"Yes it does, and we probably already have the key. We just don't see the connection yet. But if we keep at it, we will."

So we kept at it, talking softly in the dark as the Feliciano CD played over and over, providing a sweet guitar backdrop for conversations about death and giving up cherished illusions.

Down below, Delphi harbored her secrets well. Vehicles came and went by ones and twos, headlights burned holes into the black night, but no ambulances or Highway Patrol cruisers arrived with their sirens wailing and lights flashing.

We talked about Clay. And we talked about Weasel. And we talked about Junior and the choir and poor Annelise.

We didn't talk about us because we didn't have to.

We sat in Neil Pascoe's tower for the rest of the night, wrapped in a comforter and each other, and dozed when we weren't talking and listened to music when we weren't dozing. And reveled in our own warmth.

And our world, for a few hours at least, was quiet.

46

All Quiet on the Eastern Front

EARLY THE NEXT MORNING

It's easy to forget, in the heat of all the excitement and turmoil, that everyday life in Delphi doesn't revolve around unexpectedly dead bodies, or traveling choirs, or even alleged infidelities.

Sure, all those things happen from time to time, especially the last, but none was allowed to interfere with the real business of the day, which was gathering at the cafe to talk over what happened the day before. That a portion of what happened yesterday occurred *at* the cafe only added a little panache. It ensured that the breakfast crowd would be that much larger, and therefore the workload that much heavier. Which meant that I needed to get to work that much earlier to prepare for the onslaught.

From sheer habit and an aching back, I'd awakened at my usual five A.M., cocooned on the window seat in the tower. Tiptoeing as quietly as possible, I'd planted a swift kiss on Neil's forehead before tucking the comforter up around his neck.

He was still dozing when I let myself out of his house and

trudged across the street to my quiet trailer, where I quickly showered and dressed and then trudged the three snow-covered blocks to the cafe in the dark.

I let myself in through the back entrance, automatically switching on the lights as I hung my coat on the hook next to the back door. I also automatically turned up the thermostat before remembering that would do no good.

I muttered a couple of very bad words under my breath and marched over to the furnace, peering at it sharply as though just looking at it would tell me how to render the blasted machine functional. Unfortunately I was not a furnace repair specialist yesterday, and I'll be damned if the same situation didn't apply today. I muttered another unprintable word or two and aimed a swift kick at the beast out of sheer frustration.

To my complete and total surprise, the furnace fan turned on and the interior flame whooshed into life and almost instantly, wonderful warm air began to blow down from the registers. I looked at my foot, and then back at the furnace, wondering if poor Weasel had given his life in vain—if a simple kick wouldn't have saved us a world of trouble.

Then I remembered Annelise, and realized that with or without Weasel, yesterday had been destined for the dumper right from the beginning. Today didn't look to be much of an improvement.

I sighed, and with Annelise's bag slung over my shoulder, I worked my way down the hallway and through the kitchen, flipping on light switches, turning on the grill and the deep fat fryer.

With another sigh, I left the kitchen and stashed Annelise's bag under the counter by the till. I'd debated whether to put the bag back behind the booth where Junior had found it. But then I remembered that it was behind the booth only because Junior had stashed it there and no one would look for it there come morning. And given that the cafe usually got a thorough cleaning each evening, no one would expect to find the bag in the booth where Annelise had been sitting either.

Purposely treating it like the rest of the lost and found detritus, I shoved the bag into a cubbyhole under the counter, alongside the stray mittens and overdue library books and unclaimed packages.

"Where the hell have you been?" Alanna drawled from the kitchen, startling the hell out of me.

She rarely makes an unannounced entrance, and given her height and physical presence, it's hard for her to go anywhere unnoticed. But I'd been intent on my thoughts and hadn't heard her.

"Jesus, Alanna, don't do that," I said, exasperated. "At least make some noise first."

"I did make noise," she said. "I stomped snow off my boots and I slammed the door. You just didn't hear me. Anyway, where the hell were you last night?"

"She spent the night with Neil Pascoe," Del said, from the kitchen.

I was astonished—Del and Alanna *both* at work early for a change. They must have been as anxious for gossip as the rest of the town would be in, oh, say fifteen minutes.

"I did not spend the night *with* Neil," I said, cursing the blush that crawled up my neck.

"Oh ho," Alanna said, laughing. "I think she protests too much. Look at those little pink cheeks."

Del, who still had her coat looped over one arm, peered at me closely. "Nah, she didn't get any," she said over her shoulder to Alanna. This was Del's field of expertise, and I suppose she was able to look a person over and tell definitively when and where their last sexual encounter had taken place. She grinned wickedly. "Yet."

"Can we just get to work here?" I asked sharply, not quite willing to discuss the whens and wherefores of my incipient sex life with either of them.

"Well, that'd be one way to keep warm," Alanna said, ignoring me, as always. "It's for sure that no one will warm up in this ice box. That creepy little furnace man didn't fix anything. You need to call his boss today and complain, Tory."

She hugged her coat around herself and shivered a little.

I would have argued with her on general principle. After all, Alanna had made the decision to call to Weasel's employer. Theoretically, any displeasure she felt in the service rendered would be her bailiwick. But since I'd planned to call the company this morning anyway, I let it go.

"Alanna, take your coat off," I said gently, holding my hands up and indicating the warm air.

"What?" she asked, confused.

"It's warm in here," Del said, exasperated. "Therefore the furnace is working. Which means that the little creep did fix it yesterday. Can't you tell the difference?"

"Listen, when it's a hunnert and twenty degrees below zero every single day in this terrible state, it's pretty hard to tell the difference between sixty and seventy-five when you get inside."

"I have no idea if he fixed the furnace or not," I said carefully. When I'd left the cafe yesterday, the furnace was still nonfunctional. And when I'd last seen Weasel, he was even more so. "I think it just decided to work today. In any case, it's warm in here for now, and you can take your coat off and stop complaining."

"It'd be my pleasure," Alanna said, unzipping her heavy-duty parka to reveal a short, tight black uniform accented with a frilly white organdy apron. All she needed was one of those little lace caps and she'd have looked like a porn director's notion of a French maid. "What are you doing for a special this morning?" she asked as she deliberately placed her coat on a hook in the kitchen where she knew full well that it did not belong.

"Me?" I asked. "I'm not doing anything for a special this morning except serving it up." And frankly, my plans didn't involve doing much of that. I intended to hover by the window and keep an eye on the church. All morning if necessary.

"Au contraire," Alanna said, a terrible French accent overlaying her Oklahoma drawl. "You are cooking today. I am serving, madame."

She performed a little curtsy, and I was suddenly certain that her present outfit had been recycled from one of her old stripper costumes. It probably came apart in bits and pieces, which would delight all our male patrons.

Del was less than enchanted, but she said nothing as she made the rounds, straightening salt and pepper shakers and swabbing the tabletops.

"I'm not cooking today," I said adamantly.

"Oh yes you are," Alanna said, sounding more like Pepe LePew than Maurice Chevalier. "I cooked yesterday and we alternate. Remember?"

"Dammit," I muttered.

We'd agreed to alternate until we could find a permanent cook, and yesterday had been her day in the kitchen. She was obviously set on serving the public today.

"I don't suppose . . ." I let my sentence trail off.

"Non."

The *n* was supposed to be silent, but she said it anyway.

"Okay," I said to the ceiling. "The special today is scrambled eggs and toast, twelve-ninety-five a plate."

"Are you out of your mind?" Alanna asked, all accents abandoned in the wake of her indignation. "That'll clear people outta here so fast that we won't serve anyone."

I just smiled and pushed through the swinging half-door that divided the cafe from the kitchen. Del followed me with her hands on her hips.

"You aren't serious, are you?" she asked, looking me right in the eye, daring me to bullshit her.

"Of course not," I said, "I just like annoying Alanna." I cast a sideways glance at Del. "I don't suppose *you'd* like to cook this morning?"

"I don't suppose you've lost your mind," she replied. "Oh that's right. You *have* lost your mind. You spend the night with Neil without letting me know you're not coming home. You get message after message that I have to write down. And you let Weasel Cleaver get away without giving me back any of those clothes. We're going to get you ready for the rubber room pretty soon."

I thought about Weasel's borrowed finery and figured that the present owner, whoever he was and whatever Del'd had to do to get them, would not be all that thrilled to get them back anyway.

"I assume the clothes will be returned," I said quietly. "Eventually."

"They'd better be," she growled. "Were you joking about calling his boss too?'

"If it's not too busy this morning," I said, indicating the grill, "I can call as soon as they open up. I doubt if the furnace is really fixed. I just kicked it and it started again, so it's probably just a loose wire anyway. They can send someone to look it over."

"Let's hope they send someone besides Weasel this time."

"I don't think that'll be a problem," I said, wincing. "Besides, I need to complain about that damn van. I want them to get it out of here, we need the parking space."

Since the repair van was still parked in front of the cafe, there was no point in pretending not to know about it. In fact, annoyance would add to my indignation and make my whole investigative phone call seem more logical.

"What van?" Del asked.

"Weasel's van," I said slowly. "The furnace repair vehicle. The one he left here yesterday when he took a powder with your borrowed clothes. It's still parked right in front of the cafe."

I did not add, the one that had still been here last night *after* I found Weasel's dead body stashed in Clay Deibert's office.

"You better get yourself some glasses real soon, hon." Del patted my shoulder condescendingly. "There's no van parked in front of the cafe."

47

Van Gone

I suppose it's human nature to disbelieve what you really didn't want to hear in the first place. Missouri may be the Show Me state, but the sentiment is pretty widespread in South Dakota too.

"What do you mean, *there's no van out there*?" I asked Del. "Of course Weasel's van is out there. I saw it last . . ." I paused, deciding that was more information than Del needed at the moment. "It was out there yesterday," I finished lamely.

"Of course it was out there yesterday," Del said, peering at me worriedly. She spoke slowly and clearly. "Weasel was here yesterday, taking his clothes off in our storeroom and wrapping himself in paper towels. Since it's warm this morning, he may even have indulged in a little nude furnace repair. But the Canadian choir chickie stole his van, and there's no reason in the world to think she'd have brought it back and parked out in front of the cafe this morning." She peered at me closely. "Right?"

I had to be careful. I'd already forgotten that Del knew nothing about what had happened at the church after I'd left the cafe yesterday. She didn't know that Meg had denied taking the van or that her denial had been seconded by the rest of the choir.

She didn't know that the van had mysteriously reappeared. She certainly didn't know it had been still parked in front of the cafe last evening, long after poor Weasel himself had departed this mortal coil.

She thought that Weasel had hitched a ride back to Aberdeen with the express purpose of keeping an ill-gotten flannel shirt and pair of jeans.

"You're right," I agreed, nodding my head for emphasis. It was nearly impossible to put something over on Del once she was following a scent so I threw her a red herring. "I don't know what got into me. I'm just tired, I guess."

"Yeah, well, staying up all night with librarians will do that to a person," Del said, grinning wickedly. "Next time try sleeping with him."

"I'll remember that," I said, not having to manufacture a blush, "if the occasion arises again."

That made Del laugh out loud, which distracted her even more. " 'Scuse me for just a minute," I mumbled, hoping to get out of the kitchen without further scrutiny. "Gotta see a man about a thing."

"I should think so," Del agreed. "And real soon now."

I nodded and pushed through the half-door back into the cafe just as Alanna flipped the *Open* sign over and unlocked the cafe door. It would be no more than a few minutes before the first early morning stragglers showed up to be astonished by Janette or Isabel or whatever she intended to call herself while tricked out in French maid finery.

Soon the joint would be hopping and I'd be too busy in the kitchen to worry about anything but eggs over easy.

Trying to be unobtrusive, I risked a quick peek out the front window just to confirm that it wasn't Del who needed glasses. Unfortunately, her eyes were just fine. The Waldlach Furnace Repair van was no longer parked in front of the cafe. Nor was it parked in sight anywhere along Delphi's main drag.

Except for a couple of tire tracks in the snow, there was no proof that it had ever been parked in front of the cafe, much less been and gone, and been and gone again. Thank God Neil had seen it last night too, or I'd have begun to worry about my eyesight too, not to mention my sanity.

I shook my head and dug in a pocket for a stray quarter and hustled over to the pay phone by the door and dialed.

"Hello," Neil said groggily.

"Hey," I said softly. "Sorry to wake you but there've been developments."

"Hey back atcha," he said. I could hear the sleepy smile in his voice. "You can wake me up any time. What's going on?"

"You'll never believe it," I said, turning my back to the cafe and speaking as softly as possible, "but the van is gone."

"What do you mean gone?" All grogginess left his voice. "It was there last night."

"Yes indeedy," I said. "It was there, and it was locked. And the responsible party was in no condition to drive it."

"Damn," Neil said.

"That's what I thought," I said. "Did we sleep through all of the excitement? Could the Highway Patrol have come in without lights and sirens and taken the body and towed the van in the dark?"

"Doesn't seem likely," Neil said. I could see him rubbing his forehead, trying to concentrate. "Is there a yellow crime scene ribbon blocking the annex entrance?"

"Just a second," I said, setting the receiver down on top of the phone and darting back to the window.

Across the street, the church and annex were both dark and quiet. The sun was not yet up, but as far as I could tell, there was no evidence that a flurry of activity had taken place during the night—no tire tracks, no flapping yellow ribbons, no trampled snow in the adjoining boulevards. Everything looked exactly the way it had the night before, except for the missing van.

"Don't you have work to do?" Alanna demanded as I walked back to the phone.

"Leave her alone, she's talking to her sweetie," Del said, with only a shade more amusement than malice.

"Ah, isn't that cute," Alanna cooed.

I ignored them both and picked up the receiver again. "Nope," I said quietly. "Everything looks exactly the way it did last night. Dark and quiet. I don't think anyone has discovered Weasel yet, which makes sense. Clay won't be in for another half-hour or so, and he's usually the first of the church bunch to arrive."

"So what happened to the van, then?"

"A reasonable question," I replied, shivering as Eldon McKee opened the cafe door and stepped inside. He was followed by a couple of retired farmers and a trucker who'd just pulled in. "It seems safe to assume that whoever killed him also took the van."

"Maybe," Neil said slowly. "Maybe not."

"What do you mean?" I demanded. "I'd think that Occam's Razor would apply here. Whoever killed Weasel would also have had access to his keys. Ergo."

"That is if Weasel actually had his keys," Neil said. "Whoever took the van in the first place may still have them."

"You think someone stole the van twice?" I asked incredulous.

Del tapped me on the shoulder.

"Uh, as delighted as I am to see that your personal life is taking an upturn, we have a business to run," she said pointedly. "Unless you're good at psychokinetic cooking, you're going to have to get your ass back into the kitchen, toot sweet, dearie. Nanette and her tits"—she indicated Alanna, who was dipping and mincing all over the place, to the extreme delight of Eldon and his cronies—"are going to have this place packed in a few minutes. You might wanna think about dealing with that fact." She patted me on the shoulder with a forced smile. "Real soon now."

The cafe had filled alarmingly in the past few minutes, and Alanna was trying to signal me furiously while at the same time play Paree for guys who'd never had trouble staying down on the farm.

"The joint is jumping already, Neil. I gotta run," I said reluctantly. Then I had a flash of brilliance. "Why don't you come up here and help me keep an eye on things. No one will be at the library for hours anyway."

"An excellent suggestion, I'll be right there," he said, hanging up without further ado.

Del was watching me closely with narrowed eyes, so I allowed a small smile to dance across my lips. Rather than suspect me of nefarious plotting, she'd just think I was giddy after talking to Neil on the phone. She may have been almost right.

Knowing that she was watching my every move, I went back into the kitchen and pretended to be busy cooking up breakfast orders.

Very soon, I forgot to pretend. There were so many requests for scrambled eggs, bacon, and toast that I didn't have one second to think about Weasel, or his amazing reappearing-vanishing van, or Annelise's suicide. Or even Neil. The rhythm and sizzle of cooking on the grill took over my brain as I channeled the spirit of Aphrodite Ferguson, cooking mediocre food for a reasonable price.

"Uh, Tory," Del said, interrupting the flow. She stood on the other side of the stainless-steel counter, ready to pick up a couple of plates, "you might want to keep an eye out here if you can."

"Why?" I asked, too busy flipping hash browns to look up. "Is Neil here?"

"Neil's been here for fifteen minutes already; he's staring out the window like there's something interesting going on across the street. *Is* there something interesting going on across the street?"

If Del didn't know already, then obviously nothing was happening.

"Evidently not," I said, without looking up. "But if it's not Neil, what then?"

"It's her," Del said.

Something in her voice made me look up.

Glenda Harrison had entered the cafe and was sitting in the same booth where Annelise had sat the day before. She was perfectly coiffed and dressed, but there was an air of sadness and exhaustion, and maybe something like desperation, in her expression.

"She said something about picking up that bag, you know, the one the kid left here yesterday?" Del continued. "The one that Junior took with her?"

"Yeah," I said, assembling breakfasts as I talked over the hiss and sizzle. "Junior said to give the bag to her this morning. It's under the counter by the till."

Del stood and looked at me for a moment. "I'm not even going to ask how it got back here," she said. "But someday, I want an explanation. A full explanation."

This time I did look up and smile. "You got it."

As a pair of eggs cooked over hard on the grill, I risked a quick glance around the cafe and spotted Neil sitting in the window booth directly in front of Glenda's. He smiled and winked at me.

I was about to wink and smile in return, when I caught a movement behind him.

Though she'd been staring down into her coffee cup in a melancholy fashion, Glenda suddenly frowned and leaned in closer to the wall beside her in the booth. A confused look crossed her face as she squinted at whatever had caught her eye.

She reached down beside her, fished a bit, then extracted a piece of paper that had evidently lodged itself between the booth and the wall.

A piece of paper that even from this distance I recognized.

48

Sour Note

Del saw it the same time I did. And like me, she knew exactly what it was.

As she stood frozen, with a pot of decaf in her hand, ready to pour hot coffee right in Eldon McKee's lap, Del's jaw dropped to her chin. Without changing positions, she managed to signal to me that Glenda was just about to read something we both had thought was long gone.

Del wasn't the only one.

Neil, who had been watching me, turned to follow my gaze in time to see Glenda pull a wrinkled sheet of paper from the crevice between the booth and the wall. The fact that he had never seen that particular piece of paper before didn't keep him from knowing exactly what it was.

Or why Del and I were so shocked.

Why in the world would Junior have hidden Annelise's suicide note in the same booth where she'd fallen unconscious?

We'd assumed that her reason for taking it in the first place had been to keep secret the damning accusations it contained. To have inexpertly stashed it in exactly the place where someone might be expected to look for further clues to Annelise's actions made no sense at all.

"She must have panicked," Del whispered. With the ease of long practice, she'd managed to hit Eldon's cup with a stream of hot coffee, and bypassing her usual geezer flirtation, she'd set the pot on the burner and rushed to the stainless-steel counter and leaned over it for a confab. "There's no other explanation."

"Makes no sense at all," I agreed quietly as the bacon sizzled merrily on its way to becoming pure carbon. "She could just have easily stuck it in her pocket and gotten it the hell out of here."

As we whispered and watched, Glenda read the note. She looked puzzled at first, her eyes then widened, her mouth opened, and though there was the usual amount of hiss and rattle in the cafe, I could swear I heard her sharp intake of breath as she read the damning words.

"Look down," Del commanded suddenly. *"Now."*

I concentrated on scraping the remains of someone's breakfast off the grill, but out of the corner of my eye saw Glenda look up and peer at the two of us suspiciously.

"What do we do now?" I asked out of the corner of my mouth. "She's watching us."

"Hell if I know," Del said under her breath. "Our best bet is to pretend that we never saw it before. She can't prove otherwise."

I thought about that as I cracked a couple more eggs. Junior, Del, and I had read the note. We'd also touched it, so if anyone official cared to check, they'd find our fingerprints nice and clear, right under Glenda's.

But did Glenda know we'd seen the note? I thought not, given that Junior had hidden it before Glenda even knew it existed.

I watched Glenda peripherally. She was visibly shocked and horrified. And confused. And ready to confront someone about the writing on the page she held in her hand.

"Aieee," I said softly as Glenda left her booth and stormed up the aisle toward us. "Here she comes. Look busy. Deny everything."

"Hey, no problem. This is your baby," Del whispered, and

then said out loud, "Are my scrambleds done yet? I got hungry men waiting for breakfast."

"Coming right up," I said nonchalantly, though the only eggs I had cooking at the moment were theoretically sunny-side-up.

I pretended to be busy, which wasn't hard. Alanna, standing at the far end of the cafe, had been staring suspiciously in our direction too. She and her ensemble had packed the joint and I wasn't keeping up with orders fast enough to suit her or her admirers.

If her plan was to jump-start business with recycled stripper gear, she picked a piss poor day for an unannounced trial run. I didn't have energy to deal with drooling customers, bereaved choir directors, and still undiscovered dead bodies across the street all at the same time.

"Excuse me," Glenda said as Del dropped a quick wink and sidled away.

Her loyalty was touching.

"Yeah?" I said, not looking up. I didn't have to pretend to be busy anymore. I had plenty of orders backed up, and I was not nearly as adroit as Aphrodite, who could talk, cook, and smoke simultaneously.

"You do own this cafe, don't you?" Glenda asked. "I mean you're in charge here, right?"

"Sorta," I said, beginning to understand why Aphrodite had been terminally terse. People probably insisted on talking to her as she flipped pancakes. "Alanna over there"—I pointed with the spatula—"owns the place with me. We run it together."

I did my best to avoid eye contact but I could see that she was bone-deep tired, lines etched deeply in her face. I doubted she'd slept much in the last twenty-four hours.

"But you seem to be in charge," Glenda insisted.

I shrugged. I certainly wasn't jockeying for the position, but when the shit hit the fan, I seemed always to be right in front of it, and that's as good a working definition of *in charge* as any.

Glenda thrust Annelise's suicide note under my nose. "Well, do you know anything about this?"

I mimed that my hands were full, desperately trying to think of what to do. I risked a quick peek at Del, hoping for guidance, but she was at Neil's booth, talking seriously with him over a cinnamon roll. Neither looked my way. Alanna, whose radar was always on, sensed trouble. She did her best to blend into the furniture at the far end of the cafe—a hopeless task given the way she was dressed, but she gave it the old college try.

"I'm pretty busy right now," I said, trying to sound genuinely sorry not to drop everything to help a customer. "Can we talk about whatever this is after the cafe clears out a little?"

"I don't think it can wait," Glenda said urgently. "I found this piece of paper stuck next to the wall in that booth back there." She turned and pointed at the booth. "I'm certain that it was written by Annelise, the girl who died yesterday, before she lost consciousness . . ." Glenda's voice trailed off. She sounded confused and near tears. "I don't know what to do with it."

This time I did look straight at her.

I'd expected anger, or accusations. Del and I had both steeled ourselves for righteous indignation at full volume, for demands to summon the authorities. For screams and more accusations and especially demands for Clay Deibert's execution. I figured that the breakfast crowd would see a performance that would more than rival anything Alanna could manage, in or out of a French maid uniform. I had not expected Glenda Harrison, former Miss America runner-up, to show any hesitation or vulnerability.

And I especially didn't expect her to consult me on the next course of action.

Tear it up, I thought, but did not say out loud. *Pretend you never saw it*. I frantically sorted through possible replies, finally remembering that officially I had no idea what she was talking about.

"If you found something that belongs to that poor girl, then you should follow whatever procedures cover these kinds of situations," I said, deeply aware of how lame that sounded. There was nothing I could do to prevent Glenda from broadcasting the contents of the note without drawing attention to Junior herself, which would only make things worse. "Other than that, I don't know what to tell you." I had very carefully not asked to see the note.

"But it says right here," Glenda said, waving the paper in my face, "that Annelise was molested and you people need to know about it!" Her voice rose in agitation. A few heads swiveled in our direction.

"Are you sure you aren't mistaken?" I asked, keeping a neutral expression.

I had a hard enough time keeping orders straight when things ran smoothly at the cafe. The tension of waiting for Weasel's body to be discovered had garbled what little timing I had, so everything was already jumbled. Word that something was up was spreading throughout the cafe. More and more people were watching Glenda. Alanna peered at me suspiciously—she didn't know what was happening but it was plainly all my fault.

"Of course I'm not mistaken" Glenda declared sharply. Her vulnerability and confusion had been swallowed by indignation.

I'd taken the wrong tack. Obviously, small-town waitresses/short-order cooks were not allowed to question the comprehension of Miss America third runners-up.

"Here, let me see the"— I said, stopping myself just in time. I'd almost called it a *suicide note*— "it." I clamped my jaws shut and held out a hand in the hope that cooperation would result in a lower volume.

She thrust the note at me triumphantly and said, unfortunately as loudly as before, "You'll see what I mean and why something has to be done immediately! He's intending to hold a memorial service within an hour, and this—"

Her voice got even louder. She was on the brink of naming not only the alleged perpetrator but the crime as well, when Neil smoothly and deliberately slid his coffee cup and the plate with his half-eaten roll off the edge of his table.

They landed on the floor with a resounding crash, shattering not only the porcelain but Glenda's train of thought.

I believe I fell in love with him on the spot.

49

Fahrenheit 375

Of course the purpose of creating a diversion is to focus attention away from whatever it is that you don't want others to notice. Magicians and con men make an art of misdirection, skillfully drawing the eye to the hand *without* the rabbit. The audience, perfectly willing to suspend disbelief, happily follows the bouncing ball, seeing only what the master wants them to see.

Our own particular audience, which was only marginally intrigued by an outsider suicide and therefore bored and ripe for the plucking, was more than willing to fall for Neil's clever method of interrupting Glenda's recital.

Problem is, effective as his diversion was, I had no idea what to do with it, and very little time to come up with a plan of action. I couldn't just pretend that she hadn't given the note to me—too many people had spotted the exchange for that.

I was no good at forgery, and would not have been able to fashion a substitute even given enough time to work out the wording.

My options were unfortunately simple—give Annelise's

suicide note back to Glenda and allow her to broadcast the contents to one and all, or destroy it immediately.

Giving her the note would wreak havoc on the town in general, and on Clay and Junior in particular. If the accusations were false, there would be no turning back. Memories in Delphi were long and strong—Clay would be branded forever and probably ruined. Protestations of innocence would fall on deaf ears.

If the awful accusations turned out to be true, Del and I could corroborate, having seen the note personally. Neil could give hearsay backup to my report of the contents, which meant that in a worst-case scenario, the guilty party would still face justice.

Those twin realizations relieved what little conscience I had.

Without further ado, as Glenda and everyone else in the cafe turned to see the wreckage of Neil's cinnamon roll and coffee, not to mention a couple bucks' worth of cafe crockery, I deftly aimed Annelise's suicide note at the deep fat fryer and let it go.

My understanding of the aerodynamic properties of a wrinkled sheet of paper when combined with the natural air currents in the hot kitchen did not fail me. The page floated softly to my left and settled into the bubbling oil where it sank almost immediately.

"Damn!" I said loud enough to divert nearby attention back to me.

Glenda spun around.

I remembered just in time to plaster a horrified look on my face.

"Shit," I said, again loudly, using tongs to fish the ruined note quickly out of the hot oil. I had remembered my Ray Bradbury and since the fryer temp was set well below the combustion point of paper, I knew that I wouldn't have a flash fire on my hands. But the spatters and splashes were still a bother. Not to mention that I'd have to dump the contaminated oil and start with a fresh batch.

I looked up at Glenda who was watching me with consternation.

"What happened?" she demanded. "That isn't Annelise's note, is it?"

I shrugged. "Sorry, the breaking dishes startled me and I let go of it . . ." I waved the soggy, now transparent paper with the tongs. "It just fell."

It was lame, but no more lame than anything else I'd said or done in the last two days.

"But it's ruined," Glenda said, her voice rising hysterically. "I can't believe you destroyed it." She paused and narrowed her eyes and continued quietly, "You did that on purpose, didn't you?"

"On purpose?" I echoed innocently. I'd learned that very young—when confronted with your own dastardly deeds, turn the accusation into a question. "Why on earth would you think that?"

"Because you small-town rubes always stick together," she hissed. "I might have known you'd try to protect him."

"Protect whom?" I asked, wide-eyed. As far as Glenda knew, I still hadn't read the note. "From what?"

She glared at me, her lips in a tight white line, daring me to speak again.

I didn't. I just stood there, holding a hot, illegible, dripping piece of paper, forcing just a little indignation at her foundationless accusation.

"Do you still want this?" I asked, trying to seem helpful. "Maybe it can be salvaged."

I didn't think that was in the least possible, but I thought the offer might mollify Glenda. It didn't.

"Keep it," she said, clipping her words neatly. "It doesn't matter anyway. The truth won't be held back by you or anyone else."

Actually I was counting on that but decided not to say so out loud.

"Now if you'll get Annelise's bag for me," Glenda said, dripping with false civility, "unless you've managed to drop it in oil too."

"Not at all," I said, which made no sense but seemed appropriate anyway. I leaned over the counter and said loudly, "Del, can you get this lady the bag that's under the counter by the till, please? I'm sure she has a lot to do and we don't want to hold her up."

"Sure thing," Del said brightly. She'd been watching us as she cleaned up the wreckage caused by Neil's diversion. She fished the green and yellow striped bag out and handed it to Glenda, who took it angrily and stormed out of the cafe.

"Quick thinking," Del said to me. She'd come into the kitchen and was tying on an apron.

"Yeah well, I don't know how much good it'll do," I said, sighing. "She's mad now. And suspicious. I expect she'll just broadcast what the note said to anyone who'll listen. Around here you're guilty until proven innocent anyhow."

"Tell me about it," she said, taking the spatula from my hand and gently nudging me aside.

"What are you doing?" I asked, grabbing for the spatula.

"Taking over," Del said while reaching up to the stainless-steel carousel where a good dozen orders were clipped. "You're so damn slow that people are starting to walk out without their food. Even peeks at Babette's panties won't keep them here if they don't get some food. It's obvious that you aren't going to be able to concentrate. So I'll cook for a while and get us caught up."

I just stood and looked at Del in wonder. I could count on one hand the number of favors I remembered her doing for anyone. That she was willing to take over for me now, especially when she hated cooking even more than I did, was amazing.

"I don't know what to say," I said softly.

"Don't say anything. Just get your butt home and change your clothes."

"What?"

This conversation was taking too many twists and turns for me to follow.

"Neil said to tell you that Jennifer Swanhorst spent the last half hour arranging the letters and putting up the notice for the memorial service on the sign out in front of the church."

"Okay," I said slowly, waiting for more. "And?"

"He said that you'd want to know that the service starts

soon, and that everything is still quiet on the western front."

Which meant that no one had discovered Weasel's body yet. But since Del didn't know about Weasel, I couldn't comment. So I raised an eyebrow instead, waiting for her to continue.

"He said that given that things are so quiet, that you might want to consider attending the memorial service. That it would be the right thing to do under any circumstance."

He was right. The tension of waiting for someone, anyone, to open that cupboard door was almost unbearable. I'd been unable to function properly even before Glenda had further complicated my day.

"Yeah," I said nodding my head. "I really should go home and change quick and get back to the church. The poor girl nearly died here. It's right that I go to her memorial service."

"Yes indeed," Del said, agreeing. "Please leave before you drive away all of our paying customers."

"I'll just get Neil and head out then," I said, taking my apron off and hanging it on a peg.

"Too late," she said, expertly cracking eggs, pouring hash browns on the grill, and popping down some toast. "He rushed out of here a few minutes ago. Said he forgot something and that he'd meet you at the church."

"Oh?"

"And for what it's worth," Del said, peering at me closely, "he told me to remind you that Jennifer spent the last half-hour *calmly* rewording the sign in front of the church."

"You said that already." I was confused. Neil was not generally given to redundancies.

"And he said that if you didn't clap your hand to your head and fall over in a swoon that I should, and I quote exactly, *Remind Tory where they keep the letters for the sign.*"

"Oh my Lord," I said.

50

A Watched Church

It's hard to find the proper mindset for the funeral of a stranger. Even with a body in a casket and weeping relatives, it's difficult to work up more than a generic grief over the death of a person you did not know personally but whose funeral you're nevertheless obligated to attend. It's harder still at a memorial service. With no flower-decked coffin or bereaved family to concentrate on, keeping your mind on the spectacle is nearly impossible.

I searched my memory for a glimpse of Annelise, animated and lively, but the only picture I could dredge up was of her sprawled in the booth when I thought she was asleep. My acquaintance with her had lasted less than an hour, during which time she wasn't even conscious.

I was sad that someone so young had decided to take her own life, but beyond that, my concern was mostly for the living, the ones affected most by her passing.

Those people I knew very well, and the toll the last day had taken on them was obvious. Clay was gray and drawn. Though he tried to hide it with sympathetic smiles and gentle hugs for the remaining choir members, I could see that he was near exhaustion. Though Junior, who herded her other neatly dressed children into a pew, might have looked normal to outsiders, I knew that the pain etched on her face had nothing to do with dead adolescents or third-trimester pregnancies.

Annelise was a cipher, an enigma, a puzzle, and now, unfortunately, she was a statistic.

The others were real, living human beings, and they were the ones who captured my attention and concern.

Well, them and that other dead person.

The one who was stuffed in a supply cupboard in Clay Deibert's office.

The supply cupboard where the interchangeable letters for the church sign were stored.

The very same cupboard that Jennifer Swanhorst must have opened in order to redo the sign announcing the memorial service, which news Neil had relayed to me through Del, though it had taken a repetition or two for the import to sink in.

Jennifer herself, running this way and that, taking Junior's place as general factotum, conferring with Clay and the organist, looked a little worse for the wear. The bags under her red and swollen eyes were evident even from my distance.

She was tired, that much was obvious. She was sad too, and not just with a surface sadness plastered on for a public performance either. She seemed melancholy right down to her bones, weary and laden, without even the energy to produce understanding and sympathetic smiles for the congregation.

But she didn't look like she'd been presented with an unexpected dead body in the last few hours. She didn't look horrified, or sickened. Or particularly surprised.

She just looked sad and frantically busy.

I watched her carefully as she facilitated the ritual, smoothing out the thousand little details that need human intervention at a time like this. I realized that underneath the sadness, she was enjoying the duty. Women like Junior and Jennifer are born not made, and their enthusiasm for molding and guiding others was as foreign to me as, well, committing suicide in a public place.

The church was filling rapidly. The choir members sat uneasily together in a group. They were also completely subdued, and their grief looked genuine and deeply felt. Around them were many local couples, probably host families. Stu and Renee McKee sat several rows in front of me, others were scattered among the congregation.

There were also quite a few strangers. I'd caught a bit of floating conversation and realized that host families from some of the other towns where the choir had performed had also driven down to attend the impromptu service.

Around me soft murmurs of condolence echoed from the high ceilings as the organist played hymns softly and those assembled whispered politely to one another.

I tried to put my mind into the proper frame. A young girl was tragically dead and a trusted friend was possibly responsible for the despair that drove her to her death. I should have been feeling a deep, if somewhat general, sorrow at one life cut short.

And I should have been feeling some anger, or at the very least ambivalence toward the friend whose possible indiscretion had set this tragedy in motion.

But what I really felt was an unbearable tension.

Glenda Harrison hovered over the choir members, patting shoulders and wiping tears and talking to each young person in turn. She gave Jurgen, the intrepid cameraman, a brief hug before sitting down at the end of one of the pews. She'd spotted me as soon as I entered the church and had sent periodic glares in my direction ever since.

She'd also directed icy stares at the podium. I would not have been surprised to see her rise from her seat and point an accusing finger at Clay.

But the anxiety of waiting for Glenda to spill beans that Junior, Neil, and I had not only conspired to keep secret, but had probably broken a few laws for, didn't touch the knowledge that there was another dead body in the church.

Though I'd dozed in Neil's tower, nestled in his arms, I'd essentially stood watch all night, waiting for the wail of sirens and the pounding of official feet.

Nothing had happened.

I'd burned countless breakfasts and probably foolishly destroyed a piece of evidence this morning at the cafe, all the while waiting for chaos to erupt across the street.

Nothing had happened.

I'd sat in that same church for fifteen minutes now, each second more unbearable than the last, waiting for someone, anyone, to scream out the news that Weasel Cleaver was not only dead, but on the premises.

Nothing happened.

A watched pot never boils.

And a watched memorial service goes ahead exactly as planned with the congregation none the wiser, though a certain cafe owner in the audience was about to expire from anxiety alone.

After a brief confab with Glenda, the choir members rose silently and rearranged themselves on the stage to sing a tribute to their friend. As usual, Jurgen captured the whole scene on videotape, though he stopped in the middle of his filming to rummage in the big black bag that he always carried.

He set the bag down on the front pew and as I watched him sort and shuffle through it, my heart suddenly began to pound. He pulled out another cassette with which he replaced the one that had been in the camera. He dropped the used cassette back into the bag and began to film the choir's preparations again.

I sat frozen in my pew, barely daring to breathe.

Barely daring to think through the revelation that had just burst like an explosion through my head.

Barely able to process that I'd just realized how Weasel Cleaver fit into the puzzle.

51

The Red Eye

It had been hard to sit still when nothing made sense, but that had been a piece of cake compared to now.

There was a whole lot that I still didn't understand, but at least a small piece of the picture had clicked squarely into my viewfinder. Problem was, of course, that I didn't know exactly what to do with the information.

Or what it really meant in the scope of things.

But I did, finally, know *something*.

And I was itching to talk it over with Neil.

As the choir launched into a truly lovely a capella version of "Ave Maria," I looked over my shoulder to see if he was standing by the outer door.

He wasn't.

I peered around to see if he'd slipped in another way without my noticing.

He hadn't.

I double checked my memory to see if I had somehow mistaken the relayed instructions to meet him here instead of at his house.

Of course I hadn't.

I had to face the fact that Neil wasn't in the church, which meant that I had to make a very quick decision on my own.

Junior was sitting with her brood, clucking over them like a mama hen, studiously ignoring almost everything about the service, which was, after all, intended to honor the passing of a girl who'd, at best, accused her husband of adultery.

Clay was alone at the podium, standing with a solemn look on his face, listening intently to the music.

Jennifer sat straight backed at the edge of an aisle front, next to her lumpish husband.

Glenda sat in the front row, dabbing her eyes as the music swelled and filled the church.

Neil was nowhere to be seen.

And Jurgen, the one I wanted to avoid the most, was busy filming it all for posterity.

Anyone who might idly wonder why I was leaving, and where I was going, was too deeply absorbed in the service to notice.

Anyone who was not quite so absorbed, and not as idly wondering, would be stuck in place, unable to follow me.

This was my one and only opportunity to follow up on that blinding flash of insight.

Without allowing myself to hesitate, or even to think it through very clearly, I patted my pocket, mumbled a few apologies, and slid quietly past the other people in my pew and out of the church and into the annex.

Even on short notice, the church ladies would assemble a traditional luncheon after the service in the community room. In an hour the place would be overflowing with Jell-O squares and Tater Tot casseroles and hushed tones, but right now the annex was silent. And dark.

Someone, probably Clay, had turned up the heat. It wasn't as cold as it had been barely twelve hours earlier, though the notion of what a warm room would do to an undiscovered dead body made my stomach roil.

I pushed the thought out of my head and paused, listening very carefully for the sound of footsteps behind me, or movement in front of me.

The annex was silent and empty.

I was alone.

Still taking no chances, I tiptoed down the hallway to Clay's office door. Pulling the keys that I had yet to return to Junior from my pocket, I quickly unlocked the door and stepped inside.

I pulled the outer office door closed behind me and without bothering to turn on a light, I walked quickly to the inner office door.

With my hand on the knob, I stood for a moment, breathing deeply, eyes closed, gathering my courage.

I turned the handle and went inside.

There, in the corner behind Clay's desk, where I'd suddenly remembered it, was the church TV-VCR combo, its red power light a glowing eye in the darkness.

It was that pinpoint of red in the pitch black room that connected the dots between Weasel and the choir.

That pinpoint of light meant that the unit had power but no tape in the slot.

Since the VCR was portable, placed on a wheeled cart expressly for the purpose of moving it from classroom to classroom, the fact that it had been plugged in meant that someone in Clay's office had been using it.

And as I watched Jurgen paw through his black bag just now, searching for a replacement cassette tape, I realized who had been using the VCR.

And why.

52

Hide and Seek

It's not my fault that I didn't make the connection earlier.

I'd noted the pinpoint red glow of the VCR light last night while I was in the office with Neil and poor Weasel as a silent witness, but had no reason to think it was significant. And even later, with the key right in front of me, I didn't make the connection because I needed to be in St. John's Lutheran Church, watching Jurgen look through his bag once again for the realization to dawn.

Weasel had sworn up and down that Meg had stolen both his van *and* his clothes.

Meg had denied the accusation, and she'd been backed up by the whole choir.

Between them, they'd produced a standoff, with neither side able to provide proof beyond their own good word.

Which, come to think of it, Weasel was currently without, being an ex-con and all.

It was easy enough to accept the unanimous assurance of a group of clean-cut, religious, foreign youths over a creep with a proven propensity to lie, cheat, and steal.

I'd given Weasel as much benefit of the doubt as I could,

and even so had not blindly taken his word against that of Meg and the rest of the choir.

Instead, I'd led the whole troop, minus Weasel, to the front door of the church in order to prove that Weasel's van was gone. Of course, I'd proven instead that Weasel's van was exactly where he'd left it, to my extreme consternation.

But what I'd also done was leave Weasel unattended for a few moments.

And in concentrating the entire troop at the front door, I'd given Weasel the opportunity to spirit away the full video-taped cassette that Jurgen had just popped out of the camera.

The same tape that Jurgen had been using all day to film the choir's assorted activities, including the protracted rehearsal during which Weasel had declared that a major member had been missing.

While our backs had been turned, Weasel had taken the tape from Jurgen's bag and hot-footed it back to Clay's office, where he knew that a VCR was handy because he'd been in the office earlier with Junior and me.

Which was also where, I was now willing to bet, he was caught.

And shortly thereafter, killed.

I mumbled a sincere apology in the direction of the supply closet and then made sure that the inner office door was firmly closed.

I turned on the light and faced the VCR, hoping that Weasel's killers hadn't also taken the tape with them.

I counted on Weasel's speed and native craftiness.

Lord knows that Delphi had suffered from his overuse of those particular skills in the past. I hoped that they'd served him well in his final moments.

The red beacon on the VCR meant that there was no tape in the slot. I looked above, under, around and behind the unit for a hiding place but came up empty.

I checked the shelves on the rolling stand.

Nothing.

I looked on the windowsill, on the bookshelves, behind the curtain, on the floor.

I looked high and low, frantically realizing that the seconds were ticking away and that I could be discovered any minute.

I spun around and opened each of Clay's desk drawers in succession, pulling them all the way out and feeling in the deep recesses. I checked the piles of paper on top of the desk. I rifled through the half-full wastebasket.

No tape.

If the killer—*or killers,* I silently amended—had not taken the cassette with them, if Weasel had actually had a chance to hide the evidence which I was now certain would exonerate him, *before* his death, there was only one place in Clay's inner office where it could be.

"No," I said softly out loud. "Please don't make me do this."

I waited a half of a heartbeat, almost expecting a rescue. Or maybe a note from heaven excusing me from what I already knew was inevitable.

I faced the supply closet, hoping I could do what I had to do without passing out. Standing as far from the cupboard as I could, I reached out and pulled the door open in one swift motion.

And understood immediately why Jennifer Swanhorst had not run screaming from the office this morning.

53

Wherefore Art Thou?

Now that I look back on it, I shouldn't have been surprised. The van was there. The van was gone. The van was there. And finally, the van was gone.

Someone had moved it between the time that Neil and I left Clay's office last night and this morning before the cafe opened. I should have realized right away that the *someone* who moved the van probably also moved Weasel's body right along with it. I mean, why leave a body in a place where suspicion is sure to be concentrated on a narrow cast of characters?

Stash a body in a church and only the people who've been in the church will be suspects.

Park a vehicle and a dead guy alongside a road somewhere, and the finger suddenly points at the whole world. Or at least that portion of the whole world driving along that particular chunk of highway during the allotted time, which was more people than the few who'd traipsed in and out of Delphi's St. John's Lutheran Church yesterday afternoon.

The very lack of chaos and police officers this morning should have signaled to me right away that things were amiss.

Or, to put it more clearly, not as amiss as I knew them to be.

No one except Neil Pascoe and I knew that Weasel Cleaver's body had been unceremoniously stuffed into Clay Deibert's office supply cupboard.

No one except the person who did the stuffing, that is.

So the lack of a dead body on the premises would not have surprised Clay when he arrived at work. And it certainly would not have surprised Jennifer Swanhorst when she rifled through the cupboard for the letters she used to change the wording on the sign out in front of the church.

However, the lack of Weasel Cleaver's dead body certainly surprised me.

So much so that for at least a minute, I stood staring at the empty lower section with my jaw hanging open and my heart pounding frantically in my chest.

"Jesus, Weasel," I said softly out loud, "you sure know how to complicate my life."

On the other hand, I felt a great deal more comfortable searching the cupboard without Weasel's dead and lifeless eyes staring up at me, not that I'd actually seen Weasel's dead and lifeless eyes. I'd managed to avoid looking at him closely, for which my subconscious would thank me in my waning years.

Unfortunately not seeing and not remembering were two different things. I could not get Weasel out of my head as I searched the back corners of each shelf in vain for a stray VCR cassette.

I tried to think like him, to understand his mind well enough to figure out what he would consider a good hiding place for a videotape cassette. All I got were flashes of assorted body parts and prison cells, so I gave up and crawled back into my own head, which was a more comfortable fit.

My own instincts finally told me that the perfect hiding spot was in plain sight.

With a triumphant hoot, I eagerly pulled the cardboard box of Sunday school videos off the shelf and pawed through the contents. Most of the selections were perky, uplifting, children's parable-type stories, told by anthropomorphic vegetables or animated kitty cats—the kind I'd been forced to sit through at Junior's house after family meals while we waited for the kids to settle down for the night.

But down at the bottom of the box was an unmarked cassette.

I bounced it in my hand for a moment, knowing that the secrets it kept were about to be spilled, that what was on the tape could possibly convict Clay while at the same time exonerating Weasel.

It was a tough choice—send a good man down the tubes in order to save the reputation of a known felon, or just let it all go. Once the secrets were loose, they could not be put back in the box. For a moment, I even considered not watching the tape. If I'd had a deep fat fryer handy, the whole thing might have been over right then and there.

But common sense prevailed. If Clay was convictable, then nothing I could do would protect him. Indeed, I should not try. And if Weasel was innocent, or at least wrongly accused, he deserved posthumous justice.

I stood very still and listened intently. Clay was not known for dragging things out. The memorial service would be winding down soon and those assembled would amble over to the annex for food and fellowship. Though most of the people would head directly for the kitchen and community room, there was a possibility that Clay, or someone else, might detour through his office.

I had no desire to be caught there, with or without an ill-gotten videotape.

While not soundproof, Clay's inner office was protected from the goings-on in the rest of the annex, and therefore noise, inside and outside, was muffled—a fact that I supposed Weasel and his killer had taken advantage of.

I tiptoed to the door and listened carefully.

There was no sound in the outer office. I shut the light off and opened the door as quietly as possible and listened some more.

There seemed to be no sound in the hallway. I tiptoed to outer door and opened it as quietly as possible and listened again.

The annex was still dark and silent.

Leaving both doors open, hoping I'd be able to hear when the congregants began their shuffle toward the food, I hurried back into Clay's office and quickly plugged the tape into the VCR and hit the rewind button. The whir seemed impossibly loud, as though it echoed throughout the building.

Since Jurgen had been filming the rehearsal in question toward the end of the tape, I didn't let it rewind very far. I stopped it and punched play. Immediately Clay's silent office was filled with lovely, and exceptionally loud, harmonies that echoed softly out into the hallway.

I scrambled to hit the mute button, and blessed silence descended once again.

Mesmerized, I sat down and swiveled Clay's chair toward the VCR, thinking that Weasel had probably done exactly the same thing, in exactly the same place, less than twenty-four hours ago.

On the small screen, the choir members silently arranged themselves on the church stage, in front of the altar and near Clay's podium. The cinematography was strictly from the *Blair Witch Project* School of Videotaping, with odd angles and nausea-producing scene changes, not to mention a few too many close-ups of bosoms.

Jurgen, of course, wasn't in any of the shots because he was behind the camera. Faces of the other choir members popped into view frequently, along with panned shots of the church in general, including an all too brief glimpse of the back pew where Weasel, still alive and wearing his borrowed clothes, sat leaning forward, with an intense look of concentration on his face.

For just an instant, pain squeezed my heart in a vise grip.

While Junior and I had been discussing the efficacy of body fluid detectors, Weasel *had* been in the church proper, sitting quietly and listening to the choir, exactly as he'd insisted.

As I watched, the song evidently ended because the chorus stopped moving in a gentle, unified, rhythm. They broke formation and began to laugh and joke with each other. Conversing normally, rough-housing the way any group of kids might if they'd been cooped up in a church for a long winter afternoon.

Cooped up without a care in the world.

I didn't need to hear the sound of their laughter to know that it was genuine. I didn't need a translator to know that their conversations had nothing to do with a friend lying near death in a foreign hospital. I didn't need to be able to lip-read to understand that Weasel Cleaver had been absolutely correct about the choir's behavior.

Their eyes sparkled. Their smiles were contagious. Their laughter was innocent and hearty. They most assuredly weren't in mourning for anyone.

Weasel had declared that the choir was not sad, and he'd been right. He'd also declared that dark-haired and pretty Meg, the girl from Canada, had stolen his van and his clothes for purposes unknown. And he'd insisted strongly that the selfsame Meg was MIA during the rehearsal.

Pretty Meg, however, had easily convinced me that she'd been swinging and swaying with the choir, mourning right along with the rest of her comrades.

The entire choir had, in English and several other languages, doubly assured us that Meg had been present and accounted for throughout the afternoon. They'd unanimously insisted, in one way or another, that Weasel Cleaver was an ex-con, and therefore lying through his teeth.

Since they were good kids, clean kids, kids who had not been discovered in my cafe storeroom naked except for a few sheets of paper, kids who'd never swindled my former boss out of thousands of dollars, kids who had not proven over and over their untrustworthiness, I'd taken their assurance at face value.

Hell, I'd swallowed the story, hook, line, and sinker.

54

Pandora's Video

What had Del called them? The Stepford Choir? Maybe she hadn't used those exact words, but her sentiment was the same.

Back at the cafe when Annelise was discovered unconscious in her booth, we had all noticed that the remaining choir members had seemed awfully subdued. They'd milled and they'd watched and they'd whispered back and forth to each other. But they had not acted like a tightly knit group with a fallen member.

In fact it hadn't been until Del had muttered something out loud about their inappropriately calm behavior that they'd suddenly, en masse, begun to weep and wail.

At the time I'd chalked it up to a delayed reaction complicated by language and custom barriers. Now, sitting in Clay's office chair, watching a silent video of laughing and happy youths, I wasn't so sure.

Weasel had declared, insisted, and proclaimed that the choir was acting oddly, that they were far less upset about the gravely ill girl than we, strangers all, were. He'd also sworn that Meg had been absent throughout the rehearsal. We had all discounted his report. Yet barely a day later I sat and watched as tiny figures on a silent screen proved him right on all counts.

There was nothing too minute for Jurgen's camera eye, including assorted portions of female choir members' anatomy, many of which got a fair share of screen time. But whether he recorded faces or bosoms or high-vaulted ceilings, not once did I see even a hint of sadness until the camera swung suddenly to the rear of the church. Nor did I see even a glimpse of dark-haired, pretty Meg from Canada.

I did, however, see a small and furious Jennifer Swanhorst march up to Weasel, who was calmly munching a candy bar in the pew. As she said something sharp to him, his expression changed from that of crafty but careful observation to defensive self-justification.

Jennifer pointed at the door and waggled her finger.

Though I couldn't hear him, I knew that Weasel's voice was now loud enough for the choir members to overhear because several of them stopped and cocked their heads in his direction.

Weasel stood up and pointed at the choir. I could see his lips form the words, *But look at them. They're not even—*"

I couldn't tell what he said next because Jennifer positioned herself between Weasel and the camera and grabbed his arm. The camera followed them as she pulled him toward the side door, his evidently vocal protestations falling on deaf, or indifferent, ears as Jennifer pushed him out of the church—and into the annex as I well knew. Moments later she'd burst into Clay's office with a completely unabashed Weasel in tow.

Meanwhile onscreen, there was some serious conversation among the choir members, whose faces suddenly lengthened, whose eyes suddenly dimmed, whose demeanor instantly changed from vibrant and happy kids to the sad and mournful ones I'd seen not fifteen minutes after this scene had been taped.

Soon thereafter, I watched a miniature version of myself, Junior, and Weasel return to the church. I caught glimpses of our reactions to the choir's now rampant mourning.

Junior and I had been impressed. And convinced. Weasel

had been adamant and ignored, which was not surprising. Even silent on the small screen, their act was perfect. The choir looked as though their collective hearts had been broken.

I remembered standing there when Jurgen had ejected this very tape from the camcorder and placed it in his bag. So had Weasel.

And Weasel had taken the opportunity to prove his point the only way he could. When the chance presented itself, he took the tape and snuck off to find a VCR. Little did he know that tape would be the last thing he'd ever steal.

And little did I know that I'd be using it to exonerate a man I'd borne no friendship or respect.

I did now, at least, believe him.

Meg had been absent throughout the rehearsal and the choir *had* been putting on a show. Their grief for Annelise was not only fabricated, it had been donned and shed like a sweater, whenever convenient. In the cafe when they'd realized that their odd behavior was causing comment, they'd put on a marvelous show of weeping and wailing and incoherent bereavement. At the church, with only Weasel for an audience, and a discounted audience at that, they'd reverted to a happy-go-lucky mode that had lasted until Weasel made a point of emphasizing their behavior.

By the time Junior and I entered the church, they'd had plenty of time to assume, once again, the face of grief, and to manufacture some very realistic tears.

When Jennifer brought the news of Annelise's death, they were more than up to the task of convincing me that they were not only surprised, but horrified and incredibly saddened.

Even Meg, who had returned to the group by then. Her grief had seemed to be the most real of all, which was not amazing considering what an accomplished liar and actress she was.

I now had no doubt whatsoever that she'd stolen Weasel's clothes and vehicle. And I was now also certain that Annelise's suicide was not a surprise to her, or to the rest of the choir.

Were they so coldblooded as to be unconcerned while a friend and colleague lay dying? Or, the thought suddenly occurred to me, had they somehow engineered the girl's last desperate act?

Was Annelise's death a result of her own depression possibly complicated by an involvement with an older, married, and therefore forbidden man? Or was it the result of a conspiracy, modeled to serve another purpose altogether?

The TV screen went to static and I ejected the tape and looked at it, suddenly certain that the earlier portions held a great many answers to my questions. I considered rewinding and watching more of the damning video right there in Clay's office.

But I stopped and tilted my head toward the door and listened.

Voices.

Muffled and faint, but voices just the same, entering the annex from the church.

Quickly I ejected the tape and slid it deep into my coat pocket, hoping that no one would notice the telltale bulge.

The voices were getting louder. There wasn't time to do more than shut Clay's inner office door and sneak out into the hallway. I nonchalantly closed the outer office door without locking it, and blended, with a pounding heart and a neutral expression, into the crowd milling toward the community room.

55

Small Consolations

This was neither the time nor the place to expound to Neil on what I'd just discovered. Not only was it completely inappropriate to speculate about the death of the memorial service honoree while her body was being prepared for overseas transport, but far too many of the principals stood within earshot for any truly juicy details to be repeated.

On the other hand it was impossible to keep it all in.

I decided that I could pass on a few of the salient points in a hushed voice, as long as I kept my face smooth and my eye peeled for eavesdroppers. As soon as the flow of the crowd moved me into the community room, I stepped aside to wait for Neil, whom I'd spotted at the far end of the throng.

The second he reached me, I grabbed his arm and unceremoniously pulled him aside.

"You'll never believe what I just—" Neil and I both said at exactly the same time.

We paused and looked at each other.

And waited.

"You first," I said.

"No, you," he said with a smile.

I thought about being polite and insisting that he go first, but dismissed the notion instantly. Whatever he had to say couldn't compare to my news.

"Okay," I said, peering over his shoulder, trying to pinpoint the location of anyone that I was going to mention. The crowd was heavy with locals and strangers, and since the food line hadn't yet opened, they milled about aimlessly in the room.

We were close enough to Clay that we could also hear Jennifer Swanhorst complaining about some sort of candy sale campaign, as though Clay—or Jennifer for that matter—didn't have more important things to think about. Clay did his best to extricate himself from her, but she clung to his arm frantically.

"But they were there yesterday, and gone this morning," I heard her say. She was obviously near tears, and showing far more emotion than the situation demanded.

"It'll be all right," Clay said gently, though he looked uncomfortable talking about such mundane matters at so solemn an occasion. "No one will blame you."

Over in a far corner, Meg, whom I'd last seen on screen as the numbers ticked off slowly on the VCR counter, stood with a handsome boy I didn't recognize. He wasn't a member of the choir, nor was he from Delphi, though I felt certain that he was not only American, but South Dakotan. His seed company gimme cap was a dead giveaway.

They talked to each other quietly and seriously, paying no attention to anyone else in the room. They stood close, touching hands. Meg was still playing bereaved friend, and her companion seemed to be as convinced by her performance as I had been yesterday. He pulled a wrinkled blue hankie from a back pocket and dabbed her eyes.

In fact all of the choir members looked suitably stricken. There were many red and swollen eyes, many wiped tears, and many deep and mournful sighs.

Their acting coach should be very proud.

Jurgen monopolized Glenda, who took time from consoling him to stare at Clay, who was too absorbed in Jennifer's continued complaints to notice. I hoped Glenda would not make a public scene. It would be nice to spare Junior, who was plainly on the edge of collapse, a few more days before her entire life turned upside down.

No one in the room paid the slightest bit of attention to Neil and me. I pulled him into a corner where I could keep an eye on our flanks, and quietly gave him a condensed version of the empty cupboard and the very full videotape.

"Damn," he whistled. "When you snoop, you don't kid around. Did you happen to bring the tape along with you?"

I patted my coat pocket and smiled.

To my utter amazement, Neil leaned down and gave me a swift kiss on the lips, right in the middle of the Lutheran church annex community room, with almost everyone we knew swarming all around us.

"What was that for?" I asked, suddenly not thinking too clearly.

"Just because," he said, smiling. "You took a huge chance and did exactly the right thing and lived to tell the tale."

"Thanks, I think." I was almost dazzled enough to forget the seriousness of our situation.

"And we need to get the hell out of here right now," he said, taking my arm this time. "You realize that a fair number of the people in this room could have killed Weasel, don't you?"

"Yes, and all of them had the opportunity to come back last night and move the body *and* the van," I replied. I'd already remembered Junior's phone call, the one she'd made checking on my whereabouts after everyone, including her own husband, had left her house.

"Good, then you realize that we can't talk here. Besides, I have things to tell you too," Neil said, under his breath.

"Well, let's blow this joint then."

With a protective hand covering my coat pocket, we picked our way toward the door, making mindless small talk with friends and neighbors as we progressed, and offering heartfelt but hurried consolations as the need arose.

We were almost free when a hesitant hand tapped me on the shoulder.

56

Riding the Fence

I should have known that we wouldn't get away that easily. There were just too many people who were too closely involved in the tangle of lies, not to mention far more serious crimes, milling about for a quick getaway.

Though there was no visible linkage between me and Weasel's body (whether in the cupboard or out of it) or the videotape snug in my pocket, I had been seen with him by the entire choir. And the entire choir had, straight-faced, lied to me.

Which meant that whether they *knew* anything or not, whether they'd *done* anything or not, whether they suspected *me* of anything or not, I had no choice but to suspect each and every one of them.

Especially Jurgen, the intrepid camcorder operator, the one who was fixated on female body parts. The same Jurgen who, incidentally, had just tapped me gently on the shoulder.

"Excuse me, ma'am," he said smoothly in heavily accented English.

I'd not really looked at him closely before. In fact, this was almost the first time I'd seen him without a camera pressed to his face. He was dark-haired, with dark, hooded eyes and a nicely formed face. He was not exactly well-muscled, but there was an athletic grace to his stance, as though he was ready to counter any sudden moves. He carried with him an air of superior boredom that would have put my teeth on edge even if I had not begun to wonder if he'd a hand in a murder.

"Yes?" I said, striving to keep my voice even, to appear mildly curious as to the nature of the interruption while at the same time giving it no importance. You know, an air of superior boredom. Involuntarily, my hand tightened on Neil's arm. "Can I help you?"

"I do hope so, ma'am," he said with a small smile. "You were yesterday with a man here at the church. Yes?"

I pretended to think back that far, squinting a little as though the memory was in the dim recesses of my brain. I resisted the urge to scratch my head. "Yes, I was here yesterday with a man. Why?"

"I wonder if you could tell me how to contact that man," Jurgen said. "It is important that I should talk to him before we leave your town this evening."

The first half of his question was instantly forgotten in the surprise of the second half.

"Leave town *this* evening? Are you going so soon? What about the concert?"

I also forgot to feign boredom.

"Yes, ma'am," he said sadly. "We have lost our enthusiasm for singing now that one of our number has fallen. We will miss our friend too much to continue touring your wonderful country. We decided together last evening that it would be for the best to pack our belongings and go to our own separate homes. The joy of singing is gone for many of us now."

He certainly looked as though the *joy of singing* had gone for him. He was every bit as good at faux bereavement as Meg. His shoulders sagged, his eyes glazed over with a film of tears, his voice trembled convincingly.

The kid was good.

"You're not just leaving Delphi? You're cutting the entire tour short and returning to your homeland? Is that it?" Neil asked softly.

Jurgen shrugged. "We could no longer face days on the road without our friend," he said simply. "It is better that we all go home now. We will drive to the airport tonight, and I will accompany my friend home to her family."

Neil and I exchanged a quick glance, agreeing silently that getting themselves out of U.S. jurisdiction as quickly as possible was possibly also a major factor in their decision to leave immediately.

"Wait a minute," I said, realizing what I'd just heard. "*You're* going home with Annelise's body? You specifically?"

"She and I are from the same country. From the same area in fact. I have known Annelise for several years and we have been close friends. It is only right that I should accompany her to her final rest." His voice broke. "It is only right that I should tell her parents and grandparents and sisters myself how sorry I am that she is gone. And how much she loved them." He paused again. This time tears did spill down his cheeks. "And how much we loved her."

God help me, I was moved by the performance. If I hadn't known better, I'd have sworn that he was genuinely grieving.

But I remembered the laughter in the videotape. And I remembered the joy on the faces of the other choir members.

And though Jurgen had not filmed his own face, I was certain that he was no more bereaved than any of the others had been when Annelise took her overdose. Their sadness only surfaced when it was essential for appearances or when their odd behavior was specifically pointed out.

Del had done it in the cafe, and the choir had reacted promptly.

And Weasel had done it in the church, with the exact same results.

Which brought me, finally, back to Jurgen's first point.

"So you want to talk to Mr. Cleaver before you leave Delphi tonight?" I asked, trying to remain nonchalant, which was hard to do when I was increasingly certain that the person I was talking to knew very well that Mr. Cleaver was permanently incommunicado.

"It is important that I do so," Jorgen said mournfully. "Can you put me in touch with him?"

"I'm not his social secretary," I said slowly. "However, I might be able to get a message to him if you'd care to leave one with me."

I'm not a very good liar, so I had to pretend that my eye was caught by someone across the room as I spoke. As camouflage, I flashed a small smile at Clay, who had finally escaped Jennifer's clutches, but he was too busy looking at Junior to notice. The last couple of days had taken a toll on him too; he seemed to have aged ten years. His skin was gray and his eyes were immeasurably sad. If I didn't know better, I'd say that the weight of guilt lay heavy on him.

"It would be better if we could talk to . . . um . . . Mr. Cleaver . . . ourselves," Jurgen said, hesitating. He shot a quick glance off to his side. I followed his eyes and caught a small nod from Meg, who was monitoring the conversation. "But if you can get a message to him, please ask him if he perhaps inadvertently and mistakenly found himself in possession of a piece of our property."

I forced myself not to pat my coat pocket and instead looked Jurgen straight in the eye. "Do you think Mr. Cleaver *stole* something from you?"

I was pretty proud of the small note of indignation I'd worked into my voice, all in defense of a known liar and convicted thief. A *dead* known liar and convicted thief.

Jurgen shot another desperate look at Meg, who signaled for him to continue.

"No, no, no. We do not think he stole anything at all, and wish very much for you not to have that impression. What we think may have happened is that Mr. Cleaver may have thought that a particular item belonged to him. But we feel that he was mistaken and we'd like to recover it before we depart this evening. That's all."

I had to tread very carefully. I did not officially know what *item* Jurgen was talking about. And I did not officially know that Mr. Cleaver was currently out of the loop, so to speak.

But I did know that he had not mistaken Jurgen's tape for his own. I knew very well that he'd stolen it outright.

"How would a stranger like Mr. Cleaver mistake some

of your belongings for his own?" I asked innocently, not daring to look at Neil. "That would be a difficult thing to accomplish."

"Ah, but Mr. Cleaver wasn't a *complete* stranger, ma'am," Jurgen said, working up a confident and reassuring smile for me. "Some of our number had the pleasure of making Mr. Cleaver's acquaintance sometime back, while we were visiting another of your lovely small towns."

It was all I could do not to hoot triumphantly.

I had caught a look between Meg and Weasel in the cafe, and had been immediately certain that they already knew each other. Now Jurgen had confirmed the hunch.

I made a point of frowning at Jurgen, though I tried to make it a concerned frown, not an angry one. "But even so, how would Mr. Cleaver mistake your property for his?"

Jurgen squirmed. "Well, you have noticed our camera, I do think?"

It was a question, so I nodded.

"Well, not too very long ago, in another city, we purchased that camera from your Mr. Cleaver. He approached us with a very good bargain, and we decided that using an American-made camera while we were in America was a good idea. That way we could watch the filming every day while we are here, and then convert the film when we arrived back home. Mr. Cleaver generously offered such a camera to us, so we pooled our money and purchased it. Since I have the most experience in working with cameras, it was decided that I should do all of the filming. Which I have done for the past week with great pleasure."

Ah, that made all the sense in the world. Weasel's furnace repair job would take him to the surrounding counties. Obviously he'd seen the choir in Cresbard or one of the other towns on their itinerary. And obviously, since old felonious habits died hard, he'd unloaded a hot camera on them.

Good bargain indeed.

A small voice in the back of my head declared that maybe Weasel had got what was coming to him but I squashed it immediately.

"And so you think that Mr. Cleaver has taken your camera

back? That he voided your purchase without giving you a cash refund?" I was being purposely obtuse.

"No, we still most definitely have the camera in our possession," Jurgen hastened to assure me. "But he did allow us to use a few . . . he called them pre-owned . . . videocassettes because we were not near to any department stores and could not purchase our own. While it was our understanding that we had purchased the additional cassettes from Mr. Cleaver, he may have thought that they were only borrowed and that they would be returned." Jurgen drew a deep breath and continued. "So please tell Mr. Cleaver that we will be more than happy to reimburse him for the full value of the cassette tape, but that the images we have filmed are irreplaceable to us."

I'll bet the images are irreplaceable, I thought. *I'll bet you want the proof that you didn't care a rat's ass about Annelise or her death back in your hot little hands.*

I nonchalantly slipped my hand into my pocket and patted the cassette. "I'll pass the word along," I said, "if I see him."

57

Amateur City

I suppose it was nice not to have to give up all of my deeply held opinions in one fell swoop.

It was hard enough to acknowledge that, despite all evidence to the contrary, Weasel Cleaver sometimes told the truth.

That you could believe him even when a band of squeaky-clean teens raised their voices in unanimous opposition was a leap of faith that I had not been prepared to take.

It was comforting, therefore, to know that the Weasel had not entirely changed his spots.

"The little creep was actually selling hot camcorders," I said, shaking my head in disbelief.

"To foreign church kids, no less." Neil laughed. "You gotta hand it to him, Weasel Cleaver never did anything by halves."

"And it probably got him killed," I said softly.

After our little conversation with Jurgen, we'd been able to sneak away and hurry to Neil's house. The three-block walk had been too cold for conversation, though we barely got inside the house and up the stairs to Neil's living quarters before the dissection began in earnest.

"Do you think they did it together?" Neil asked.

"*They,* meaning the whole choir?"

"Not all of them. I can't believe that the whole group is evil," he said, pulling a couple of brandy snifters from the wooden rack above the counter where we sat. "But some of them *had* to have been working together, don't you think? I know that Meg couldn't move a dead body on her own. I even doubt Jurgen could. They don't call it *dead weight* for nothing."

"Well, they *all* lied to me. Maybe they *were* all in on it," I said, remembering an Agatha Christie where a group of characters all did it together. "I'm not a conspiracy buff, but for all of them to be happy and then all be sad at the exact same moment is just too much to chalk up to coincidence or bad translations. Whatever they're doing, they're in on it together."

Neil pulled the cork out of a fat bottle of sherry and poured us each a half-glass full. He slid one over to me.

"What about Glenda? She knows them better than anyone. Could they have plotted and executed something like this without her catching on?"

"But did they *plan* anything?" I asked, taking a sip of warm fire, studiously not thinking about the fact that it was barely past noon. "Stashing a dead body in a supply cupboard doesn't strike me as a particularly good use of manpower. I doubt anyone would plot that sort of thing in advance. In fact I doubt if it *could* be planned. Not a single one of those kids has ever been to Delphi before, much less inside the Lutheran minister's office."

"Not to mention that no one could have predicted finding Weasel there at the opportune moment," Neil said, agreeing with me.

"Then what happened?" I asked. "They evidently had a reason to get rid of him. I mean, the guy's dead and he didn't kill himself. So the fact that he met at least a few of the key players before they came to Delphi seems germane. There has to be something more behind Meg's van theft than just a prank. She targeted Weasel specifically. They'll be leaving Delphi soon if we don't find a way to stop them."

It seemed hopeless.

We both sipped in silence.

"Should we call the police?" I asked finally. "If they bring a forensics team in, they'll find evidence of a body in the cupboard. And maybe a whole lot more. I didn't see any blood, but there would be fibers and hair left behind."

"That stuff takes weeks to analyze," Neil said glumly. "They're not about to detain a whole troop of photogenic foreign teenagers on the word of a couple of small-towners. Especially with no body to back them up."

"But the body *has* to be somewhere," I said plaintively. "And I'll bet anything it's in the van."

"And I'll bet anything that they moved the van between the time we got here and Junior's call," Neil said. "I know it was dark, and I know it was late, and I know we dozed, but I still think we'd have noticed a body being lugged across the street and driven off. We'd have seen the headlights if nothing else."

"Which means," I said, sitting up straight, "that they may have seen us peeking in the van windows. Junior didn't say how long after I left her house the crowd cleared out, but it must have been quickly for her to have put the kids to bed before she called."

"Which *means*," Neil said slowly, "that they may be more than just a little suspicious of us. Jurgen's questions just now might have been nothing but a performance."

"Lord," I said, exhaling. "He might have been testing us to see what we knew. Is there any way he could know that we were in the church?"

Neil thought for a minute.

"The timeline would have to be pretty short, but we can't rule it out. It didn't occur to me to look over my shoulder last night. I have no idea if we were watched. In fact, I was so spooked that I probably wouldn't have noticed someone standing right beside me."

"Me neither."

"Jesus, what a pitiful investigative pair we are." Neil laughed ruefully.

I reached out and placed my hand on his. "Hey, what do

they expect from amateurs? It's not like this is our day job."

"Thank God, because we'd be fired on the first day," he said, smiling. "But I still think we need to earn our keep. It would help if we could figure out exactly where and when Weasel met the choir."

"Well, Watson," I said, grinning. "It just so happens that Mr. Holmes can find that out for you."

58

Out of the Frying Pan and Into the Furnace

It didn't matter that I'd been in the position of trying to uncover disquieting truths about death on several occasions, I'm still a novice investigator, a rank amateur, flying by the seat of my pants, with no desire at all to follow in Miss Marple's footsteps.

Tripping over dead bodies is not on my to-do list any day of the week, and waitressing, even in a run-down cafe, even in a town like Delphi, beats the hell out of investigating under all circumstances.

But you deal with what you're given, and even though my hand was definitely Duck in a Grand game of whist, I was determined to play to my strong suit no matter who had the trump cards.

"Waldlach Furnace Repair, serving the needs of the five-county area for twenty-five years," a perky female voice said from the other end of the line. "How can we help you?"

I raised an eyebrow at Neil, hoping I was ready to give a good performance.

"Yes," I said sharply, without even a hint of a smile in my

voice. "My name is Tory Bauer, I'm the owner of the Delphi Cafe down in Delphi."

Okay it was redundant information, but I wanted her to place me immediately. I also wanted my displeasure to be instant and obvious.

To emphasize my belligerence, I said nothing further, hoping to make her uncomfortable, to rattle her.

The silence lengthened, and I wondered if I had already made a tactical blunder, though Neil gave me an enthusiastic thumbs up.

"Um . . . yes, Miss Bauer," the receptionist said. I could hear papers rattling in the background; I assumed she was searching for the work order that sent Weasel to our doorstep in the first place. "What can we do to help you?"

"You can send your furnace repairman back to my place of business today so he can actually fix my furnace. Which he didn't do yesterday. *That's* what you can do," I said, feeling just plain awful about it.

I hate it when customers yell at me, and reducing this young girl to tears was not an assignment I relished.

"Let's see," she said, a note of panic creeping into her voice. "Okay, according to our paperwork, we sent Lenny to your place of business yesterday morning, right?"

Lenny? Weasel's real first name was Lenny?

Lordy, the things you find out.

"Yes, you sent Lenny Cleaver to my place of business yesterday," I said, making a face at Neil. *Lenny Cleaver* indeed. "He came and he left, but my furnace is still not working."

Well, that last was a bit of a fib, but Weasel's tender ministrations had had nothing to do with the current warmth in the cafe—my well-placed kick this morning had rattled things back into temporary working order.

"Cleaver?" the girl repeated, with a note of amazement in her voice. "No, no. It's written right here on the work order that Lenny Deifenbach was sent to check and repair the furnace at the Delphi Cafe."

I pulled the receiver away from my ear and looked at it, as though that would help what I'd just heard make sense.

"You sent *Lenny Deifenbach* to fix our furnace?" I repeated stupidly.

Had Weasel changed his name while in jail? He was Cleaver before, and as far as we knew, he was Cleaver still.

I mimed confusion at Neil, who shrugged in return.

"The work order right here in front of me says Lenny Deifenbach was assigned the furnace repair in Delphi yesterday morning. Mr. Cleaver"—even over the phone, I could hear her shudder—"was sent on an entirely different repair run. He was nowhere near Delphi yesterday."

"Just a second," I said into the phone, thinking furiously.

On the one hand I was relieved that Weasel was actually who he said he was. On the other, no Lenny Deifenbach had appeared yesterday to fix our faulty furnace.

"You say that you sent Lenny Deifenbach to Delphi yesterday?"

"That's what I've been trying to tell you, ma'am," the girl said, exasperated.

"Can I speak to Mr. Deifenbach then?" I asked, deciding to play along. "It's obvious that he'll have to come back today and finish the work he started yesterday."

"I'm sorry, but Lenny is out sick today, and all of our vans are gone at the moment. But I'll put your name down on the list. In fact we expect Mr. Cleaver"—again she hesitated just a bit, and then continued—"in any minute, and we'll get him out to you as soon as we possibly can."

"You do that," I said absently and hung up the phone.

"That was interesting," Neil said, understating just a tad. "So Weasel wasn't supposed to make the Delphi run yesterday, huh?"

"Nope. Some guy named Lenny was assigned the job."

"But no guy named Lenny actually showed up," Neil said "And we certainly didn't find any Lennys in any cupboards last night."

"They don't know that Weasel is missing yet," I said. "Miss Perky thinks he'll be in soon. She'll be more than happy to ship him our way. In fact by the tone of her voice, I think she'd be delighted to find him stuffed into a supply closet herself."

I could not imagine the horror of working with Weasel on a daily basis. Miss Perky had my complete and total sympathy.

"And this Lenny is MIA too?" Neil asked.

"Well, he called in sick," I said, pulling the phone book over to me, rifling through the D's, hoping that Lenny lived conveniently in Aberdeen and didn't commute from the hinterlands. "I assume he's still among the living. Let's see if he answers his phone."

I dialed the only number I could find for a *Deifenbach, Leonard.*

It rang six times.

Lenny evidently didn't have an answering machine. Or call forwarding. Or voice mail.

"Hello," a male voice said groggily. He evidently dropped the receiver and fumbled to catch it because I could hear some colorful, albeit muffled, phrases as his voice faded. "There," he said, firmly in control again. "Yeah?"

"Could I speak to a Lenny Deifenbach please?" I asked sweetly.

"Ya got him," he said. "What time is it anyway?"

"Twelve-thirty," I said, checking the clock on Neil's wall.

"Jesus," Lenny said conversationally.

I wasn't sure how to reply to that so I plunged right in.

"My name is Tory Bauer. I run the Delphi Cafe down in Delphi."

Maybe we need a new name for the cafe. Tory's Cafe in Delphi sounded better.

"Yeah?" Plainly the name didn't ring a bell. "Did I meet you last night? If so, I'm sorry I didn't get your phone number. You sound hot."

I closed my eyes and shook my head. This Lenny was a Weasel clone.

"Mr. Deifenbach," I said testily, "I did *not* meet you last night. I run the Delphi Cafe. The furnace in the Delphi Cafe is not working properly. My business partner called your place of business expressly so that someone could drive down to Delphi and fix my furnace."

I waited to see if he could connect the dots on his own.

I was not overly optimistic.

"Well, Miss Bauer, if your furnace isn't working, then you should call my boss. I'm sure he'll be more than happy to send someone down to you right away. However, I'm sick and have no intention of getting out of bed except to pee. I am not traipsing to Delphi to fix any furnace."

"And you didn't traipse to Delphi to fix my furnace yesterday either," I said sharply. "Though the receptionist at your work certainly thinks you did. I believe we were visited by a Mr. Cleaver instead."

"Oh, yeah." He chuckled. "I remember now. I was all ready to come down and take care of your little problem when Weasel said he'd take the job for me. In fact Weasel said he'd take all of my jobs for the afternoon and no one would be the wiser if I just disappeared for a few hours."

"Weasel Cleaver *asked* to come to Delphi?" I said out loud for Neil's benefit.

"Yeah," Lenny agreed. "Said he had some unfinished business to take care of and could kill two birds with one stone." Lenny paused and chuckled to himself. "That Weasel's a good guy. Did the same thing awhile back. Took a pissy Cresbard run for me. Let me have the day and did me a great big favor while he was at it. I love that guy. Though I gotta stop spending these surprise days off at the bar." He moaned for emphasis.

"He went to Cresbard *for* you?" I asked, hoping the hangover hadn't scrambled Lenny's brain completely.

"Yeah, I think it was Cresbard. One of those one-blink towns anyway," Lenny said. "Something about the church there. They had a concert scheduled and no heat."

59

Tower of Babble

Damn, I like it when I'm right.

Of course, being right this time was no guarantee that I'd be right the next. It didn't even guarantee that I was right about anything else. But I was right on one point, which helped to make up for all those times when I'd been dead wrong.

"He *did* meet them specifically," I crowed. "I knew it. I knew it. I knew it."

"Yes indeedy," Neil said, clinking his snifter against mine. "You knew it. Now what does it mean?"

"Hell if I know," I said, grinning back at him. "I'm just going to enjoy the moment."

"Okay, you bask," he said, pouring more sherry into our glasses. "I'm going to ruminate."

He got off the bar stool and ambled into the living room.

"Hey, wait up," I said, following after him with my glass. "We're a team. No solitary rumination allowed."

He settled himself into a corner of a big leather couch, the kind you sink into and never want to get back up. Brave with a glass of sherry under my belt, I sat next to him, pretending nonchalance.

Just as nonchalantly, he pointed a remote at the stereo in the corner and Anita Baker's smooth alto filled the room.

Not daring to look at him, I deliberately settled into his side, enjoying his warmth.

Without looking at me, he sort of yawned, stretched his arm up, and then settled it around my shoulders.

It felt right. It felt like coming home.

Problem is, it also felt awkward, almost like I was fifteen again. It didn't matter that we'd been best friends for years, that we were always comfortable in each other's company, that we could trust each other completely. Suddenly I was unsure of what to say or how to react, afraid of looking or sounding stupid.

My tendency in situations like that is to babble, and I could feel a good one coming on.

"So Weasel knew them from Cresbard," I said quickly, taking another sip of sherry. "At the church no less. I should have asked Lenny if he bought any camcorders lately."

"So what was in Cresbard that he needed to take someone else's run in order to be there?" Neil asked. "I doubt he knew that the choir kids were going to be in town at the same time."

"Maybe he knew Meg from a long time ago," I said, testing the water by leaning my head on Neil's shoulder.

"He had a fondness for Canadian jailbait?" he said, tightening his arm.

"Weasel believed in spreading himself around," I said, laughing. "But I don't remember him venturing across the border. He had plenty of opportunities here."

"That's what I thought," Neil said, nodding. "We can pretty much discount any earlier meetings, then, since he spent the last three years as a guest of the state of South Dakota. So, I ask again, what was he doing in Cresbard?"

"Fixing a furnace," I said. "Or not, given his propensity to leave jobs undone. And selling stolen camcorders to foreign youth. Maybe he got the loot there and unloaded it in the same town."

"Sounds stupid enough," Neil agreed. He'd turned his head and was looking at me as Anita's smooth voice soared and dipped in the background.

Afraid to look back, I started babbling again.

"I mean, if we only knew what he was thinking. If we only knew what any of them were thinking."

Neil reached out a finger and placed it under my chin and turned my head toward him.

"Meg," I said, unable to shut up. "We need to know what Meg was thinking and doing. I think she's the pivot here. I think she—"

"Tory," Neil said softly.

I swallowed.

I knew he was going to kiss me.

I wanted him to kiss me.

I was going to kiss him back.

And maybe never stop.

But instead I said, "If only your Babelfish could translate Canadian for us. Then maybe we'd be able to understand Meg."

Neil pulled back sharply, his eyes widening.

Oh God, I thought, *I've ruined the moment. I've reminded him what an idiot I am. It's going to be over before it even started.*

"Translation," Neil said, smacking his forehead with the heel of his hand "*Babelfish*. My Lord, Tory, how could I have forgotten?"

60

Rough Drafts

For just a moment, I thought I'd ruined everything, that I'd babbled myself right back out of Neil's heart. And probably out of his life as well. Not to mention his library.

But it wasn't what I said that distracted him. Well, what I said did distract him, but not the way I thought.

"Jesus!" Neil exclaimed. "What the hell is wrong with my brain?"

He jumped off the couch, grabbed my hand, and pulled me up and after him, back through the kitchen and down the hall to his bedroom, swearing at himself the whole time.

I managed to set my brandy snifter down on the cupboard along the way, but didn't interrupt him. I knew he'd fill me in as soon as he stopped berating himself.

"*This* is what I left the cafe for," he said, thrusting a haphazard stack of pages at me. "*This* is what we forgot last night. And it's why I was late getting to the memorial service."

I looked at the sheets. They seemed to be normal computer printouts. I squinted back at Neil, who raised his eyes to the ceiling and said, "I can't believe I forgot about them until just now."

"Well you were *going* to kiss me. I suppose that's excuse enough."

I couldn't believe I'd actually said that out loud.

For just a second, a long, horrible second that lasted about two years, Neil froze and peered at me intently. Then he let out a great whoop of laughter, swept me up into his arms, and planted a lovely kiss that ended almost before I could react.

"Yes I *was* going to kiss you," he said, pulling away and grabbing a handful of wrinkled pages that were in another stack beside his computer. "And I will some more. But first we have to talk about this stuff."

"Party pooper," I said, my heart pounding, but in a nice way. I took the papers he held out and recognized them immediately.

They were the handwritten sheets from Annelise's bag.

The wrinkled pages that we'd forgotten to replace with the rest of her belongings last night.

"Oh my God, Neil," I said, romance suddenly forgotten entirely. "How in the world did we forget about these?"

"Junior called and said that Clay was going to his office, remember? We went up to the tower and sat in the dark waiting for the cherries to arrive."

"Shit," I said, sitting down in the chair next to Neil's computer chair. I looked over the pages Annelise had written, but I didn't understand Swedish any better than I had last night.

"Those aren't important," Neil said, grabbing them from me. "Well, they are important, but they aren't what I forgot to show you."

I looked up into his eyes, brown and warm behind his glasses, and smiled for no good reason. Well, maybe for every good reason.

"*These* are what I forgot to show you," he pointed at the other sheets, the ones he'd handed me first. "I didn't remember them until you mentioned Babelfish."

I inhaled sharply. "Neil, you scanned these and sent them to your friend, didn't you?"

He nodded happily. "Read them and tell me what you make of 'em."

I looked at the first. It was a standard e-mail printout, with a greeting from Jorg, and the following paragraph:

"I do not want you to worry, my dear family, when you hear that I have been ill. This is the only way I can come home to you. I am so sad and I miss my homeland so very much that I must come though they want me to stay. But staying is impossible now since he has left me."

I looked up at Neil, confused.

"Read the next," he said.

I flipped to the next page. It had the same format and greeting, but with the following message:

"Please do not fear for me, my loved ones, when you hear what I have done. I must come home to you and this is the only way I can do it. My heart is gone and I have no joy in staying. I long to be with all of you again. I will never love again and cannot heal until I come to my own home where I can rest in peace."

Now I *was* confused. Both pages said basically the same thing, though the wording was different.

In fact they both nearly echoed the contents of the letter that Annelise had written home to her parents. The one we'd opened and sent to Jorg for a translation.

"Go on," Neil urged.

The next page was a little different:

"I must do this thing because my heart is broken. I have been loved and that love is no more and I can no longer survive without my dearest heart."

"But . . ." I said, unable to follow Annelise's train of thought. She was in love, that was certain. And her lover had ended the relationship, that was also certain.

But was she longing to die, or just wanting to go home?

"Keep going," Neil said softly.

The last page was the shocker:

"I must end my life because I have been violated. My love and my trust was shattered by . . ." The narrative was interrupted by a different font, evidently Jorg added his own commentary: "Though they are blacked out, it is obvious that the girl wrote several names; most of them are crossed out so heavily that I cannot read them. But in the end she underlined the Reverend Clay Deibert, the minister of this Lutheran church in Delphi."

I looked up at Neil, shocked to the core.

"These are rough drafts, aren't they?" I asked bleakly.

"That's what Jorg thinks too," Neil said. He sat in his office chair and took the pages from me gently. "The first two were obviously early versions of the letter she wrote home to her family."

"And the rest are practice suicide notes," I said, barely breathing. "Suicide notes that each gave a different reason for doing it."

I stopped to think what this could possibly mean.

"Did she choose Clay because he actually molested her, or did she pull his name out of a hat because she didn't want to name her real lover? The one who dumped her?"

"That's not the important question, Tory," Neil said softly.

"Not the *important* question," I said a little indignantly. "Try telling that to Junior, who's been eating her heart out over this. Or Clay, who is about to be smeared, maybe for no good reason."

"They're important," Neil agreed. "But not as important as the question these ask together—the real question. The *life or death* issue."

I looked at him, not comprehending for a moment.

61

To *Be* or Not To *Be*

Well, it's a good thing that I was right about Weasel having met Meg in Cresbard, because it looked like I'd been wrong about everything else, right from the beginning.

I was stunned.

"You think it was a stunt?" I asked, barely whispering though I don't know why. "That she purposely staged a suicide attempt so that she could go home in the middle of the tour?"

"That's what it looks like," Neil said, leaning back in his chair. "If you take the letter she meant to send and compare it to the early versions, it looks very much like she was trying to warn them not to worry if they heard bad news from the U.S. That no matter what they were told, she was safe and expecting to be home with them soon."

I remembered that Jurgen had mentioned handing Annelise's body over to her parents *and* grandparents. Including, presumably, the grandmother I'd thought she wanted to join in heaven.

"But why would she take an overdose on purpose? Why would she risk something so incredibly dangerous? Something that could go very wrong?"

Something *had* gone very wrong. Annelise wasn't winging her way home, sad but ready to rest and heal in the bosom of her multigenerational family.

She was dead.

Neil shrugged. "She was a kid. Whoever broke her heart *really* broke her heart. You know how kids are at that age. They think they'll never get over a heartbreak. That they'll never love again."

Actually, I knew exactly how she felt. But I'd never, no matter how much Nicky's betrayals had hurt, considered checking out. I'd just soldiered on in my misery, assuming that I would never love again. I wanted to hug that poor girl and tell her that she'd get over it, that she had a long life ahead of her. That the jerk, whoever he was, would not matter to her in a few years.

But it was too late.

Neil continued. "She wanted to go home and evidently there's some kind of contract, written or verbal, that keeps the kids on for the whole tour, so they wouldn't let her go. I suppose this seemed like the only solution to her."

"But to take an overdose on purpose. To stage a suicide attempt by swallowing medicine you're allergic to seems beyond understanding," I said. "No matter how sad she was, how could she take such a chance? How would she know the right dosage?"

And again the obvious answer came to me: She didn't know.

She took too much aspirin with codeine. Aspirin by itself, ingested in large enough quantities, can kill. But she purposely combined aspirin with codeine, to which she was allergic. The combination was not just debilitating, it was lethal.

Suddenly I was angry. A genuine suicide attempt was bad enough, but pretending to do it to gain a quick trip back to Sweden to recuperate, no matter the reason, was beyond acceptance. To have put her family through such agony was inexcusable. To have miscalculated and really killed herself when that was not her aim was a horror. A tragedy.

As quickly as it had come, my anger disappeared, leaving only an overwhelming sadness.

"Oh Neil, she pulled a stupid stunt because some boy left her, and now she's dead."I remembered the rest of the translations. "But if she had a broken heart and was just wanting to go back to Sweden, why bring Clay into it? Why ruin an innocent man?"

"Maybe she didn't realize what that kind of accusation would do to him or his family. She wrote her original note in Swedish and then recopied it in English. Maybe she didn't really mean to say she was *violated*. English wasn't her first language. It may not even have been her second. And remember that she wrote the note as she drifted into unconsciousness."

"Maybe it *was* just a vocabulary snafu," I conceded. "But I still think her intent was to point a finger at someone, and Clay just happened to be the victim." I was getting angry again.

"That doesn't make sense, Tory. From all reports, she was a nice kid. Maybe affairs between teens and adults aren't illegal in Sweden. Maybe she thought it would be no big deal. Maybe she was protecting her real lover and she assumed that Clay could take the hit without major damage."

"And maybe we're still misinterpreting the whole thing," I said. "But I think I know a way to find out."

62

Smile, You're on Candid Video

Amazing what you can learn when you turn up the volume.

The video snips I'd watched before, hunkered down in Clay's office, scared to death I'd be caught, had been informative. They'd silently confirmed Weasel's insistence that Meg was missing during the choir rehearsals at the church yesterday afternoon.

They'd also backed up his claim that the choir wasn't in the least mournful about Annelise's suicide attempt. It was obvious, with or without sound, that the assorted members of the European Traveling Lutheran Youth Choir were not sad until it became expedient for them to look that way in front of an audience.

But when, or if, the choir was sad about the impending loss of one of their own, with the sound turned up, at least one person showed some real emotion over the situation.

"Whether they should be ashamed or not is none of your business," I heard Jennifer Swanhorst say faintly off camera. "I think they're behaving disgracefully too . . ."

At which point Jurgen had swung the camera around to focus on Jennifer as she wrestled Weasel from his pew.

"But *you* need to get out of here right now," Jennifer exclaimed. "This is a church, no place for *people* like you." Disgust was written plainly on her face; obviously St. John's Lutheran was not a refuge for human failings.

Weasel's response to Jennifer's insult was pretty much what I'd have expected, with or without sound. He protested and argued and declared loudly that the kids in the choir were robots, that they didn't care about the sick girl at all.

At which time Jennifer grabbed the candy bar from Weasel's hand and pulled him unceremoniously out of the church, though she paused for one last glare at the camera. "This *is* a place of God," she said directly to Jurgen, which meant that she said it directly to us from the TV screen in Neil's living room. "And it would do well for you to remember that."

"Whoa," I said. We were sitting on the big comfy couch next to each other, watching the last portion of the video again. "You get a whole new perspective when you can hear what they're saying too."

"Did you catch that just now?" Neil asked, leaning forward.

"With Jennifer? Yeah," I said. "Whatta bitch."

"No, just after."

Neil aimed the remote at the TV and rewound a few seconds worth of tape and hit play again.

The camera was focused on the choir members, who all watched the door as Jennifer towed Weasel to the principal's office. Not a few had smirks on their faces.

A male voice from off camera said something in a different language.

"That must be Jurgen," Neil said, pointing at the screen, "because it sounds loud, like it was said right next to the microphone."

"Do you understand what he said?" I asked.

"Nope. But I'll bet it was a command to act sad. Watch how quickly the faces change."

Neil rewound the section again, and sure enough, the choir was laughing and happy, Weasel was watching carefully, munching on a candy bar, angry Jennifer entered and distracted Jurgen, Weasel exclaimed his displeasure, Jennifer agreed but still insisted that he leave, and then the voice—very likely Jurgen's—said something, and instantly the faces around him crumpled.

They didn't dissolve into tears, but their smiles disappeared. Their eyes lost their sparkle. Their voices, sometimes speaking in English, sometimes in other languages, lost that jolly lilt.

In other words, from that moment on, they became very sad. And sad they remained until after I reentered the church with Junior and Weasel. And sad they still were, a day later.

"You think he's in charge then?" I asked. "He gives the orders?"

"Maybe," Neil said, settling back again. "Or maybe he just reminded them of how they're supposed to act."

"Well, whoever's in charge, they're obviously in on it together," I said. "Did they truly not care about Annelise? Was she evil? A pain in the butt? Could she have been so awful that they were happy to get rid of her? Pleased that she got rid of herself?"

Despite what I'd seen, I couldn't bring myself to believe that the whole choir was heartless. Or that a girl who only wanted to go home and heal a broken heart was some sort of pariah, an outcast whose death was preferable to her company.

"One way to find out," Neil said, aiming the remote at the TV again.

The tape rewound in a dizzying array of scenes as the ticker on the VCR highlighted ever decreasing numbers in swift rotation. We saw kids swaying in rhythm backward on stage, people entering and leaving the cafe in reverse (I caught a quick glimpse of my own backward frown directed at Alanna's tight sweater), more scenes at the church in Delphi, some shots I recognized as Junior's house, and then suddenly we were back in bright sunlight traveling backward along a highway.

"This looks like a good spot," Neil said, putting the tape into forward motion again.

The kids were in a Suburban from the look of the interior. Not all of them were squeezed into the same vehicle; there were several panned shots of a van traveling behind them on the snowbound highway whose occupants waved wildly every time they caught the camera pointed in their direction.

However, Meg, Glenda, and Annelise *were* in the van.

Glenda, in the front passenger seat, was turned to face the next seat back. She had one arm looped over the armrest and she was talking seriously to Annelise.

"Turn up the sound," I said. "Can we hear them?"

There was a lot of road noise and other happy background chatter. Jurgen was evidently sitting in the seat farthest back while Glenda was in front and Annelise behind her. We could still faintly make out the conversation and see them over the heads of the others who were actively engaged in the general roughhousing that took place any time you crammed young people into a moving vehicle.

"I know, dear," Glenda said, giving Annelise, whom I had never seen mobile, a pat on the arm. "I'm sorry, but we need to finish this tour intact or we'll never get funding for the ones who come after us. You wouldn't want to be responsible for keeping the next group of singers home, now would you?"

Her words were reasonable, and her touch was sympathetic, but her voice was tinged with just a hint of contempt. As though Annelise's request signaled a deep and abiding character flaw.

Annelise caught the undertone too, because she replied quietly, in accented but understandable English, "But I miss my home. This has been a wonderful opportunity, but since . . ." She paused and shot a pained look toward the back of the van. "I have no heart to sing anymore. I do not want to let anyone down, but I must go home.' "

It was the first time I'd heard her speak out loud. There was nothing extraordinary about her voice, she just sounded like an unhappy, homesick girl. A normal, pretty, unhappy, homesick girl.

She didn't sound like a suicidally depressed, unhappy girl, however, not that such a thing would be instantly recognizable to your average waitress.

"That's just not possible right now, dear," Glenda said, leaning even further back to speak to Annelise privately. Again she seemed to be understanding and sympathetic, but her eyes were hard. And luckily for us, the camera was trained in her direction so we heard her next comment. "We need, and I do mean *need*, to get through the next town without a mishap for this tour to be a success. All I'm asking you to do is hang in for two more concerts, and then you can go. Can you last that long?"

Annelise nodded and mumbled something. Glenda turned back toward the front and settled in again while Annelise slumped in her seat and leaned her head on the window and watched the treeless expanse of a South Dakotan winter landscape speed past.

Neil paused the tape. We sat in silence for a moment, watching a sad girl who stared out a window at an icy barren plain.

"Let it go a few more seconds," I said, softly. "I want to see what happens next."

The scene jumped back into life. Annelise surreptitiously wiped a tear from her face with a quick finger. One of the girls in the seat behind Annelise reached forward and patted her on the shoulder.

Coming in from out of camera range, a feminine hand offered a tissue which Annelise took with a grateful smile. Meg leaned over from her seat and gave her a swift hug. Though her back was to us, I could swear that she said something in Annelise's ear because Annelise pulled back and looked at her intently. Meg then said something but her head was turned far enough away that we couldn't read her lips. Annelise smiled wanly in return and nodded too. Meg, with a small smile, then retreated to her own seat, and the camera swung once again to film the waving passengers in the van that followed behind.

Neil stopped the tape again.

"What do you make of that?"

I thought for a minute, replaying the scene in my head, and then trying to blend it with the things I'd seen later.

"Well, first and foremost, Glenda Harrison seems to think

of no one but Glenda Harrison. The kid is obviously sad and homesick and she wants to go home, but Glenda is more than willing to use emotional blackmail to keep her on the tour."

"Maybe Glenda's job is on the line," Neil said. "Maybe something happened in one of the other towns. Something bad enough that someone in charge gave her a warning about further incidents."

" 'We need, and I do mean need, to get through the next town without a mishap,' " I quoted. "Sounds like something must have happened on this tour, something that got some adverse publicity. Or at least publicity that reflected badly on Glenda."

"She's a tough cookie," Neil said.

"Yeah, well you don't get to be a Miss America third runner-up without having a backbone of steel."

"Not to mention Vaseline-coated teeth." Neil laughed.

"Did it look to you like Annelise was an outcast?" I asked, thinking over the smiles I'd seen in the video, and the sympathetic pats. The whole group looked like the usual assortment of kids on the road—some were reading, some were sleeping, some were talking.

None, except Annelise, looked like anything was amiss.

And not a single one looked like the kind of person to dance on another's grave.

"Not to me," Neil said. "In fact, I thought Meg was being especially friendly. I didn't see any overt hostility at all. No one said anything nasty, no one did anything nasty, except Glenda. And what she did wasn't nasty exactly, just selfish."

"Or maybe just pragmatic. Maybe this particular tour has a history of snafus and its funding really is in jeopardy," I said. "Maybe if we watch the whole tape, we'll get a better handle on their personalities. We're only about halfway through and we know that they bought the camcorder in Cresbard. There might be something on the earlier sections that'll help."

"I suppose you're right," Neil said. "We'd best do this by the numbers."

I froze and looked at him, my eyes widening in surprise.

"Numbers!" I said, slapping my forehead exactly the way Neil had done earlier.

63

Running the Numbers

Since his conclusions seemed to bear no relation to the evidence at hand, and leaps of intuition always took place in his mind, not on the page, I'll bet Sherlock Holmes would have made the connection sooner. Given the unsettling tendency for his solutions to be dropped wholesale on the reader without warning or explanation, I always figured that Arthur Conan Doyle had no idea how Holmes did it either.

But there was no way that this un-Sherlockian waitress would have made the connection before the videotape was found in the VCR in Clay's office.

In fact, there wasn't any way for the dots to be connected until after watching portions of said video. Or at least the portion showing Weasel Cleaver sitting in a back pew of St. John's Lutheran Church eating a Snickers bar.

And even then I hadn't made the connection until I'd watched (on more than one occasion) the VCR counter numbers whirling past as the tape forwarded, reversed, and played. I think it was the Snickers bar that did it—Weasel had one in the church, as the tape clearly proved. And there was a half-eaten Snickers bar on Clay's desk last night when I'd made my grisly discovery. It just took me a while to correlate the two.

"But how did the page get into the typewriter?" Neil asked, frowning.

He hadn't questioned my sudden announcement that Weasel had been sitting at Clay's desk in his office, in the dark, munching on a candy bar (probably stolen, hadn't Jennifer mentioned missing candy to Clay?), watching Jurgen's tape and writing down the counter numbers of salient episodes.

Those were the number sequences on the back of the typewritten love note we'd found rolled into Clay's typewriter shortly after having discovered Weasel's body. In fact I was suddenly certain that Weasel had been caught watching the tape, and had been killed for his efforts.

Neil couldn't argue that conclusion either. But he cut to the chase with another conundrum.

"If Weasel was writing tape counter numbers down on the paper, and I'm pretty sure he was," Neil said, thinking it through as he spoke, "then how did the paper get rolled into the typewriter? Did the killer think it would stay hidden in plain sight like that? If he or she or they understood the significance of the numbers, then why leave the paper at all? Not to mention the tape?"

"Well, maybe Weasel heard them coming and shut off the VCR and rolled the paper into the typewriter himself," I said. "He wouldn't have wanted to get caught in Clay's office. I'm sure he figured he'd come back and pick up the page and tape later. I think he just rolled it into the Selectric to get it out of the way."

"Rather than just putting it in his own pocket?" Neil asked. "He could have wadded the sheet up and stuffed it away with a lot less effort."

"Well, I'm glad he didn't do that," I said, somberly. "Because if it had been in his pocket, it would be missing right along with his body right now. And his van. And a whole lot of answers."

"Yeah, like when was the typewriting done?" Neil said. "Did Weasel pull a sheet of paper out of the typewriter, one that had already been written on, flip it over, and take notes? Or did use a clean sheet that he or someone else rolled into the typewriter later and used?"

"I like the last one better," I said. "Weasel wrote the numbers on a random piece of paper he found on Clay's desk. He didn't bring it with him because the sheet wasn't creased and Weasel wasn't carrying a notebook or clipboard. I can see him, chuckling and whooping at the screen as he wrote numbers down."

"Then he hears something in the hall," Neil said, leaning forward on the couch excitedly.

"Or even in Clay's outer office," I added.

"And quick like a bunny, he shuts off the VCR and rolls the paper into the typewriter." Neil sat back again, deflated. He looked at me. "Doesn't make sense, does it?"

"No it doesn't, dammit," I said. "Okay, how about this. He hears someone coming, he has time to shut off the VCR but not time to hide the paper, so he leaves it on the desk hoping that no one will see it. Or if they do, he hopes they won't understand the significance. Lord knows, it took us long enough to figure it out.

"Then the killer comes in, confronts Weasel. Dispatches him, stashes him in the cupboard, leaves the Snickers bar untouched, but picks up a sheet of paper without noticing that it has writing on it, rolls it into the typewriter and types an incriminating love note for the police to find in the morning." I sat back. Something was wrong with that scenario. Maybe everything. "But that would only work if the killer was one of the choir people since the note pointed directly to Clay and Annelise."

"Isn't that what we've been leading up to?" Neil asked, raising an eyebrow. "The connection between Weasel, Clay, and the tape *is* the choir. Everything seems to revolve around this video. There'd be no reason to kill him if he didn't know something dangerous. And since the note ties Clay to Annelise, the *something dangerous* has to tie in with her suicide. There's no other explanation."

"But what could be dangerous about a suicide? She'd already left a note naming Clay as a molester. That's enough to ruin him socially and professionally."

"But the note disappeared. Maybe whoever killed Weasel

thought that the note was gone, never to reappear. Maybe whoever killed Weasel did it to make sure that a connection between Clay and Annelise was inescapable."

"But the only people who knew the note was gone were Junior, Del, and me," I said. "I'd like to have, but I swear I didn't kill Weasel. I'm pretty sure Junior didn't, and Del never sets foot in the Lutheran church."

"Others could have known that she planned to write a note," Neil said. "We found rough drafts after all. She may have had help writing them. She may have confided her intention to someone before she took the overdose. A friend who cared enough to make damn sure that someone paid dearly for the act."

"But who cared deeply?" I asked. "We already saw how nonchalant the choir was when Annelise was still alive in the hospital. They'd have shown more emotion over a rain shower."

"Well, I'll bet *someone* cared," Neil said. "They're good at hiding *and* faking emotions. And I'll bet that *someone* was Weasel's killer."

"So we have Weasel in Clay's office watching the tape in order to prove his point about the choir's behavior, right?" I asked.

Neil nodded.

"Okay, then, the important question, maybe even more important than what's on the tape, is *why*."

"Why what?"

"Why the hell was he still in Clay's office? If he wanted to prove a point with the video, why stick around the church at all? Why not go back to his snug little home to watch and be vindicated? Or better yet, if he wanted to prove his point to someone, why not watch the tape in front of the people who mattered? Make his point in public, embarrass the offenders and force apologies from them? It wasn't a life-or-death situation. Why trespass in a dark and cold office when there are VCRs everywhere in the world?"

"Because he wanted the offenders to *know* that he knew," Neil said, getting excited again.

"Right," I agreed, catching a little of Neil's enthusiasm. "Because he was meeting someone there. That's the only explanation that makes sense. Otherwise he'd have gone home."

"But who was he meeting?"

"Let's watch and find out."

64

Don't Come Knockin'

We sat on the couch and watched the VCR counter numbers swirl in reverse.

Weasel had sold the camcorder to the group in Cresbard, so it was logical to assume that the relevant taping started there. Given Jurgen's enthusiasm for using the camera, I couldn't imagine that he waited long before trying out his new toy.

"Will the numbers from Clay's VCR correspond with yours?" I asked.

Neil shrugged. "I doubt they'll match up perfectly, but they should be pretty close."

The numbers whizzed from 4,000 to 2,000 in less than a minute, and then from there down to 1,000 even faster as the tape neared the end of the reel.

"This oughta do it," Neil said, aiming the remote at the VCR, which stopped at about 650 on the counter. The lowest set of numbers on the paper was 800–1247, so we weren't too far from Weasel's earliest notation. "Here goes," Neil said.

He pushed play and instantly the blank screen was filled with writhing bodies. Or maybe it was just one writhing body—it was hard to tell. Assorted limbs flashed and flailed, appeared and disappeared, came into focus and then drifted back out of view, all to a chorus of moans and heavy breathing. Though the camera seemed to be stationary, the figures on screen moved about too quickly and erratically, and mostly too close to the lens, to know if there was one person or six since the angle didn't allow for faces in the tightly framed shot.

"My Lord," I said, stunned.

Neil whistled long and low.

"Is it one of *them*?" I asked Neil, meaning the choir.

"Is it *five* of them?" he replied, hypnotized by the screen.

From what little I could see beyond the bodies, the camera was set up in a darkened room. It was a storeroom or low-ceilinged workroom of some kind. It seemed to be long and narrow and there were shelves along the wall opposite the camera. Shelves laden with wire mesh cages and latched metal doors. The cages held ductwork and fittings and such.

"Jesus," I breathed softly. "This is the inside of a vehicle."

"It's the inside of Weasel's van," Neil said. "Look at that stuff in the bins and along the wall. Those are furnace repair tools and supplies."

I tilted my head sideways trying to get a better handle on the action. "Can you tell who it is? Is it Weasel? Was this his tape originally? Jurgen said they'd bought a *preowned* cassette."

"You'd know that better than me," Neil laughed. "You've had more experience with him undressed."

"I don't think the guy is hairy enough," I said finally. My main impression of naked Weasel Cleaver had been of an inordinate amount of fur coating his whole body. "If that *is* a guy." We still hadn't gotten a look at a face and the dim lighting made it hard to differentiate between bodies or spot any identifying features. "You suppose Weasel was making home movies and then decided to sell the camera and a used tape to some church kids just for shits and giggles?"

"Again, you'd know that better than me," Neil said. "But it seems like a guy who'd get naked in a cafe storeroom would not be above filming afternoon delights in a work vehicle."

"You'd think not," I said, squinting at the screen.

"Recognize any of the voices?" Neil asked.

"Nope, thank goodness," I said. All we'd heard were inarticulate moans and ragged breath anyway.

The scene abruptly changed to bright outdoors.

Jurgen's accented voice could be heard speaking, in English, as he filmed. "This is the city of Cresbard, South Dakota."

The camera moved jerkily up and down the snowy main street of an entirely typical prairie town. The wind whistled and howled in the microphone.

"There!" I shouted to Neil excitedly. "Rewind a bit. Right there in that last shot."

Neil reversed the tape one frame at a time, and there in broad daylight, just a few cars away from where Jurgen stood, was a tan Waldlach Furnace Repair van.

"Well, we knew he was in Cresbard anyway," Neil said. "Everyone corroborates that, from Lenny, to Jurgen, and now this. The question is how long a time lag was there between the filming of that little . . . um . . . interlude, and the transfer of camera ownership."

"Or was there a lag at all?" I asked. "Weasel was pretty certain that Meg was ripe for the plucking. Did he know that from experience?"

"One of a zillion unanswered questions," Neil said, aiming the remote at the TV again. "Too bad the van doesn't have side windows. We'd have had a notion of where it was at least. And the time of day."

Neil started the tape again. The camera panned once again, far too quickly up and down the street, and then abruptly we were inside a building. From the indoor-outdoor carpeting on the floor, to the suspended ceilings, to the felt and braid religious wall banners that festooned the brick walls, I had to assume we were now in the Cresbard Lutheran church's community room.

Again, the camera wobbled and moved quickly in nausea-inducing leaps and jumps, among the roomful of people who milled around aimlessly talking and laughing with each other.

"There's Annelise," I said, pointing. As if on cue, she turned her head toward the camera and flashed a wan smile. Her eyes were red-rimmed and I thought she'd been crying. She stood next to Meg, who was talking earnestly to a young man who looked vaguely familiar. "Who's that guy with Meg?"

Neil squinted at the screen. "He's the one she was with this morning after the memorial service. You suppose he drove down to Delphi just to be with her?"

It was a possibility because right then he leaned over and gave Meg a light kiss on the forehead.

The kiss didn't go unnoticed among the other choir members. A few nudged others, and someone tapped Glenda on the shoulder. She looked much less exhausted on-screen than the last time I'd seen her in person. In Cresbard, she'd been the Miss America third runner-up in charge of a group of traveling youth.

Jurgen focused on Glenda's face, zooming in and out at a dizzying pace. Her mouth tightened and her eyes narrowed. Her bustline didn't show any emotion at all, but Jurgen seemed to think it worth recording as well.

The camera followed Glenda as she strode over to Meg. There was far too much noise in the room for the microphone to pick up their heated conversation, but it was plain that Glenda was angry and that Meg didn't exactly care.

Glenda fumed and Meg calmly stared her down.

"That Meg is one cool cookie," Neil said, admiringly. "I'd be quaking in my boots if Glenda focused all that wrath on me."

"She's something else," I agreed. If Meg was able to withstand the full force of Glenda's disapproval, then she would indeed have had the wherewithal to charm Weasel out of his clothes and vehicle in Delphi.

Annelise wasn't quite so calm and collected. Visibly horrified by Glenda's harangue, she looked around frantically, and then sprinted out of camera range.

"I'll be damned," Neil said softly. "Will you look at that."

He didn't have to point it out. My jaw had already dropped to my chest.

65

The Minister and the Chorus Girl

"I love you, Weasel Cleaver," I said out loud.

It was a posthumous and entirely platonic love, the kind you might feel for a creature who was too slimy to touch, like a slug, who somehow raised himself above slugdom and served a higher purpose.

"If it wasn't for him, we'd never have seen that." Neil hoisted his glass to the ceiling. "Weasel, wherever you are, we owe you one."

We clinked glasses and then rewound the tape to watch the scene all over again.

Annelise sped out of camera range, evidently upset by Glenda's treatment of Meg. She returned swiftly, with a somber Clay Deibert in tow.

"Can you believe the timing?" I asked, watching the scene unfold, as fascinated as I had been the first time. "I mean, what are the chances that Clay would have been in Cresbard on the exact day that Weasel showed up with a hot camcorder to sell?"

"Actually, it's not that big a coincidence," Neil said. "Remember that the choir was rerouted to Delphi at the last minute because of snafus in Cresbard? Maybe the furnace outage triggered the change in venue. It makes sense that arrangements to send the choir elsewhere were started as the furnace was being looked at. It was definitely in their best interest not to count on Weasel's furnace-repairing skills."

On TV, Clay, dragged by Annelise who clutched at his arm fiercely, smiled diplomatically at both Meg and Glenda.

They returned the favor by glaring at him stonily.

Or rather Glenda glared stonily; Meg just looked at him as if daring Clay to try to make her behave.

I cursed the terrible acoustics and spared a bad word or two for Jurgen, who filmed the scene faithfully without stepping even one foot closer so that we could hear what was being said.

Glenda's eyes flicked in Jurgen's direction and caught a glimpse of the camera. Immediately her face relaxed and she flashed a carefully controlled smile at Clay as she spoke to him. Whatever she had to say, it involved Meg and the young man because Glenda gestured at both.

Clay listened intently, and then said something to Meg that was evidently not well received because her face went instantly from impassive to furious.

"Whoa, the ice queen does have emotions," I'd said the first time we watched the scene.

"And a quick temper," Neil had agreed as Meg turned on one foot and stomped off, after saying something nasty enough to make Clay pull back and blink two or three times rapidly in surprise.

After that Glenda buttonholed Clay for a brief confab, during which she kept a careful eye on the rest of room and its occupants. Annelise hovered nearby, looking forlorn. The second Glenda flounced away, she grabbed Clay's arm again and said something to him.

Whatever she said surprised him almost as much as what Meg had said earlier. His eyes flicked from side to side, as if checking to see if anyone was eavesdropping.

He pulled Annelise over in a corner, unfortunately out of camera range.

"Jurgen, swing the camera, you dumb ass! Follow them!"

I shouted at the TV, which did as much good as it had the first time I'd said it.

Instead, Jurgen focused on Glenda, picking her out of the crowd. She'd cornered Meg and was evidently arguing with her. The young man, the one who seemed to have sparked the confrontation, stood nearby, stoic and silent. He was evidently also adamant because Glenda turned to him at least once and said something that made him shake his head *no* vigorously.

Jurgen finally tired of the trio and panned the room again. We got quick flashes of familiar choir faces, a peek at Clay with his arm around Annelise in the corner, and then a millisecond shot of Weasel eyeing the room narrowly from a doorway.

Then the camera swung back to Glenda, who was standing alone, chewing her lip, lost in thought. Jurgen recorded once again Glenda's well-preserved figure before swinging one last time in a quick scan of the room.

With barely more screen time than Weasel's last appearance, we caught a glimpse of Annelise and Clay and were as stunned once again.

On the screen Clay looked tenderly down at Annelise, who gazed up at him with adoring eyes. She then stood on tiptoe and planted a kiss right on his lips.

Neil paused the tape and we sat in silence for a moment or two.

"I keep hoping that doesn't mean what I think it means," I said softly.

"Me too," Neil said. "I know she accused him of molesting her. And we've been treating the accusation like it had merit on general principle, but I never really believed it."

The tape started playing automatically again and we watched the last few seconds of the damning scene.

Annelise pulled away from Clay, who didn't look in the least surprised, or shocked or horrified or unwilling. He also didn't push her away. Then again, he didn't have to. Jennifer Swanhorst suddenly rushed into view with a face horrified enough for everyone in the room. She flashed a tight smile at

Clay and then firmly but gently led Annelise away from him.

"What the heck was Jennifer doing there?" Neil asked.

"She's been taking over for Junior a lot," I said. "I suppose it took a lot of juggling to rearrange the choir's schedule, not to mention finding host homes and setting up a concert agenda on such short notice. It doesn't surprise me that she rode up with Clay. Junior's in no shape to spend hours in a car these days."

"She's angling for Junior's job as Queen of the Universe, that's for sure," Neil said sourly.

I had to agree. Though we'd made great strides in our personal relationship, one Junior was more than enough. Jennifer had learned from the master. She was quickly becoming my candidate for World's Biggest Pain in the Butt.

On the TV the scene changed again. We ventured into uncharted territory.

A territory involving endless, and I do mean endless, sweeping panoramic shots of snow-covered prairie.

We saw snow on the ground.

We saw snow on the trees.

We saw snow on the rooftops.

We saw snow up close, so that the individual crystals sparkled.

We saw snow far away and unfocused.

We saw way too much snow.

Jurgen, who lived in Sweden, for crying out loud, and whom you would have thought would be inured to the sight of unending white landscapes, seemed every bit as fascinated with our flat, snow-covered, terrain as he had been with bosoms and rear ends.

We waited and watched patiently, finally deciding that if we wanted to look at snow, we'd open the curtains. Neil quickly fast forwarded to the next set of numbers.

"Right about here," he said, as the scenes slowed down around the 1593 mark that Weasel had noted.

I looked at the screen, confused. "More scenery," I said unnecessarily, since Neil was sitting right next to me. "And it all looks just the same."

"Land of infinite variety, not," Neil agreed.

We checked the numbers on the sheet. 1593–1679 was penciled in at the top of the page.

We looked at the screen and saw only rolling white emptiness for those eighty-six endless counter ticks.

Neil forwarded beyond 1679 just in case the counters hadn't lined up perfectly, but there was nothing there except landscape.

He rewound to well before 1593 and there was more of the same.

"What the hell did he want us to see?" I asked.

"Ya got me," Neil said. "Maybe Jurgen has cinematic aspirations."

"I got news for him. They already made *Fargo*," I said glumly. "I don't think anyone needs another whole movie about snow."

"Well, maybe Jurgen would get it right," Neil laughed.

The rest of the world may have worshipped at the feet of the Brothers Coen, but not us. At least not for that movie.

"They probably they got Arizona wrong too," I said, laughing.

"Good grief, Tory," a panting voice said from behind us. "Don't you have a home?"

66

Between a Rock and a Hard Woman

The tradition at the library, which filled the entire first floor of Neil's house, was that patrons could consider it always open, within reasonable boundaries. If you wanted something new to read at two A.M., you were pretty much shit outta luck. But otherwise, whether Neil was at home or not, it was okay for borrowers just to go in, select a book, write their name and the title down on a pad he kept on his desk, and leave.

Though he didn't leave town often, he did frequently work out in one or another of his sheds, tinkering on old trucks or building cabinets. Since he owned the library and therefore didn't have to answer to a board or any other sort of oversight committee, and he most assuredly didn't want to be tied to a specific schedule, he encouraged people to go in and get what they needed without him.

However, they weren't supposed to go upstairs to his living quarters. Since Delphi folk are pretty good about following rules, Neil rarely closed the door between the top of the stairs and what he considered his house.

If he was in the house and not working in the library itself and if people really needed to talk to him, they sometimes stood at the foot of the curved oak staircase and hollered up.

But they never entered the second floor uninvited.

In fact, this was the first time I could remember someone actually coming all the way upstairs without warning.

Why was I not surprised to know who dared to broach the inner sanctum?

"I have a message for you, Tory," Junior said, lumbering over to one of Neil's chairs and sitting down heavily. She didn't bother to take off her coat, hat, earmuffs, gloves, scarf, or boots. The trek upstairs in full winter gear had plainly taken an extreme amount of effort. Though she'd been coy about her due date, it could not be long now.

She hadn't yet noticed the frozen scene on the TV. I shot a sideways, guilty glance at Neil, who shrugged imperceptibly and kept his hand off the remote, though the temptation to shut the VCR off must have been enormous.

"Oh yeah?" I said, mostly to be polite, but also to keep her attention on us instead of on the TV. There was no point in asking her *What message from whom?* If she intended to deliver the message, nothing on God's white earth would stop her. And if she meant for me to dangle a bit before spilling the beans, the same applied.

Have I mentioned that Junior sometimes drives me crazy?

"You know if you spent more time at your own house, I wouldn't have to walk up all these stairs just to find you," she said, looking around at Neil's neat and stylish living room. "Your cleaning lady does a good job, Neil," she added.

"That's why I pay her the big bucks," Neil said warily.

I don't even know that he has a cleaning lady, but I'm sure he was curious about the nature of Junior's visit and was therefore determined not to ruffle her feathers. She rarely paid third-trimester social calls, and I highly doubt she was just making the rounds.

"If you'd rung the doorbell or hollered you wouldn't have had to climb the stairs," I said gently.

"I did shout. You two were too engrossed in your movie to hear me." She leaned over and peered at the paused tape. I should have known she wouldn't miss a detail like what was on TV. "*Fargo*, huh?"

"Yeah," Neil said hastily. "But we already know how it ends."

This time he shut the TV off. We both heaved a silent sigh of relief when the screen went blank. Whatever we'd just discovered by watching Jurgen's video, I certainly didn't want to discuss it with Junior.

Junior continued to inspect the living room, saying nothing.

The moment of silence lingered.

Finally, Neil said, "What can we do for you, Junior?"

"We?" Junior asked, raising an eyebrow, I'm sure storing the pronoun for future examination. "Well I'm not sure *you* can do anything. But Tory here can help me, if she's willing."

I'd learned from dint of long experience never to agree to help Junior unless I knew exactly what was expected, so my answer was a strictly noncommittal "Hmm."

"Well, it'll be to your advantage," Junior said sweetly. "Because Del said to tell you unless your presence was absolutely needed elsewhere, that it'd be ever so jolly of you to return to work."

"Oh shit," I said. I'd forgotten about the cafe altogether. I'd left Del and Alanna to run it alone over the noon hour. I rather suspected that Junior had paraphrased Del's request.

"Oh shit is right," Junior agreed. "You're not the most popular person there right now. Del also said to tell you that she'd be submitting a bill as your answering service but that pretty soon she was just going to tell callers that you'd moved and left no forwarding address."

I put my head in my hands and moaned inwardly.

It's not like I'd been lollygagging, though I was keenly aware of Junior's disapproving glance at the empty brandy snifters on the coffee table. And it's not like I'd been looking for an excuse not to go back to work. Time had just slipped away.

And given the distractions of the last few hours, it wasn't surprising.

Either way my choices were bleak.

I could tuck my tail between my legs and scurry back to work to endure the combined wrath of Del and Alanna. Or I could go with Junior, during which time I could possibly wrestle a few of yesterday's mysteries into submission.

That was, if Junior's favor didn't involve either babysitting or housecleaning.

"Where are your kids?" I asked, pretending to be nonchalant.

"Off with Mother," Junior said. "Where they'll be all day, out of our way."

"This wouldn't involve any heavy lifting, would it?"

Junior just shook her head at me and stood up slowly and awkwardly. "Well, are you coming, or aren't you?"

I shot a glance at Neil, who shrugged.

It was my call.

In either case, there would be no more snuggling on the couch, and given a choice between facing both Dell and Alanna, or Junior alone, I amazed myself with my decision.

At the very least, Junior wouldn't be as loud.

67

Fargo II, the Sequel

One thing about riding in a car with Junior, it left you with plenty of time to think.

Most of the time she'd chatter your ear off, bragging about her kids, making plans for world domination, complaining about the people in Clay's congregation, rearranging my life to suit her agenda.

But this time she sat, bundled so completely that she barely fit behind the steering wheel of her mother's Toyota, almost silent.

"I'm as up for adventure as the next guy," I said when we got into the car. "But I'd sorta like to know where we're going."

"I'm not exactly sure," Junior replied, reversing the car out of Neil's driveway and then driving east on the county highway that Delphi's main drag morphed into at the city limits.

"Oookay," I said slowly, nodding, as the frozen tundra whizzed past my window. "I can dig it. But why did we need Neil's cell phone?"

She'd asked for, damn near demanded, the use of Neil's mobile phone for the duration. Neil had been confused but he'd complied.

"Junior?" I said, peering at her. She was sweating now. I suppose that pregnant women's thermostats were all out of whack, a little bit of exercise in winter gear would overset their bodies' regulation system and they'd overheat.

Junior grimaced and then said, "I heard you."

I waited as another quarter-mile rolled past and then looked at her directly.

She got the hint. "I thought it wouldn't be a good idea to drive around out in the country in the middle of the winter without a way to contact the rest of the world. Remember what happened to you last month?"

I had no choice but to remember what happened to me last month, considering that folks took such delight in reminding me. But that didn't answer my question. "Why did you need Neil's phone? Where's yours?"

She drove on a ways before answering as the miles of snow-covered prairie stretched out around us in an endless circle of horizon. "Clay has our phone with him," she said finally.

"So call him and get it."

"It's shut off. Or he's not answering."

"Well, maybe we should go and get it from him so you'll have it with you when you drop me back off at Neil's," I suggested.

Junior looked at me, her face hard and pale. "I don't *know* where Clay is," she said, pronouncing each word carefully. "I need to find him immediately and I didn't want to drive around by myself. You were the only person I could trust to come along with me."

There had to be a zillion women in Junior's church whom she liked and who would drop everything for the chance to help such a selfless and devoted wife and mother. Why hadn't she called one of them? Why force me, a cousin she didn't even like, to ride shotgun?

"Well, I'd have thought that Jennifer or someone would have been happy to help you," I said. Jennifer Swanhorst had been more than willing to step in and ride to Cresbard with Clay. She'd been micromanaging church affairs as Junior's pregnancy advanced and her efficiency declined. She'd been involved in all of the choir activities. She would have been thrilled to perform this service for her church.

"Tory," Junior said tightly, again facing the road, "after the memorial service, Clay took off again. He left a note on his desk saying that he went ice fishing and then he disappeared."

"Again?" I asked, shaking my head. Nothing Clay Deibert had done in the last few days made the least bit of sense to me. It was as though he'd chucked his former life and turned into a taller, blond Nicky Bauer.

Junior didn't answer, she just concentrated on the road.

I realized that I was probably the only one who knew Junior's suspicions about Clay and Annelise. That I was the only one privy to her deepest marital fear: that her husband had been having an affair.

That was why she couldn't ask Jennifer or any of the church ladies to come along on this trek through the wintry South Dakota countryside. She didn't want any of them to know her suspicions. And given that all of them belonged to her church, she didn't want any of them to know if her suspicions had been right.

Junior was afraid of what she'd find when she found Clay.

And she wanted me along for backup.

I should have been touched, but Junior's fears were contagious. Anxiety settled into the pit of my stomach as we drove in silence.

Junior drove grimly; overwhelmed occasionally by the sheer burden of her worries, she'd close her eyes for a few deep breaths, a maneuver not nearly as dangerous on our perfectly straight and level roads as it might be anywhere else in the country.

I had finally understood, without being told, where we were going. I no more thought Clay was ice fishing than Junior did—men, even midwestern men, don't just suddenly develop an appetite for sport fishing in mid-life.

Low-slung red sports cars, yes.

A dependence on Grecian Formula and Viagra, yes.

An affinity for mindless young women with big boobs, most emphatically yes.

But they didn't suddenly, with no prior warning, decide to

isolate themselves inside in an unheated shack on a frozen body of water just for the joy of dropping a weighted string into a hole in the ice.

But in order to find out where Clay *was*, we needed to prove where he *wasn't*.

So I knew we were heading for the lake, one of the gazillion shallow ponds formed the last time the glaciers dropped in for a visit.

Minnesota was dotted with glacial lakes; in fact they called their state the "Land of 10,000 Lakes." But South Dakota had its share too. Maybe we were the land of one hundred lakes. Luckily, only one of them was close enough for Clay's stated purposes.

So on the twenty-mile drive as Junior grimaced and drove silently, I had plenty of time to think about everything that had happened in the last two days.

Unfortunately, not a damn thing made sense. Especially the counter notations on the videocassette.

Well, actually the first set of numbers did. The 800–1247 section pretty well covered the time from Jurgen's exterior shot of Cresbard's Main Street, including Weasel's furnace repair van, up to when Jennifer had hustled a very reluctant Annelise away from Clay's arms and out of camera range.

I could see why Weasel had earmarked that section. Not only did it prove that he'd met Meg previous to yesterday's encounter, it gave us at least a little insight behind Meg's seemingly calm façade.

And the last set of numbers made perfect sense. The 4011–5729 interlude more than amply backed up Weasel's assertion about the heartlessness, and acting abilities, of the European Traveling Lutheran Youth Choir, not to mention proving his claim that Meg had been absent.

But that middle section had me confused. The numbers had been written out of sequence across the top of the page, 1593–1679. But Neil and I had watched those eighty-six units of videotape and had only seen exactly what I was seeing outside the car window as I rode along in silence with Junior.

Neil had reversed and forwarded the tape, but even allowing for differing counter speeds, there was absolutely nothing on that section of tape that related to anything that had happened lately.

Weasel's other earmarks has been accidentally fortuitous for our purposes, telling us much about the main characters involved in this little melodrama, while at the same time reinforcing Weasel's protestations of innocence.

But that middle section, those eighty-six whatevers, told us nothing about anything.

There were no people in the clip.

There was no action in the clip.

There were no voices in the clip.

There was only snow, and a whole lot of it.

Why did Weasel want us to look at snow?

"Look at all the snow," Junior said finally.

"Huh?"

"There's still so much snow left after the blizzard last month," Junior said. "It'll be good for the farms when it melts. Maybe we can start the spring with an adequate amount of moisture for a change."

"Yeah, that'd be nice," I said, wondering if we were going to make small talk now. I decided that she was nervous and chattering just to cover up her own anxiety.

Up ahead, I could see the lake, a large gray slab of ice with low-lying drifts tracing white fingers out from the shore, interspersed with a few darker patches of thin ice. There were cabins scattered along the perimeter and miniature buildings that mostly looked like outhouses set at random on the ice itself.

"You have any notion where he might be fishing?" I asked, after thinking carefully how to phrase the question and making sure not to put any special emphasis on the last word.

Junior made a face. I figured I'd ventured too far into painful territory, but she answered me anyway. "The Swanhorsts have a cabin on the far side of the lake and they've invited him to use it for years. I know that George likes to ice fish, so I figured that would be a good place to start. I'm not exactly sure which is their cabin, so we'll just look for vehicles. Clay has our car; that's why I have Mother's."

"Just like *Fargo*," I said.

"Huh?" It was Junior's turn to be confused.

"This is just like the movie *Fargo*," I said lamely. "Here's a pregnant woman driving in a car around a frozen lake looking for a vehicle at a cabin."

It sounded stupid, and I was sorry I'd said it out loud.

Junior blew all her air out and for a moment I thought I was in for it. But she continued calmly. "Except that no one in their right minds is going to be using a wood chipper in the middle of winter. Besides that, we're not looking for a murderer."

Junior was looking for a possibly errant husband.

Unfortunately, I *was* looking for a murderer.

During the last hours, I'd been able to treat this whole exercise as a mental puzzle to be worked out for my own pleasure. I'd managed to forget what no one else in Delphi save Neil Pascoe knew: that we had two dead bodies on our hands.

Of course, one was dead by her own hand.

But the other wasn't.

Though their acquaintance was peripheral, not to mention brief, I was convinced that the two deaths were inextricably intertwined. I think Annelise's death would have happened with or without proximity to Weasel Cleaver.

But without Annelise's suicide, I was certain that Weasel Cleaver would be alive and among us, disgusting everyone within farting distance.

And as little as I'd liked the man, I wished he'd been able to go the way he would have wanted (in bed with a couple of twenty-year-olds) rather than stuffed ignominiously into a supply cupboard and then later transported to God knows where, left to freeze solid before being found.

So even though I wasn't looking for a murderer out the window while riding around a frozen lake with a pregnant woman, I was most assuredly looking for a murderer.

And I suddenly realized how Junior could help in that search.

68

Stunt Girl

It was pretty shameless of me to milk Junior when she was so desperately worried about her husband and marriage. On the other hand, she had used me without remorse, and she'd not hesitate to do it again when the need arose. So doing my best to avoid painful subjects, I decided to exploit her sudden willingness to chat.

"Well," I said conversationally as we turned off the highway, onto the road that circumnavigated the lake. "What brought the choir to Delphi in the first place? I've been away from work so much lately that I never did get the whole scoop."

Junior squinted. "They were scheduled to appear in Cresbard. It'd been set up for a whole year; these things have to be arranged a long time in advance for visas and funds and all to be in place. They'd come down from a concert in Jamestown ready to take a few days off with the assorted host families before a putting on another show in Cresbard, but the furnace went out in the church there."

I'd known that, but confirmation was nice.

"So the church was cold. Wasn't there anyplace else where they could have held their concert?" I asked.

"Youda thought so," Junior said. "I don't know why they needed to leave so suddenly either. I think something happened with one of the kids. Some sort of incident."

"Oh?" I asked, trying not to sound too curious.

"Clay wouldn't tell me much, but I'm pretty sure it involved sexual escapades. The minister there called him up for a conference."

Which reminded her of her own problems, which were way too close to home for her to bear. A pained look crossed her face.

Filing that bit of information away for future examination, I scrambled to change the subject. Sorta.

"Tell me about the kids then. You had almost a week with them; you must have gotten to know them fairly well." Shit, that cut too close to the bone for Junior too. "How about Glenda? What was she like?"

There. A safe subject.

"That bitch," Junior said harshly. "She's the root of all the problems. If she'd been watching them the way she was supposed to, the way she says she does, monitoring their every move, being their very best friend and confidante, keeping track of everything they think and do, none of this would ever have happened."

Junior had a point. If Glenda'd had a better handle on the drugs, prescription or otherwise, Annelise would still be alive and kicking.

"She certainly wasn't able to rein them in at my house," Junior said bitterly.

I'd intended to avoid subjects that were too painful for Junior to talk about. But since she mentioned it, I figured there was no reason to demur.

"Well, they seemed to be fooling around right under her nose," I agreed carefully, not mentioning any other noses they might have thumbed.

"Under her nose, in the bedrooms, on my couch. Everywhere."

"Oh, you flashed your body fluid detector around some more, huh?"

She was disgusted. "I found . . . stuff . . . everywhere. I

don't think there was a single room where someone hadn't been doing *something* . . ."

Of course, the body fluid detector wasn't scientifically accurate. I knew that it couldn't differentiate between snot and semen, to be indelicate, so Junior might actually have been monitoring the nose-picking propensity of her own children.

But I sort of doubted it. There were way too many road signs pointing to sex.

"So how did the kids get along with each other?" I was hoping for a clue to whom Annelise might have been in love with.

If she hadn't been in love with Clay, that is. Though from the videotape, I almost had to conclude that she was.

Junior winced again.

She sure was doing that a lot. I wondered if she'd developed a facial tic.

"They seemed to get along pretty well. Some better than others."

"Was Meg good friends with anyone?"

What I wanted was a clue to why she'd stolen Weasel's van yesterday, though I didn't suppose Junior could supply that.

Junior shrugged. "She was okay on the surface. I don't think much slipped by her. She was pretty close to Annelise though."

Just saying the name caused a flash of pain across Junior's face.

"You know Weasel swore that the rest of the choir didn't give a rat's ass about Annelise, including Meg. He said that they weren't sad until people started to notice that they should be acting sad."

Junior snorted. "And what would a little creep like him know about real friendship and loyalty? He spent his whole life stealing from friends and people who trusted him. Look what he did to Aphrodite."

"Yeah, well, I think he was turning over a new leaf," I said firmly. I couldn't very well trot out my proof that Weasel had been telling the truth, but I could stand up for him. "And besides, I saw some of that myself at the cafe. Not a single one of the choir members showed any emotion about Annelise's condition until Del said something snotty. Then they all started weeping and wailing at once."

"Like that means anything," Junior said, taking a curve carefully. We had driven past scattered cabins that ranged from shacks and run-down single-wide trailers to upscale log dwellings that would have been at home on the slopes of the Rockies.

"Well, *I* think those kids are excellent actors. All of 'em," I repeated. "I doubt if anyone could really tell if they were sad or not."

"Renee McKee told me that Meg cried herself to sleep last night, that she could hear her sobs right through the bedroom door. No one else was in there with her, so if she was acting, then she was doing it for herself alone."

I thought about that for a minute. Maybe Meg *was* sad about Annelise's death, but was she sad for the automatically assumed reasons? Was she sad because her friend was dead? Or was she sad because something went horribly wrong with a scheme? A stunt?

Did she have a very good reason to be sad now, that she hadn't had yesterday afternoon?

For a second I stopped breathing as we slowed down some more.

Along the road were a few parked pickups. There was evidence of human habitation—empty beer cases were stacked in truck boxes and smoke rose lazily from teeny little buildings set fifty feet from shore.

But so far, we'd not seen a trace of Clay Deibert.

I tried to focus on the thought that had drifted in and out of my view as Junior slowed the car to a crawl.

She pointed out the side window. "I think that's the Swanhorsts' cabin. *You* see any vehicles nearby?"

There was a note of desperation in her voice. I don't know if she was more afraid of finding Clay or not finding him.

We drove by slowly. Not only were there no vehicles near the cabin, the driveway had drifted over pretty well. And there were no tracks in the snow.

Unless he'd driven in through the yard, Clay was not only

not at the Swanhorsts' cabin ice fishing, he hadn't been there yesterday either. Or any day in the past week.

"Doesn't look like he's been here," I said softly, wanting to change the subject delicately. It wasn't possible. "Where are the kids now? The choir I mean?"

Junior hung her head and closed her eyes and breathed heavily in and out a couple of times. "They're probably at the church, getting packed up and ready to leave," she said without looking up or opening her eyes.

Trying to keep the urgency out of my voice, and without wanting to upset her further, I said, "Do you think we can go back to town now? I'd really like to talk to Meg for a minute."

Junior looked over at me and swallowed. She was pale and sweating.

"I think that'd be a good idea, Tory. And maybe you should drive." A look of real pain crossed her face again. "I'm pretty sure I'm in labor."

69

Lawsy Miss Scarlett

I can hear you clucking right now, shaking your head muttering to yourself that any idiot would have figured it out sooner. With twenty-twenty hindsight being what it is, I can see how you might feel that way. I wonder myself why I didn't make the connection.

But at the time I only thought that Junior was expressing nonverbally the emotional pain she felt over the possible infidelity of her formerly dependable husband.

That she was experiencing actual physical pain never occurred to me. That explained finally why *I* was the one who had to come with her on the mysterious drive around the lake.

If she was in labor, and Junior would surely know that better than anyone, then finding Clay was an imperative. And if finding Clay meant driving out into the countryside to look for his car even knowing that he might not want to be found, even knowing that whatever mental collapse he seemed to be suffering might affect his sense of responsibility, then having a companion was also an imperative.

There was no one else except me that she could trust with the possible outcome of this trip. I already knew what she suspected, and at odd intervals, I'd suspected right along with her.

She'd never have allowed anyone from her church to know her deepest fears. She wouldn't have allowed me to know them either, but that had happened both accidentally and gradually, and the knowledge could not be taken back now.

She needed someone to ride along, and circumstances had dictated who that person had to be. In true Junior fashion she'd hornswaggled me into volunteering by not revealing pertinent information until it was too late for me to back out.

"You know, you might have told me about this earlier," I said testily, rearranging the seat to accommodate my shorter legs, and lowering the steering wheel. "We're halfway around the lake. It'll take as much time to go back as to continue on. We're going to have to finish the circuit and then head back into town."

Without waiting for her to agree, I looked over my shoulder for nonexistent traffic and then pulled out, driving a good deal faster than was recommended on curving, occasionally ice-covered, country gravel roads.

Junior just nodded, her face pale, her eyes closed tight.

"Jesus, Junior, how close *are* the pains?" I asked, not that it made a bit of difference. My experience with childbirth was entirely literary, with a few gaps filled in by PBS and The Learning Channel, not to mention the odd, badly acted sitcom.

"About fifteen minutes apart now," she said, relaxing a little again.

"Fifteen minutes!" I shouted, keeping my eye on the road while speeding up even more. "You took me a zillion miles out in the country when your labor pains were fifteen fucking minutes apart? Have you lost your mind?"

I was beginning to panic. I had no clue as to how to go about helping to deliver a baby, and no desire to learn firsthand. I didn't even know if we had any clean towels or blankets in the car. And I know for sure that we didn't have any hot water, which seemed to play an important role in cinematic births.

"Calm down, Tory," Junior said, adjusting her position a

little. "We have plenty of time to get back into town. And plenty of time for Clay to get me to the hospital in Aberdeen. But I do need to find him."

"No shit," I agreed. "You know this is his fault. We'd never be in this situation without Clay."

"No kidding," Junior agreed calmly. She was between contractions and back in charge.

"I don't just mean *your* situation," I said pointedly. "I know he's responsible for that. What I meant was that we wouldn't be in any of this if Clay hadn't been acting so strange lately."

I was being harsh, and probably saying things that were painful for her to hear. But Junior was in labor and her husband was missing and there didn't seem to be much point in pussy-footing around the issues anymore. Besides I was too upset to guard my words.

"Well, it's not *all* his fault," Junior said, looking out the window.

"You bet your sweet ass it's not *all* his fault. You had a hand in this too. And I don't mean *that* way either. If you hadn't taken that damn suicide note and the bag then I'd never have been in Clay's office last night and I wouldn't have found . . ." Finally my brain caught up with my mouth. I scrambled for a quick cover-up finish to the question because Junior had turned to look at me. ". . . Snickers bars all over his desk," I finished lamely. It was a piss-poor recovery, a non sequitur of the highest order.

Junior frowned. "Snickers bars? Clay hates Snickers. In fact he hates them so much that he'd have been willing to skip them altogether for the candy drive. But Jennifer insisted. Snickers are *her* favorite. In fact she snarfed down a bunch of them on that eighty-some-mile round trip they made to Cresbard last week." She grimaced again. "In fact," she said, her breathing becoming a little ragged, "she had the gall to confront Clay about disappearing candy when she's the one eating up all the profits."

I had a notion where some of those profits may have disappeared, considering that I'd found a half-eaten Snickers on Clay's desk and Weasel had been caught on camera waving another around.

Junior closed her eyes through the remainder of the contraction. I sped up even a little more. She opened her eyes again, ready to take up what she'd ignored the first time around. "And what do you mean about taking the note *and* the bag? I didn't touch that suicide note."

"Of course you took it," I said, exasperated. There was no point in pretending otherwise. "It disappeared from the cafe the same time you did."

I stopped abruptly and thought that through. I suddenly realized something about the note.

I'd only had a brief moment to read it, and I certainly didn't bother to memorize it beyond the fact that Annelise really did write that she'd been molested by the reverend of Delphi's Lutheran church.

But did she really mean to say that?

Was that the meaning she'd meant to imply?

She was writing in a second, or third, or fourth language, after all.

And Neil's little experiment with the online Babelfish had proven that even literal translations don't catch the subtext of a message. Words don't always mean what you think they'll mean when flipped back and forth between languages.

I knew full well that Annelise had written a couple of practice suicide notes, and while they'd said essentially the same thing, the wording was different in each. And the final impression, the one any reader would take away, was different in each.

In one she was heartbroken over a lost love.

In another she was hurt and mortified because a trust had been shattered.

In yet another, she'd named a specific perpetrator, a single man who'd been the author of her unhappiness.

But in all of the notes, the one single consistent thread had been a longing to go home. That had been the message to her parents in the letter ready to mail and among the trial runs. On the video, while in the van, she'd told Glenda that she wanted to leave.

We'd assumed that she'd opted to go home in a box rather than wait.

But were we right about that?

Had she truly wanted to commit suicide, or did she just want to go home really badly?

"Oh my Lord," I said out loud as we turned back onto the paved highway at last and sped west toward Delphi. "Junior, call Neil right now. Tell him what's going on with you and have him contact the church so they'll know we're coming. And tell him I need to talk to him."

70

Accidentally on Purpose

Our roads are so straight that engineers insert correction curves every forty or so miles that take the curvature of the earth into consideration so that people driving north in South Dakota can be ever confident that they are traveling along a true northerly path. Our portion of the state is so flat that if we stood in one spot long enough, we could watch the sunrise and the sunset over both horizons just by facing the other direction. And it's a known fact that you can drive fifty miles of interstate highway and meet maybe three cars going the other direction.

But that still doesn't mean that it's automatically safe to drive in South Dakota, because most of our of traffic fatalities result from one-car accidents.

Deer leap from the roadside ditches with no warning. Icy patches in the wintertime are often hard to see, even in broad daylight. A driver's own carelessness, encouraged by endless straight stretches of empty road, renders the lack of opposing traffic or geographical obstacles moot.

Accidents happen and they happen frequently.

And even in our technologically backward neck of the woods, accidents happen often when drivers think they can yak safely on the phone inside a moving vehicle.

I wasn't about to chance it when my passenger was a woman in labor.

"Tell him that they weren't faking," I said to Junior. It didn't matter that she was acting as an intermediary in a conversation that would leave her confused. Now that I finally understood one of the major contradictions of the last two days, it didn't matter who listened in.

Junior looked at me oddly, but she relayed the message to Neil.

"He says they had to have been. At least part of the time." Junior's face convulsed again. She hunched forward a little bit and inhaled slowly.

I waited for the contraction to end before answering, hoping that the increased frequency didn't mean what I thought it meant.

She sat back up and opened her eyes and waited for my answer.

"Tell him that they weren't faking except when they knew they had to. Tell him that—" I paused, wondering if I really should say it out loud—"that Annelise's suicide was an accident."

Junior looked at me in surprise, plainly not believing me.

"What do you mean? She took pills and wrote a note!" she said vehemently, without relaying my message to Neil.

"Tell Neil what I said and then I'll explain to both of you."

As I drove I repeated the scenario that had just popped into my head. Junior held the phone out so that Neil could hear me too.

"We know that Annelise was homesick and sad. We know that she had been in love and that the love affair had ended badly for her"—Junior started to interrupt, but I held out a hand—"we know that she wanted to leave the tour and go home more than anything else. We know that Glenda wouldn't let her go, that there were some kind of funding snafus, and maybe even a scandal attached to a previous tour that made aborting in the middle a dicey affair that would jeopardize the whole enterprise."

"Oh, I know about that," Junior interrupted. "Glenda has been the American liaison for the Lutheran traveling choir for a couple of years now, and the rumor, unsubstantiated, mind you, is that she's not exactly celibate on the road. She enforces strict behavior rules on the kids but is hot to trot herself. Though there've never been any specific charges lodged against her, the local ministers all warned each other to keep a careful eye on her and the kids during their visits. In fact Clay made that eighty-mile round trip to Cresbard to talk to the pastor there several times. Clay was the one who insisted that the choir come to Delphi in the first place. He thought he could keep an eye on them better here; the broken furnace was just an excuse."

"Jesus Christ, Junior," I said, exasperated, "why didn't you tell me that earlier?"

"It's church business," she said primly. "I shouldn't be telling you now either, but since you're speculating wildly, I thought it'd be better if you heard the truth."

Her face contorted again, I waited for the pain to pass.

"You got that, Neil?" I shouted.

Junior listened to the phone and then nodded.

"Okay, then Glenda was on some sort of probation, right?" I looked at Junior, who nodded. "It was particularly important for her to get through this tour with the whole group intact and with no scandal attached, right? And except for Annelise, everyone else wanted the tour to continue. No one was unhappy except her."

Junior nodded again.

"That makes what I'm going to say completely logical. Annelise knew that she wasn't going to get to go home under ordinary circumstances. So with the help of Meg at least, and possibly the whole choir, she decided to engineer her own suicide."

"Well *that* got her home in a hurry, didn't it?" Junior asked, exasperated

"That's the problem," I said sadly. "She only wanted to *attempt* suicide. She wanted to shake Glenda up enough to let her go home no matter the consequences. I think that the whole choir knew she was going to do it. They acted together, to *help* her, and to *cover up* for her. I am absolutely certain that Annelise did not intend to die."

Junior listened to the phone some more. "Neil says to tell you that Weasel was right then, that the kids really weren't sad until everyone else thought they should be."

"Right," I agreed. "They knew that Annelise wasn't going to die. They knew that she was going to go home, which is what she really wanted. So they had no reason in the world to act unhappy until it was obvious that their behavior looked odd."

"So why did she say those awful things about Clay?" Junior asked me, the pain on her face not physical this time.

"I don't know for sure, but Neil and I think that it might have been a language problem as much as anything." I deliberately ignored the video shot where Annelise had kissed a very surprised Clay on the lips. I tried to discount his leaving her bedroom in the middle of the night. I purposely devalued his recent erratic behavior and continued on before Junior could interrupt. "The rest of the kids thought that Annelise was going to be okay, so when Jennifer came in with the awful news, the shock and grief were real."

I'd been there. The horror on the assembled faces was too genuine to have been faked. It was too raw and deep. "So none of them was acting, at least not past the announcement. They were *all* shocked and brokenhearted. They *are* all grieving."

We waited a moment for Junior's next contraction to pass. It wasn't just my imagination, they were occurring at less than ten-minute intervals now. We were about ten miles from Delphi and even though praying wasn't my normal mode of communication, I sent a silent but entirely heartfelt plea that there be no unpleasant surprises on the last leg of the trip into town.

After her face relaxed, she listened to Neil again. "He says that we all owe Weasel a big apology." Junior took the phone away from her ear and said to me, "I don't know why you two are such big Weasel fans all of a sudden. Renee McKee says that Meg told her that Weasel made a pass at her in Cresbard and that he did it again when she saw him in Delphi."

And with that statement, another piece of the puzzle slipped into place.

71

Eighty-six Whatevers

Don't kid yourself. You'd have thought that the number sequence related to the VCR counter too. After all, the three sets of numbers were written on the same page and in the same hand. The fact that one set was penciled in along the upper edge of the sheet wouldn't have made any more impression on you than it had on Neil or me.

And the lowest set of numbers, 800–1247, did relate exactly to the videotape. Weasel had sat in Clay's office in the deserted church annex and carefully made a notation of the relevant 447 units (or whatever they were called) that proved conclusively that he'd met the choir kids before coming to Delphi yesterday. I imagine that my doubt had hurt his feelings and he wanted to show me that I'd been wrong about him *and* the choir.

And then I imagine he fast-forwarded to the Delphi sequences and just as gleefully made note of the 1,629 recorded moments between 4100 and 5729, which again showed the whole world that ex-con or no, he was able to tell the truth at least some of the time.

So it's not my damn fault that I assumed the other eighty-six units, the difference between 1593 and 1679, related to the videotape as well. It's not like Weasel expected to die for his efforts and had therefore labeled his notes clearly: This pertains to videotape, and this signifies something else entirely.

I had to figure that out for myself, and until Junior'd made a point of mentioning the miles used on a round trip to Cresbard, I had truly believed that there was some deep significance to the endless videotaped shots of snowy plains.

But the snow scenes were just snow scenes, filmed by a boy fascinated equally with flat ground and bumpy chests.

The significance was the difference between 1593 and 1697. Those eighty-six whatevers just happened to be miles.

I had forgotten, in my surprise and amazement at the things that the videotape had shown us, that Weasel wasn't in the least interested in Annelise beyond wanting us to know that he saw what he saw.

He wasn't concerned with her death, or how it came about.

He wanted everyone to know that the choir's behavior had been every bit as odd as he'd said it was. And he wanted everyone to believe that Meg had taken his van, something I'd been unwilling to accept after the reappearance of the vehicle.

So until Junior had mentioned those miles again, I hadn't made the connection.

The choir had been in Cresbard.

Meg was talking to a boy *in* Cresbard, who I'd bet was *from* Cresbard. Their relationship was obviously deeper than mere conversation, or Glenda, who monitored the choir's activities closely, would not have interfered. Nor would she have called Clay to intervene and assist in the separation.

On the video, Meg was plainly annoyed by Clay's interference.

And she was plainly upset over being separated from the boy.

Who lived in Cresbard.

Which was about forty miles from Delphi.

A round trip, with a little extra for back tracking (the boy wore a gimme cap, he was obviously farm bred, and farms were out of town) was just about eighty-six miles exactly.

The notation didn't refer to the videotape, with which Weasel hoped to prove that the whole choir was duplicitous. It referred to mileage accumulated on his van during its absence by Meg, whose duplicity he abhored.

I hadn't spent one minute wondering what Weasel had done in between leaving the church with Jurgen's videotape and when he'd been caught watching it in Clay's office. There was a period of several hours unaccounted for in that time—more than enough to trot across the street, unnoticed, and make note of the last numbers of the odometer reading.

I'd blithely assumed that he'd taken his van and driven back to Aberdeen. It wasn't until after finding his body in the cupboard and later peeking into the windows of the locked van that I'd known that had not been the case.

But Junior had mentioned the distance to Cresbard. And she'd also repeated Renee McKee's gossip about Weasel.

If Weasel had made a pass at Meg last week, and there was no reason in the world to doubt it, which had been rebuffed (and there was no reason in the world to doubt that either), that would surely not have stopped him from trying his luck again on a chance re-meeting in Delphi.

Weasel was nothing if not tenacious. Taking no for an answer had gotten him nowhere, and he was not the kind of guy to remember that taking yes had mostly landed him in jail.

So he'd tried again with Meg and was again turned down.

But Meg, disgusted as she was, had seized the moment—she'd gotten revenge on Weasel by stealing his clothes and leaving him naked in the storeroom of the cafe.

And I'd bet everything I owned that she'd used the opportunity to drive Weasel's van to Cresbard for an interlude with her farm boy. She'd gotten revenge on Weasel while at the same time pretty well ensuring that he wouldn't call the police and report the van as stolen. Who would admit publicly to being tricked out of his clothes in a restaurant storeroom?

He hadn't come whining to us either. If I hadn't found him accidentally, I'd never have known about the incident.

It all tied together.

It tied so well that I suddenly wondered if it also tied Meg to Weasel's death.

"You say that everyone's at the church?" I asked Junior as we finally entered the Delphi city limits.

"I've been telling you that for the last few miles," she said testily. "But you've been off in space, not paying attention to a word I've said."

Neil had hung up with a promise to call ahead and let them know we were coming. We all thought that driving the extra distance to Junior's house, especially given the regularity and severity of her contractions, was dicey. Clay would just have to be found and they'd need to leave for the hospital immediately.

Neither Neil nor I had mentioned the need for a backup plan should Clay still be mysteriously unavailable. And rather than give Junior the opportunity to volunteer me for additional shuttle duty, I'd kept my mouth closed for the last of the drive as my mind raced hither and yon.

In fact, I'd been so preoccupied with the sudden notion that Meg could have been Weasel's attacker, that there'd have been no reason for him to have stayed in Clay's office unless he was meeting someone specifically, that I'd barely logged the fact that Junior had been chattering nonstop between pains.

It wasn't until we came within sight of the church, in front of which stood a whole group of anxious people, including, thank God, Clay Deibert, that I'd realized what Junior had been saying for the last few miles.

". . . and I want you to understand once and for all"—she'd grimaced through the pain—"that I did not take that damn suicide note."

72

Okay, Don't Blame Canada

I don't think I've ever been so glad to see anyone in my life as I was to spot Clay in the crowd standing out in front of St. John's Lutheran Church. The others wore coats, not to mention boots, hats, mittens, and scarves, but he stood in his shirt sleeves in the snow, peering anxiously as I made an illegal U-turn and pulled up with the passenger door to the sidewalk.

Clay rushed over and pulled Junior out of the car, a look of tender concern on his face. With one arm carefully supporting an elbow, he aimed his wife up the sidewalk.

"Where the hell have you been?" Junior demanded, forgetting that she had an avid audience gathered on the frozen lawn. "I've been trying to get hold of you for the past two hours."

"*I* called him, honey," Jennifer Swanhorst said, taking Junior's other arm. "He got here as quickly as he could."

But I doubt Junior heard her because she suddenly doubled over and said something through her clenched teeth that I couldn't quite make out.

I scrambled from the car and hurried around to the sidewalk. "What's happening? What did she say?"

"Water," Clay explained, going instantly pale. "Her water just broke. I don't think there's time to get to Aberdeen now. We'll be safer staying here than getting stranded on the road. We'd better get her inside where it's warm and then call the doctor."

I was not about to argue with his plan, especially since it didn't involve me driving Junior to the hospital. Someone rushed ahead and held open the annex doors for the trio.

As the rest of us followed in behind them, I dimly realized that Jurgen was once again functioning as Captain Camcorder, merrily recording the melee.

I brought up the rear, deliberately positioning myself next to Meg, whose guarded expression was unreadable. I'd thought about trying a subtle approach, easing my way into a conversation with her during which I could pump her gently about the things I had lately realized. But the profusion of suitcases piled in the annex hallway told me that time was short.

Besides, I wanted to shock Meg into telling the truth. I had a feeling that she was not a girl who could be manipulated, that subtlety would be met with obfuscation. Or worse.

"So whose idea was it to stage a suicide anyway?" I asked her quietly without a preamble, making sure that no one was eavesdropping as we stood in the annex hallway. Most of the others milled about as Junior and entourage went into Clay's office and firmly closed the door. No one paid any attention to us.

"What? I don't know what you're talking about," Meg said. Her eyes widened, but otherwise she maintained a calm exterior.

"Oh you know what I'm talking about," I declared. "Annelise wanted desperately to go home and Glenda wouldn't let her go. I want to know who came up with the plan to stage a nonfatal overdose so that they'd have no choice but to send her back."

Meg looked desperately around her, probably hoping for assistance from one of the other choir members, but they were all babbling excitedly. The impending birth of a baby or three was far more engrossing than a conversation between a middle-aged cafe owner and one of their own.

After all, I was just a small-town American rube, what the hell could I possibly know?

Well, I knew that Meg knew that Annelise intended to stage a suicide attempt.

And now Meg knew it too.

Her shoulders sagged. "It seemed like such a good idea," she said softly. "That bitch Glenda wasn't going to let her go home. She'd already ruined her life and I think she took pleasure in forcing the poor kid to stay on the tour with the rest of us even though every day was torture. Even Jurgen agreed that this was a good way for Annelise to get what she wanted."

"So what went wrong? If she only wanted to go home, how did she end up dead?"

Tears rolled down Meg's cheeks, her façade cracking. "I don't know. We tried to calculate the number of aspirin she could take without doing permanent harm. We looked it up in a medical book and had it all worked out to where she'd be sick and everyone would be worried but she'd get to go home and recover there."

"Well, playing with overdoses when you're allergic to one of the components is pretty tricky," I said harshly. "I don't suppose that any of you took her allergy to codeine into consideration."

Meg blinked at me several times. "Annelise wouldn't have taken anything with codeine in it. She was allergic to codeine. Very allergic."

"But she did," I insisted, remembering the empty 222 bottle in Annelise's bag, and the doctor's conclusion that Annelise had died of an overdose complicated by an allergic reaction. "She took a whole bottle of aspirin with codeine, the kind you can buy over the counter in Canada. I assumed you'd given it to her."

"My Lord," Meg said vehemently, the flow of tears interrupted by a sudden anger. "You think I'd have been so stupid? Or that I'd have given her the something that would be tied directly back to me? Annelise absolutely insisted that none of us be blamed for her suicide attempt. She worried about that a lot, so we all faked headaches over the last week. Even Jurgen. We blamed the headaches on rapid climate changes so that asking for extra pills wouldn't seem strange. We gave Annelise the pills and she saved them up until she had enough to fake an overdose. But that's all she took, just plain aspirin. None of us had access to anything stronger."

I thought about that, almost making a connection, but not quite. Meg looked like she was going to bolt, so I rushed on quickly. "Even so, you helped to fashion her suicide note, didn't you? You even took her through a couple of practice runs, right?"

Meg leaned back against the brick wall and looked at me tiredly. "Annelise was pretty good with English but there were terms and phrases that she just didn't understand, so she asked me for help in making the note absolutely clear, yes."

"And that's how she ended up accusing Clay Deibert of molesting her when he only wanted to help, right? She may or may not have had a crush on him, but he was just doing what he could to help her to work through the heartbreak of a lost love. It was you who decided to wreak a little havoc on the townfolk."

A small smile played on Meg's lips. "Well, they deserved it. The whole lot is a bunch of hypocrites. *Don't fraternize with the locals. Don't fraternize within the tour group. Celibacy is next to Godliness*," she sing-songed. "Not a single one of 'em can live up to their own standards. Besides which, the damn note disappeared anyway, so it didn't do any damage."

"No thanks to you," I said sharply, thinking of the possible fallout. Remembering the anguish it had already caused Junior. "But you're a prankster, all right. You took Weasel Cleaver's clothes and his van and drove to Cresbard and let him stew in our storeroom naked."

"And *he* deserved it most of all." Meg chuckled. "The little creep actually thought that I'd be willing to buy his silence with a quickie. What a fool."

"Why did you need his silence?" I asked, suddenly on alert.

"Because he caught me and"—she paused for a second, giving me a sideways glance—"a very nice local boy . . . having some fun in a storeroom at the church in that last town. And he thought he could parlay that little bit of information into a blowjob or more for himself."

"And you didn't kill him to keep him quiet?" I asked, enunciating each word clearly so she wouldn't mistake my meaning.

This time she really did laugh out loud. "Kill the little slimeball? Not on your life. I agreed to meet him later but I stood him up. I figured he'd been punished enough. You see, there's a difference between me and the rest of these goody-goodies. At least some of them actually believe what they're preaching. Some of them would be devastated by their family's disappointment. They'd consider it a permanent blotch on their good character to be dismissed by a man-eater like Ms. Glenda Harrison. Me, I'm here for the adventure. It's a lark and I intend to enjoy myself fully. *I'm* not mourning the loss of a hometown sweetheart, so brokenhearted that I have to talk to anyone I can get to listen to me in the middle of the damn night every single night. *I'm* not pretending not to be attracted to younger men. *I'm* not worried about the opinions of sanctimonious small-town Americans who think they comprise all of North America."

"What did you just say?" I asked, trying to sort through Meg's diatribe. I had a feeling that she'd just said something very important.

The door to Clay's office cracked open and he poked his head into the hallway and announced, "Everything's going fine in here. I think we'll have a new baby in just a few minutes. We're on the phone with the doctor and everything should be okay. Tory, can you come in here for a minute? Junior's been asking for you."

So I didn't have time to wait for Meg's reply.

But then again, I didn't need to because suddenly it almost all fell into place.

73

Birth and Death

There was a brief time, in my far distant past, when I longed for a child of my own. But that was not to be, and rather than moving heaven and earth to defy biology, I simply accepted my fate without too many backward glances.

I can coo over infants with the best of them, but beyond a sort of unfocused notion that when they smelled good, they really smelled good, I didn't think about them much.

And I had certainly never yearned to be present at a birth. I'm squeamish enough as it is. For me, a little bit of blood and a whole lot of pain goes a really long way. I'm more than content to wait to inspect the squalling bundle after mother and child have been cleaned and dressed and had a moment to get to know each other.

Throughout our contentious relationship, Junior has not seen fit to invite me into her personal life beyond a few family suppers and the occasional request to watch the children if no one else was available. Why she wanted me specifically at her side now was a mystery.

I knelt on the floor beside her. She was covered with a crocheted afghan from the couch in Clay's outer office. She was drenched in sweat, her hair was plastered to her head in a stringy mass. She made strange, inarticulate noises, her face contorted almost beyond recognition as she half sat, supported on one side by Jennifer Swanhorst and on the other by Glenda Harrison. Jurgen, the mad cameraman, was nowhere to be seen, thank goodness.

Positioned at the other end, Clay was wedged between Junior's upraised knees. He was sweating almost more than Junior, and pale. But as her contraction eased he shot her a look of such concentrated love that my heart leaped.

"You're almost there," he said gently. "Just a couple more." He held a telephone cradled between his shoulder and ear and was evidently listening to instructions from the doctor.

Junior caught his look and nodded back at Clay, love shining from her eyes as well.

Whatever had been going on with them, it had been deeper than a transitory affair with a visiting member of a traveling choir since Junior had mentioned early on that Clay'd been distracted and acting odd for more than a month, well before the choir's appearance in Delphi.

But however serious the rift, it was obvious from the looks passing between the two, as Junior began to push in earnest, that it was over. They were on the road to recovery and I rejoiced for them.

I caught Junior's eye between pushes, and nodded. This is what she'd wanted me to see. She wanted me to know that things would be okay now, that the aberration, whatever it was, was gone.

And by the same token, I knew that she wasn't going to want to sit down with me in a month and hash it all over. The subject would be closed forever.

Which was fine with me, since I'd finally connected the dots, finally understood what had happened.

I looked at Junior and nodded again. She flashed a small smile at me and then her world, indeed her entire universe, narrowed down to the imperative of her body and the creature impatient to make an appearance.

I wasn't really needed anymore, but my work was not done.

I switched positions, to behind Junior's head, as the others focused completely on the impending birth.

"I can't figure it out," I said, almost conversationally.

"What can't you figure out?" Glenda said. She grimaced along with Junior.

"Why you put the suicide note back in the cafe after taking it."

I lied. I knew exactly why it had happened.

Glenda's mouth dropped open and she inhaled sharply, I think in preparation for a vehement argument.

I put one finger to my lips and used the other hand to point to Junior. "No sense in getting everyone upset, is there?"

"I don't know what you're talking about," Glenda whispered back, refusing to look at me. She leaned down and smoothed Junior's hair back off her forehead with a free hand.

"That's okay," I said conversationally. "Because I know exactly what I'm talking about and I'll be more than happy to explain it to you."

The kicker had been Junior's final, adamant denial of taking the suicide note. I should have known that it never would have survived in her hands. It was just too damning a document. If Junior had tempted the law *and* the vengeance of her own God to spirit away evidence linking her husband to a heinous act, she surely would not have left it in existence to do further damage.

No, the note had disappeared because Glenda had taken it while we were occupied with the ambulance and the attendant madness of getting the unconscious Annelise out of the cafe.

And it had reappeared this morning because Glenda wanted the finger of blame, and the focus of attention, pointed as far away from her as possible.

"I assume that you took the note to begin with because you thought it mentioned you in some way. You thought that Annelise had perhaps made good on a threat to expose you and your habits."

That last was a shot in the dark, but it evidently hit the mark because Glenda's eyes narrowed.

"You're crazy," she whispered. "You're nothing but a pathetic small-town loser with nothing better to do than sit around and gossip while you wait for something to happen that's more exciting than shoveling a sidewalk."

"That may be," I said calmly. "But I think that even sophisticated big-city types like you would be fascinated to discover that an accidentally successful suicide was really a murder."

There, I'd said the "M" word out loud.

I figured I'd be saying it again fairly soon.

Glenda leaned down and whispered something soothing to Junior and then gestured for Jennifer to take over. She stood up and was about to leave the room when I caught her arm.

"It won't do any good for you to go and talk to him. I'm not the only one who knows."

That last was a blatant lie. I hadn't had time to tell Neil any of the latest conclusions or revelations, but I wanted to bluff Glenda into staying put for the rest of our conversation.

"*You* switched the regular aspirins with the 222. Whether it's legal in Canada or not, aspirin with codeine is a prescription medication in the United States, and while on tour, you control all prescription meds. You told me that yourself yesterday morning. And as the tour liaison, you knew full well about Annelise's allergy to codeine."

"You can't prove any of this," Glenda said, pulling herself to her full height. "And if you tell people this, I'll sue your ass so fast it'll make your head spin."

"Damn, you big-city people play hardball, don't you?" I said, whistling low. "I guess I'll just have to tell the police that several of us saw the 222 bottle in Annelise's bag then." Glenda had surely planted the empty pill bottle in Annelise's bag when she'd taken the suicide note. "Who do you suppose our small-town police are going to listen to? Small towners? Or outsiders who commit murder?"

"My lawyer can eat your lawyer for breakfast," she spat. "You don't know who you're tangling with, sweetie pie."

"And, Miss America third runner-up, you don't know who you already tangled with. First you stole Annelise's hometown sweetheart away from her . . ."

Meg had given me that piece too. Annelise was pining for the recent loss of her childhood boyfriend. It just so happened that Jurgen, the intrepid camera boy, was from Annelise's hometown.

And it also happened that Jurgen was fascinated with Glenda.

I continued out loud. ". . . and then you pumped him for information after Annelise caught the two of you together."

Another nugget from our Canadian friend. Annelise had a habit of wanting to confide her deepest emotions to someone, anyone, during the middle of the night. She'd awakened Meg, by phone or in person, on more than one occasion. I'll bet that's why Clay was in her room at two A.M. In fact, she may have confided far more to Clay than I'd realized because even engrossed as he was in the impending birth of his own child, he'd kept a careful eye on our conversation.

In her innocence, Annelise must have interrupted Glenda and Jurgen together on a midnight search for comfort. Maybe she'd even gone to Jurgen for consolation. Junior had said that her little body fluid detector had flashed wildly everywhere in her house. For all I know, they could have made free on all of the furniture.

"Jurgen, in his innocence"—he was a kid after all, a kid in a strange country, infatuated with a glamorous, older, deeply accommodating woman—"came to you with Annelise's cockamamie plan to go home via hospital flight. You were afraid that she'd tell the others about your affair. That bit of news would not only shitcan the rest of the tour, it would smear your reputation." I shook my head mournfully. "Couldn't let that happen, could you? So you carefully doled out aspirin with codeine for each and every fake headache, knowing that the pills were going directly to Annelise. Knowing full well that Delphi was too far away from a hospital to help her in time. Knowing that Annelise's allergy to codeine would do what a marginal overdose of aspirin would not. You knew that it would kill her."

At the center of the action, Junior let out a hoarse and agonized yell, followed by a large squishy noise, followed by the thin wail of a new life.

A life to balance one of the ones that had been taken.

I was about to continue on, to tell Glenda that she'd just as coldbloodedly met Weasel Cleaver right here in Clay's office the night before and killed him in order to protect her secret and to recover the videotape.

But I stopped myself just in time.

Epilogue

A WEEK LATER
IN A WARM CAFE

At least once during every one of these impromptu investigations, I make a completely wrong assumption, and this one had been no different.

One night, a little over a week ago, I'd stood in Clay Deibert's office and declared to myself that we had two deaths in Delphi, one self-inflicted and the other not. I'd also declared to myself that some men are too good, too dependable, for human failings.

Turns out I was wrong on all counts.

Annelise had been murdered by Glenda Harrison to cover up her affair with young Jurgen.

Clay Deibert had not molested young Annelise, and for that I was entirely grateful.

But I had, somewhat late in the game, made a few correlations that pointed, sadly, to another inescapable conclusion.

Jennifer Swanhorst had been angling for Junior's job. She'd stepped in, usurping every duty, happily assuming the weight of being a minister's wife.

It hadn't occurred to me that she'd been angling for Junior's husband too.

And it most assuredly hadn't occurred to me that Clay would be receptive. I still couldn't explain it except that ministers must suffer from mid-life crises the same as other men.

Jennifer had accompanied Clay on several trips to Cresbard, on one of which they'd been observed by Meg in some sort of compromising position because Meg had declared them *all* to be hypocrites. A merry prankster, Meg had taken delight in framing Clay for a peccadillo he had not committed while knowing that he was guilty of another.

And Annelise, ecstatic in finding a willing listener, had been enthusiastic in showing her happiness, which had, coincidentally been caught on camera by her former boyfriend.

And Meg, the wily observer, saw it all.

Junior had known that her husband had been behaving erratically, but she'd been led down the garden path by a Canadian with no sense of guilt.

And Junior had taken me right along with her.

I realized finally that Jennifer had been the one to call Clay when the news of Annelise's death was announced. And she'd been the one to call the unreachable Clay when his wife went into labor. She seemed to have unlimited access.

It had been Jennifer's half-eaten Snickers bar that had been left on Clay's desk on the fateful evening.

The videotape had shown Weasel with a Snickers bar too, but that had been hours before I'd let myself into Clay's office on Junior's errand to retrieve Annelise's bag.

It had been Jennifer who'd typed the love note, after Clay had broken off the relationship. That she'd typed it on the back of a sheet of paper that Weasel Cleaver had been using for his notes was the wildest of coincidences. But life if full of them.

She'd left the note in Clay's typewriter for him to find in the morning.

Little did she know that his office would be invaded more than once in between.

After having watched Clay and Junior together, marveling over their new daughter, a single daughter, to Delphi's deep disappointment, I knew that the breach caused by Clay's temporary insanity had been healed.

I have no proof of any of these suppositions, of course. And I'll never confront either Clay or Junior with my notions. Both of them would deny the accusation vehemently, and there'd be no point in reminding Junior of that terrible pain.

Things between us are different now—not entirely better, but certainly improved. I imagine that eventually I'll forget that I ever thought that Clay was capable of being entirely too human.

Eventually everything will go back to the way it was in Delphi.

Which was fine by me because if my most recent suppositions about Clay were correct, I had the leveling knowledge that in at least one other case, I'd been 100 percent wrong.

I realized that if Glenda had been going to meet Weasel in Clay's office with the express purpose of retrieving that videotape, and was willing to kill him in order to accomplish this task, then she'd never have left the tape there. She would have taken it and destroyed it.

And I have no doubt that she would have killed again to keep her secret. As she'd explained calmly to the police as they'd led her away, she'd really had no choice in the matter.

But because of that tape, I had, on a fateful night last week, declared that Weasel Cleaver had not stuffed himself into Clay Deibert's office supply closet.

And I'd also assumed that no one else was in the annex with Neil and me because we'd not been able to hear anyone else moving about or breathing.

I must stop making unfounded assumptions.

I sat in a window booth at the cafe and slid an unmarked videocassette across the table. "I think this belongs to you."

"Damn, I wondered where it had gotten to," Weasel Cleaver said, grinning. "Though I should tell you that it's not really mine either. It belongs to my friend Lenny."

"I figured as much," I said wearily.

Lenny had said that Weasel had taken the Delphi run to kill two birds with one trip. He'd wanted to confront Meg. And he'd wanted to recover a videocassette that wasn't supposed to be included in the sale of the camera.

"It wasn't a hot camera," Weasel swore, crossing his fingers over his chest. "I do not want to go back to jail. I'm on the straight and narrow for the rest of my life. Lenny needed some cash so he asked me to see if any of my contacts would be interested. That's why I took that Cresbard call. But none of 'em were interested. However, those kids wanted it real bad. I figured a sale was a sale. I just gave them the wrong used tape, is all."

I sighed. "You know, I ought to smack you upside the head for everything you put me through."

He laughed, and as glad as I was to hear him laugh, a part of me wanted to strangle him on the spot.

Over the last year, I've been confronted with bodies far more often than I ever wanted to be, and never once have I had the slightest desire to poke and prod them to make sure that they were truly and sincerely dead.

I was evidently too trusting.

A mistake I don't intend to duplicate.

Neil had kept a safe distance while Weasel had been in the supply cupboard, venturing no closer than absolutely necessary. I'd moved in swiftly to grab Annelise's bag but I'd avoided looking at the body directly.

It never occurred to me to wonder why Weasel's face had been so carefully turned away from us.

And it never occurred to me to take his pulse, to check to see if he was stone-cold dead.

So the little rat bastard, knowing that we thought he'd been assisted on his journey from this Vale of Tears, had sat very still in that closet, scrunched (I hope painfully) and listened to us scheme and plan.

"It was worth everything just to hear you defend me, Tory. I swear it did my poor little ex-con heart a world of good." He laughed. "But I nearly shouted when you mentioned calling the police. If you hadn't talked yourselves out of it, the jig would have been up right then and there. Besides that, if you'd wanted to see the truth, you would have. I can breathe quietly, but I'm no Houdini. You two were so busy talking and conspiring that I could have farted and you wouldn't have noticed."

Trust Weasel to get to the heart of the matter delicately.

"But why hide in the closet?"I'd finally figured out that's what he'd been doing, hiding—not pretending to be dead, just trying not to get caught.

"And where would you have me hide, eh? That office had more traffic than Grand Central Station. First Miss Priss comes in while I'm watching the video. She cries for a while and then types something and leaves. Later you guys come in and rattle around. The only person who didn't show was the one I was waiting for."

Meg had said that she'd stood him up.

She'd arranged to meet him that evening; that's why he didn't leave Delphi in the interim between taking the tape and when we'd interrupted him.

What he'd done instead was to sneak into the empty cafe and fix the damn furnace.

And then he'd driven back to Aberdeen and checked in with his boss, and talked a little to Lenny and the chirpy receptionist. That's why none of them thought he was missing.

In fact, the only people who'd ever thought that Weasel Cleaver was dead were Neil Pascoe and me.

"So why did you leave the tape in Clay's office? If you'd taken it with you, everything would have turned out differently."

"And aren't you glad I didn't?" he countered.

He was right. If not for the video and our certainty that Weasel had been murdered, and our mistaken notion that the two were inextricably woven together, we'd have taken Annelise's suicide at face value and a murderer would have gone free.

As awful as those two days had been, they'd more than served their purpose.

"You two spooked me," Weasel continued. "I was afraid you'd get home and decide to call the police. I had to get outta there right away. I didn't even remember the tape until I got home. But I tried to call you and tell you about it."

Yeah, Del had mentioned her displeasure over taking innumerable calls for me, both at home and at the cafe. I hadn't bothered to ask for the messages.

There's another mistake I don't intend to duplicate.

"So you're here and you're alive and you're turning over a new leaf, is that it?" I asked, leaning back in the booth, looking at him intently.

"You got that right, babe," he said, digging into the chest pocket of his zip-up Waldlach Furnace Repair overalls.

He fished out a piece of paper and handed it to me.

"What's this?"

"Just a little compensation for some damage I did. I was going to give it to Aphrodite, but she's gone. So I guess you're next in line."

It was a check.

For more than the amount that he'd swindled from Aphrodite.

It was enough to pay her back with interest.

It was enough to dig the cafe out of its present hole.

I said a minute ago that things were back to normal in Delphi, and that's true because normal in Delphi is like a snow drift, carved by the incessant wind, moving infinitesimally, but moving just the same.

Like the river that you never step into twice, Delphi is always changing and it's always the same.

I'm going to be here forever, running the cafe, trying to deserve Aphrodite's legacy.

But I'm also going home to Neil. He's still my best friend, and now he's the most important person in my life.

Always changing and always the same.

Tonight, Mother plans to drop her bomb. She's finally going to make the confession that was delayed by Annelise's death. She declares that no matter what, by this time tomorrow, all hell is going to break lose.

And for Delphi, that's just about par for the course.